# PRAISE FOR *ORSTRALIA*

"Australia has some claim to being a punk founder nation, most obviously through the influence of the Saints and Radio Birdman. In *Orstralia*, Tristan Clark explores the wider terrain to recover a vibrant prepunk, punk, and postpunk history that captures the vibrancy and excitement of a culture brimming with ingenuity and teenage verve. A brilliant book and essential reading for all those interested in punk's cultural past."

—Matthew Worley, author of *No Future: Punk Politics and British Youth Culture, 1976–84*

"If your knowledge of Australian punk grinds to a halt at the Saints, Radio Birdman, the Hard-Ons, and Vicious Circle, *Orstralia* is a deep dive into that country's turbulent alternative underground of the late 1970s and '80s, when rebellious youths clashed with the police (not to mention the church, the government, the media . . . authority in general), rival subcultures, their parents, and even themselves. Proving that an oppressive police state is no match for subversive creativity in the long run, Australian punk evolved and thrived in the face of such adversity—very much its own beast given its isolation from London and New York—and this forensically researched tome is its story, written in such detail and with such fascinating insight, you can relive it all vicariously without having your nose broken and discover a treasure trove of passionate noise into the bargain. This is an important and entertaining piece of work."

—Ian Glasper, author of *Burning Britain: The History of UK Punk 1980–1984* and *The Day the Country Died: A History of Anarcho Punk 1980 to 1984*

# ORSTRALIA
## A PUNK HISTORY
## 1974-1989

TRISTAN CLARK

PM

*Orstralia: A Punk History, 1974–1989*


ISBN: 979-8-88744-039-2 (paperback)
ISBN: 979-8-88744-049-1 (ebook)
Library of Congress Control Number: 2023944312

Front cover design by Carlos Patiño
Front cover photo: World War XXIV by Al Creed
Rear cover photo: Liz and Vera of Gash by Smeer
Interior design by briandesign
Interior collages by Zach Malakonas

10 9 8 7 6 5 4 3 2 1

PM Press
PO Box 23912
Oakland, CA 94623
www.pmpress.org

Printed in the USA.

# CONTENTS

# ACKNOWLEDGMENTS

I respectfully acknowledge the Wurundjeri People of the Kulin Nation who are the Traditional Custodians of the land on which this work was mostly created. I further acknowledge the Traditional Custodians of all the lands across Australia on which the events of this book took place. I pay respect to Elders past and present.

I also wish to thank Ramsey, Joey, Wade, and all at PM Press, Staz, Em, Mum and Dad, Lil, Totti, Pep, Iain, Carlos, Sam, Neil, Zach, and Clint, as well as everyone who contributed through interviews, photos, information, insight, feedback, and encouragement.

# PREFACE

Punk's highly disputed meaning and multiplicities of definition ensures it is reduced to an author's ultimate determination and therefore inhabited by biases based in experiences and prejudgements. Is punk a specified sound, a definable attitude, or a more nebulous amalgam? Seeking to resolve such questioning, as well as providing sufficient definitional clarity and reasons for exclusion of bands, would constitute another book in itself that is not this one.

Included in this title are interviews with people whose views or previous behaviours contravene not only the author's values, but in all likelihood those of many of this book's readership. They have been included, however, through belief that their exclusion would lead to a compromised history and that punk's more unflattering facets should not be deliberately effaced or disregarded.

Despite attempting to offer a definitive historical account, omissions have surely occurred. Apologies are extended to those who feel themselves to have been unduly precluded or forgotten.

# INTRODUCTION

In 1977, the hype emanating from punk in England would permeate Australia, encapsulated by a *Sydney Morning Herald* headline: "The Punk Rock Craze Is Heading Our Way."[1]

Presented as the latest form of corrupting youth culture, mild panic ensued as Australian media forewarned of the purportedly violent and amoral new phenomenon.

Four decades later, the "Executive Life" section of *Business Insider Australia* featured an article titled "40 Years Ago Today, Punk Music Was Born in Australia."[2] Its appearance in the business press exemplified how momentous late '70s punk, as both musical and cultural conformation, had been, as well as its continued legacy.

In 1979, though, a documenter of early Australian punk had eulogised that "the punk wave quickly exhausted itself" and "punk is well and truly dead."[3] More words have been expended on the examination of punk's supposedly fleeting lifespan than any former or subsequent youth culture relative to its supposedly brief period of existence. Yet if punk encompassed a moment of the late 1970s, as many ethnographies had supposed, declarations of its death proved facile.

Reemerging to mainstream consciousness in the 1990s through more palatable, marketable, and ultimately profitable forms, scant attention was given to what had transpired in the interim. Neglected—aside from its most popular groups—were the myriad of permutations and bands that punk's transfiguration was to produce since its 1970s origins.

This book is an attempt to illuminate that full history.

1974-1981
STAMP OUT

# "I ONLY PANIC WHEN THERE'S NOTHING TO DO"

## QUEENSLAND

### BRISBANE

Few places could be more incongruous in the history of Western cultural innovation than 1970s Brisbane. Within such a culturally stunted music environment, bands repetitiously plied cover songs in the few live venues that hadn't lost out to the discos. Yet even the Bee Gees, a band that so symbolised the disco era, felt constricted by opportunity in Brisbane, eventually returning to their home country of England.

By the time of the Saints' first release, the "(I'm) Stranded" single in 1976, ABBA held three of the top ten positions among the highest-selling singles in Australia. Only twelve months previous, Sherbet had released the national number one "Summer Love."

In a year when Australia's prime minister was dismissed and the folly of the Vietnam War was symbolically concluded by the falling of Saigon, it isn't hard to fathom the innocent appeal of a summer of love. But while Australia was not experiencing urban decline and cultural tumult as acutely as the US and UK, punk here would also strip back the facade of idyllic commercial soft rock by means of unrepentant social realism.

The drab, grey, and slush of London and New York winters could hardly be further from Brisbane's oppressively hot, humid, and sleepless summer nights. Where London and New York lacked jobs and cash, Brisbane did not lack for a drudging conservatism. Under the rule of a blushingly oppressive state government, to a young creative the city could not feel any more removed from the great cultural centres of the North Atlantic. Located fifteen kilometres southwest of Brisbane's central business district, Inala was instead the perfect environment for the crafting of an ode that spoke to the deadening effects of confinement to a satellite suburb: "(I'm) Stranded."

Released to near insignificance among the stasis that was Brisbane's music scene in 1976, punk in Australia emerged from nothingness—the formless vision of a small grouping of malcontents. As the central character of Brisbane writer David Malouf's 1975 novel *Johnno* described, the city was "a place where nothing happened and nothing ever would happen."[1] It would take the intransigence of youth to ignore such proscription. And while something was indeed to happen, those in the know were few and came to face, at times, serious opposition.

Australian icon of the countercultural era Richard Neville later boasted, "We made Australia safe ... for the Sex Pistols."[2] Australia's early punks would likely not concur with Neville's inadvertently glib assessment of their safety. Queensland's repressive state apparatus certainly hadn't heeded his assurance, as bands and fans were hounded by police. In an unofficially declared war by youth against the tradition of older generations, new music—loud, noisy, amateurish, and brash—would be the armament chosen for its conduct.

A factory wall adjoining a train line in inner Melbourne once carried the painted proclamation "No one invented punk." Arguments over punk's beginnings are undeniably vexatious, involving navigation of a deeply emotional field. No demarcation of punk's genesis exists, nor a definitive timeline; punk was not birthed fully formed with the Ramones' "Blitzkrieg Bop," the Sex Pistols' "Anarchy in the UK," or the Saints' "(I'm) Stranded." Punk was not the genius of individuals but the culmination of multifarious events, identities, and trends in the history of rock music, filtered through diverging cultural and socioeconomic climates. Still, bombastic claims continue to this day that the Saints constitute the very first punk band. If they were in fact the inception point, their origins inauspiciously lay in guitarist Ed Kuepper performing Chuck Berry at a party as an inebriated Chris Bailey sang along. Kid Galahad and the Eternals would be its more cohesive formulation in 1973. In 1974, they became the Saints.

Cynical, sarcastic, and aloof, the band felt assurance in what they were doing, even if others were unresponsive or mostly just unaware. Derisive of the little music that was being made around them, drummer Ivor Hay says, "Generally any bands we saw, most of the time, were just playing 'Smoke on the Water' [Deep Purple] or something.... We didn't really know much of any band scenes or anything like that."

With little contemporary reference, Kuepper would almost imply a teleological drive rather than anything consciously drawn from influences: "But why the Saints did what they did, I don't know."[3] Hay, however, makes some attempt of rationalisation—that "if you sort of take Eddie Cochran and just make it a bit louder and noisier, you probably got the same sound.... It's not like you sat down and said we're going to become anything, it's just a whole pile of things happening... anything from Eddie Cochran to the Stones, Kinks.... Ed was listening to some heavy metal stuff at the time as well.... MC5 and the Stooges and Lou Reed, Velvet Underground, we would have been listening to those, and New York Dolls are in there somewhere.... But there was also a lot of things like the Easy Beats as well.... I don't know whether there's any sort of direct line of sight between anything."

In the Saints, the intersecting of environment and musical influence added to the exuberance of youth and ultimately an upping of tempo. "What Ed would try to do is to get in front of the beat all the time, which I think was a euphemism for playing faster. So I'd always be trying to catch up, and the more I tried to catch up, the faster he would go."

Acting of their own intuition and experimentation, the Saints arrived at the same point and time as the revered pillars of the Ramones and Sex Pistols. The Damned drummer Rat Scabies reflects on the seeming coincidence: "When you consider The Saints were doing the same in Australia at the same time as the Ramones in New York, it was obvious that people wanted to do it all over the world. The Saints were totally removed from anything going on anywhere else.... The synchronicity was amazing."[4] You Am I's Russell Hopkinson adds further observation that "there's always those little pockets where people aren't tainted by what's going on and they kind of change the course of things. I think the Saints were just a really pure expression of that."

But while the Saints were undeniably pioneering and comparable with the two other great punk protagonists, the truth is considerably less hyperbolic. The Ramones' and Sex Pistols' debut records would be revelatory—momentous life-changing occasions to many. Meanwhile, in their hometown, the Saints were likely better known to the constabulary than music fans.

The "(I'm) Stranded" single, with its stark white cover and only the most minimal of detail, gave no hint of what awaited the listener. In the contemporary age of grindcore, death metal, power electronics, and black metal, it's hard to fathom its contents having once been some of the severest sounds in the world.

One of Brisbane's most ardent underground music fans of the first-wave era, the "Brisbane Devotee," observed that "in 1976–77 The Saints were too hard to understand, and what was hard to understand was hard to care about."[5] On perception of the band in Brisbane, though, Hay underlines the unfamiliarity: "It's really hard to say what they thought, because we didn't really engage in that much with anyone.... You can almost count on two hands the number of gigs we would have done."

The same month as the release of the Saints' single in September 1976, the "100 Club Punk Special" gig in London featured a now-coalescing scene, including the Sex Pistols, the Clash, Buzzcocks, and the Damned, none of whom had yet made releases. Three months later, Brisbane's *Courier Mail* reported the English tabloid newspapers' vitriolic indignancy caused by a profanity-laden Sex Pistols television appearance. That half-minute of vision came to define not only the Sex Pistols but the near entirety of a movement.

Yet at home, the Saints continued in relative obscurity—or at least until ABC radio informed them otherwise. Citing UK music magazine *Sounds*'s bold titling of "(I'm) Stranded" as "single of this and every other week," it asserted that the record "pounds" Status Quo and the Ramones "into the dirt."[6]

If what the Saints were performing was so unprecedented and inventive, Australia's music commentariat weren't quite as convinced. A *Sydney Morning Herald* review defined them as "musical nastiness." *Juke* was no less unflattering: "I can imagine the Stones doing demos this bad when they'd just left school. The mix is bad, the playing's bad, the label's bad, the name of the band's bad, but as they say ... we all got to start somewhere and for the Saints this is a start but only just."[7]

Incredulous about their newfound attention in England, it would take some time before band members even viewed a copy of the *Sounds* review. Record label interest, however, was not nearly as sluggish, with EMI in London despatching its Australian outpost to sign the group.

Though the Saints' local shows were scarce, their meeting with Australia's eventual top rock band, AC/DC, occurred two days before Christmas 1976 at a Gold Coast high school hall. Recently returned from a UK tour, AC/DC had been greeted on arrival at the airport by a contingent of screaming fans. The Saints played the show largely to no one.

Shortly after, the band would embark on their own UK tour, but not before relocation to Sydney, making a brief visit to Melbourne and appearing twice on Australia's most popular music television program, *Countdown*. Performing "(I'm) Stranded" before a national audience, its theme of alienation would be a more discernible message than the Pistols' overtures of political chaos or complete upending of social decorum. Depicting their home country's suburban stagnation, rather than the fissures of England's class system and urban decay, the Saints' theme of antipodean melancholia was to remain present across their following two albums.

Disembarking in England, the Saints stepped into the impending summer of 1977 and the height of punk's very public exposition. Amid the spotlight, however, Bailey implies their own naivety: "We had stumbled into a scene that we had known absolutely nothing about!"[8]

The Saints made their international debut at the Roundhouse in London, supporting labelmates the Ramones and Talking Heads. Recorded at the adjoining Roundhouse Studios, the "This Perfect Day" single followed two weeks later, reaching number thirty-four on the UK charts as well as being performed on *Top of the Pops*. Hay expresses their optimism that "we had the music press initially behind us, we had BBC with John Peel behind us, and so that made things a lot better, I guess, in terms of acceptance."

The same month as the single's release, the group began a UK tour with the Jam. If the Jam were taken by the Australian band, it did not hold for the rest of the down-under population, as the following year members and management of the Australian Rugby League team brawled with the Jam in Leeds. Toll of the incident included a glassing of the team's comanager and hospitalisation of a member of the Jam.

Hay remembers his own—if perhaps unintended—harming of an audience member: "The gigs that we did, there's a lot of spitting going on in those days, which was annoying. I remember I threw a stick at somebody, and when I went to pick it up and get back to playing again, this guy was holding his head a little bit. . . . I never threw a stick again."

The incident exhibited the dichotomy between the band and the caricature of punk that was playing out before them. The Saints did not necessitate extremity of performance or style; their relative normalcy would be curious to those now accustomed to the flamboyance of UK punk. Anchored to a genre so attached to image, the Saints were viewed by some as labouring in a gulf between the old rock world and the new wave. Absent of an inciting aesthetic, Kuepper expressed the band's unwillingness to acquiesce to the expectations of punk: "It's got too involved in fashion, which is superfluous.... We don't care about all that, we play this music because it's what we've always played and we don't care who likes us—just because we've been named as a 'punk' band doesn't mean that we're going to start dressing the part."[9]

The Saints would deliver their own sputum in the form of second album *Eternally Yours* (1978), its deviancy apparent from the initial burst of horns on opening track "Know Your Product." The album was not received as favourably as the ferocity of their previous material.

Even if punk, as a readily identifiable sound, was near completely dissolved from their third album, *Prehistoric Sounds* (1978), the Saints were to undeniably implant themselves within the pantheon of early punk worldwide. Hay concedes it is flattering to be considered one of the genre's initiators: "I've got no problems accepting an appraisal. And I guess the beauty is that it was never designed to be that.... You've sort of got this combination of innovation where you're doing something potentially no one else is doing but you don't really care either way. And then you've got the sort of luck and opportunity which comes out of nowhere.... You couldn't have scripted something like that; you couldn't have planned for it. Just a lot of things came together, and serendipity."

Much has been written of the political environment fomented by Queensland premier Joh Bjelke-Petersen's Country/National Party and its effect on both the Saints and punk's fertility in Brisbane. Ed Kuepper, however, suggested the band employed a more scorched-earth policy than just reaction to Brisbane's political climate: "We're trying to kick out restrictions, repressive social systems, crummy governments, social circles, imbeciles, complacency, apathy, hippies, squares, farts. You name it, we want to kick it out."[10]

One of the first punk bands to tour Australia, the Stranglers had been left aghast by Queensland, so much so that their song "Nuclear Device (The Wizard of Aus)" referenced Bjelke-Petersen and his grip over the state's politics.

To those too young to have been present at or recall the time, depiction of Joh's Queensland may seem fanciful in a "model" liberal democracy like Australia. Coming closest to an Australian political demigod, Bjelke-Petersen sought to extinguish any intransigence. Hazards existed for all who expressed alternative beliefs or exhibited identities and lifestyles that supposedly transgressed his Christian-tinged worldview. It would be into this perilous environment that the first wave of Brisbane's punk bands emerged.

With their intent focused on the UK, Hay confirms the Saints were largely oblivious to musical happenings back home, despite Ed Kuepper's younger brother's presence in early punk band Same 13: "I don't think we sat around worrying too much about what was happening in Brisbane and whether there were any legacy bands or anything like that. We were probably too preoccupied with just getting on with things in London."

With little guidance for what they were doing aside from obsessive study of the trickle of overseas records and magazines, young people in disparate international cities such as Brisbane showed that punk would not be confined just to the US or UK, but quickly constituted into a late '70s global phenomenon.

While a number of scholars have invoked art provocateurs the Dadaists as precursor to punk's confrontational style, it is perhaps tenuous to see kindred spirits in avant-garde performers and errant youth in leather jackets offering a chorus of "Cigarettes and Alcohol." Though the song was a reasonable portrayal of the Leftovers' predilections, the ability to overintellectualise punk was to become rife. Legs McNeil's book *Please Kill Me*, the quintessential oral account of punk's origins, was instead largely a document of hedonistic destruction, drugs, alcohol, and violence. The Leftovers arguably warrant their own volume.

In 1979, *Roadrunner* writer Scott Matheson declared the Leftovers as "Brisbane's only bona fide punk band, possibly Australia's only real punk band." Band member Ed Wreckage backed Matheson's declaration: "We're everything other punk bands try to be but can't. . . . No one's going to destroy us."[11] Wishing to interview the band, however, Matheson was only able to locate two members: "Drummer Michael was in hospital recovering from a car crash, and Warren Lamond, the singer, had had a forty-four-gallon drum thrown at him."

While outside entities sought to attack the group, the band also did their utmost to destroy themselves. Wreckage says, "Some of the stories I've heard and the things that happened to me are horrific."

The Leftovers' beginnings traced to the dead-end northern reaches of Brisbane. Wreckage describes an area where, at night, "The cops were out hunting for teenagers, and it was just the worst place."

Friend to the band Peter McGrath sketches home life in the suburb of Sandgate: "All our parents worked at Golden Circle [fruit] cannery... all shift workers, that's why we had no parental guidance.... Domestic violence was the norm. The cops were either coming to see why you aren't going to school or because your mum and dad had a barney over something."

The violence to which some were exposed at home was only magnified in the streets, Wreckage revealing, "I've got a lot of wounds from that period.... We were just musos, but we had to defend ourselves when that came up. That's sort of how we became tough; we had to be at really early ages."

In 1977, band members had been badly beaten at a hotel near Sandgate, with Wreckage especially receiving serious injuries: "We were sicced upon by a bunch of older guys—they just didn't like the look of us.... No one had ever seen anybody like us before with dyed hair and leather and stuff.... That song 'Dead on Arrival' is about me. The guys went home and started writing that song when I was in hospital.... That night I had a T-shirt on with 'DOA' [dead on arrival] spray-painted on it.... I remember the doctors brought me to and they were laughing about how silly this must have looked."

The Leftovers soon ventured beyond the safe setting of their rehearsal space. Wreckage remembers their first fully public show being "full of Saints fans and for some reason they just didn't like us.... Somebody threw a beer can, a full unopened beer can—pegged it as hard as they could—and it hit me in the chest. And then all of a sudden there's just all this shit flying at us—broken plates, glasses."

Discord continued at a show at the Dive in Fortitude Valley—the "Brisbane Devotee" recalled the scene: "There was a fight. Leftover fans couldn't stand the Saints. Maybe fifty or so people who all started laying into each other. Chairs, tables flying around the place.... Then these two cops wandered in.... They were turfed out the window."[12] David Donald implicates Wreckage: "Ed threw someone out the window which we thought was a Saints supporter, but I actually believe it was a plain-clothes cop."

The more considerable threat than a rival band's fans remained police and their breaking up of gigs: "Nearly all of them would get busted up by the cops.... I don't know how, but they'd just be there. The first Hamilton Hall gig we did ... was just nonsense. They [police] were throwing bricks through the windows from outside so they could gain entry to the joint.... We were just a soft target."

At the "Great Brain Robbery" show in West End in 1979, two dozen attendees were arrested after an undercover officer tried to detain Warren Lamond for offensive language onstage, resulting in a scuffle. David Donald had been napping on the same stage only to wake to "windows being smashed and people being dragged off."

With limited options for regular gigs, Wreckage says, "We thought we'd go north and hunt out nightclubs in little towns or hunt out halls and book them ... that's how naive we were [*laughs*].... We drove into town and we were busted in about fifteen minutes—in jail for drugs charges. I was a seventeen-year-old kid.... There were a few promoters around at that time in Brisbane, but they wouldn't have a bar of us because we were so different." Even Brisbane's progressive community radio station shunned the band: "Triple Z [4ZZZ] wouldn't back us.... We were like acid."

Able to amass only a modest number of shows, the band decided to trek south, but failed to manage playing even a single bar of music. "We ended up finding our gear smashed up, thrown out the back of this pub.... They purely didn't like the look of us.... That was the first and last night of Sydney."

One of the reasons cited by Wreckage for the dislike in Sydney was the group's roadie, Simmo: "When he went out, he didn't dress punk, he dressed as a female." Music was to bring the band in contact with a range of identities and experiences: "We were meeting all sort of different people.... The gay culture, that's where we began.... The first nightclub we ever had a paying gig in was Romeo's Nightclub in Fortitude Valley. We used to play two songs while the gay revues—or 'all-male revues' as they were called in those days—changed.... We had gay people who were our closest friends, but they kept it silent until we started playing in gay nightclubs.... It opened the doors for a lot of people to be what they wanted to be, and that was the beauty of punk."

If punk allowed for some to exhibit their true identities, Wreckage says Smith made attempts to conceal his own for safety: "He actually grew his hair, and he was wearing suits at one stage and walking around with a briefcase trying to hide that punk persona.... The only thing that got me away from it was just hiding.... We would have gotten out if we could. We were planning to go to Europe because we knew people there.... It just didn't happen. We were too far into dope as well."

Similar reasons would mean their first and only recording while still active, the revered *Cigarettes and Alcohol* seven-inch, remained unreleased until 1979. "It was all down to money. We had plans and it all just went to shit, and it was all because of drugs." Whereas marijuana and LSD had been the fuel for hippie love, punk was propelled by copious booze, bad speed, heroin, and a whiff of glue. Wreckage says, "We all got busted; Glenn did time; I did time; it was the ruination of everything.... That's just the way it was, living on the razor's edge—needle's edge—basically."

Towards the band's conclusion, Smith had told a *Roadrunner* journalist, "I reckon there's a future. I don't know what it is, but I know I've got one."[13] Tragically, Smith developed a drug habit and would later succumb to liver cancer. The eventual trajectory of the remaining band members was just as stark, Wreckage sharing that "Warren was a mess ... shot himself.... Glenn died of liver cancer.... Jim died of stomach cancer.... John hanged himself.... Michael died of liver cancer." Wreckage unsurprisingly observes, "I dodged a bullet.... I never thought I'd make it past twenty-five using smack and smoking and drinking—basically on a one-way ticket out of here."

Before all the deaths and despair, though, Wreckage says, "We were dependent on each other for so long that even our families were all sort of dependent on each other. It just grew into that sort of thing.... That's how we survived."

As bulwark to an unleashed competitive individualism, punk offered community to disenfranchised young people in the context of the 1970s' economic turmoil and rising unemployment. In Brisbane, more than elsewhere in Australia, it also constituted resistance to a legitimately repressive regime. "It was 'How bad can it get? How low can this thing go?' What you put your life into just gets trodden on.... Somebody was against everything you were doing. That's just how it seemed.... But we sort of wanted to stick it out and just change it.... It wasn't our sole objective, we were just musicians, but there was no way of you separating the two things, of being a performer and being active, politically. We had to try and shock people into realising how fucked up this place was.... Most people didn't know it was as bad as it was."

Yet for all the misfortune, harassment, and hostility, Wreckage still manages to salvage some positive within their legacy: "Every gig wasn't botched, there was some good ones. I remember getting clapped offstage a few times [*laughs*]." Rod McLeod is adamant, however, in highlighting their impact: "They were fucking scary bastards playing short, sharp, brutal songs with such attitude. No band in Brisbane could even compare to what they were doing, then or now."

For Wreckage, though, "It's really hard to put it into context, because it's almost ethereal now. It was a really exciting time to be alive.... You have a look at it now, it's been mainstream for the last thirty years. It just goes to show that we had foresight. We were ahead of our time."

Wreckage passed away in 2021.

The Leftovers were to exhibit punk's tension between the past and its innovatory urge. As well as their own original material, the band scattered Velvet Underground and harder '60s songs among their set, Wreckage revealing, "That's how we got to know the Survivors."

Survivors guitarist Greg Williamson notes their name as signifying endurance from a previous and unedifying era: "The early '70s were kind of slow music and country pop; all very melodic and soft, and for me that's what the name Survivors meant: we survived that period until music came alive again in about 1976."

Even if the older Williamson was largely oblivious to daring new sounds like the Ramones, "Bruce [Anthon, drums] and Jim [Dickson, bass] knew about it.... Their love was still the earlier music, I think, but we found the new music inspiring, because it had so much energy and they were making things happen.... We were a couple of years older than those people [the punk scene] and I think people kind of accepted us just for the fact that we loved the music and played it hard and loud and that was good enough. Maybe some people thought we weren't 'punky' enough.... It didn't matter, because we were 100 percent committed to what we were doing."

Further differentiating himself from the youthful musicians who he was now finding himself in company with, Williamson reveals that he "was also married at the time." Divergence between his own living and the proclivities of bands such as the Leftovers were obvious: "I could never understand how all those other things happened in people's lives because, for me, it was just about playing music. Other people wanted to get into the lifestyle . . . for us it was just the music. They had different lives and maybe they were trying to escape things."

As Survivors released their *Baby Come Back* seven-inch in 1977, the recording reflected a band straddling two time periods. For Williamson, it also brought the conflict of choosing between the stability of career and domestic life with the unpredictability and often bones-of-your-arse existence as a musician. "There was the question 'Are you going to go touring?'" For Williamson, that would entail having "to think about giving up my job. . . . If the music and the songs had been just a little bit stronger and it had become its own momentum, maybe that would have happened. But it was good, and it was fun, but it just didn't have that extra power to become permanent, I think."

If Survivors were viewed by some as remnants of an older sound, Razar would embody the new, youthful recalcitrance of punk. They would also become the band most synonymous with Brisbane police's intrusion into it.

On their final and auspiciously least-punk-sounding album, the original incarnation of the Saints provided the most poetically astute lyrical depiction of the city's taut existence in the track "Brisbane (Security City)":

> Thirteen hot nights in a row
> The cops drive past but they move slow
> A million people staying low
> With mangoes ripe who needs to grow

The song, however, had been penned as expats, with Ed Kuepper speaking of a nice flat in London and a record company car chauffeuring them to the recording studio. Razar vocalist Marty Burke insists, "The Saints left the place before it all blew up. . . . The fact remains that they were not here. . . . I know, having said that, Ed does acknowledge the importance of the bands like us that followed."

As the Saints sang of the unease of living as outsiders in an unresponsive or disdainful environment, Razar documented the more immediate danger. The same year the Saints released "Brisbane (Security City)"—1978—Razar offered "Task Force (Undercover Cops)." What it lacked in Chris Bailey's subtlety was more than made up for in blunt indignation:

They're gonna stop my music because they say it's too loud
Then they begin to beat people within our crowd

Though not a directly specified target of the local police's "task force," the city's punks were readily identified by its officers. Composed of around twenty members based in Brisbane, this task force's official role was to combat "unruliness" and "hooliganism" in areas supposedly reputable for such behaviour. The "Brisbane Devotee" described the atmosphere: "Now in QLD [Queensland] you had this group growing that was political with vague ideas of Anarchy and now you have the QLD Special Branch as the first cops through the door at punk dances. They're not there to stop swearing etc. like you're arrested for, it can only be to harass this new movement, to nip in the bud this new 'sickness.'"[14]

This "movement" was just another target of Bjelke-Petersen's intolerance for dissent. In 1971, a state of emergency had been declared in anticipation of protests against the tour of South Africa's Springboks rugby union team. Forward to 1977, and more than four hundred were arrested at a single anti-uranium protest in Brisbane.

A year prior, when questioned if Queensland was becoming a "police state," Bjelke-Petersen's own police commissioner had responded, "I think there are signs of that development."[15] In September 1977, the government banned street marches and demonstrations, prompting democratic rights and civil liberties campaigns. Hundreds would be arrested in contravention of the order in right-to-march protests that continued for the next two years.

The "Brisbane Devotee" observed among protestors "short-haired weirdos, some of which had green hair. Now you can imagine what effect a green-haired idiot has on the QLD police. Loathing, distaste, hatred."[16]

While the most overt focus was street demonstrations, three decades later Allan Gardiner ruminated on the policing of punk in Brisbane, suggesting it "begs the question of why police in large numbers using extreme force were unleashed against a bunch of teenagers. The answer is that this was a political police force and the teenagers had been positioned by history as their enemy."[17]

The years have not diminished Burke's sense of drama that confronted Razar when entering "the vacuum left behind by the Saints": "a true police state with young bands like Razar being taken seriously enough for the task force to regularly trash our gigs, building up a file on Brisbane punks as a whole—considered a real threat. Where else in the world has there been such a situation like it? Not even London ever had that true connection where a musical genre and authoritarian rule (dictatorial police state) clashed head-on.... Although we thought and fought more from a live performance level, that format took on a lot more meaning."

Gardiner suggests that "politics in the independent music scene was, in itself, usually too diffuse to make it the target of extreme state violence."[18] Even if the subjugation was not extreme by international standards, Ed Wreckage is not so dismissive of the harm faced: "Lots of people really copped it. The police force, the way they worked here, were brutal—absolutely brutal." Burke's memory is that "you would... be arrested for obscene language or worse, taken to the watchhouse cells and bashed with a cricket bat and a telephone book ... [which] hides the bruises from looking like punches."

Amid such severity, though, Burke is able to offer the humour of sometimes absurd episodes: "I tried to evade being dragged away and arrested at the 'Cane Toad Hop.' ... I calmly walked outside the gig and said to who I thought was a cabbie, 'Hey, it's a fucking shitfight in there, can you give me a ride outta here?' ... 'Sure can,' he says. 'You're under arrest for obscene language, I'll give you a lift all the way there!' Oh, for fuck's sake, an undercover cop."

The cover of their *Stamp Out Disco/Task Force (Undercover Cops)* seven-inch in 1978 (followed by the *Money* seven-inch in 1979) suitably featured a photo of Queensland police. Driving from practice one night, the band was pulled over for failing to have their headlights on. Searching the car, an officer examined the just-completed record and, recognising at least one of the police officers on its cover, requested copies to share with colleagues. Four decades later, those same singles would be worth in the vicinity of $1,000 each.

The band's only respite from police was to come from playing Sydney. Burke appeared onstage in a shirt scrawled with "QLD Refugee." The feeling of being symbolic fugitives, coupled with the threat of physical harm, provokes the question of them ever having considered ceasing, yet bassist Bob Wackley counters: "No, just bitter and more defiant in my mind." Any defiance, though, seems by necessity to have been propelled by teenage bravado. "I'm a scrawny bloke (most of us were) and being monstered by cops, usually bigger than me, with batons, holstered guns

... that was intimidating. It was like a game sometimes." That game was to ultimately take its toll, with Wackley conceding that "eventually I moved out of Brisbane to be free of it."

A local fanzine in 1978 had noted the "worn-out Sex Pistols/Clash/Damned" songs being performed by Brisbane bands.[19] One band to spurn the UK impudence was X-Men, with guitarist Bruce Callaway explaining, "I was more interested in the New York sound at the time," and that the British side of punk "seemed a bit more undeveloped and fashion conscious, whereas the ones coming out of New York I think had more depth to them."

Before immersing himself in the sounds of the US, Callaway admits, "I was like a lot of people drifting through that period, and there wasn't a lot going on." A defining moment was to refocus his life: "I saw the Saints.... I remember I saw them at Festival Hall. It was '76, battle of the bands or something like that: satin pants, satin shirts, Status Quo covers, all that stuff, and the Saints came out totally dressed differently ... smoking cigarettes and carrying on.... It was shocking, such a drastic change in the speed of the songs."

Callaway's friends were not similarly moved. Deciding "I'm going to cut my hair, I'm going to dress differently, I'm going to play this sort of music," Callaway says, "you alienate your friends immediately, most of them. It was that black and white."

Forming X-Men together with John Hoey in 1977, their sense of isolation slowly receded as "we heard about all these other bands.... There must have been a whole bunch of people hanging around like us, and there just seemed to be an explosion of bands all in a rush." The influx was reflected in the number of people willing to attend the mostly hall shows: "One hundred to two hundred people ... I don't think anyone had trouble getting an audience."

Less impacted by police harassment than other groups, trouble for X-Men was to come from punks themselves: "There were a bunch of people in that scene who were just there to create violence and chaos.... I decided I'd had enough. Every time we'd go and play at a new venue ... these guys would show up and smash things."

To Callaway, Sydney "just seemed more of a viable place." Relocating in 1978, he came uncannily to find his place as guitarist in the very band that had wrenched him from his directionless Brisbane life. Performing in a revamped lineup of the Saints, Callaway stayed with the group until their return to Europe. Hoey, following Callaway, also made his way to Sydney, there becoming a member of heralded alternative band Died Pretty.

A band that pursued punk and music industry attention in similar measure, Gerry Mander and the Boundaries also flaunted one of its most overtly political names. His music career well predating punk, band founder Wally Watkins remembers, "When I first started, I had a Vox AC15 [fifteen-watt amplifier].... People would come and say, 'Can you turn it down a bit?' ... It was classed as rebellious in the sense that a lot of the guys grew their hair long."

The allure or perceived viability of punk saw Watkins form Gerry Mander and the Boundaries in 1978. For Watkins, punk had "made me more get into the original stuff, cut my hair, dress up a bit in different clothes."

Possessing a name that referenced the calculated redrawing of electoral boundaries to favour Bjelke-Petersen's party, the band were invited to play "Rock Against Joh" in 1978. "When we came on, the girl we had in the band had an army uniform on with a cap and a big red [communist] star on it. Well, of course the TV went nuts, so we ended up on the six o'clock news."

Of the name, however, Watkins implies it being more performative than explicitly political: "It was a bit tongue-in-cheek... in the middle of all that kerfuffle." Nonetheless, "We thought the boys [police] would be out there looking at us all the time.... We had a few come in there, plainclothes guys checking us out, but we were smart enough.... It didn't get too outrageous."

Obvious was the chasm between a seasoned musician like Watkins and the younger punk bands properly engaged in a game of cat and mouse with authorities. Watkins instead was attempting to "make a living, and more so, get into some recording."

Without finding that major success, Watkins "came back to the Gold Coast about 1982.... I wasn't making any money, couldn't get any dough out of it, so I thought, 'Nah, I'll just have to go play covers and go surfing.'"

Where Watkins describes Gerry Mander as composed of "clean skins," bands such as the Disposable Fits and Fuji Angels would be sad examples of life too often imitating art. In 2011, a *Brisbane Times* article on the city's homeless included Peter Adams, who "years ago played in one of Brisbane's earliest punk bands, The Disposable Fits '78–80."[20] At the time of its publication, Adams was a recovering morphine addict, a legacy of his heady early punk years.

Reaching back to those days, Adams recalls his "first encounter with punk" being "a couple of fellows ... walking up the street, and one was quite a standout with a bright rubber dish glove on one hand, a variety of cuts, tears, stencils, etc., on the clothes and safety pins, chains and razor blades affixed to the clothes, skin, and body parts. I thought, 'This guy has style.'" Those two youthful punks were Johnny Burnaway (the Leftovers) and Peter McGrath.

Already a fan of Sex Pistols and the Clash, Adams, together with Mark Halstead, formed Disposable Fits. Not quite the novice as Adams, Halstead had also performed in Fuji Angels; "Fuji" being the name of a syringe manufacturer, both bands' names barely concealed the tendencies of some members. Fittingly, Adams reveals that despite the dangers of a hostile populace and police force, "The most harm I faced was from myself."

Disposable Fits and Fuji Angels were far from the first to name themselves in adulation of drug culture, though such titles were often ascribed as fashion as much as function. Losing three days to frenetic partying was one thing, but decades strung out on smack was wrenching for both friends and family. Heroin use in Australia had risen considerably from the 1960s, Adams tracing its arrival: "The pervasion of heroin into Australia ... was initially centred around Kings Cross and the 'R 'n' R' [rest and recreation] scene with US troops on leave from Vietnam." Ed Wreckage forlornly describes its impact: "I remember there was never any pot ... so everybody went to smack. It left a huge trail of misery, and we're all still dealing with it. I lost all my friends that way."

Adams himself died in 2020.

A reflective Adams viewed punk as having "attracted a lot of different people, some with a touch of genius, some with a touch of tragedy, everybody touched by various brushes." Halstead's journey through the music industry would be an exhibit of all such facets, which, subsequent to Disposable Fits, included the release of a country version of the Sex

Pistols track "Pretty Vacant" in 1983 on the Kingswoods' *Purty Vacant* seven-inch.

Country music posed little challenge to punk as a soundtrack for urban youth—rather, the great enemy was the mirror-ball-lit dance floor. By 1980—despite Razar's ambition to "Stamp Out Disco"—the Village People were atop the charts with "Can't Stop the Music." Brisbane's Exchange Hotel pumped disco on Friday and Saturday nights, formerly the venue's designated punk/new wave evenings.

If disco personified passivity, decadence, consumerism, and escapism, Fun Things guitarist/vocalist Brad Shepherd says his band was more simply a juvenile act of defiance, a "puerile attempt just to do something. Just kicking against a middle-class upbringing."[21]

Entertainment options for teens were limited, tending to progress through corner-store pinball, underage drinking and drugs, and youth gang punch-ups. Fun Things' most defining moment, though, relays brother Murray, came from the gathered Shepherd family watching punk being brought into suburban Australian homes: "The whole family was watching television after dinner. Mike [Willesee] prepared everybody and told them to steel themselves against the latest music sensation coming out of Britain. He then proceeded to play 'Anarchy in the UK.' Brad and I turned to each other and with wide open eyes and mouth knew what we were going to do. The look on his face told us that our dad was not impressed."

Mr Shepherd would be further unimpressed when later forced to bail Brad out of jail after being arrested at a Leftovers show.

The band first performed as the Aliens when Murray was a mere twelve-year-old scout member. He says, "I do get a chuckle out of the fact that I was only thirteen years old when we made that *Fun Things* record [self-titled seven-inch, 1980]."

Derided for their age and managing a measly ten shows in their brief existence, they were further differentiated as fans of the Stooges, MC5, the Dead Boys, and "the American punks." With Brad also having been a member of the Radio Birdman fan club, their influence was unashamedly displayed on the track "When the Birdmen Fly."

Visiting one of the few purveyors of such underground music in Brisbane, Murray inadvertently came to be caught up in a police operation: "I was in Rotten Records one Saturday morning when it was raided by the censorship and drug squad . . . searching the shop from top to bottom looking for illegal substances and records with rude words or 'pornographic' pictures on the cover. All present, owner and patrons, were searched. My mini flick knife was confiscated."

Fun Things were to offer only the solitary recording. Continuing to perform, Murray joined the Screaming Tribesmen while Brad attained national status as a member of Hoodoo Gurus.

Few better instances of teen folly captured to vinyl likely exist in Australia than the 1979 self-titled seven-inch by Young Identities, another youthful band formed—in the most fun and obnoxious manner—to combat urban boredom. Guitarist Rod McLeod speaks of the inevitable casualties: "Gate-crashing early shows of the Aliens was fun. . . . Smashed my first guitar at one. . . . We came out of our own little hole in the ground. . . . We were suburban kids . . . who just loved aggressive music—no art students or uni grads here. . . . My younger brother Clayton [vocalist] was picked on for liking punk music when he was in high school. Everyone was still into Peter Frampton and shit. We converted a lot of them in the end."

The foremost venues for the conversion were parties and rehearsal rooms "because most of the band members and our followers were all underage. . . . It was just one huge teen frenzy—drinking and fucking and vandalism. Some of the gang were smashing things up when the guys who ran the room showed up. . . . Next thing you know, five paddy wagons were hauling us all away to the Caxton Street barracks. They worked me over a bit and were even typing out my 'confession' when someone owned up."

In a case of great historical coincidence, the Caxton Street Police Barracks were located opposite "Club 76," a sharehouse where the Saints had rehearsed and performed at their own parties.

As teen delinquents, McLeod surprisingly reveals, "We had one of our first shows at Griffith University. The promoter got a huge bill for damage caused, and that sort of jinxed us as well." Theirs being more unwitting artistic protest than concerted political project, McLeod says of ridding the noxious Bjekle-Petersen government: "It was a bigger job than what a bunch of snotty-nosed kids from the suburbs could do anything about."[22]

The recording of three McLeod-affiliated bands—Young Identities, Just Urbain, and Bodysnatchers—in a single day sounds like the makings of an aural train wreck. No formal gigs and no marketing were not an ideal sales strategy for the resulting seven-inch records either, and any attempt to impose themselves on the Brisbane music market could be deemed a failure. Yet with copies of the Young Identities single now worth in proximity of $1,000, their teenage lack of seriousness could subsequently be viewed as collectable charm.

The clan's productivity could not be dampened—a Kicks/Just Urbain split tape, *Leather Godzilla*, released in 1980, was offered in a "hand-stitched McLeod tartan cloth bag." Kicks further featured on a split cassette with Public Execution. A collector's nightmare, only twenty-five copies were produced.

Kicks shows did not come with any great regularity until a quasi-residency at the Silver Dollar, but "filthy graffiti in the ladies' toilets and syringes stuck in the carpet killed that." Despite a tendency towards the shambolic in a live setting, the band began to draw attention and then something very much resembling a proper audience. They would also release a single which was not completely loathed by whatever press actually paid attention to it. A previously wary 4ZZZ even offered a live show, though by then the band's existence was terminal. McLeod says, "I think our stuff was even too crude for the likes of 4ZZZ. The first show they ever offered us was 1983, the last ever show we did as Kicks.... It was of its time and it will always be part of what we stood for. A great time to be alive and kicking against the pricks!"

McLeod passed away in 2023 after developing lung and liver cancer.

With "the pricks" being figuratively fought by kids who didn't know how to simply shut up and be compliant, other bands' sounds consigned them to the outskirts of punk: Credits, who featured two Survivors members and an eventual guitarist of Helmet; the Apartments; Riptides; the Pits; Pork.

Of all the alternative Brisbane bands of the period, it is the Go-Betweens who possess the most lauded legacy. Remembering their "first-ever gig was supporting the Leftovers," David Donald insists that "they were absolutely terrified—scared of the Leftovers fans."

Leftovers aside, Go-Betweens' Lindy Morrison says of the punk she was initially exposed to that "it was everything that I would have hoped to have done. Songs like The Slits 'Typical Girls,' it was everything that I was then thinking. 'Anarchy in the UK', ... 'Blank Generation'—I was just so fucking lost as to what my direction would be until I heard this stuff."[23]

Morrison, together with Go-Betweens members Robert Forster and John Willsteed, briefly joined Zero in 1979, standing alongside other Brisbane punk/post-punk groups Out of Nowhere, the Poles, the End, and the Swell Guys.

Zero was one of the city's most stridently political bands, and the group's constant figure, Irena Luckus, had a background in radical libertarian groups. As a fertile political scene developed in Brisbane, Luckus says the state government "were bent on holding back the sea to a new age of younger people who dared to see the world differently." Nonetheless, the government was still unable to prevent the "cross-pollination of politics, art, music, and design.... People opened up their own art galleries, performance art hit the streets, the city was pasted up with political and music posters, and local halls—long standing emptied and unloved—were rented by musicians who put up their own 'dance events.' This blossomed into Brisbane's cultural resistance."

Inspired by all-female UK groups such as the Slits and the Raincoats, Luckus describes Zero as "an all-girl band, largely—unrepented feminists. Some of us who visited the live music venues would scream at boy bands to get a girl in their band." The many young, unrefined boys whose attraction to music preceded politics were now finding themselves in the company of—and confronted by—those espousing feminism.

As a feminist, performer, activist, and young mother, Luckus uniquely balanced time between the "cultural resistance" and domesticity: "I had two children and that kept me at home more often ... but I also had beautiful parents who would take them for weekends, allowing me to pursue my inspirations. I stayed clear of the police because of my responsibilities to my children."

Peter Adams, an early vocalist for the band, remembers the group managed to find at least one haven from police harassment: "For a while, Zero used to practice at an institute for the developmentally disabled. The residents loved it and there was no police presence."

Adams had been another who was to traverse both politics and, with its arrival, punk. What he viewed was largely cultural protestation rather than an embrace of more organised political formations: "I ... went to antiwar and [Aboriginal] land rights marches. I spent a few years hanging out at the Red and Black Bookshop and other environs, producing and disseminating radical propaganda . . . but Brisbane punk didn't have much politics except what individuals brought with them."

Whatever the strength of their political interest and critique, bands featured at events for political causes and fundraising—even if the money wasn't always to make its way to intended recipients. In 1979, Zero performed with the Hard-Ons (posthumous self-titled seven-inch, 2019) at a "Rock Against Poofta Bashing" show. Decades later, John Willsteed recalled the evening, where "the cops came in with their dogs and took all the money from the door."[24]

The show was held in a period when "poofter bashing" was viewed as barely more unpalatable a pastime than denigrating "wogs" or catcalling women in the street; homosexual acts were still legally prohibited in Queensland until the beginning of the 1990s.

Able to navigate the dangers presented, Zero boasted a significantly greater lifespan than the remainder of Brisbane's early punk bands. In 1982, now as Xero, the group released their sole recording, the *Lust in the Dust* twelve-inch.

As if to act as chapter headings for a biography of the band, the record included tracks "The Girls," "The Misfits," and "Love and Anarchy." As a group of (often) female performers, they stood among fellow miscreants on the fringes of a conservative culture, engaging in attempts of radical mutuality within temporal spaces of autonomy—or at the least just pissing off the right people. Expressed perhaps with a certain romanticism, Luckus traces the evolving of a small, diffident scene into one "where finally, one could go into a few select pubs [women had only been allowed to drink in Queensland pubs' public bars since 1970] and totally enjoy real music that was inspired by the context in which it lived—like a big heartbeat filled with anticipation and lots of celebration. . . . Our revolution was a happy one."

The interim, however, had brought moments of inactivity as a lull punctuated punk's initial burst. Ed Wreckage describes the period around 1979 as "a wasteland. . . . After a while, everybody lost their will. . . . There was no point playing punk, it was still a magnet for the police up here." Little remained of the early bands, and by decade's end the police's task force had taken an undeniable toll. David Donald remembers at "the end of '79–80 there was an exodus of people going to Sydney, London, jail, death."

For Donald—or "Dodo"—his experience was likewise brief, becoming another of those to depart: "Fifteen I left school, sixteen I left home, seventeen I left the country." Within the brevity of his time active in the scene, Donald joined Bex Crystals, a band that sits with others of the period who remain barely documented: the 31st, the Alphabet Children, Flying Squad, the Fractions, the Lounge Lizards, the Patients, Bad Twists, Scrap Metal, V2 and the Hiltons, and the Misstakes. Also having a stint in the Leftovers, Wreckage jokes about Donald's attendance at band rehearsals: "Dodo never did [*laughs*]."

Finding place in a group who once bellowed a chorus of "Cigarettes and Alcohol," Donald reveals he has now "been in the wine trade twenty years." He speaks of those who once viewed him and his cohorts with contempt now seeking out his expertise: "These people who would never speak to me or give me the time of day are suddenly inviting me around to open these bottles worth hundreds and thousands of dollars because they wanted your opinion on what they'd actually bought."

Returning from the lavish cellars of Brisbane's well-heeled, Donald casts his mind back to his youth. Contrasting the self-betterment that he views came from immersion in a vibrant and intelligent punk movement, Donald remembers that the glint of a cop's badge was never far away: "They didn't need search warrants—they just walked into your house. And they knew people by name, and they'd pick you up and take you on a little drive.... You had to sort of watch your back at all times.... There was a real backlash from the general public as well.... I don't think I could walk into a pub without having a glass thrown at my head.... I needed to get out.... It was pretty much an exodus for our own safety."

To Donald, such peril ensured a premature growing up, even if still coupled with a youthful sense of adventure: "That whole pushing the boundaries ... you basically went from teenage kid to being an adult—there was virtually no adolescence.... At the same time, I had a great big grin on my face.... We were basically pushing the envelope in every possible way.... We were never a threat to society; we were a threat to ourselves."

Donald suggests that the passing of four decades has done little to lessen the ties that were born from enduring such unique events—that beyond just some unyielding kids in a hall making a hell of a racket, what people such as Donald experienced formed bonds analogous to those who have faced battle together: "Most people from that period who haven't died are all still in full contact, that whole network of people. . . . It's sort of like you went through the war together. . . . We suffered a lot together. . . . It meant an awful lot to a lot of people."

## IPSWICH

Formed out of the dwellings that crowded around its coal mines, the Brisbane satellite city of Ipswich still had a dozen operational open-cut mines at the time punk filtered into its homes. A series of bands in vicinity of the city would come to be collectively known as "Bremerbeat," named after the river which snakes through its centre. Such groups were to include Toy Watches, the Pits, the Lemmings, and Differentials. The pop-friendly, punk sound of these bands sometimes belied how tough it was to be punks in the region—and how tough they were in response.

Reflecting their environment, Donald says, "The Ipswich mob were pretty rough ... not all of them, but there was a component of the Ipswich mob." Ed Wreckage is even more concise in his psychological assessment: "All the people from up that way were fucking mad [*laughs*]. . . . I think if you spoke to Vespa from the Upsets, he'd tell you a few things ... people getting shot at and all sorts of crazy stuff."

Vespa's bandmate Brad Cox acknowledges, "It was a wild band and the front two [inclusive of Vespa] took no shit from anyone." Bewilderingly then, "The Upsets' first practice was at the Camira State Primary School staff room in mid-'79. Don't ask me how Vespa ... got us in there."

As a band, Cox says (familiarly) that it "was born and sustained by the boredom. . . . Lots of housing commission homes; no one worked except for me, so I was the only one with a car." Vehicles, however, weren't always as effective a means of fleeing as one's own legs: "The first gig was a birthday party at a Gailes caravan park hall. . . . We were onstage at the back of the hall when suddenly cops were everywhere, grabbing pot smokers and shut down the PA. We went for a quick look outside in the car park, and then on the pretext of getting our instruments we went backstage and jumped over the back fence with a few close friends and legged it."

The party received a front page headline in the *Queensland Times*.[25]

Dauntless, the band recorded and released their *Back to Afghanistan* seven-inch (1980) a year after the Soviet invasion of that country. Despite the single now catalogued as another among the high-priced early Queensland punk seven-inch records, Cox says the band felt a certain distance from the Brisbane scene: "I always thought there were cliques in Brisbane.... We played with other local bands putting on our own shows at ... any hall we could hire. La Fetts and the Differentials come to mind."

The band progressed to Caesars Palace, an Ipswich venue noted for carpet-lined walls and amateur strip nights. Punk should not have seemed outlandish in such surrounds, yet "these six guys were mouthing off at the band, and we all went outside for a fight (not me, I was on the sidelines).... A one-on-one started with the bassist and another guy in the middle of the street right in town." If ever there was opportunity for police to exert their authority and make arrests, it was such a scenario. "A cop car stopped at the lights, took one look, and sped away from the scene."

## ROCKHAMPTON

From an even less assuming city for raucous music in the late '70s, the Rejects formed in 1979 from Rockhampton high school students, their first and only show coming at a band member's Year 12 graduation.

As one of approximately two active punks that composed Rockhampton's second punk wave in the 1980s, Cameron Borg says of the Rejects, "Everyone at school had heard of these guys. They were Catholic guys, and they were playing in this punk band around town."

On the evening of their sole and defining performance, drummer Spike Glover recalls, "We started our set dressed in our punk clothing and by the end of it, Brother Fredricks pulled us aside and told us in no uncertain terms that we were not to go back on for another set." The band didn't hesitate to comply. "Brother Fredricks was a black belt in karate and judo, as were a lot of the Christian Brothers at the time."

## TOWNSVILLE

Having spent his pre-punk years studying in Townsville, Survivors' Jim Dickson quipped, "We used to say for every thousand miles north of Sydney, you went back ten years in time." Being two thousand kilometres from the New South Wales capital, it didn't take much of a mathematician to determine how far in the past the city was allegedly residing. Though being a university town ensured there to be at least a small smattering of progressivism, the size of such a group, Dickson suggested, "could fit into a match-box."[26]

The insular university-based scene even came to have further connection with the first wave of Brisbane punk, as Les, formerly of Disposable Fits, relocated to Townsville for work. He found a place as drummer of the Lips, whose first show came at a disco after convincing organizers they required a real-life punk band to augment their "punk themed" night. Scant detail of the group's existence is matched by the lack of information surrounding the evening's performance, which was ambiguously described as "interesting."[27]

While small pockets of punk would also germinate in the most unassuming of places, it would be Dickson's insinuation of Sydney as the centre of what was most current that held true.

# "DESCENT INTO THE MAELSTROM"

## NEW SOUTH WALES AND AUSTRALIAN CAPITAL TERRITORY

### SYDNEY

As Bjelke-Petersen reigned to the north, Queensland punks could be excused for forgetting that in 1974 the country had reelected an unprecedentedly socially progressive federal government headed by Gough Whitlam.

Sydney best reflected the nation's more culturally liberal atmosphere. Whereas the licentiousness of Brisbane's nightlife under Bjelke-Petersen was largely subterranean, in Sydney's Kings Cross it was on display for all to see. Adjoining the Cross, Darlinghurst was the centre from which Sydney punk emerged, germinating among the inner city's seediness. Punks brushed shoulders with addicts, sex workers, and underworld figures.

Flight to the suburbs by those with means had brought an emptiness to the inner city, and so slews of abandoned buildings and dilapidated terrace homes became occupied by punks, artists, and activists. Though hypergentrification was still some years away, such process was being pushed in motion as young people took over pubs that had otherwise been left to aging drunks. Oxford Street, now long renowned as a hub for Sydney's gay scene, was site of the Oxford Hotel, whose upstairs, commandeered by Radio Birdman, has become one of the most vaunted of Australia's former underground music venues.

Radio Birdman bassist Warwick Gilbert expresses his preference for the band around the period of the "Funhouse" at the Oxford Hotel. At a point in their timeline celebrated by many but attended by significantly fewer, Gilbert, with full confidence, proclaims that was "the best band on the planet. It was incredible, and the audience was part of that too."

Remembering the powerful confluence of doggedness and teen angst, Gilbert says he had "wanted to burn the whole shithouse down, really, and that music was the biggest 'fuck you' I could find."

Attending the same school as vocalist Rob Younger, Gilbert recalls that "we both liked the same kind of music.... We both kind of bought import records." The fiendish scouring of local stores ensured finding "just these real isolated gems." Sitting unwanted among the racks were records by the Stooges. "*Raw Power*, it's the best rock 'n' roll album ever," Gilbert says. Yet almost more importantly, it "provided a way forward."

"From the first practice" of Radio Birdman, Gilbert says they "just plugged in and *kaboom*, it's like a bloody atom bomb going off.... You just knew it was the best thing in the world at the time." Gilbert insists that "you weren't fooling yourself; you just actually knew it, and the people in the audience knew it." To begin with, the "enlightened" were most modest in number: the band amassed seven dollars at their first paying show.[1]

Radio Birdman's 1974–75 years saw the band as an unknown or unwanted entity; gigs usually consisted of only a few dozen patrons. Their proficiency as performers, however, was to eventually conquer; crowned victors of the *RAM* (*Rock Australia Magazine*) "Levis's Punk Band Thriller," the group were presented with recording time, from which came their *Burn My Eye* seven-inch in 1976.

Heralded as Australia's best punk band through their victory, Gilbert dismissively says, "I never really thought about punk" despite being "very aware of it.... We'd been doing that sort of music for a few years by then, like the Saints from Brisbane. We didn't know about the Saints until '(I'm) Stranded' came out, and that was pretty amazing."

Legendary has become the sometimes-tense interaction between the two bands; at a shared Paddington Hall show in 1977, Chris Bailey made use of an utterly sardonic line during their set: "We want to thank as a group the local chapter of the Hitler Youth who put up the fine props."[2] Referencing Radio Birdman's use of banners and symbology, Younger remembers being "told Chris's sister tore down our flag that night and said something about homosexuals and Aborigines being bashed in Queensland because of fascists like us. That was funny."[3]

Labelling himself "apolitical," Radio Birdman guitarist Deniz Tek dismissed notions of it having any explicit meaning: "There was certainly no political intent in all of that. It was more of a club mentality, having our own organisation."[4] Where the Saints had been insular,

Birdman were populists, evidenced in their fan club and crowd chants of "Yeah hup."

The Saints' and Radio Birdman's refusal of the punk label could be viewed as if it was an affront to their intellect and an ignoring of the years they had honed their sounds unaffected by trends. Gilbert does, however, acknowledge the opportunity it afforded lesser professional outfits such as theirs: "I guess for the time we weren't such great players either, and the punk era, thank God for that ... gave us a foot in the door to play music."

Seeking their own musical entertainment, Gilbert's work colleagues "found out I was in the band and they said, 'We'll do Warwick a favour, we'll go and see his band,' and they came along to the Oxford." They unwittingly chose a memorable performance. "Rob [was] crawling around the floor screaming and then ... Sisto [Birdman's roadie] ... he's carrying this skull and then Rob took the lid off and there was some stuff that was sheep brains and he stuffed them in his mouth and it was so revolting he started spitting them out and speckles all the audience.... Everyone just fled for their lives and ran down the stairs.... I went back to work on Monday and everyone's going, 'There he is.'"

Of the career as an animator that he has maintained since those days, Gilbert says, "I've worked for Disney for eighteen years, and Hanna-Barbera, and I've directed thirty films."

Having also performed at the Oxford, Greg Morris punctures some of the storied venue's mythology: "Considering what it's known for ... it was just a small stage in one corner and the walls weren't finished and no carpet on the floor." The transmission of taxi radios would also be involuntarily picked up by its PA. The Funhouse crowd was just as scrambled, described as consisting of a "fractured peer group: Cheesecloth hippies, leather [Hells] Angels, Paddo trendies, some kids O.D.ed on photos of Pistols devotees."[5]

In 1976–77, punk's more formal emergence trickled into a growing interest towards Birdman. The band's first album, *Radios Appear* (1977), entered the national charts, peaking at number thirty-five. Gilbert, however, reveals the group never harboured any great affinity with the new movement "because I think they were younger, and they were more into the fashion of punk and we weren't."

The conflicting of the old and the new would be most evident in England, but not before the band's final performance at Paddington, exhibiting all the trappings of a punk show. Younger jumped into the audience to punch an audience member who had been spitting, all while the band dodged projectiles directed at them. At show's end, the hall's windows had been smashed, blood streaked the stairway, and a row of cars parked outside were damaged.

Playing in England would bring similar destruction, though more psychic and relational, culminating in the band's breakup. Any vision of success, however, had already been eviscerated. Tek says, "We started playing in England like January or February of '78, and so it was immediately after the punk craze had just started to subside. And you had all these people wondering what the next thing was gonna be, but it wasn't gonna be us for sure."[6]

The contrast of Birdman and the punk "craze" was best exemplified in Younger's flowing, lengthy blond hair. Gilbert recalls one particular instance where the two came into violent confrontation. "We played a gig that Slaughter and the Dogs were supposed to be playing and they pulled out.... They had a big punk following and we played instead, and the punks didn't like us at all." Sisto "was from Detroit.... He was in the military, he's a stone killer, he's a dangerous guy ... so when the mohawk guy threw a bottle at us—*bang*—Sisto is on him and had him around the head and it looked like he was trying to yank his head off.... All the other punks jumped on Sisto ... and you can see Sisto's fists coming out the top of the clump and the guys' heads going back where he hit them.... He really hurt those guys.... Punk was more of a fashion statement so they couldn't deal with actual violence."

They were slated to tour Europe with the Flamin' Groovies before the United States with the Ramones, but indifferent reviews only compounded an unfavourable environment as the US tour was cancelled. The group soon disbanded, but not before recording a second album. Even then, it failed to materialise for another three years (*Living Eyes* LP, 1981).

On being considered an early expression of punk, Gilbert says the group "were more precursor, like I see the *Fun House*–era Stooges were a precursor to punk. They were a link from the great garage punk" which had been "basically Stones-type bands with fuzz guitars and stuff, and we were more in tradition of that ... the attitude, the punk attitude."

Having shared punk's vision, though, to "kick all the cobwebs, you know, the old farts away," Gilbert says to find a place then in the conversation of punk's pioneers: "It's nice to be included . . . and to be recognised."

The first issue of Sydney fanzine *Spurt* in 1977 had conducted interviews with some of the city's early punks. Interviewee "Noel" noted punk's still-marginal status, that "there's about 15 of us [*laughs*]. It's just starting. I think it will get big."[7] It would initially get big, but not through foreseen means.

As a music industry darling, Ross Wilson was not only a name anathema to punk but also dismissed the genre's suitability to Australia: "We don't have the kind of culture punk needed. We're quite comfortable."[8] But even if Wilson was accurate in assessment of Anglo-Australia's lack of acute deprivation, it didn't prevent him from attempting to cash in as cowriter of the satirical track "I Might Be a Punk (But I Love You Baby)" in 1977. Performed by Norman Gunston, the TV alter ego of Australian comedian Gary McDonald, the song mocked punk as a readily adoptable trend. It also outsold every Australian punk single of the 1970s and early '80s and would be the first Australian "punk" release following the Saints and Radio Birdman.

Others had less success being associating with punk. Sydney band Punkz were anything but suited to their name. As a '60s-style pop group, Punkz eventually wised up to its ridiculousness, band member Robin Jackson telling *Women's Weekly* of the change from Punkz to Cheek "because of all the stupid problems associated with being labelled as a punk group—which we're not, of course."[9]

Securing the Oxford Funhouse, Radio Birdman had placed an ad in *RAM* for bands to join them at "Sydney's only genuine rock 'n' roll venue. We are having trouble finding good bands to book."

One of the few groups to meet such requirement, Psychosurgeons were fellow worshippers of the Stooges deity. Gilbert, however, suggests that Psychosurgeons "didn't have any choice" but to attempt emulation of their heroes, as "they couldn't play." Psychosurgeons vocalist Paul Gearside was himself a pure novice: "I'd never sung in a band, or in the shower for that matter."

Lacking musical acumen, the band was very much an experiment in punk's egalitarian and inclusive ethos. They would also be one of the most reviled bands in the city. At their first show, Mark Taylor plugged a phase pedal into distortion, all played at maximum volume in an effort to create the most extreme sound. Gearside unsurprisingly tempered any expectation: "I thought we were going great if people were laughing at us.... One pretty rough night... Craig got hit with something and lost it—he was the shy one. He jumped off the stage and ran up the left aisle and went at it; Mark and Dave stopped and joined in. When we jumped into the melee, we landed on the reflector board over all the little stage lights. All the bulbs smashed, and the place was plunged into darkness."

Receiving an invitation to play outside of Sydney, the band road-tripped north to Lismore. This time they were at least able to avert the fight: "We played a couple of covers and the people cowered at the back.... We were in a bit of strife; all we could play was about eight songs and we didn't know 'Rawhide.' ... Some goons in flannos and cowboy boots came in, and one had a whip. I can crack a whip, so I asked him for it. We started [the Stooges'] 'Search and Destroy' for the third time, and I tried to get the punters dancing. I jumped onto the floor and started cracking the whip all 'round. I hit the drinks and food table, just about cut the birthday cake in half—all the candles were gone. Two or three punters went down writhing in pain, and that was it: power off, told to fuck off.... 'Wild Weekend' was written in the car on the way home."

It would be released along with "Horizontal Action" as a seven-inch in 1978.

Channelling Jackson Pollock for design of the record, the band liberally splashed its covers with cow's blood; rumours circulated that it was of human origin. Catching a cab home with some of the blood still on his clothes, Dave Taylor was dobbed into police.

Away from their troubles, Gearside says, "[The Funhouse] felt safe and it felt like it was ours. We couldn't wait to get there on a Friday or Saturday night—didn't matter who was playing. We all sort of ended up knowing each other.... There were some real characters that frequented the Funhouse." Including Hells Angels members.

If Psychosurgeons' music was more than a nod to the Stooges, it wasn't only that with which they shared commonality. Preceding the Stooges' final show in 1974, Iggy Pop had used a radio show to goad a motorcycle gang, following a confrontation at their previous gig. The gang duly complied, and the smashing of thrown bottles can be heard on the live recording of their last show, the *Metallic KO* LP.

Following the taunting of Psychosurgeons onstage at the Funhouse, Gearside recklessly threw cans of beer at the responsible Hells Angels members; he was beaten for his boldness. A knife was also brandished at Mark Taylor. It was to be both the final show at the Funhouse and Gearside's last with the band: "I remember that the last song I sang in the band was 'Search and Destroy.' . . . After I was beaten up, I was pretty sick on the floor. I just wanted to get out of the place because they were hanging around downstairs to have another go. . . . I had to move from my place in Queen Street because the bad guys had my address and were hanging about for weeks after."

Gearside would not "see the Psychos play again."

The Funhouse advertisement for bands had not made much proscription aside from being "good." Sydney's first punk band in the English vein, Johnny Dole and the Scabs, were one of only a few to meet Birdman's criteria. Though Warwick Gilbert is blunt in giving assessment that the Scabs "were kind of cashing in on the punk thing. . . . They were more a regular sort of a band but couldn't play very well. . . . I think they just wanted to be part of it."

Greg Morris confirms the Scabs had started life as more of a "regular" band. But like so many other musicians, all that was to be cast aside by the impact of four guys in barely fitting leather jackets from New York: "The first time I heard the Ramones was on radio going to a rehearsal. . . . My first reaction was 'That's what we sound like.' Our style of playing had morphed into a harsher sound, but the style didn't have a name yet. Strangely, when I got to the studio, the others . . . had heard it too, and we all had the same feeling. So we discussed it, and we thought this was a direction we would like to go towards. We found out a little later it was called punk rock.

"Of the gigs we did manage to get in that early stage," Morris says, "we didn't play to that many people." Despite the fact "it wasn't very big," he does recall that "there were a lot of diverse people in the audience. . . . When it first started, you'd see surfies, office workers, and people on the dole all coming along to see what it was all about."

As the first local approximation of the Sex Pistols, the band also quickly drew attention from a media desiring similar scandal and swear words. Morris, though, highlights that "those articles have a lot of what I refer to as 'expected' journalism. For example, we were all supposed to hate Led Zeppelin and Black Sabbath etc. and expected to put it down. But I grew up on that stuff."

A segment on television program *A Current Affair* featured the band, with presenter Mike Carlton suitably playing up the drama of this strange and threatening new species: "If this sounds terrible on your television set, then you should hear it in the flesh. It's called punk rock because that's what it is, nobody really cares what it sounds like.... Maybe it's naked violence, maybe it's pure animal—I just don't know. You wouldn't want them in your lounge room, and you certainly wouldn't want your daughter to marry one."

Morris estimates that "you could take what was ever written about Johnny Dole and the Scabs and halve it and you might have something closer to the truth. But they spelt our name right, so that's all that mattered. It's good fun seeing your name in print, even if what's being said is not entirely true."

A bearded Morris, however, was not being perceived as entirely "true" to the band's punk aesthetic: "I was kicked out because of an image issue. I wouldn't conform to what some of them thought the image should be.... The others felt we needed to look like what was happening in England.... In England, it was a very different reason why punk came about: nobody had jobs, and everyone was struggling, and putting together a band was an outlet. For us, when we first started, three of us had day jobs. I was married and had a mortgage, so we didn't have the hardships associated with being a punk. Don't get me wrong, we weren't rich, but we certainly weren't feeling it like they were in England."

David Virgin recalled the multifarious discussions that surrounded a genre still in its infancy and without clear definition: "There was much debate in the pubs and clubs of Sydney in the late-'70s.... Does clothes maketh punk, does political allegiance come in to play? What is anarchy? Who deserves the title of punk, who doesn't? Is it music? Is it lifestyle? Can you have a beard?"[10]

But for Morris, and to the detriment of the Scabs, "punk really only started to kick off after the band had finished, which is a real shame because I think we could have been something if we'd continued playing and released a record.... The greed of the manager and Johnny's [Dole, vocalist] eventual drug problems stuffed it all up."

Almost a decade following the Scabs' demise, Dole was finally overcome by its effects, dying from overdose.

The Scabs' eight recorded tracks were finally released as *Scab Animal 1977* in 1997.

At the closure of Funhouse, the Scabs had approached publicans of various inner-city locales for potential venues in which to have shows. At the time, booking agencies held a monopoly over reputable establishments, as well as possessing the more known bands on their books. Punk would be shut out. They finally secured the hesitant approval of the Grand Hotel, but bands were consigned to a back room. Its drab interior seriously contrasted the tawdry collection of punks it would eventually attract as the fluidity between floor and stage, punter and performer, was blurred.

Surprising to those not of the era, venue PAs are a more recent phenomenon, with bands of this earlier time usually required to organise sound equipment. Reviews of live shows from the late 1970s well into the '80s are routinely found to discuss nonfunctioning or poorly performing gear.

For the Grand, the task of PA was handled by Jeff Fatt, later of the Cockroaches, a hardworking if middling group who had some modest success. After the band's breakup, Fatt joined other Cockroaches member Anthony Field in a children's entertainment group: the Wiggles, one of Australia's highest-earning entertainers. Fatt had fatefully not been lured by punk, even if the Cockroaches once presented audiences with the chorus of "I Want a Leather Jacket."

No band at the time could be more removed from the Wiggles G-rated classification than the deservedly named Filth. A hideous, swearing, and sneering blight to the niceties of television-sanctioned rock 'n' roll, Filth attained the informal title as the most virulently punk—and hence loathed—band in Sydney, if not the whole country. Mark Taylor went even a step further: "They were the most nihilistic, despicable band ever certainly in Australia, if not the entire world."[11] What the band was lacking in musical dexterity was more than compensated for by their frenzied live show. *Roadrunner* magazine suitably suggested that "if any band took rock 'n' roll to its logical final solution it was Filth. . . . Keeping time had nothing to do with it. Neither did the future for that matter. . . . Filth were always more of a comment (an abusive one) than a group."[12]

Prompted about reflection on his hometown of Wollongong, guitarist Bob Short makes his own derisive comment: "I probably would have to give the Luke Skywalker response about a bright shiny centre of the universe and the point furthest from it. Or, like many before, call it the arsehole of the universe."

Short sought escape to Sydney, despite the excessive actions of the big city's police. Finding a discarded cutout for Sherbet's *Greatest Hits* following a gig, Short flung the advertising into the street, where it not so fortuitously hit a passing police car. The outburst resulted in a service revolver being placed to the back of his head.

Desiring to form his own group, Short speaks of vocalist Pete Tillman's suitability: "I'd seen him sing in a band called West Coast Live. They were awful and the audience hated him; that was the best reason to be in a band with him. We got our name when a woman in McDonald's dragged her child from the building after seeing us. As she departed, she screamed, 'I'm not eating near that filth!' . . . My biggest inspiration for Filth was the old zoo in Taronga. There was a kind of avenue of apes in cages in the old days; apes would shit in their hands and throw them at their audience, they'd clamp themselves to the bars and piss and wank at you, and they screamed with rage. This is the best description of a typical Filth gig."

As a model of punk's shocking edifice, Short says, "We were wilder and more loathed than any legend. . . . We wanted to be hated and succeeded beyond our wildest imagination."

In 1977, while *Star Wars* gave a futuristic depiction of the past, punks must have looked like they'd crawled from a seedy spaceport bar in the outer reaches of the galaxy. Short says people responded accordingly: "Every time Filth played there was violence. Just walking into a pub could be dangerous—I was bashed several times. When people talk about how dangerous and rowdy the streets of Sydney have become, I just laugh. No one jumps out of their cars with tire irons in their hands anymore."

The "Zippy Pinhead" column in *Spurt* was less than complimentary of Filth and documented their crowd's propensity for violence "where moronic meatheads beat themselves up."[13] Mark Taylor recounts their target instead being the innocent Bondi Masonic Hall, where the crowd "broke every window in the hall and reduced the entire contents to a pile of splinters overnight. Filth's manager told me that early the next morning he took six vanloads of broken chairs, windows, and furniture and dumped it on Bondi Beach."[14]

But where some simply saw wanton destruction, others like Bruce Tindale saw art: "Bob only had three strings ... and played slide with a broken beer bottle and whipped his guitar with the chain he used as a guitar strap. The singer, Pete Tillman, decided to cut himself with some broken glass and turned to the audience with his T-shirt fading to red. They only had a few songs, so the gig didn't last long. It reminded me a little of the weirder German performance/body artists I had studied at art school."

The trajectory of Tillman seemed to confirm the often temporal, youthful nature of punk that would sometimes precede careerist respectability. From the chaos and calamity of Filth, Tillman's post-music career came as a barrister and included the publishing of such spiritless titles as *The Legal Adviser's Guide to Franchising*.

The chaos would also temper with Short's new band Urban Guerillas, as they took on semblance of a proper—if not more explicitly political—group. Guerillas member Dan Rumour was to become a fixture on Sydney's music scene through other punk bands Blackrunner, Friction, Ugly Mirrors, and Bedhogs. Eventually expanding stylistically, Rumour became a founding member of the Cruel Sea.

Where Black crafted Urban Guerillas "as a vehicle of left-wing anarchist political ideology," Kamikaze Kids singer Julie Mostyn suggests her own politics as more emblematic of the counterculture's "personal is political.... Everything comes down to politics, and I think what you do in a personal way is a political act. Just choosing to go with that feeling ... that sort of rejection of what had been before is political in its own way, even though they're not standing up and protesting verbally."

For Mostyn, "having grown up in that sort of bohemian atmosphere" of Kings Cross combined with "disenfranchisement as well just in terms of my own personal sort of history in my family. I had parents who were very domineering, so I was looking for my own voice, and so it was just all of those things converging and me searching for some way of expressing myself."

Precipitated in part by "seeing Radio Birdman for the first time," Mostyn cites the gig as being "like a revelation.... We wanted something really exciting and that showed us a new way of being." Together with Dare Jennings, she helped promote the message: "We printed the first Birdman T-shirts." Creating the label Phantom T-Shirts, Mostyn says,

"We were just working out the back of the house that we lived in, in a shed, screen printing the T-shirts to start with" before it "got bigger and bigger." Jennings was to continue with apparel, founding clothing labels Mambo in 1984 and Deus ex Machina in 2005.

Addressing her own band, Mostyn says of Kamikaze Kids' brief existence that "I suppose we were one of the first in that scene after Radio Birdman.... We couldn't play very well, so we got the punk following" as "we were pretty wild, and we had the spirit—that rebellious spirit." The "spirit," however, began to slip into self-immolation, Mostyn confiding that "there was a lot of alcohol involved, and drugs." Any inebriation, though, was certainly not confined to the bands themselves: "There were many, many nights when people would be just passed out in the venues.... It sort of wasn't really leading anywhere very healthy, and really what I'd always been about was just wanting to express some sort of rage about something to do with my childhood ... but it wasn't looking very healthy there for a while, so I think we imploded."

Mostyn continued in the more capable Flaming Hands, but the new group came with its own issues, namely the pressures and expectations of being overseen by INXS manager Chris Murphy: "His way of managing was sort of world domination, like what happened with INXS.... To me it was really sort of scary.... I didn't want world domination, I just wanted to be able to develop in my own time and in my own space."

It would seem hard for many to believe that she could reject such opportunity, and Mostyn concurs: "I know, because it's everybody's dream." Far from thoughts of chart dominance, though, Mostyn expresses a more humble and simplistic drive: "I love connecting with people.... I love that sharing of emotions and you're having a discussion with people through music that you probably would never have in person.... We all have the same sort of emotions and feelings; we don't often get to talk about them, but through music you can, and that's what I love."

Thirty kilometres southwest of Darlinghurst, the passage to punk of Malcolm Baxter and bandmate Andy Groome diverged significantly to Mostyn's, meeting at a Cabramatta migrant hostel. As pasty Englishmen baking in the Australian heat, they strived to acclimatise not only to the weather but also the hostility: "Going to Cabramatta High—which was one of the roughest high schools around—that was always interesting: they hated migrants."

The duo's fixation with British music style Merseybeat was disrupted when Baxter's girlfriend, now wife, returned from the UK "with all these records and stories" having seen "the Clash, the Jam, and all these bands play." Baxter, however, describes punk as having been "more a dawning than a revelation.... It was a natural progression."

Less natural, at least for Australian punk, was their band the Last Words' signing to a major record label, with their *Animal World* seven-inch released on Wizard in 1977. "When we got signed, we were the only punk band in Sydney that got signed like that."

Wizard was home to chart toppers Hush, Daddy Cool, Air Supply, Rick Springfield, and Rolf Harris, yet the Last Words' presence on the label was not the great opportunity it initially appeared to be: "They really liked us, but they just didn't know what to do with us."

Beyond the puzzlement of the label, resentment came from within the scene itself: "When we started playing at the Grand, the people down there were just saying, 'You're sellouts.' ... Here we were with a single, we were in the *Telegraph*, and we were playing at the Grand, so it was weird for them." But "we were coming from a whole different perspective. We were coming from a background of 'We want to get into the music industry whatever way we can.'"

Having made the initial step of being signed, the group found the reality was not quite what they'd hoped: "We just got bored here really quickly, and we just thought there was no hope, so that's why we went to Britain."

In London, however, bassist Leigh Kendall recalls a scene that "was extraordinarily snobby in an inverse sort of way" and where "by 1979 ska had emerged and punk was beginning to become a bit 'old hat' to the cognoscenti." Regardless, says Baxter, "Did we have success? No, but it was fun.... I'd seen what was happening to everybody else, famewise, and I thought, 'I don't know if I want that.' ... It all sounded great back when we were fourteen.... Andy, when he left England, he just put his guitar down and never picked it up again."

Baxter, ruminating on people playing music, often in obscurity, says, "It's just something that's in people, that they have to do.... Some of the best performances ever were probably performed just in a garage."

Additionally, for Baxter, fame often comes at a significant personal cost: "They're not happy with just seeing you play music; they want you to die. They're not willing to pay the price for it, but they want you to pay it. . . . It's not about how big Nick Cave got—ask him about the price he's had to pay."

The Last Words further released two more seven-inch records and an album in England before returning to Australia. For Baxter, his punk era had come to completion. Reflecting on the need for progression, he confides that "I feel sorry for people that haven't grown up. If you're still acting like you're twenty at fifty you've wasted thirty years of your life. Do I still like that music? I love it, I play it all the time. It's great to go back and play the stuff, but I don't live there. I don't think any of us should. . . . I became a Christian pastor. We all go different places . . . as a consequence my life is very different. . . . But I can still rock."

Whether intended as a statement about their own ability to rock, or just named after a mass of minerals, Ian Hartley fawned about the authentically punk origins of Rocks: "They come from Sydney's depressing factory area, not from clothing boutiques. . . . They sing of an anguish and oppression that few of us will ever experience."[15] Drummer Greg Morris clarifies that Rocks lived in "a normal, clean, leafy suburban area." But far from the most troubling error associated with the band, the title of their 1978 single "You'r So Boring" is one of the most blatant instances of a record sleeve lacking a spellcheck.

While Rocks were being touted as "real punks," another band would be eyed with suspicion.

Supernaut's first single, "I Like It Both Ways" (1976), while commercially very popular, had not been without controversy due to its lyrical content personifying much of the sexual ambiguity of glam rock.

The band, originally from Perth, shifted direction for their 1978 *Unemployed* seven-inch, the sound of which was akin to the English punk bands with backgrounds in pre-punk glam. Though Supernaut wasn't without a taste for punk, singer Gary Twinn dismissed the perception that the group had sought to capitalise on punk's moment of notoriety: "The original punks were into glam and bands like the Faces, just as we were; they didn't arrive on the planet with short hair and bondage clothes. . . . We'd already had a modicum of success at a young age and were still developing. We didn't say, 'Oh, let's be punks and cut our hair.'"

Relocating to Sydney and undergoing a rebranding to "the Nauts," the band failed to revitalise their flagging popularity. A disgruntled

Twinn says, "We were not embraced by punks because they were all busy pretending they were real punks."

Sharing a manager with the Nauts, the Last Words were paired with the new arrivals at Frenchs' Tavern. Malcolm Baxter recalls a hostile, predominantly Last Words audience: "The Nauts went on and people were threatening them with broken bottles." Source for the disdain, according to Baxter, was credibility, "because they didn't come from that."

The band chose not to continue, Twinn identifying a restive group who "were all bored with the nonsense about image, management, music biz politics, and each other."

Today, Twinn plays in the International Swingers with original Sex Pistols bassist Glen Matlock.

Epitomising DIY (do-it-yourself) and disavowal of the mainstream music industry, the Thought Criminals were the antithesis of first-wave punk's sometimes ambivalence towards or even embrace of major labels. They self-released their *Hilton Bomber* seven-inch in 1978, the title of which referenced a bombing earlier that year at Sydney's Hilton Hotel during convening of the Commonwealth Heads of Government Regional Meeting. By this time, bassist Leigh Kendall was well versed in a movement routinely mischaracterised for bombings and terrorism: "I had been involved with the anarchist scene in Australia since 1974.... I never had any illusions about punk's radical content or potential. I was already of the view that anything outside of workers' revolution was doomed to fail.... In 1980, I was walking down Finchley Road [London] when I saw a billboard advertising Remington shavers, depicting a punk with a mohawk shaving the side of his head. Whatever radical potential punk had was gone, and it was now a product hijacked by capitalism. I had read *Society of the Spectacle* [by Guy Debord], which had informed my understanding."

Kendall departed the band following the *Hilton Bomber* record, as the initial fierce punk sound came to recede over subsequent releases.

The seven-inch had contained the track "Fun," its lyrics a rebuke of music as aspiring stardom. The band eventually brought a cessation to their live shows and issued a statement denouncing the music industry and its intermediaries, who were drawing money at the expense of bands and musicians.

Guitarist Roger Grierson's independent Doublethink label had been integral to the local scene, giving opportunity for bands who would likely have remained undocumented. David Studdert, whose band Tactics had been released on the label, stresses Grierson's indefatigable efforts: "Up to about '82, the whole scene wouldn't have happened in the way it happened without him. He put a shitload of energy into all of that."

Grierson was to eventually become one of those very industry people he'd once helped denounce, rising to chairman of Festival Mushroom Records. But then, as Studdert observes, "so did a lot of punks. Once neoliberalism and globalisation hit, they all just took off the safety pins and walked down that road."

The fourth of Doublethink's releases, Popular Mechanics' *From Here to Obscurity* seven-inch, was issued in 1979. The record showed the direction Grierson and Doublethink were to take, away from a more rudimentary punk sound, and Popular Mechanics were situated among other Sydney post-punk bands such as Systematics, Voigt/465, Scattered Order, and Nervous System.

An outgrowth of punk, post-punk was criticised as being the makings of university students, and deliberately inaccessible. Whatever the critique's validity, its tendency towards aesthetics as politics contrasted the often crude and didactic nature of punk. For every punk versed in Dadaism and Futurism, there was another barely literate enough to fill out a dole form.

Composed of art and humanities university students, Slugfuckers (*Instant Classic* seven-inch, 1979) existed as Deleuze- and Guattari-inspired art and performance rather than simply some borrowed chords and a 4/4 beat. The group would also be cited as an influence on the later development of industrial music.

Art as purity of performance was arguably embodied by no Sydney band more than X. Dismissing any academic pretension of their own, vocalist/guitarist Steve Lucas observes that "a lot of the bands came out of universities . . . X wasn't. I got kicked out of school when I was sixteen and I'd kind of been drifting for three years when I hooked up with X. . . . I was a hippie: long hair, no shoes. . . . When I wasn't tripping or smoking pot, I was helping friends round up goats running wild."

Lucas's hippie sensibility, though, would be affronted by an early session of what was to become X: "I remember walking out of that rehearsal and thinking, 'What a load of rubbish.' All this fucking anger, you know, and I was chill. . . . I sensed that was the last thing on earth I wanted to do . . . and so they carried on."

A few more rehearsals brought a "massive split" in the band. Lucas remembers being sent "a telegram saying, 'Come down. New band. Bring voice.' And so I did. . . . We did one rehearsal and you just knew instantly that that was the lineup." Still unable to completely give himself over to punk, however, Lucas was forced to borrow a safety pin from Johnny Dole to keep his jeans up before a show.

Recently ousted from Rose Tattoo, bassist Ian Rilen was a relative geriatric by the time punk arrived, having been born in 1947, though Lucas asserts that "Ian wanted to be a punk. . . . He loved everything new that was happening. . . . He loved playing X, but he knew we weren't commercial."

Any attempt at forcing their way into commercial avenues would be hindered by the band's infamy: "We were banned from thirty-two different venues at one time in Sydney. . . . We had the highest alcohol consumption records in Sydney, we had the highest attendance records in Sydney, and we were banned from the most places consecutively in Sydney. And the only reason we kept getting gigs was because even though the punters wrecked the joint, they still made shitloads of money."

On one occasion, the violence even culminated in a fatality: "We did a gig at . . . the Denison in Bondi and a riot broke out there between the Maori/Islander drinkers and all the punks. . . . Someone actually got a pool cue through the eye and was killed—lying in the gutter."

Barbarity at their shows would not be the only precursor to the band's brush with police. After they were scheduled to record a film clip, two members had chosen to drop acid the previous evening. Compounding an already anxiety-inducing experience, the setting for the clip was an empty floor in the police CIB (Criminal Investigative Branch) headquarters: "There's all these coppers there, I'm barefoot, red hair, moth-eaten singlet . . . and they left me there: twenty-second floor in a building with no walls, tripping off my head. I locked myself in the toilet."

X's debut album, *Aspirations*, with Oz rock legend Lobby Loyde as engineer, was recorded in four or five hours in 1979. Lucas remembers the band "set up and just one by one played every song we knew." Postproduction was a similarly uncomplicated process: "Can I overdub the guitars where the strings broke? . . . No. . . . Can we redo the vocals in this song because we came in wrong? . . . No. Love it. Love it the way it is."

With five years in between albums, *At Home with You* saw the dissipating of speed coupled with a greater precision, which resulted in a sound much removed from the debut. Despite that, Lucas says it "sold phenomenally well." Believing "someone will pick us up now," Lucas says, "of course nobody did. But then again, if you'd ever been to one of our gigs you'd know why."

X's notoriety, though, didn't seem to dissuade Mushroom Records from eventually signing the group. It would be to their ultimate regret. "We had this big party. Mushroom really went overboard. . . . I had a few cocktails, went home, and Ian and Kathy [Green, drums] hung around. . . . They got smashed, went back to Mushroom/Premier, and decided they wanted to see the 'Dream Baby' film clip and they couldn't find it in the Mushroom offices. . . . They started pulling all the gold records off the walls and throwing them around. They turned the table upside down—the big boardroom table—called the head of publishing a fucking paedophile. They just went mental. . . . I went in the next day to finish signing off on the publishing deal. . . . Everyone's just looking at me like I was a leper. . . . Eventually one of the secretaries said, 'Actually, you weren't there, were you?' . . . We just did what we did, and I don't think any of us really thought it was gonna last. And it didn't last; we constantly broke up, but then we just couldn't find anything else that was remotely as energising so we'd have to get back together. . . . It was like being addicted to drugs or sex or gambling or whatever it was. You hated yourself for doing it, but you couldn't avoid doing it."

Of their intoxicating qualities, Lucas asserts that "when we sort of were together it was really, really intense." X as a live band? Lucas insists "there was no one like it."

Few others would also endure such misfortune, Lucas says, intimating the purifying effect of a Greek tragedy, before conceding their actual impact: "Any band worth its salt has got to have a wreck every now and then, but, you know, we had so much death. . . . In 1978, there was kind of a poll or book going around, who's going to be next to die, and it was me. . . . And somehow, I didn't. I don't know why. . . . I certainly did everything. Some of the stories people have told me about myself that I have no memory of are pretty horrible. Not horrible because I did nasty things to people, but just horrible that I could do that and not be dead."

Ian Krahe, Ian Rilen, and Steve Cafiero would not survive.

Able to surmount the tribulation, Lucas is tinged with nostalgia. Speaking to old '60s Australian rock musicians, his recollection is that "they'd say, 'Oh, you've got no idea what it was like: 1966 in Carnaby Street, 1967 in Abbey Road studios ... fucking unbelievable,' and I can see that it would have been. But I don't feel ashamed by saying, 'Well, you should have seen Sydney in 1977, you would not fucking believe what went on—it was insane.'"

If Sydney's scene was maniacal, Suicide Squad guitarist Mark Easton says of his hometown Wollongong, "I don't think they knew what punk was yet.... There was still hippie bands playing at the local pubs.... They hadn't moved on."

For a proudly blue-collar city, it comes as a surprise to learn that the first record released as part of the new wave would tend towards the more highbrow. Sunday Painters' *Alternatives to Perfection* seven-inch in 1980 reflected the vibe of the art-punk movements of Sydney and other larger, Western urban centres.

By contrast, in seeking to form his own band, Easton says an advertisement for a drummer had been answered by "some guy who was out in the bush who ... had no idea even what Sydney was about in the first place. I don't know if he'd even been there."

Never performing a single show in Wollongong before decamping to Sydney, Easton found himself "in a lot of debt" and in need of work: "I couldn't get a job anywhere because of the way I looked.... I ended up getting a taxi licence because ... there was no uniform, you could turn up to work looking any way you wanted.

"These old ladies would go to get in my cab and they'd go, 'Oh no!' and they'd jump out.... And then I'd get people in the cab and they'd say, 'Oh, cool cab driver' and they'd pay for their fare in drugs and I'd be high as, driving—it was pretty silly. Before that, actually, I had a job in a pie factory and I used to get all the stale, out-of-date pies and I'd sell them to all the punks ... for a real good price."

In 1980, Suicide Squad produced one of Australia's most revered early punk singles, "I Hate School." The song featured the vocals of Annie Barrett, but the song's lyrics came from the genius mind of Easton's younger sister: "I came home one time and I said to my sister, 'What do you really hate?' and she said, 'I hate school' ... so we sat down and wrote a song. . . . When I was in school, I was always in bands that everybody hated. All of a sudden when punk came along, I thought, 'Wow, now I can be in a band that everybody hates but you're popular to a certain bunch of people.' . . . It was a trend, but it was the right trend at the right time for a lot of people. For me, I would never have gone to Sydney and played in a band if that hadn't happened."

Concurrent to Suicide Squad, XL Capris were another of the few Sydney groups with a female vocalist. Singer Johanna Pigott, reflecting on their beginnings, jokes that "in 1978 the tolerance for incompetence was high . . . so we started a band."[16] In spite of any amateurism, the group had something of an immediate impact on audiences: "Mid-January 1979; first 'real' gig at Garibaldi's. The band was banned from this venue because an excited fan threw the men's toilet out the window."[17]

Even if the group was self-admittedly not the most proficient upon their inception, what they lacked in competence was compensated for through energy and quirkiness on their first single, "My City of Sydney." Released in 1980, it was the sole Australian title found in John Peel's collection of his 142 favourite records, revealed following his death in 2004.

Guitarist Kimble Rendall departed, helping form Hoodoo Gurus as well as taking up director roles for both film and music videos of major Australian acts. Pigott, together with Todd Hunter, affirmed their acumen as songwriters, cowriting "Rain" for Dragon and "Age of Reason" for John Farnham. Along with bandmate Tim Gooding, Pigott also became a writer for teen television drama *Heartbreak High*.

Set in Sydney, the 1981 film *Puberty Blues* (adapted from the book) provided a telling if controversial snapshot of the issues facing lower-middle-class Australian teens and highlighted the youthful desire for identity. With much of its content applicable to the punk scene, the film adaptation featured Geoff Rhoe of Minuteman. Bandmate Steve Lorkin explains that "he was the main character. . . . He was the guy that died from a drug overdose. . . . He did a lot of TV commercials like Coca-Cola. . . . When I tried out for the band, I said, 'I know you from somewhere,' and he just sort of laughed."

Eventual editor-in-chief of *Vogue Australia* Kirstie Clements had come from the same area and era of the *Puberty Blues* book's setting. Speaking of its parallel to her own formative years, Clements observed, "It was best to hide any individual or intelligent thoughts if you were to fit in with the dominant behaviours that prevailed."[18] Invited to a show at the Grand as a sixteen-year-old, Clements recounts, "I walked into the gloom nervously and looked around. It was full of punks with safety pins in their noses and ears, studded leather jackets, and skinny black jeans.... It was the most exciting thing I had ever seen.... That night changed my life."[19]

Another of Clement's observations of the Grand had been that "there were hardly any girls, and the ones that were looked formidable."[20] The singer of the Screaming Abdabs (*We Don't Wanna: The Paris Theatre Tape 1978* LP, 2016), Carmel Strelein, was arguably not only the scene's most formidable-looking woman, but also its greatest embodiment of an iconoclastic figure. One of the most striking characters on the streets of inner Sydney, it was reported that "her head was totally shaved; outrageous mascara and eyeliner swoops launched out from her eyes and whooshed back across the temples, twin ocular flames that met at the back of her skull."[21]

Leaving home at thirteen, Strelein modelled for hip '70s British designer Zandra Rhodes. Norman Parkinson, one of Britain's preeminent photographers, travelled to Sydney to photograph her. Published in his book *Sisters under the Skin*, photos of Strelein appeared alongside the Queen Mother, Princess Anne, Elizabeth Taylor, and Miss Piggy.

Arriving to Sydney in early 1977, Bruce Tindale notes the pivotal moment of befriending fellow student Chris Masuak, Radio Birdman's guitarist. Developing his own (modest) six-string ambition, Tindale says, "I could hardly play the guitar, but for whatever reason they rang me and said come along to rehearsals. We started out at the Paris [Theatre]."

The Paris Theatre had been initiated by Johnny Allen, previously codirector of Australia's most (in)famous countercultural/hippie gathering, the Aquarius Festival in Nimbin, in 1973. Travelling to New York and legendary venue CBGB, Allen became sympathetic to punk, viewing an affinity through "a totally revolutionary concept of how one approaches one's entire lifestyle and set of values."[22]

Of similar uncommon thought and approach, Tindale says, "The Abdabs were a bit unique.... I think the small crowd at our debut was a bit startled, partly by the minimal music and somewhat by the visual style of the band."

Their idiosyncrasy, however, would go from being merely quaint to perilous, as Tindale says their "second Paris Theatre concert was the one where things got a bit scary. . . . The audience took umbrage and screamed stuff at us like 'Fuck off!' and they threw things. I recall seeing shoes, empty and full alcohol containers all over the stage, and, strangely, lots of money in silver coin."

Regardless of the reaction, Tindale remains thankful for "the chance to play in bands. . . . I had come to town . . . from a markedly mundane country upbringing. . . . By mid-'78 I had been in three inner-city bands [including the Professors (posthumous *Go Out Tonight* seven-inch, 2018)], made lifelong friends, and seen a whole new musical era born."

Far from retreating to normalcy, Strelein's life took her to San Francisco, where she lived the gamut of its experience, through drug dependency, sex work, and rehab, before establishing her own successful hair salon. She also remained involved in the punk and drag scenes. At thirty-seven, however, Strelein was killed in a contract killing undertaken by her ex-husband, a Hells Angels associate and prospect.

If punk, for men, often meant the disavowal of traditional roles and behaviours, for women such as Strelein it was doubly as daring through the spurning of patriarchal expectations. As an act of deviancy, Johanna Pigott says punk allowed women to assert themselves in unconventional ways: "Being liked for being loud and aggressive and not nice. Nothing unusual now, but in the late-'70s it wasn't nice for a suburban girl to go wild like that."[23]

If punk and its celebrated amateurism would be a challenge to rock's rigid and near-exclusively all-male hierarchy, female punks would be both a serious deviation and confrontation. Brushing aside the doormen, punk and its democratising effect allowed for the influx of a greater range of identities, as women asserted themselves as active participants rather than a passive spectatorship. Helen Carter, member of the (initially) all-female punk band Friction, asserted that "when punk came along, that was women coming out really."[24]

Music, like most cultural forms, is regulated by self-anointed guardians. Even for bands composed exclusively of males, some found themselves beyond the adulation of a punk scene noted for its supposed inclusivity. The title of the Press's 1979 album *Fodder for the Critics* alluded to the position the band believed themselves to inhabit. From the outer west of Sydney, the band, Bruce Cumming declares, "were a clique of one."

Conveying his life in the suburbs prior to punk, Cumming admits, "I was a teenage kid, I had an attitude, I had a fucking mouth on me, I was a heavy drinker ... and didn't mind shitloads of drugs either.... Basically I was ripe for it [punk]."

Notwithstanding Cumming's perceived shunning of the band, he says, "We did pick up a following around the inner city. It was small and a few of them were as cool as fuck ... but they weren't the people in the bands." Instead, he identifies "between a lot of bands ... a lot of territorial pissing.... I don't think that's historically unprecedented, because you would have got that even when they were doing hayrides back in, I don't know, 1910 or something; there would have been bands trying to bash banjos over each other's heads to get the gig."

When the Press was billed with Psychosurgeons, beer glasses took the place of banjos, hurled at the band while onstage. "I didn't know who was throwing the shit, but I didn't need to," says Cumming. Drummer Rick Doolan and two of his friends promptly dealt with the perpetrators.

Despite their willingness to confront detractors, Cumming says, "I think the most violence we ever had at any of our gigs ... was actually us." One of Cumming's stage memories is when singer Steve Kot "called for a song which we dropped" but "nothing happened, and he blew a fuse. That ended up down in the street." Not a stoush one probably wanted to find oneself among; with an air of nonchalance, Cumming observes, "We were pretty tough fucking dudes."

Following the Press, some were to gain even more fearsome reputations. Of drummer Doolan: "He was the secretary of the Nomads [outlaw motorcycle club]." Band associate "Angelo was the president.... Rick and Angelo are both dead.... I thought the world of Rick.... It's a bit hard to sit here and say that a guy who made a fortune selling amphetamines was a child of the universe or something, but he was a fair-dinkum bloke.... A lot of people had a lot of love and respect for him." But most importantly, "he got along like a house on fire with my mum."

Another band to gain notoriety was New Zealand's Proud Scum, who had become exiles of their own making.

At a 1979 show in hometown Auckland, a fire broke out onstage as the group performed. Instead of fleeing for the exit, "the band played on, ignoring the flames and, seemingly, everybody else remained entirely unfazed."[25] The fire brigade "arrived to an empty, smoked-filled room. Nothing more was ever said about it."[26]

Even if the event was best left unspoken of, the band came to have difficulty securing venues in its aftermath. The group arrived in Sydney, viewed as a more viable location, in early 1980. Singer Jonathan "Jamrag" Griffiths outlines the move: "Toy Love had just moved there, and other Kiwi bands in the years before. It seemed a logical step. And Auckland's punk scene seemed to be falling apart. Most of the punk bands were becoming more mainstream and distancing themselves from their past, while the punk fans were becoming increasingly violent and destructive. I couldn't see a future for our band in Auckland."

Griffiths admits that some minor ambitions were held by Proud Scum for the new city: "A bigger audience, more venues, so much opportunity." The reality was less heady and more sobering: "I was surprised how difficult it was to break in and how big an impact our network of friends and contacts had had on our success in Auckland."

While the band's prospects languished, Kiwi punks such as Griffiths hadn't always found favour with the locals either: "We were at a party in Paddington and this ferrety little guy sleazed up next to her [Griffiths's girlfriend] and was chatting her up right in front of me. . . . I was feeling a little vomitus (probably having consumed a lot of alcohol); I leaned over and spewed on his head."

The arrival of hardened Kiwi punks was to cause a stir beyond just lustful, mammalian-appearing men, with Roger Grierson recalling, "There was a sub section of punks—Proud Scum and bands like that—that was just 'punk punk.' They weren't Nazis but . . . there was a whole bunch of punks that thought Sham 69 was a good idea. They kinda went the 'dumb punk way.'"[27]

Countering Grierson's unfavourable opinion, Mark from Positive Hatred insists that "Proud Scum weren't a violent band at all." Alternatively, they were perhaps just some lonely Kiwis seeking the company of sex aids: "They used to have blow-up [sex] dolls . . . and stupid me, drunk one night—one of them deflated itself—decided I was going to blow it up through its hole. I didn't realise it had been used; I thought it came straight out of the packet."

• • •

As New Zealand punks came to leave a lasting—if sometimes sordid—imprint on the Sydney scene, others remained true outsiders. Marcus Phelan of Sheiks describes their detached stance: "I didn't care much about fashion or belonging to some kind of tribe." The impetus for Phelan was primarily creative. "We just wanted to write and play music that was exciting and had energy because the music that the radio and record companies were churning out was largely West Coast FM, soft rock, Hawaiian-shirted, margarita-sipping, coke-sniffing, *Don Kirshner's Rock Concert* snorefest schlock, or 'prog rock.'"

Thinking their music to be of sufficient quality, Phelan says, "In England, young talent like us would be put in a studio with a good producer and be guided and nurtured." In Sydney, they were forced to remain a DIY outfit. A year passed after the release of their conspicuously "not punk" first single, and Sheiks miraculously found a new sound on their *New York/Ten Times Around* seven-inch in 1980. Displaying a jagged, art-punk style, they had seemingly stumbled their way into punk's proximity for a brief moment. Phelan, though, was unimpressed with the tracks: "I hated them at the time."

Along with the Sheiks, other oddities, obscurities, and short-lived and unrecorded entities included Blackrunner, Broken Toys, Frenzy, Shock Treatment, Subversion, Local Product, the Bland, the Parasites, Johnny Demon and the Devils, the Inmates, Flying Calvittos, Invaders, Seems Twice, British Jets, Tommy and the Dipsticks, KAOS, Society Blitz, World War IV, and Inmates (the latter from rural Armidale).

One of the most curious Sydney records to surface was that of Danny Decay and the Molars. With punks not being noted for exemplary dental hygiene, Johnny Rotten's name had come from the parlous state of his teeth. In perhaps a committed attempt to bring oral health awareness to the scene, Danny Decay donned some dubiously authentic dental attire for the cover of their *If Dentistry Is Right* seven-inch in 1982.

Where marginal acts crafted their own offbeat releases to meagre responses, post–Radio Birdman Sydney was accused of being mired by the "Detroit sound" which came to occupy the city's band scene for years to come. Rooted in the MC5/Stooges aural template, they reflected one side of the division between the more artistic and the more rock origins of punk. Ashley Thomson, however, notes humans' propensity for binaries: "Some people are always divided, they need a side: Ford/Holden, Detroit/spiky punk, Beatles/Stones. Fuck it, I like it all. Australia went fucking nuts for that Detroit thing. . . . I guess that surgeon/jet fighter pilot/guitarist [Deniz Tek] has a lot to answer for."

Ex-Birdman members, through a series of bands, were not to stray far from the proven formula, including the Visitors' self-titled twelve-inch in 1980 and New Christs' *Face of a New God* seven-inch in 1981. The same year, New Race—a supergroup containing Rob Younger, Deniz Tek, and Warwick Gilbert (Radio Birdman), Ron Asheton (Stooges), and Dennis Thompson (MC5)—toured Australia. In the absence of a studio recording, an LP—*First and the Last*—captured them live.

Gilbert was far from ebullient about the sound becoming so entrenched, declaring that "it became a kind of hateful thing for me—people who played that sort of stuff."

By no means the only person aggrieved with bands prone to emulation, a rejected candidate for the Lipstick Killers (*Hindu Gods of Love* seven-inch, 1979) wrote of his disgust to *RAM*. Responding to an advertisement, the hopeful bassist arrived to find stereotypical-looking punks who immediately made judgement of his ample hair: "They take one look at my shoulder-length hair and beard and say, 'Hello . . . goodbye.'"[28]

Where Psychosurgeons' inexperience had seen their Stooges attempt collapse into punk, the band's continuation as Lipstick Killers more competently corrected the trajectory. From crowds of around a hundred for Psychosurgeons gigs, the Lipstick Killers almost immediately tripled their fandom. They gifted the Sunnyboys their first show as support in 1980, a gig which saw a crowd swollen to 1,200.

Feeling themselves to have exhausted Sydney, the band left for the US at the end of the year. Though the trip was primarily viewed as "adventure," the band was also adamant they could scrape out some modicum of success. As their peers had sought careers in London and failed, Lipstick Killers chose the relatively untested location of Los Angeles.

Shows, however, were intermittent; they secured only ten gigs in twelve months. Of those they did manage, Mark Taylor spoke of audiences' puzzlement: "They didn't applaud, they just stood there, they didn't dislike it, I think the clothes were wrong, the songs were wrong, but maybe the energy was right."[29] And if shows were scarce, money was even scarcer: "We ate sugar and bread a lot of the time."[30] The remaining members quit before they could record their intended LP, and the band was defunct by the end of 1981.

The most popular and enduring of bands consigned to the "Detroit" category, the Celibate Rifles released three and a half decades' worth of albums while presumably also enjoying a significantly more diversified diet than sugar and bread.

Possessing lyrics that contradicted the heavily masculine vibe of Detroit-styled bands, and devoid of the predictable black styling, the Rifles unconsciously cultivated an image more as unhip dags. Regardless of their fashion shortcomings, the Rifles drew the attention of major label scouts, with singer Damian Lovelock recalling, "One of the guys that came out to see us, said to me that we were one of the best live bands he'd ever seen, but at the same time we had virtually zero commercial potential."[31]

Steadfast, the band amassed one of the greatest careers for an Australian independent act through the 1980s. Yet far from any rock hedonism, Lovelock came to embrace spiritualism, and he practiced as a yoga teacher in addition to his soccer fixation. It was also this latter passion for which he became most recognisable, eventually appearing as a soccer analyst on SBS TV and also publishing two books on the sport.

He passed away from cancer in 2019.

As someone who came to resent what the Birdman legacy did to the local scene, Warwick Gilbert did little to help abate it when forming the Hitmen with old bandmates. Due to the fractures from Birdman's breakup, Gilbert says that "the Radio Birdman crowd-controlled Sydney, so the Hitmen were forced to find another audience.... We just wanted to play our songs and were dubbed uncool by the inner-city scene, and it really was stifling."

Their predicament would not be aided by followers of the Kelpies. Drummer Ashley Thomson relives the particular prank when "we got a decent gig with the Hitmen. Our fans added graffiti of a big fat 'S' on all their venue posters, thus we didn't get another show with the SHitmen."[32]

As a teen residing in suburban Brisbane, when Thomson arrived to Sydney, the contrast could not have been more striking: "I'd come back to Sydney a very sad and isolated fuck, and transitioned to a hundred new friends/drug buddies, playing in this great band, having adventures, girlfriends; I had this whole new life experience happening. Rock 'n' roll saved my life—it nearly killed me as well, but ultimately, hey, I'm still around."

The Kelpies successfully managed to consolidate both the Detroit and more punk cliques, and they were drawing sizeable crowds. Despite this, says Thomson, "The industry were scared of us—actually scared. To this day we're left off era music compilations. . . . A lot of that apprehension was about the chaos and fights at gigs." Thomson, in detail, paints the aftermath of one such show: "As I left the venue—for some reason I remember this in slow motion—there was a large, wide set of stairs. . . . I waltzed down with my girlfriend through about ten fights: punks versus surfies; punks had handfuls of blond hair; a surfie was hammering some punk who was laughing maniacally; a punk chick was pissing on the stairs. . . . There was one venue security guy who was just watching, having a smoke. Faces I knew were appearing in front of my face, cut and bleeding like boxers, smiling, saying, 'Great gig, Ash.' A couple of people were unconscious: Fighting? Booze? Both? No police anywhere; there seemed to be feathers floating around like people had had a pillow fight. . . . It was like a punk rock David Lynch open-air play. That was just two minutes; fuck knows what else went on."

Guitarist Mark Easton mourns the drama they had found themselves lead actors in: "That was part of the reason we broke up. . . . People were just taking it too far. With the Kelpies, we'd sort of moved out of the traditional punk thing, but they were bringing it with them, the following. The following thought they owned the band."

Compounding the turbulence of their audiences, the band themselves harboured a tempestuousness, Easton recounting, "They basically self-destructed after a year and a half. . . . We were getting banned from gigs, we were unreliable, there was too much heroin going around." Thomson exhibits a greater insouciance to their demise: "We, like a million other bands, burned bright and fast."

The Kelpies released a seven-inch in 1982, and a posthumous *Official Bootleg* album followed in 1986, subtitled *Live at 51 Stanley Street*. The grimy party house of that address also featured on TV show *Simon Townsend's Wonder World*, a reporter standing in the claustrophobic basement space for one of the Kelpies' rehearsals.

The show itself was aired as a children's program, but the actual happenings at the address were often not suited for a youthful audience. Thomson reflects on the frenzied nature of the scene's participants: "I understand now that a large percentage of those original Sydney punks were traumatised, abused, and neglected as kids, had violent, drunk parents, or no parents, had undiagnosed mental health. As a result, they became severe substance abusers and went on to stints in jail, spending time in Morrisette Hospital, suicided, died by misadventure, overdosed, etc. But also, we had a fair whack of people just being rebellious, looking for some action, defining themselves, and growing up. We did try to look after each other, as ill-equipped as we were. We'd carry each other home, talk someone into not climbing the Harbour Bridge, take people to hospital, stand up for each other."

But even as the scene acted as surrogate family and counsellor, Thomson doesn't absolve himself: "I loved getting fucked up. I was so good at it—mister drug-fucked lampshade. I kinda went through that boringly typical *Women's Weekly* escalating drug progression—I was a greedy drug pig. But such a cool, cool time. Of course, as it does, it ended in tears for me: junkie, seizures, dead bodies, arrests, dealing, scamming, crime, emptiness, insanity, psych wards, doctors, pills, car crashes, deep psychosis, detox wards, hospitals, homelessness, physical illness, starvation, violence, and death. I died about three times. I became a totally evil cunt. I still carry a stain from it all."

Fortunately, through all the tragedy and young lives cut too short, there is the relief of the occasional clichéd happy ending: "When I was twenty-six, a cool sixty-year-old female detox worker talked me into going to rehab . . . have been straight ever since. I've had the same partner for twenty years, and we had two kids who play in bands and go to uni. I've kept up playing music, and the last ten years or so I work with fucked-up young people. It's a funny old world."

## CANBERRA

If any one city provided an example of how to unintentionally create suburban monotony, it was the nation's capital. Planning fostered decentralised enclaves, a prime breeding ground for the politics of boredom; the once-utopian vision of its architects was not being shared by those left as its guinea pigs. Virtually no nightlife populated the city's centre, with desertification coming at the working day's end. Allan

Coop, bassist of Cough Cough, described the despairing lack of options: "Nothing to do, nowhere to go. Just an already weary and well-defined path to the future. The only entertainment: a bong crowded coffee table in a suburban lounge room."[33]

Entertainment, at least in the modest form of a community radio program, had come in mid-1977 with *The Punk Show*. The program was hosted by chemistry tutor Ian Watson and computer programmer Steve Kilbey (eventual singer/bassist of the Church); the nerds had appeared to catch on to punk before the misfits.

The city's first two punk shows, presented under the banner of "Anti-Disco," came to attract more than those simply unenamoured by disco music and the heyday of *Saturday Night Fever*. They also, says Chris Shakallis, were "the first time that any of us got to witness how many others outside our own small circle of friends were getting into the new music."[34]

Transitioning from "Anti-Disco" into "Rock Against Boredom," one of their regular performers was Vacant Lot. Vocalist George Howson had been present at the city's initial shows, where, like Shakallis, he "was amazed there was all these people and had no idea where they had all come from. There was this sense of, 'Wow, there's this scene here.'" An immediate impetus for the proliferation of more bands, Howson remembers "all these other bands popping up out of nowhere ... and they're doing something completely different."

Before the scene's eventual codification into something very identifiably "punk," Howson remembers "one phrase Chris [Shakallis] used was that the template hadn't been fully written then, musically, and in terms of fashion." Thus it was "kind of like a very expressive environment: individually you can do what you wanted and there was no uniform." In addition to the fashion, Howson reminisces that "everyone had their own dance style. There was a lot of pogoing.... You could get up there and really—physically, at a visceral level—just respond to music, and the more intense it was, the more intense you moved.... The energy was contagious.... It was such a physical experience."

The progeny of a federal Liberal minister, in 1978 Howson had gone to study at ANU (Australian National University), presumably with all the expectations that accompanied being the son of a prominent political figure. Howson, however, was no supporter of the then Fraser-led

Liberal government: "There was this thing that you were really fighting against these dominant entrenched political forces that control the political landscape."

Though Australia conformed to the shibboleth of punk being birthed against the backdrop of a conservative government, Howson reminds that "when you think about it retrospectively," punk "was actually pre-Thatcher in England," emerging during the Labour government of James Callaghan. Travelling to Sweden in the early '80s, Howson says that punk there coexisted with a comparatively generous Scandinavian welfare state: "Materially, it was making a big difference, the standard of living, but a lot of it was soulless, and that's part of what was being rebelled against ... fighting the emptiness or meaninglessness of modern life."

Formed by ANU students in 1978, Vacant Lot bore a name which seemed to reflect that desolation. Their sole release, the 1981 *Living Underground* seven-inch, was covered with a simple black-and-white image of a backyard, its kept lawn containing an empty clothesline and disused play equipment: a wordless statement on the barrenness of suburban living. Howson, in rejection of his own upbringing, dropped out of university to pursue the band: "A lot of it was just people on the dole who could devote their time to music," as "the dole was a lot more flexible in those days."

At university, drummer Alex Anderson had involved himself in radical student politics as Vacant Lot performed at related events and demonstrations. Howson, however, became increasingly cautious of "a very totalitarian attitude within the ideology of left-wing politics which started to repel me in terms of that [idea] that people are empty vessels to fill up with the right way of thinking." Resultantly, his lyrics became "more just personal themes and atmosphere and physical descriptions of places and moods."

The shift inward was possibly aided by Howson's drug experimentation, which, he posits, was also part cause for the band's breakup: "I was doing a lot of drugs and being fairly chaotic."

As the band concluded, Howson says he "dropped out ... went interstate ... fucked up, ended up in the psych ward.... I guess I cut off from music for a while ... just because there was a pain attached to that." Howson confesses that in losing Vacant Lot, "I was quite heartbroken, because my whole world disappeared at that stage."

Bassist Bruce Hart had also given up his studies for the band, "but went back and completed his degree as a microbiologist," Howson says. "He was working at Latrobe Uni . . . they were trying to cure fly strike in sheep, and he was trying to manufacture ecstasy." Hart was "taking small quantities of drugs home and he obviously had a recipe from somewhere. . . . He was making it in his bathroom, I think, and suddenly there was a bit of a bad smell and he went out, maybe sensed something was wrong . . . and it exploded. . . . He had time to remove the chemicals as people came running." The property owner, believing the hot water service to blame, gave Hart a month's free rent.

Hart overdosed in 2009.

Few punks can boast—or are even willing to reveal—that they have played guitar at Tamworth's Country Music Festival. Paul Hayward has—and not just once, but on seventeen occasions.

As a kid, Hayward's father had sent him "to country and western lessons . . . and as soon as I could do a C chord, he was happy he'd got his money's worth." Continuing beyond his father-funded lessons, Hayward says, "What the teacher was teaching us fitted in, like 'Anarchy in the UK' was in the Mixolydian mode on the white notes on a piano—just go from a G then down to the F to the E on the white notes."

But the budding musician was still some way off the Sex Pistols, the sound of electric guitars a wonderment against the plucking of Hayward's acoustic: "I heard this noise in the upstairs bit when I was studying at school. . . . We realised it was a guy playing electric guitar. It sounded like a lawnmower, but in tune. So I went around with my nylon string graphite and said, 'Do you want to have a jam?'"

Another person with whom Hayward rehearsed had his own—albeit distinctive—issue with the Sex Pistols: "He was always conflicted because his father was a minister in the church. . . . He was too scared to walk into the import shop and buy the Sex Pistols album."

Exhibiting his fledgling group at college, Hayward recalls that Young Docteurs "were the young, shit punk band, and the older blues guys changed our poster name to the 'Young Dogturds.'" The Turds, however, would defecate all over the more seriously minded musicians, at least in terms of people willing to catch glimpse of them: "We did one thing called 'Canberra Calling'—all Canberra bands—there was well over seven hundred." Entry to the show included a free seven-inch of bands performing on the evening: Young Docteurs, Quintrex Bop, the Naturals, and No Concept.

Paul's dad, despite being unflinching in his devotion to country, had maintained interest in his son's musical endeavours, and in doing so became a certain fixture of the local scene. "I remember one of the punk girls came out and said, 'Hey Paul, there's a couple of old fags at the bar' at the uni, and I was like, 'Oh that's my dad and his mate,' and they've got their fake leather jackets on. They became part of the scene."

Not all were to be similarly supportive, as evidenced when Young Docteurs heedlessly performed at a rugby gathering. Regardless of the band only being "seventeen-year-old kids, these guys wanted to punch us. And they were big footy players." Fortuitously, they were rescued by one of Canberra's most fabled punks: "Trog being the mad bastard he was . . . had stockpiled all these schooner glasses. So, when they came to attack us, he just sat back and held them off by chucking schooner glasses . . . and we escaped."

Surveying that Canberra had "gone about as far as it could go," the band relocated to Sydney, but not before releasing their debut record in 1979, the *Bronze Portrait* seven-inch. Hayward admits that in making the move, the Docteurs were consigned to being "little fish in the big sea." As small fry, the band took on influences of the broader independent scene in Sydney at the time. Although having "signed a multi-record deal with Festival Records," the group only managed two further singles before petering out.[35] Reflecting on their own attempt at success, Hayward, however, remains philosophical: "Everyone had a go; it's just the luck of the draw."

The same year as Young Docteurs' formation, the *Canberra Times* despatched a foreign correspondent to immerse themselves in the new phenomenon that was drawing many of London's youth. Attending a show by the Clash, what this reporter found was a rebuke to any hoped attempt at sensationalist journalism: "Violence, the theatre destroyed, teenagers dressed in the most hideous clothes they could find, ears and noses pierced by safety pins, arms mutilated by cigarette burns and the word 'Hate' tatooed [*sic*] on hands—that's what I expected to witness at my first major punk rock concert. In this respect, unfortunately, it was a bore, and the concert by one of Britain's top bands, The Clash, was a disappointment."[36]

As media routinely sought to portray a cartoonish version of punk, a Canberra group spurned such tropes to present a thoughtful, distinctly Australian selfhood.

The central protagonist of Tactics, David Studdert, is direct in his disinterest for punk as a singular identity: "I was never interested in punk as the whole lifestyle, kind of dress code. Even the music didn't seem that interesting to me; I'd already heard the Stooges and MC5 and all that stuff." Studdert instead asserts that "I was extremely angry, and I was looking for something.... I was just temperamentally inclined to all that [punk], really.... It was kind of what I was digging out of myself." Desisting from formal education, Studdert "was looking for things that gave me answers to things that I was wanting to know but the answers I wasn't finding.... I was an outsider, I was by myself a lot, I was thinking a lot and reading a lot, and I didn't particularly like what I saw around me very much."

The challenging of traditional life patterns tied punk with hippie predecessors by their not wishing to be lashed to conventional and unbroken modes of school-work-marriage-children-work-retirement. Accordingly, Studdert observes that "when we started in Canberra, there wasn't really any punks, there was disgruntled hippies.... We fell in with those people, because that was the only place we could get any gigs.... When we started playing ... we played so intensely that everyone thought we were punks."

Speaking fondly of the initial "Anti-Disco" shows, Studdert says that "everyone turns up dressed in this really individual way ... made it up themselves—it was fantastic." But as with the systematising of all new and inventive movements, "within six months they were all dressed exactly the same again.... This is the thing that white Australia ... always overlooks: they get all anxious because they're a long way away, and all their art is just photocopy art—it's basically a rush to the photocopying machine.... There was a lot of energy in that scene, but it was an energy that was unthought. It was enough that they were all together in a scene looking at bands and talking about what they liked.... All the punks thought they were the cultural avant garde."

Comfortable with being distant, Studdert doggedly sought authenticity through denial of aping the latest acts from either side of the Atlantic: "I was looking for something that was kind of unique to how we lived in Australia; something that was true on its own terms. That was the whole driving force behind what we were doing. . . . In those days, on *Countdown*, Little River Band would be singing about being in a hotel in Las Vegas. It didn't have anything to do with me. . . . All I wanted to know about was what was outside my front door. So not only was the music borrowed and secondhand, but all the lyrics were too. It was a massive false consciousness, and that was precisely what we wanted to change. We were very ambitious, and we were on a mission."

That mission would have to start from the fabrication that was Canberra. "The thing that always struck me about Canberra was the kind of simulacrum it was. . . . You drove to the edge of it and there was literally a line where the green grass stopped and the brown grass started. . . . It was a place that really made me think about the whole relation of white Australia and the land; what they'd erected there and how removed it was from the Other." Uniquely, Studdert addressed issues of white settlement and colonialism after having spent time ingesting Australian Indigenous history and culture: "It was all part of the same search. . . . You could go to the National Library and sit there all day and read books . . . about Indigenous music, Indigenous chanting. The whole 'Standing by the Window'—I took the form from Indigenous song, that repetitious thing where they don't have any metaphors, but they just describe something slowly through a series of repetitions."

"Standing by the Window" was to be one track of Tactics' 1979 debut seven-inch, *Long Weekend*.

Exhibiting restlessness in the confines of their hometown, Studdert recalls thinking, "There's no audience for what we're doing. We've gotta go find one." But "in those days, going to Sydney . . . was a long drive up a shitty road." And only to find a sometimes-shitty response: "Some guy at the Lansdowne Hotel said to me one drunken night—I don't think he knew I was from Tactics—'Tactics: What the fuck were they?' And that was right; they couldn't find a niche to slot us into. We were just trying to sound like the bush at night. . . . We were doing something that didn't belong in any kind of niche, and that always makes problems for people—people have trouble placing it."

Despite the difficulty in classification, Studdert says that they were still able to have an effect, at least initially: "There was a period where we were the biggest thing in that scene in Sydney—it didn't last very long. Mostly it was a misunderstanding; they were able to slot us into a post-punk niche."

Far from that isolated and disaffected young man, a reflective Studdert now seems somewhat at peace with his place in Australian music history—that a lack of tangible accolades or renumeration is not constitutive of failure, and that the endeavour of music for anything beyond creative aspirations is likely to be to the detriment of the psyche. "People have inflated ambitions which can never truly be achieved.... You can't have 130 versions of the Beatles, you can't have a hundred Michael Jacksons. At some point you have to understand that. But it makes people very anxious, because in neoliberalism if it doesn't work, it's your fault: you haven't tried hard enough. It means people are carrying a lot of psychological pressure because of that." He goes on: "I had a period when I was doing my PhD, and they got me to teach an introduction to music course.... First thing I used to say was, 'You're doing this because you think it's hip, it's exciting. But you've got to live with the fact that sometime in your mid-thirties, the boring accountant that you think is utterly square, while you're pushing your beaten-up old VW ... he'll go by in a Porsche. And you've got to learn how to live with that. And if you can't live with it, don't fucking do it. Music's not a career, it's a calling.'"

For some, an expired car by the roadside would sound a mere inconvenience compared to the wreckage that was to become their personal lives. Another of punk's multitude of casualties, Trog, as George Howson says, "was always pretty much a level of intensity beyond most people." His is a biography to match.

Befriending "a couple of blokes who were in a band called Thalidomide," Trog says that "they asked me to come along to a gig to see the Young Docteurs, Guthugga Pipeline, Thalidomide, and Myxo.... I was there for every gig after that."

Though he became a fixture of Canberra punk, his band Capital Punishment did not have such perseverance, as Trog's hedonistic pursuits seemed to supersede any musical calling: "I became more interested in maintaining an image and getting wasted on booze and drugs."

Attendant to drug use, he was jailed "for armed robbery with corporal violence."

Upon release, Trog reconvened with a friend, and what transpired next potentially compromised his freedom even more severely:

We decided to catch up, do some speed, and party at the Irish

> Club. That was fine, but when the club closed, we decided to go back to his place. As soon as we walked in his front door, he started smashing into his partner until she was knocked down. Then he started putting the boots in—it was full-on. I grabbed his arm and tried to tell him that he was going to regret this.... The next thing I know is that after being king-hit and picking myself up off the floor, I'm being attacked with a carving knife. I managed to ward off the blows with a milk crate, and then try to make a run for it through the kitchen to the front door. But I tripped on a metal strip holding down the carpet.... While I was flying through the air, I reached out and grabbed the kitchen drawer handle and yanked it open. Everything in the drawer landed on the floor at the same time I did, including more carving knives. I stood up and faced him—*wham*! His complexion turned grey as he said, "I've been stabbed," and then after taking three steps, collapsed. The knife had pierced his right-hand side through his liver... and puncturing his left lung. I got charged, and I was already on parole.... The trial went on for nearly a year; he changed his stories nine times from the original police statement and during the trial itself.... It took a jury six minutes to come back with the verdict of not guilty.

In spite of the incident, music remained a constant for Trog as he "became involved with another band—Daddy's Comin Home—in the late '80s." Its cessation, however, culminated in the bleakest period of his life:

> In the '90s, I moved to Melbourne.... The isolation led to severe depression and heroin abuse.... I became a homeless junkie living in Chinatown. After being stabbed in the guts, in broad daylight, I ended up in Kings Cross for over ten years, where I witnessed and went through some scary shit. After ripping off the wrong people, they eventually caught up with me. I was taken to a place nearby with a garage underneath where I was stripped naked, strapped, and taped to a chair. I was then bashed and humiliated, tortured for what seemed an eternity as they laughed and made jokes.... Eventually they took off a toe with a pair of pruning scissors.... I was dumped around the back of St Vincent's Hospital.... This was actually a major turning point in

> my life. Shortly after this, an old mate . . . another Canberra punk, killed himself by jumping off the eleventh floor of a government high-rise housing complex after we had an argument over a morphine pill. This was when I decided that things had to change. I went to the Matthew Talbot Hostel [homeless shelter] and asked for help.

That desperate plea for assistance would curb a till-then harrowing life story and be punctuated by a happy ending: "The woman who interviewed me, who gave me a room at the hostel, also gave me the guardianship to get me on the right path. She gave the patience, love, and understanding that I'd been searching for my whole life. I became clean and alcohol free in September 2008. A year later, we were married. Life is great. In fact, it's fucking wonderful."

## NEWCASTLE

As a movement with supposed working-class origins, punk's appeal would instead span classes and backgrounds through commonalities of boredom, disaffection, and social ostracism, rather than strict socioeconomic grievance. Not that such conditions were absent in Newcastle in the late '70s, as unemployment in the city surpassed the national average, with young people most affected.

Within such conditions, it could be expected that bands would help voice the hardship and trepidations of the city's younger demographic. Ward 10 guitarist Les Gully confirms that Newcastle was indeed "abuzz like never before, with arrests and unrest and garages full of punk bands." Many groups were forgotten to the decades, or remained little more than names provoking curiosity—for example, the Rejects and Head Damage. Others, such as the Mansons, were at least able to produce lasting artefacts, like their 1982 seven-inch *I Died Four Times! (But I Don't Wanna Talk About It)*.

Pel Mel, the band most successful in generating attention beyond Newcastle's confines, offered music that defied the more obvious rock/punk formula. Vocalist Jude McGee contextualises the environment in which they began: "Newcastle in the '70s was a steel and surf town. . . . For the most part, Novocastrians were solid, working-class people, unionists with a strong sense of community (so long as you were white), but pretty conservative and parochial.... A lot of young people were unemployed, and there was a bit of a hippie scene around surfing and the beach. But there wasn't a lot going on, especially in terms of live music.... And you'd rarely see a woman onstage, unless she had a tambourine."

For McGee and a small coterie, however,

> we were starting to hear about all these new bands ... Joy Division, the Sex Pistols, Siouxsie and the Banshees, Buzzcocks, the Slits, X-Ray Spex, Orange Juice, Josef K, the Fall, Television, Talking Heads.... We started to share records and find like-minded people into the same stuff.... Essentially this built its own scene at the Grand Hotel in Newcastle, with Pel Mel and the Limp as the house bands.... It was a small but distinct subculture and attracted all the outsiders.... Pel Mel were always musical outsiders in Newcastle. We once entered a battle of the bands competition (we needed the money), and we actually thought we'd win because we were playing original music and something new. But of course, a very average Status Quo cover band took the prize. To a lot of suburban people, we probably looked like we were from outer space. And as for having two women in the band... crazy!... For me, one of the most important things about punk was the message that anyone should be free to play whatever they want—including women.... But some blokes, especially when we ventured out of the inner city or played in other pubs in Newcastle, were challenged by that.

Pel Mel secured a show in Sydney, and McGee says that it "led to more gigs, and pretty quickly we were playing in Sydney a lot.... There was stuff happening all over Surry Hills, Darlinghurst, Redfern, Newtown. It seemed like everyone was in ten different bands—bands that might only ever play once or twice. People were always writing books, or making art, or shooting Super 8 movies. All this culture was funded by the dole and/or shitty jobs."

Initially possessing a defined punk influence, Pel Mel adopted a more refined new wave/pop sound that was to be captured on their 1981 seven-inch *No Word from China*.

As punk and new wave diverged into disparate streams, new wave ushered softened sounds and styles that proved invaluable in fertilising the mainstream music industry through the 1980s. Alternative popularity, however, did not translate into Pel Mel's chart success; conversely, their swirling among the machinations of the music industry only furthered their demise: "To be honest, the Australian music industry and Australian radio had worn us down and killed the joy. We never did belong in the pub rock scene."

# "AFTER A FASHION"

## VICTORIA

### MELBOURNE

As the scenes to the north flourished, some were sceptical that the great punk musical revolution would permeate Melbourne. Interviewing a resident of Sydney, the *Age* newspaper reported their taunt: "Punk will never reach you down there. You're too conservative, too straight.... Nobody down there's got the guts."[1]

At the least, both Radio Birdman and the Saints were to give Melbourne audiences a glimpse of the potential for punk's musical adventurousness that was occurring elsewhere. Attending both tours, Phill Calvert gives an account of Radio Birdman's gig which also reveals a live music scene subjected to outmoded regulations: "The pub closed at ten. That was it, you were out.... Because they had entertainment on, they had to supply you with a meal, so you got a little mini pizza. And then you watch the band, and they were fucking insane."

Melbourne at the end of the '70s, while not troublingly conservative, was a drab and uniform city. Not too dissimilar from John Brack's famous *Collins St., 5 pm* painting of two decades earlier, it was far from the exemplar of multiculturalism and vibrant culture for which it reveres itself today. To the surprise of at least one person to the north, then, punk not only took hold in Melbourne in the late '70s but produced a succession of its own bands. In August 1977, the city's first "New Wave Rock Show" was held at Swinburne University—bands performing were Boys Next Door, the Reals, and Babeez.

On New Year's Eve of the same year, Melbourne's first punk festival—"Punk Gunk"—took place outside the home of Babeez's members in Carlton. While bands in Brisbane were being subjected to endless scrutiny, intimidation, and the routine breaking up of shows, Melbourne police were unfussed as Boys Next Door, Babeez, JAB, Tch Tch Tch, Spred, and the Zorros played to see in 1978.

One of those present at the festival was Barry Earl. Possessing a name more suited to the sale of real estate or secondhand cars, Earl was a rather conspicuous figure. For even in spite of punk's supposed inclusiveness, who could trust a man with a beard, unbuttoned shirt, and sports car as an apparent punk patron? Earl had gravitated to punk in London and now foresaw opportunity in Australia by beating out any other potential rivals as a punk band manager.

Backed by Michael Gudinski of Mushroom Records, Earl established the Suicide record label with the purpose of collecting groups under his control. Describing the Suicide venture as "a bit of a misadventure," Boys Next Door guitarist Mick Harvey viewed it as "just a couple of ignorant record company people who decided they would start a new wave label."[2]

Early punk shows at the Tiger Lounge had drawn a regular crowd of eighty to a hundred people, so opportunity for exploitation seemed meagre. But as music writer Stuart Coupe noted, "Things evolved and the audience grew," and so with it "out came the opportunists."[3] Clinton Walker, writing in *Pulp* fanzine, was rightly suspicious that "from the outset, Suicide's intentions appeared pretty obvious. Monopoly. It's simple: the more bets they placed, the greater chance of picking a winner."[4]

Earl had indeed made overtures of money, and in doing so lured Teenage Radio Stars, JAB, X-Ray-Z, Survivors (Brisbane), Wasted Daze, Negatives, and Boys Next Door to the label. Yet only three singles were ever to be produced for Suicide. A compilation album—*Lethal Weapons*—also featured the label's acts. Released in 1978, it was to be the final output for Suicide, and by the time of the label's demise most of the participating bands were also defunct. The record and label had been a source of considerable enmity and debate, as accusations of deliberate meddling and interference against bands for not signing were aired.

Bruce Milne, organiser of the initial "New Wave Rock Show," recalled a more harmonious, pre-Suicide period: "Before Suicide came along, all the bands used to get on well together because unity was vital if punk–new wave was to properly establish itself as a musical alternative. After the arrival of Suicide the two different factions—Suicide and nonSuicide bands—didn't talk to one another. There was a mutual suspicion and antagonism that didn't exist before."[5]

As Melbourne's early punk history was blighted by the Suicide episode, two of the bands that performed at the first Swinburne show—Babeez and Boys Next Door—became central figureheads for the fracturing of the scene that resulted.

Boys Next Door drummer Phill Calvert's recollection of any split is muted, recalling that "I never felt there was an 'us and them' attitude." His opinion of the experience, however, mirrors that of other participants in that it "wasn't such a good idea.... We hated everything about it, but it got us a single ['These Boots Are Made for Walking,' 1978].... It got us in the studio, and we made an album."

Mushroom chose to take up its option on Boys Next Door with the band negotiating to record newer tracks to accompany those already completed. These would feature new member Roland S. Howard of Young Charlatans and become the second side to their 1979 twelve-inch, *Door Door*.

Pessimistic about *Door Door*, Gudinski saw no obvious radio single. After release of a further seven-inch the same year (*Shivers*), the band was dropped by the label. Calvert remembers that "[Nick] Cave went to Gudinski and said ... 'You should stay with it,' and Gudinski said, 'Don't care.'" Interviewed in 1979, a prophetic Cave said of Gudinski, "We could surprise him."[6]

Bringing attention back to Boys Next Door's origins, Calvert says, "We were playing Alice Cooper covers, we were playing Bowie covers" before "seeing early shows by Birdman and the Saints and discovering the stuff they were listening to ... and also that first Ramones record.... I suppose we started to write more in that direction."

The band was accompanied by scrutiny of the alleged contradiction between punk and their private school origins. Calvert remembers it being examined before a very public audience: "There was a daytime women's TV show.... They got us on there and interviewed us because we were these private school boys, but now we were punks."

The clip to their cover of Nancy Sinatra's "These Boots Are Made for Walking" had indeed shown a safe-looking and -sounding band. Yet measured against 1970s society, the group was transgressive like few others in Melbourne. Suitably, Calvert's partner, Julia, describes the orientation of the band's parents: "They were so conservative; almost beyond conservative compared to how most parents probably are now."

Theirs was an attitude not born of material deprivation, but the stultifying culture of middle-class Melbourne. Calvert asserts that "we had just as much to rebel against as anybody else."

The most popular of Melbourne's punk bands, Boys Next Door became especially attractive to those drawn from art, literary, and film backgrounds and schools. Punk seemed to offer all the energy, challenge, and attitude that a then-rigid Australian art establishment did not. Observing the music scene at the time, Melbourne artist Vivienne Shark LeWitt wrote, "It is shrewdly intelligent, surprisingly articulate, witty, threatening, curiously repellent yet magnetic, radical, inventive, and has proved innovative in the spheres of music, philosophy, the visual arts, theatre, film, typography, and fashion."[7]

Outside of the safer enclaves of punk venues and art schools, however, Calvert says in "super-straight Melbourne . . . you walked down the street looking like what we looked like, people turned their heads and went, 'What the fuck happened to them?'" Giving the impression they'd been "pulled backwards through a cheese grater," Calvert says, "I got beaten up, Tracy [Pew, bassist] got beat up a couple of times, Nick got beat up."

Performing one of their earliest shows at Mick Harvey's father's church, Boys Next Door found a small crowd supplemented by the arrival of the Holmesglen Sharpies, a gang who began antagonising them onstage. As Cave spat at an audience member, a fight ensued, with himself and members of the Reals being injured. About this act of apparent recklessness, Cave, not averse to a scrap, one day relayed to Ben Juniper what had animated him during the Boys Next Door period: "I was just angry. I wanted to hurt people."

Calvert also reveals this unassuming attribute of Cave's: "One thing I will say about Nick is that whilst being incredibly scrawny and thin, Jesus Christ, you never want to fight that guy, he's incredibly strong. And I think it's mental; he's not in fear of getting hurt."

That absence of fear would arguably extend to Cave's well-documented drug use, yet Calvert cautions any idea of luck or an unchecked self-destructiveness: "Nick was never trying to get rid of the pain; he was doing it for a whole lot of reasons, but he was never looking for sympathy and he was never proving [anything] to somebody else, and that's why it didn't kill him. . . . I never took drugs thinking that the outcome would be that I would die. . . . I started taking speed to be able to drive and stay awake and do three shows in a night. That's how you did 250 shows in three years or something."

Boys Next Door played a hundred shows in 1978 alone.

As novices, the early incarnation of Boys Next Door consisted of ample Alex Harvey Band and Alice Cooper covers, their theatrics having a clear effect on Cave as a performer. A *Roadrunner* journalist noted that "often his antics overbalanced into excess and melodrama, and should have been embarrassing" before admitting that they "only served to make the performance more paradoxical and quite irresistible."[8]

Calvert recounts conversation with a former Melbourne record store co-owner, who reminisced to him of Cave's transcendental effect: "The first time I ever saw you guys, I came into the room, you went onstage, and it reminded me of when I saw the Rolling Stones at the Palais in 1960-whatever, because I walked in and I just said, 'That guy's got it.'"

But if Cave was harbouring the charisma of Jagger, Melbourne's suburbanites were having difficulty identifying it. Calvert speaks of the band's ability to elicit a unique ambivalence outside the city: "You might get a show out there on a Friday, Saturday. . . . You're calling upon the slightly more interesting elements of society to go see it so you could actually play, and the response from them could be really good. Doesn't mean that later on in the car park people may not throw things at you as you're loading out the gear."

It was a demanding prospect for preened art punks to woo a room of pub rockers generally wanting to beat their heads in, yet the band was also called upon as support for larger, more mainstream acts, including Cold Chisel, Icehouse, Australian Crawl, and Skyhooks.

If your common suburban beer-barn dweller was suspicious or antipathetic of punk, the band themselves was quick to jettison the association: "The word 'punk' lasted about five minutes in Melbourne. At that point in history, people started distancing themselves from the word 'punk' really, really, really quickly, and it was because it was corralling you into one sound."

But while stylistically they continued to progress, among Melbourne audiences Clinton Walker wrote that the band "had hit the proverbial glass ceiling. They couldn't go on playing to the same adoring two hundred people every other week. . . . They were just going to have to get out of Australia."[9]

The band departed in February 1980, and with it so too did the name. Living the requisite life of indigent Australian musicians in London, the Birthday Party accrued only ten shows by year's end. Through menial jobs and a squatted home with no amenities, the band could easily have languished or returned to the middle-class comfortability of Melbourne. Their break was to come with signing to new record label 4AD.

They returned from England at the end of 1980, and Calvert recalls the cultural shift that had occurred and of which they would be at least in part responsible: "There was a girl on the corner, and she was dressed like all the girls used to dress back then, like T-bar shoes, black tights, tartan shirt, miniskirt, hair dark, lots of makeup, and I go, 'Who's that?' and he [Calvert's friend] goes, 'I don't know,' and I go, 'What do you mean? Anybody who looks like this in this town we know, they're the only people who come to our thing.' And he goes, 'Oh, it's not like that anymore, it's everybody.'"

Every drama must have its heroine, and in the brief saga that was the Suicide record label, Babeez/News were to be at least one band that could chide its participants for having been duped. Band stalwart Gavin Quinn offers an expectedly sectarian—and ultimately vindicated—view: "The Suicide label was created to soak up and control the dangerous new punks. . . . It was divisive at the time, but once the character of the Mushroom-Suicide deal became obvious, people realised our objections were well intended."

Henry Vyhnal, a member of Babeez through 1977–78, also performed on Boys Next Door's *Door Door* record. Having interest on either side of the divide, Vyhnal avoided the role of peacemaker: "I let them fight it out without taking sides or stoking the furnace. . . . For me it was always about the music, not the scene."

The first Melbourne band to release a recording, Babeez featured a photo of an aborted foetus on the cover of the *Dowanna Love* seven-inch. But far from preoccupation with just shock value, the group were serious in intent and drive. Now with a name change to News, Quinn reveals they "rehearsed an average of five hours a day, five days a week, every week."[10]

A concerted graffiti campaign helped publicise the rebranding, Quinn explaining that it more than sufficiently achieved its intended goal of exposure: "The graffiti had brought us to notice with newspapers claiming all sorts of political meanings—'Nuclear Energy Won't Survive' (NEWS), for example. For several weeks we had shifts of bored but cheery ASIO [Australian Security Intelligence Organisation] agents sitting patiently outside, observing us."

The first show as News came, supporting Paul Kelly's band High Rise Bombers at alternative arts venue the Pram Factory. Of this meeting of the older, dominant Carlton rock scene and the new generation, a reviewer of the show wrote in the *Age* that "they won a grudging and eventually enthusiastic response."[11] Playing at a dance for the Hawthorn Football Club's cheer squad, the band were forced to take comfort from the decent paycheque after being mostly met with predictable confusion.

Whether flummoxed by the unfamiliar sounds or political message, Quinn says, "Politics had been a no-go zone in music." The band routinely played shows within Melbourne's inner-city political and activist scenes. Following mass arrests and bashings by police of those attending Sydney's first Gay and Lesbian Mardi Gras in 1978, Quinn coordinated a benefit show to help contribute to legal funds.

If Boys Next Door and News were already divided by Suicide, Vyhnal highlights ideological and geographical differences that exacerbated the chasm: "South of the [Yarra] river bands like Boys Next Door were more into style and clothes at the time. Gavin saw punk as a political movement, whereas Nick Cave saw it as a way of getting ahead in the music industry. Both are valid. I've always seen music as a force for good, and as such music is always loaded, politically. I identified far more with Gavin's vision than Nick's. Unsurprisingly, Nick has been more successfully commercial than Gavin."

News came to use the forum of the *Age* to mock "those trendy 'punks' from South Yarra with tie-dyed haircuts and bones through their noses."[12] Quinn didn't exhibit any eagerness for conciliation: "We weren't interested in compromise, either with the fashion punk scene or the music establishment. We knew that what we were doing was good. We were creating music we didn't feel anyone else was creating. It needed to be created, these things needed to be said."[13]

Establishment figures thought otherwise. With release of their *Dirty Secrets* seven-inch in 1978, Tim Finn of Split Enz reviewed the record: "I've seen their name spray-painted all over the place in Melbourne.... Hate it. They may have energy but they don't have any class."[14]

Performing on the record was drummer John Murphy. As a student at Melbourne's exclusive Scotch College, Murphy had put together a Sex Pistols cover band—Vicious Vicars—for a school dance. Describing the event as a "disaster," Murphy says, "I ended up almost being expelled for the debacle that followed."[15] Any repercussions of schoolboy hijinks left Murphy undeterred, his career as percussionist to include Michael Hutchence's (INXS) side project Max Q, through to darker cult acts including Death in June, Whitehouse, Current 93, Nurse with Wound, and Lustmord.

As Murphy quit News, bassist Julie Jordan also departed, and the group was seemingly finished, leaving their Carlton home. A fortnight later, the house was firebombed, with only the toilet and fireplace left standing.

Though unable to resist one last barb, even Quinn is able to romanticise the era in spite of all the antagonism associated with Suicide: "I'm pretty sure most people involved are proud of those days because, those shills aside, it was a fantastic time."

As a trained violinist and student of genetics and microbiology, Henry Vyhnal did not possess the expected pedigree for a life of spiky hair and spikier music. Recording his own single in 1977, however, Vyhnal expressed the enthusiasm that came at the height of punk's international exposure, titling its B-side "Punk Power." Having had minor success with vastly more credentialed bands, Vyhnal found that punk had rejuvenated his desire to perform: "I was one of the few Carlton musicians at the time that appreciated punk. When my former bandmates heard I was playing with the punks and spending lots of downtime with them, they thought I was crazy. As the wheel turned and punk became more mainstream, the bands they formed often included a punky vibe, even though they were still laughing behind their faces at what punk stood for."

Henry Vyhnal's violin was not the only to feature on a Melbourne punk record, as Negatives' Peter Cave found to his disbelief: "'Planet on the Prowl' on the Suicide record was completely ruined by . . . our 'producer,' who took it upon himself to remove the dozen or so incredible guitar overdubs by Michael Holmes and replace them with his own electronically processed violin. . . . We found out about it when we heard our copies of the album."

Perhaps the Negatives' greatest performance, though, was neither their live show nor "Planet on the Prowl," but an intoxicated Gary Gray allegedly carving "Negatives" into Barry Earl's desk.

By then, Gray and bandmate Chris Walsh had spent half a decade as suburban recusants with a questionable command of their instruments. Under the name Judas Iscariot and the Traitors, recordings exist from 1974, the tracks so rough and indiscernible they make a solo bedroom noise-project demo tape seem the pinnacle of high fidelity.

Eventually Cave's flirtation with punk ceased, coming with a resumption of middle-class sensibility: "One factor in my decision to leave was that I had been accepted into the ABC as a trainee and was about to start full-time work. . . . When I left the band, punk was looking like a dead end with no future—pun intended."

Unlike the middle-class upbringing of other early Melbourne punks, Rob Griffiths, vocalist/guitarist of Fiction, says, "Mum cleaned and ironed clothes for a living, and she brought up five kids on her own." Griffiths, though, supressed any sense of class war, finding commonality in knowing which side of a cultural divide he wished to choose: "Some joker played the Saints' '(I'm) Stranded' on commercial radio and asked if this was really music. If they were drawing a line in the sand, I knew what side I wanted to be on."

The original punks of '77–78, Griffiths notes, "were creative types who wanted to do their own thing, get drunk at the Ballroom, and eat the free sandwiches." Griffiths could well have done with more of the free food offerings himself: "The doctor said it was malnutrition. . . . 1978 was a year on the dole, living in a shared house and not eating or living properly, I guess." In an era long predating outlandish superfoods and supplements, "The doctor's prescription was Vegemite on toast each morning."

Fiction first performed in 1978 and into '79, and Griffiths "went to the UK at the end of that year and came back with a lot of ideas about mod." Implanting those ideas into Fiction, many mods were to come out of the punk scene, as Griffiths reminisces a commingling: "The Seaview Ballroom was a real mixture of punks and mods. . . . I never saw any animosity between the two groups. We all kinda knew each other."

More revival than revolution, mod consisted of a flurry of motor scooters rather than stumbling, drunk punks; sharp '60s dress of shirts, ties, Fred Perrys, and miniskirts, instead of tattered and torn clothes and spiked hair. Mod peaked quickly and just as swiftly receded, its largest scenes existing in Sydney and Melbourne with bands the Sets, Division 4, the Introverts, Jump Vision, the Coathangers, the Clones, the Go, Bleu Scooters, 5:15, and the group that succeeded Fiction, Little Murders.

The first punk band to perform at the Seaview Ballroom, JAB had relocated to Melbourne in 1977. In competition with News, the group and/or their fans were prolific in attempting to ensure the band's name was attached to every edifice across the inner city.

Employing greater experimentation than the standard rock band composition, the group made utilisation of tapes and synth. Member Ash Wednesday gave the reasoning that "I think lead guitar has been done to death ... it's lost its meaning. The alternative to that is to go back to power chords ... or devise some new musical system."[16]

Ash Wednesday later joined one of the more accomplished pursuers of a new system, becoming a touring member of Einstürzende Neubauten.

Against the refined and heavily stylised Ballroom scene stood the relative philistinism of the Chosen Few. The unassuming location for their beginnings was a farm and hard rock/heavy metal band Deathwish. Jam sessions often acted as an excuse for parties, with a bungalow becoming a near casualty through accidental fire. Pest eradication also preoccupied the band, as practice was occasionally paused for rabbit hunting.

Supplementary to his more respectable role as a local high school teacher, Ian Cunningham played bass in the band. His bandmates had previously been his students.

The band changed their name to the Chosen Few in late '77, and Cunningham expressed their music-first principle that saw them contemptuous of many of their contemporaries: "We did think a lot of bands were all show and no go. We concentrated on the music and gave fuck-all thought to anything else."

Neglecting to mention their crude attempts as self-promoters, the Chosen Few placed ads in the local music press lauding genocidal dictators. They also took up punk's penchant for Nazi iconography on their 1978 seven-inch *The Joke's on Us!*, its artwork including an image of Hitler and a large swastika.

As peddlers of the outrageous, the band attracted suitably immoderate acts such as "the couple who had a root in front of the stage using a metal tube chair as a sex aid (I kid you not!)."[17] A prevaricate Cunningham also references another show "where someone handed out a bit of shotgun justice."

The band was not averse to dispensing their own brand of justice. An almost haughty Cunningham says, "We took to carrying axe handles on stage. We all had one, lovingly embellished with personal identification. The idea was that any cunt who gobbed on us was going to get fucking smashed right then and there."[18]

Despite the group's chastising of art punk, in retirement Cunningham became something of a dabbler himself, exhibiting his abstract paintings in 2012. The Chosen Few's most lasting piece of "art," however, came to be that which adorned themselves. The plausible outcome of too many beers, band members used a shaped and heated metal coat hanger to brand themselves with the letters "TCF" (the Chosen Few). A lifetime reminder of the group's mere fifteen-month lifespan, Cunningham says, "By then, most of the original bands, at least in Melbourne, had split up or morphed into something else.... Those bands who emerged after that first glorious explosion were more focused and more aware of commercial possibilities."

Ousting both their singer and their name, as well as adding keyboard and restraining their sound, the freshly instituted Bohdan and the Instigators seemed to confirm Cunningham's summation. He left the band.

As for the Chosen Few, Cunningham recalls: "We basically played for beer."

Amid punk/new wave's indubitable impacting of music, Adelaide pub band Rufus Red moved to Melbourne, embracing the new sounds and a new name: X-Ray-Z. Signing to Mushroom for their 1977 single "Poor Image," the baggage of their previous life was evident, as the band was both stuck between genres and had members a decade older than most of the new scene. Ian Hartley's review of the record was unsparing: "They sound not unlike Tom Verlaine's Television, but I must live in a lousy reception area, cos I keep getting a poor image."[19]

In 1978, the band was scooped up in Suicide's signings, but the nearly six-minute track "Valium" suggested they were still not quite grasping punk's short, sharp shock. Later in the year, perhaps again sensing the shifting trends, the band became Popgun Men, with a variation in lineup and sound.

Lofty ambitions were not an uncommon trait, even among those attracted to the new movement. James Freud, having "crept out" of his family home "with my guitar and amplifier" one night, vowed "never to return as a mere mortal. I'd return as a superstar."[20]

With more modest beginnings, Freud and school friend Sean Kelly had been performing sedate acoustic songs at a party when an uninvited group arrived and turned his world on its head: "A bunch of punks, wired on speed, gate-crashed the place and told us to shut the fuck up, which we did. They turned the stereo up to ten and put on the Sex Pistols."[21] The following day, Freud placed an ad for musicians. Answered by three Greeks from the western suburbs—including one only just released from jail—they became the Spred. Now with a shock of pink hair, Freud's transformation was complemented by no eyebrows, casualties of a drug session.

Their first "real" gig came supporting Rose Tattoo in the outer suburbs. Freud remembers a crowd "who hated us as soon as we walked on."[22] The mood failed to improve—the culmination of LSD, broken strings, thrown beer glasses, and a resulting brawl started by the Greeks.

The rhythm section being ousted, the band was renamed Teenage Radio Stars (*I Wanna Be Your Baby* seven-inch, 1978). Barely concealing their desire for stardom, the group's appearance on *Countdown* further tainted other bands' impressions of them. Addressing relations between groups, bassist Pierre "Voltaire" says, "There was a lot of intense rivalry between all the bands."[23] After slandering Boys Next Door in an interview, either Nick Cave or Tracy Pew threw a dog shit at Freud onstage at the Ballroom.

In an attempt to transcend the excrement in pursuance of pop fame, Barry Earl convinced Freud of his need to transition to solo performer. He released an album as James Freud and the Radio Stars in 1980; its single "Modern Girl" reached number twelve on the national charts. In 1982, he rejoined Kelly in Models, a band that would vault to number one in 1985.

Freud also authored two autobiographies, *I Am the Voice Left from Drinking* and *I Am the Voice Left from Rehab*, in 2002 and 2007, which not only chronicled '80s pop/rock success but gave account of the addiction that eventually overcame him. Freud committed suicide in 2010, a week after Models were inducted into the ARIA (Australian Recording Industry Association) Hall of Fame.

By time they broke up in 1988, Models had debts of three hundred thousand dollars.[24] In 2014, Voltaire, aka Pierre Sutcliffe, won half a million dollars on TV game show *Million Dollar Minute*.

Removed from the Spred's rhythm section, Graham Schiavello and Peter Kidd together joined La Femme, a band whose origins were in Melbourne's working-class north and its youthful "sharpie" gangs. Sharpies composed an infamously violent and uniquely Australian subculture. Singer Chane Chane explains, "There were four lots of sharps: there were the '60s, the early '70s, the mid-'70s, and then there was the late '70s.... The late '70s, they got into punk and ska and all kinds of different stuff, and then it just dwindled away." To Chane, the passage from sharpie to punk was "just a natural progression—you're still a rebel."

Chane had begun his sharpie association at age fourteen: "I started in Ascot Vale; we took over the flats there.... I found the two gangs that were running that; we beat one gang up and the other gang was too tough, so I got an air rifle and just went to every one of their houses and smashed the rifle through the window and shot the television. They never fucked with us again."

Adjacent to the intimidation, Chane describes one avenue of their income: "We used to hang around the Ascot Vale flats and look at the people coming out from the trots [horse racing] and go, 'He's a winner. He's a winner.'"

Discouraged by the danger and likely career path, Chane says impetus for departing the sharpie scene was when "I came home, and six people were waiting to kill me.... I thought, 'Fuck it, I gotta get out of gangs. It's getting too heavy and I don't want to be a career criminal.'"

Making the transition to a band, Chane says, "We already thought we were famous as sharps, because we were pretty well known, so this was just another step." Their impact was immediate, with La Femme's first recording (*Chelsea Kids* seven-inch, 1978) reportedly becoming, at the time, "the biggest selling local independent record ever."[25] The single was an evocation of his departed life—Chane reveals the song "was written about me getting away" from the sharpie scene.

Although disallowed from playing the song on *Countdown*, in the aftermath of their appearance on the show, Chane says, "We were kind of popular.... I was being chased through the streets by kids." In a familiar anecdote, however, he relays what came next: "What they tried to do was turn us into pop stars ... the record company, our agencies and manager.... I quickly figured that what was popular on the radio they would come in and tell you to do."

Chane sought to push back against the encroachment of outside influence: "I just said, 'Fuck off' ... and they said, 'Well, we've got your contract, we can do whatever we want.'" He responded with an uncommon, if also particularly self-harmful, tactic: "Pete and I were kind of dabbling in heroin, and we just said, 'Let's go flat out, let's just fuck it up.' So, we just started hitting up all the time. In interviews, we'd turn up and have a hit." Further thwarting any ambition was Chane vomiting "all over" a representative of RCA Records following the band's album's launch.

A surprisingly sanguine Chane says, "We were completely fucked over, but we didn't really care."

The band laboured on until 1982. Kidd, says Chane, "ended up going to jail—shooting a cop or something." As for Chane, a not too dissimilar appearance saw him front a Billy Idol cover band. Thereafter, he "gave up music, basically. I started compering strip shows."

Reflecting on his exposure to the tumultuousness of the music business, Chane offers wisdom that "it's never what you expect it to be, so you're stupid to expect anything.... We weren't meant to get anywhere either; we were just meant to go out, get free booze and get laid, and have some fun."

So much fun that "a liver that's supposed to last me eighty years, I wore it out in thirty."

As the industry sought to meld punk to its own end, in one rare instance it emerged from within. In 1978, Dave and the Derros released their *Death to Disco/Punk Princess* seven-inch. Dave, says band member Nigel Haines, "was the breakfast disc jockey at 3XY." Haines himself has worked for a handful of major Melbourne radio stations. Together, he says, "We basically started doing parodies of songs ... as most breakfast shows do." Yet, as Haines explains, "Ours really wasn't a parody as such, it really was a thing [of] having a go at disco, and it really was done in the style of punk rock.... Both Dave and myself were right into punk, we just loved the raw style of it and the no-bullshit lyrics."

As for the B-side "Punk Princess," Haines reveals it to have suitably been the most primitive of recording sessions: "I did the drumming on that ... it was two pieces of wooden stick belted on the back of a vinyl chair.... Punk is very rough and raw, and I'm probably the roughest and rawest of anyone [*laughs*]."

The single, says Haines, "made quite a bit of money," but "we gave it all to charity."

Where Dave and the Derros were figures ensconced in the establishment, Primitive Calculators were unashamed outsiders, even among an already marginal scene. Keyboardist Denise Rosenberg explains, "We thought we were better than the other inner-city bands because we came from a working-class background."

Highlighting how punk augmented the angst they were already harbouring, vocalist/guitarist Stuart Grant says, "We were unemployed, we were really negative, we hated the world.... We were part of the same critique the hippies had made, of wanting to refuse capitalist society, but we hated hippies. We'd seen that they'd failed, and we thought they were just lightweight. The sense that the revolutions of the 1960s had failed led to this incredible nihilism."[26] The message and aspirations of the new social movements had, in punk, shifted to resignation and anger.

Grant's rationale nearly mirrors that of Rosenberg: "I think we were just pissed off with anything political ... and just figured that the world was fucked then, as it is now. I decided early on never to have kids and never regretted that decision."

But where Grant identifies a political disaffection, Rosenberg says the music scene they encountered was occupied by those with differing priorities: "As time went on ... most wanted to become successful in the music business. We never went down that path. We just wanted to make fierce noise and hurt people's ears and sound like no one else. That's why we went down the synthesiser path."

Rosenberg emphasises the success of the Calculators' abrasiveness, which "didn't go down well with mixing-desk people or most of the crowds.... I recall one of our first gigs at the Ballroom ... a handful of people jumping up and down in front of us, and the majority standing way back in the room with their fingers in their ears. When RRR recorded a live-to-air there in May 1979, apparently the mixer guy in the van threw down his headphones and said, 'I'm not mixing this shit,' or something to that effect."

Besides their proximity as Calculators' next-door neighbours, Whirlywirld were to offer a similar style of synth-driven music. Member Ian "Ollie" Olsen was one of the very first punks in Melbourne and had been a member of the Reals and Young Charlatans. Yet, feeling constricted by conventional instrumentation and discovering a commonality of interest with John Murphy of News, he and Murphy left their respective bands to form Whirlywirld. Murphy says, "We didn't just want to play thrash.... But we were definitely punk rockers in the clothes, looks and attitude. Ollie used to have arguments with dyed-in-the-wool punks about synthesisers. Back in those days synths were no-go."[27]

Together, Whirlywirld and Primitive Calculators were cocreators of a "Little Band" scene, a subset of the larger punk bracket. Inherently elusive and temporal in nature, Rosenberg details that "we allowed anyone who wanted to use our equipment to do so.... It was popular because we would let anyone get up and play." Little Bands included Thrush and the Cunts, Bottle Shop Quartet, Oroton Bags, Child Molester Plus Four, the Delicatessens, Alan Bamford Experience, Incredibly Strange Creatures, Lunatic Fringe, and Pastel Bats, among a multitude of others.

By contrast, of the more "conventional" punk bands that showed a modicum of longevity, Rosenberg says, "Many ... wanted to become professional musicians.... Bands would change their sound to become more attractive to audiences and the music business.... We went the other path and put out our own singles [*I Can't Stop It* seven-inch, 1979].... When we hosted [TV music show] *Rage* in 2014, they stated on their website that we were 'Australia's most influential band that you've never heard of.' Perfect."

Obscurity notwithstanding, the music of Primitive Calculators was included in the soundtrack to Richard Lowenstein's 1986 cult film *Dogs in Space*.

Underwhelming at the box office despite the casting of marquee lead character Michael Hutchence, the film portrays Sam Sejavka, singer of the Ears, with whom Lowenstein had formerly shared a home. The setting for the film was predominantly the house where they resided together.

Catherine McQuade of the Ears gives her impression of the residence and their mode of living at the time: "In some ways, it was the archetype of punk dysfunction: lots of drugs, sleeping till late afternoon, living in unbelievably filthy conditions. But it was always like a game. It was not like punk in the UK, where real economic challenges and anger about society were core; everyone was living comfortably on the dole, reading Baudelaire and Rimbaud and eating cold tinned spaghetti out of the can.... Although *Dogs in Space* captured the ambience, I would have to say that *Withnail and I* was the closest I ever saw to showing the humour."

In 2009, Lowenstein released *We're Living on Dog Food*, a documentary that chronicled the late '70s/early '80s music scene based around the Ballroom.

Also appearing on the *Dogs in Space* soundtrack, Marching Girls were rooted in New Zealand punk band the Scavengers before relocating to Melbourne. Singer Brendan Perry, alongside drummer Simon Monroe, left following their seven-inch in 1980, titled *1*, joining with Lisa Gerrard, previously of Microfilm, to form Dead Can Dance. Extending the cinematic connection, Microfilm's Nique Needles's appearance in *Dogs in Space* preceded a succession of B movies. Additional to playing in Dead Can Dance, Gerrard produced the music and sound for Hollywood films *Heat* and *Gladiator* as well as the television programs *South Park* and *CSI*.

A band to have their own—if fleeting—connection to commercial television, Plastic EP and the Records were perhaps the greatest anomaly among Melbourne's early producers of punk. Releasing their *At Home/Three Special Words* seven-inch in 1981, it's intriguing to consider how a band with a taste for the Monkees, the Yardbirds, the Beatles, and Elvis conjured such a record. They were far removed from a scene like the Ballroom, but the words "New Wave" emblazoned atop the record indicated they were at least attuned enough to recognise what they were attempting.

Shortening their name to the EPs, the group appeared on variety show *Hey Hey It's Saturday*'s "Red Faces" talent segment in 1987. Beginning with choreographed moves and singer "Plastic EP" dressed in a gold jacket, the band were halted after barely reaching the chorus. Bassist Walter Schiavon was nonetheless assured of the experience: "Any exposure is good exposure."

Having "lost a lot of band members on the way," Schiavon says the group "became a studio band." Understating their efforts, Schiavon says, "We wrote a lot of songs," which has culminated in a dozen albums. Not content with just their musical output in the search for fame, the band became a prolific YouTube entity, as well as having "created five iPhone movies hoping to get discovered. But it has always been a long way to the top."

A band likely to have met a similarly swift end on *Hey Hey It's Saturday*, schoolboy humour saw the Relatives debut as the Velvet Underpants at a high school dance in 1977. One can only imagine the chagrin of staff as the band attempted Sex Pistols and Saints songs dressed in their best private-school-punk fashion.

The Relatives' *Now She's on the Beat* seven-inch was released in 1979, and its pink cover of hand-drawn green fish could not be any more divergent from the black-and-white war theme of an emerging anarcho-punk subgenre. At its launch, five dollars gave payers not only the record and show but, fitting their exclusive private school pedigree, supper and champagne on arrival.

The band produced another seven-inch (*Uncle Theo Comes to Visit*, 1979) before disbanding in 1981, and again the launch stipulated five dollars for entry, the record, and supper.

As an avowed Trotskyist, Nic Chancellor's keen class consciousness might have anticipated disdain for such bourgeois trappings as supper and champagne. As a motorcyclist, his attire had pre-styled him for punk: "I had jeans with holes in the knees and a leather jacket." Informed of his uncanny likeness to the Ramones, he sought out the band and became an immediate fan.

He formed his own group, the Zorros, who debuted at the Champion Hotel, a bar harbouring a serious reputation. While band audiences congregated upstairs, Chancellor says the violence "would happen at the main bar downstairs and in the commission flats across the road." As a regular performer at the hotel, Lisa Gerrard remembers, "They were like smashing bottles over each other's heads and a woman bit a man's nose off there one night."[28]

Sharing a member with Z-Cars, both groups incorporated a greater pop sensibility with their punk foundations. Remaining faithful to the late '70s melodic sound, but now extending into the early '80s, they were joined by Corporate Body, Delegates, and the Start/Fifth Column.

In 1980, Z-Cars released their *This Is Z-Cars* seven-inch, and Zorros followed in 1981 with the *Too Young* seven-inch.

Zorros' next release did not materialise until 1988, though the band remained active during the seven-year gap. For Chancellor, a redirection of his musical interest occurred that same year: "My first rave in 1988 was called 'Soma.' . . . The DJs were obscured by a black curtain, and the people danced in circles together. This was an evolutionary experience and totally changed my direction. . . . A certain section of the punk milieu drifted headlong towards this tighter and potentially eclectic sound that house and rave included. People such as Ollic Olscn from Young Charlatans were enthusiastic proponents of the shift." Through the 1990s, Olsen became one of the most prominent figures in Melbourne/Australian techno. For Chancellor, the revolution was no longer the urban rebel in a leather jacket, maintaining the spirit of Marx, but party drugs and the communalism of a dusty open-air dance floor in northern New South Wales: "Before long I relocated to make the doof/rave rebellion my daily lifestyle."

Another to find punk amenable to her already established politics, Sylvie Leber, says, "Coming from a working-class background myself, it appealed to me." Revealing herself as the descendant of "a long line of lefties," Leber boasts, "My grandfather was a revolutionary, my father was in the French Resistance, so I was kind of already well trained in political analysis and . . . being critical of society."

Initially forming as the Girl's Garage Band to play the "Women, Patriarchy and the Future" forum, the all-female group, including Leber on bass, were prompted by favourable responses to continue. They took on the name Toxic Shock, and, as band member Hellen Sky told the *Age*, "It was a new experience to see women playing music."[29] In 2015, Leber acutely highlighted the traditional dearth of female musicians—that "of the seventy-three artists and music industry figures inducted into the Australia Recording Industry Association (ARIA) Hall of Fame, not one is a female instrumentalist."[30]

In addition to its upturning of tradition, punk's ability to scandalise was embodied in Toxic Shock's name alone, a term ascribed to the late '70s outbreak of illness caused by high-absorbency tampons. "Iconic" radio host Peter Grace deemed it so confronting that the precious listeners of Melbourne required protecting. Leber says, "We sent him our record to play, and he said—because of the name Toxic Shock—'I wouldn't play this filth in the lounge rooms of Melbourne.'"

The offending record was a self-released seven-inch in 1981. With an easy comparison to the Slits, however, they embodied punk viewed as spirit rather than strict delineation of sound. Leber herself feels she was removed from any specifically narrow clique: "I don't even know whether I could say I was in a punk scene. . . . Punk was just part of a whole lot of other stuff. . . . The south side was definitely more a scene [based around the Ballroom]."

Expressing punk's politics as sometimes more than symbolic or sloganeering, Leber was active in establishing Victoria's first rape crisis centre, which "was a small group of women who thought it was important to have a service for women . . . out of which all the CASAs [Centre Against Sexual Assault] have evolved. . . . So that was extremely significant."

Pursuing her own political interests, Toxic Shock vocalist Fran Kelly became one of the country's foremost media personalities through seventeen years as Radio National's *Breakfast* host.

## GEELONG

Leber's inner-city circle churned with music and protest. Andy Turner likens Victoria's second-largest city to the decayed urban centres of England: "Grey, bleak, and run-down. . . . Nearby cement works carried a coating of grey dust over our entire neighbourhood and the veggies in my dad's garden. . . . Unemployment was rife, as the manufacturing industries in Australia had begun to disintegrate in the '70s. The best metaphor for Geelong at the time was, for me, Hi-Lite Park. It was a mini fun park down at Eastern Beach that begun as a vibrant and popular family outing but was now a faded, rusting, outdated and just generally exhausted shell."

As a cry against the UK's own socioeconomic woes, as well as cultural traditionalism, the Sex Pistols naturally appealed to Turner. Yet at the formation of Endangered Species in 1979, Turner says, "We felt totally alone as a band. There was a small, tight scene of punk/new wave lovers in Geelong, but we mainly went to the Ballroom in St Kilda for our kicks. . . . The much older music scenesters . . . thought we were a joke, and venues to play in for new bands were virtually nil."

Although "punk was the original fuel" for the band, Turner explains, "We had incredibly eclectic tastes—we loved Wire from the beginning." Exhibiting indifference to any thought of curbing their sound to find more receptive audiences, Turner highlights an inverse route: "As we wrote more originals, we had weirder timings, bizarre chords, and weird lyrics about dropping out and tripping in the countryside or kids wandering around postwar wastelands."

Much like Turner's own family's disapproving response to the Sex Pistols, Endangered Species' confronting style was to elicit its own sense of shock: "Somehow a friend had got us to play at his high school fete.... In a tiny classroom to an audience of a couple of mates, a bunch of young school kids, and some old ladies, we belted out three utterly distorted, ramshackle slabs of noise.... Watching the faces of the kids and older ladies as we utterly assaulted their eardrums in a tiny classroom sticks out as a really funny memory."

Adjacent to Endangered Species, Turner remembers the Orphans "as much by their reputation as actual musical output." Retelling his sole experience of the band live, Turner says, "They kicked off their first number with the most brutal and skull-busting ... punk sound." The drummer "smashed through his snare skin after a few songs, and I think they stopped.... That's the only time I heard of them playing, though I'm sure they must've done something else."

As well as a tape the band released in 1980, that "something else" took place at the very same show Turner had witnessed. Orphans member Pete Herakovic gives brief summary: "We didn't go down well—they were all new wave trench-coat wearers. Being booed, our drummer Nick got up and told them what he thought of them and wanted to fight his way out. The place went dead quiet."

The band—or at least one certain member of the Orphans—didn't seem averse to letting their fists do just as much talking: "Nick punching out the bass player from James Freud at the Golfview was the best. Peter Harris [vocals] was giving the bass player a hard time onstage; the guy kicked Peter in the head, so Nick got up onstage and hooked him. He fell backwards onto his amp and the whole band stopped playing. We were ejected—great night."

The Orphans also hold the inglorious title of being the final band to play the Argyle before it chose the relatively quiet path of wine bar and restaurant: “We had some rocker friends from Ballarat doing the door for us. It was supposed to be no more than 150 people inside” yet “they just let everyone in. . . . The toilets were trashed, kicked in, and the light fixtures were ripped off the walls.”

As if by some form of cosmic retribution, someone broke into the Orphans’ practice space, smashing all their equipment.

# "SHITPILE"

## TASMANIA

### LAUNCESTON

Once a penal settlement—the destination of her Empire's effluence—the southern backwater of Tasmania received uncharacteristic attention in 1977 by the visit of Queen Elizabeth. She arrived the same month as the intended release of the Sex Pistols' "God Save the Queen" single, but in Tasmania no punk bands yet existed to act as symbolic frustration to Elizabeth's presence. Forming months after her tour, Launceston's White Riot became not only the first of Tasmania's punk bands, but one of a modest number in the country then playing original material alongside Sex Pistols covers.

The only notable riot in Launceston's history had occurred a century prior, the *Mercury* reporting that it "was confined to the rabble and larrikin classes."[1] Though White Riot's strange sounds were not to cause any great paroxysm, the band did provoke some of its own disquiet: playing their first show at a local football club, the band, drummer Martin Greer recounted, "upset most of the people there. They started throwing cans and bottles at us, so we pissed off."[2]

Banned from a number of the city's pubs, White Riot failed to secure another show for almost six months. Further opportunities were mixed—an enviable support spot for the Angels was juxtaposed by a New Year's Eve show where they played before a couple of dozen aging hippies. Unperturbed, the band—now the Flecks—continued until 1981 while they developed a more new wave style.

Though White Riot were undoubtedly an oddity in their hometown, the city would not be without further presence of punks. As part of their Tasmanian tour in 1979, Boys Next Door performed in Launceston and Burnie and played four shows in Hobart. News also undertook a two-week tour of the state, Gavin Quinn reassuring that "there certainly were punks in Tasmania."

## HOBART

Having at least determined the existence of punks in Tasmania, Kim Pearce says critically, "The Hobart music scene was a lame duck, as far as I recall . . . full of cover bands. . . . When punk came to Hobart town, I remember the Speed Boats, who were basically old veteran Hobart musicians cashing in. Fine if you wanted to hear perfect versions of the Sex Pistols, the Clash, and the Stranglers." Anthony D'Ettorre adds some greater emphasis, however, contending that Speed Boats were in fact "quite legendary. . . . They were very Stooges, MC5, Radio Birdman" and the "only punk band in Hobart."

Additional to Pearce's modest list was Mr X, which had the rarity of a female singer in a band that included Stiff Little Fingers and Clash covers in their set.

Forming in 1978, Pearce says that the Reserves at the least "were certainly inspired by punk, largely in terms of the DIY ethos and the fact only one member had any musical experience. We could not play to save ourselves, although we did get better. This was helped by a drummer who could keep time some of the time." Of this amateurism operating within a scene of small-time professionals with big-time attitudes, Pearce says, "We loved abuse. I recall a certain member of a muso band considering we were the 'worst' band he had ever heard. That was a compliment we took on board."

Existing for "about three years," the Reserves advertised their post office box address on promotional material. They failed to receive a single letter.

# "LIFE ON THE DOLE"

## SOUTH AUSTRALIA AND NORTHERN TERRITORY

### ADELAIDE

As local punk bands laboured for what little attention they could accrue, Australia's media only too willingly featured the scandal that was the Sex Pistols. In 1977, however, ABC television's *This Day Tonight* program featured a segment that spotlighted Adelaide's infant punk scene. Attempting to placate concerned viewers, the announcer asserted that "if you're wondering if it's going to take off in a big way here, it's worth remembering that the quiet streets of Adelaide are a long, long way from London."[1]

Even local music magazine *Roadrunner* questioned Adelaide's suitability, owing to its supposed lack of motivating conditions. "A tasteful, pleasant, safe little city is Adelaide," began an article by music journalist Stephen Hunter. Reaching a gushing crescendo, Hunter called it "an Athens of the South, a centre for the Arts, tolerant and conducive to those with a creative whim.... What's there to react against?"[2]

As industry and booking agencies dominated Adelaide's live music, bands performing more marginal, obscure, or just plain weird material were confined to the outermost margins. Patrick O'Grady catered to such bands and their audiences by organising shows—known as "bijous"—in rented halls in the Adelaide Hills. Lineups were multivaried, displaying a commonality of vision rather than any rigid similarity of sound. Two bands to play these shows were JAB and Black Chrome.

Formed in 1977, Black Chrome peeled back the curtains from the scene's anonymity, appearing in the *This Day Tonight* segment with the B-side of their 1978 *We Are Tomorrow* seven-inch. Usually noted for more quality journalism, the program momentarily devolved into tabloid as if to stimulate parental concern over the dinner table. If this represented "tomorrow," then the city's citizens, with their churches and Victorian-era morality, should be worried. Given the career path of Black Chrome's vocalist/guitarist Simon Stretton, however, perhaps they should have just condoned the bad haircuts and bad attitudes of their kids: Stretton is today a district court judge.

Central to the formation of the new scene in Adelaide had been Radio Birdman's multiple shows in 1977. One of those present, Riff Raff guitarist Geoffrey Stapleton, enthuses that "they put in a mythmaking onslaught of a performance.... Suddenly everyone was forming a punk band. Funny the things you remember: our bass player, Grant Wills, wore a garbage bag."

Securing the support act spot for Radio Birdman, Riff Raff emerged in 1977 from earlier rock band Gold. With a new name and new interest, Stapleton says, "The music scene in Adelaide was still way behind the times, and we had trouble getting gigs.... Adelaide was a place you had to leave if you were serious about getting anywhere in the Australian music scene ... but when it came to the crunch, Danny Johnson and I were the only ones to leave."

Later, as a member of GANGgajang, Stapleton recorded what has become a seminal Australian rock anthem: "Sounds of Then (This Is Australia)."

With Riff Raff decamped to Melbourne, the first recording to document Adelaide's punk scene—the *Live at the Marryatville Hotel* cassette in 1978—featured the Dagoes, the Accountants, and the U-Bombs. Together the three bands would form a loose union, playing a series of shows together and featuring in a short video. If much at all can be garnered from the footage, it is more the audience's level of intoxication, as well as one man's apparent summation of the scene's modus operandi: "We're here to lick clits and suck pricks."[3]

Much like the legend that has come to be attached to Birdman's Adelaide performances, Accountants drummer Andrew Steel says, "The whole thing with the Accountants was the mythology.... We were talking about the Accountants ... and getting people to talk about the Accountants, from recollection, before we even owned our own instruments." At an early age, and with all the impudence with which teen boys can irritate, Steel says, "We were not big on self-censoring.... On our advertising we had things like 'Nobody over thirty will be admitted,' 'No hippies allowed.' ... We were all about being stirrers."

As young reprobates, Steel says, "Everything was bigger than life in those days.... In Elizabeth in the 1970s you've got a satellite city and it's divided into its little suburbs populated by identifiable youth gangs."

Differentiating it from the dead end that was gang skirmishes, music, Steel says, "was our escape from Elizabeth." Their name came from thinking of "the most boring profession we could think of outside of being librarians." Steel documents the reaction to the band as significantly more intense, including "fifteen miles of car chase in the middle of the night" back to Elizabeth, escaping from "somebody that we'd somehow pissed off.... I'm sure they had a rifle, but I'm sure they were just giving us a scare." Going in the opposite direction on another occasion, Steel says, "The Accountants did get a police escort out of Elizabeth after playing a pro-legalise-marijuana gig. The Iroquois, which were the dominant bike club back in those days, did not take well to us, and the police thought they better give us an escort."

Adelaide wasn't the only city to exhibit an aversion to the band. Steel continues, "We managed to get thrown out of Port Augusta.... Sid got his Marshall amp out of the truck, dragged it up to the second floor ... and plays some guitar at one or two in the morning.... Eventually the cops said basically ... 'Pack up your shit and get out of town now or we've got somewhere for you to stay.'"

Even as the Accountants found themselves in a series of incidents, to Steel, punk offered something far more fundamental than just cheap thrills: "For me it opened me up and gave me the sort of confidence I needed ... that I could go ... 'I don't want to do this job anymore ... I think I should go to art school.' So, it gave me the kick and confidence to let myself be inspired and a bit more true to myself rather than being worried about being stable and conservative."

Not the only member to eschew a conventional life path, Steel informs that "Nick Hope went on to acting." Most famously, Hope was cast as the lead role in the 1993 feature *Bad Boy Bubby*.

Like the film, which has generated a cult status in the decades subsequent to its release, Steel alludes to continued interest in the

Accountants' story: "They never let the truth get in the way of a good story.... The myth and legend are what keeps it alive."

Another band with origins at one of Birdman's shows was U-Bombs; vocalist/bassist Anando Bharti recounts that he "arrived in Adelaide from Sydney a few days before the U-Bombs formed on the dance floor of the Marryatville Hotel at Radio Birdman's first gig in Adelaide."

Bharti's beginnings as a musician traced to Queensland and to Toowoomba band Streetlife, together with future Hoodoo Gurus member Clyde Bramley. Playing the city's "main street at the Carnival of Flowers," Bharti says, "I think Toowoomba has never been the same since. My father was appalled—it is the only gig of mine that he ever witnessed."

Departing the scene of their misdeed, Bharti recalls that he "wasn't enjoying Sydney" so "left with my girlfriend, hitchhiking to wherever we got a ride, which turned out to be Adelaide.... A few days after we got there, Radio Birdman played.... I noticed that the guy dancing next to me was my best friend from school in Toowoomba, Paul Tuxworth. He moved to Adelaide immediately after high school and we lost contact.... Starting a punk band was the obvious next step, which we did then and there."

Offering the memory that "many venue owners and clientele were shocked at our early gigs," U-Bombs incurred banning from a residency "after a nasty fight in the carpark between our fans and the pub regulars. I think that was the reason for all the bannings: violence and broken beer glasses." Bharti insists, though, that "we did not incite any violence. We were all peaceniks who enjoyed playing loud, 'aggressive' music."

Exhibiting the peacenik's penchant for mind-altering substances, Bharti's nonmusical memories "mainly consist of wandering around the Adelaide Hills looking for magic mushrooms. My memories of that time are few and far between, perhaps because of the mushrooms." Accordingly, he says, "Apparently we played about 150 gigs in two years."

Their 1978 single "Give Me a Medal" was a determinedly political title that befitted a socially conscious band who "did benefits for Aboriginal land rights, anti–nuclear mining, pro–marijuana legalisation, anti–police violence."

In 1979, the band sent copies of a demo tape to record labels. Despite their sometimes-serious political tone, the group exhibited a sense of humour and lack of self-pretension by including prefilled rejection slips and return envelopes. A muted response from the industry was compounded by a shift in sound, *DNA* reporting, "Their days were numbered when they decided to include a saxophone."[4]

As the band concluded, Bharti sought greater meaning than that of some youthful defiance: "My spiritual quest led me eventually to become a disciple of Bhagwan Shree Rajneesh (now known as Osho), guru of the 'Orange People.' ... When I started wearing an orange suit and a picture of my guru on a necklace to U-Bombs gigs, it freaked out many of our fans, and, I think, the other members of the band, although they put up with it.... I wanted to get to India to meet Osho in the flesh."

A long, long way from hazy nights spent on the stale beer-soaked carpets of Adelaide's pubs, Bharti says, "I spent seven years (over a twenty-year period) living in Osho's commune in India, where I had the opportunity to play with musicians from literally all over the world.... I became less interested in rock 'n' roll and more into harmonious instrumental music.... In 2015, I visited Jamaica while working as a recording engineer.... The tropical climate was immediately appealing to me, and while I was there the Jamaican government decriminalised cannabis.... I decided to move to Jamaica and start a vegan music community, which I did. I spent all my inheritance building a cool place": Bhartopia.

Witnessing the U-Bombs at the Tivoli, a writer from *Roadrunner* said, "It struck me that the essential difference between the U-Bombs and the more organised aspect of so-called New Wave was fun."[5] Sometimes, though, that sense of fun or jocularity could go a little too far or be too confrontational. The third band of the city's new punk triumvirate had begun life as Daryl Breakaway and the Niggers. Guitarist Neil Perryman reveals that the group's "singer was a Black guy called Daryl Le Merssier, I think. Anyway, Breakaway sounded better. I think Daryl thought of Niggers as [the band's] name. He didn't last long, because he didn't have a particularly good voice."

Relaunched as the Dagoes, the band had questionable legitimacy in their new title: "There was no one with Italian heritage in the band." Further, "We couldn't get the *We Sell Soul* seven-inch [1980] pressed under the name the Dagoes. It had to be the Tony Rome Band, then we rubber-stamped the Dagoes over it. The daily newspapers wouldn't put us in the gig guides as the Dagoes, it had to be the Day-goes."

A band of predominantly record store employees, the Dagoes differed from the majority of Adelaide's punk sphere because of their overriding garage influence.

The group now featured a teenage Richard Cant as vocalist. Cant remembers, "They put me down in this basement in the middle of the city . . . and there I did this audition for these other guys. In my school uniform, mind you. . . . Then they had to decide between a hippie and the private school kid, and they picked the private school kid. And, basically, a week later I was on stage at one of the biggest underground pubs in Adelaide, in front of a thousand people."[6]

Cant's mother, providing his transport to the show, stood aghast at her son's new appointment. Live video footage of the band at the Marryatville in 1978 shows the group out of tune and out of time, performing their track "This Perfect Band."

Forward to 1979, and the Dagoes went through a series of lineup changes, reappearing as a nine-piece. Anyone who has ever tried to coordinate practice for a conventionally sized band would weep at contemplation of the near-impossible logistics of such a swollen lineup. A double seven-inch in 1981 moved even further from punk influences before the band eventually ceased in 1982.

One of the people to "latch on" to the Dagoes, Harry Butler was the self-described "well known and much hated editor of *DNA*."[7] An Adelaide-based fanzine whose first issue appeared in October 1979, *DNA* became the longest-running punk zine in Australia. The country's initial punk fanzines had traced back to 1977, with *Plastered Press* in Melbourne, *Ssuicide ALLey* in Brisbane (succeeded by *Pulp*), *Spurt* and *Self Abuse* in Sydney, *The Rat* in Brisbane, *Alive 'n' Pumping* in Melbourne, *Remote Control* in Perth, and *Street Fever* in Adelaide. Together they comprised a specifically punk-focused press alongside the more professional *RAM*, *Juke*, and *Roadrunner*.

Butler explains their function within a broader, self-perpetuating culture:

> Fanzines sprang up partly because the existing music press wouldn't write about punk bands, and partly because people found it just as good to engage in creative writing as they did in creating music. Other people got together and moved onto

> the airwaves, the 1970s being the era when community radio stations began broadcasting.... The thing I can't emphasise enough, though, is that everything and anything in terms of involvement was encouraged in punk rock, not just playing in a band. That's one thing which set punk apart from other genres: total involvement, and doing it yourself. Most other music styles are content to do their thing and then slot into the existing music establishment, whereas punk sought to create an entire new setup (which was eventually partly successful).

Explaining his productivity, or lack thereof at times, Butler jests, "The fanzine's publishing schedule had nothing at all to do with the music and everything to do with whatever was going on in my apology of a life."

That "apology of a life" has allowed *DNA* to continue intermittently for over forty years.

Tim O'Connor, as someone who was initially denied access to punk, let alone anything rock 'n' roll, says, "Dad ruled the roost when it came to TV and the radio."

Making outside acquaintance with some punk fans, O'Connor admits mirroring his father's prejudices: "I was poo-pooing the Pistols, but they said they'd lend me some records." Knowing that "this music would be verboten at home," O'Connor "played them when the folks had gone to work, before school.... I still love and own copies of these records to this day."

A much greater affront to his father's prohibition, O'Connor says, was when "we four decided to form a band called Skidmarks.... For Christmas that year, I got a cheap electric from K-Mart but had no amp, so I plugged it into the home stereo."

Skidmarks's output rivalled that of a low-quality, department store guitar. "After about six months, the others quit playing music, but I wanted to continue. I think I put an ad in the paper and the only one who answered it was Ian List. This was the start of No Action." Signifying punk's negligibility, O'Connor says, "We put an ad in the paper for a drummer. Again, only one reply. Goes to show how many folks were dying to play punk rock in those days." As for a vocalist, O'Connor had met Rip Savage when "we were both members of the South Australian Star Trek Club."

The band's debut show saw them performing at Ian List's former school at lunchtime. After the initial "success" of playing to a couple of hundred curious students, they were dealt the reality of the live band scene. Appearing before no one and having the venue's owner cut short their set, the band again found a more receptive audience elsewhere. "We also did a gig at the Spastics Society, as it was called in those days," O'Connor says. "Ian's brother had Down syndrome. . . . As soon as we started playing, they went off."

Having reached the high point of their fugitive existence, the band were only able to complete half a dozen songs at their final show before being told over the PA by the venue's DJ to get off.

After such inglorious beginnings as a musician, O'Connor "moved to Melbourne in 1988. The Melbourne music scene was much more vibrant and exciting than Adelaide, and after a couple of false starts, we formed Frente!"

Frente!'s 1992 debut album, *Marvin the Album*, went platinum in Australia.

Just as Frente!'s popularity was receding, that of California punks Rancid was reaching international status. Yet more than two decades before Rancid enlivened hundreds of thousands of disaffected mall rats with their contemporary take on ska and punk, an Australian obscurity known as Nasty Nigel and the Teenage Hellcats did similarly, but to little acclaim. With a significant whiff of the Caribbean, at least musically, the *Jonestown Suicide* seven-inch in 1979 overlaid aggressive punk vocals to the title track's ska/reggae sound.

The record's B-side received play on independent radio in the eastern states, though a reviewer at *Roadrunner* was far less taken by it, describing the record as "a great Xmas present for someone you don't like."[8]

An incalculably more popular Christmas present had been Sister Janet Mead's pumped-up rock version of the Lord's Prayer. An Adelaide Catholic nun, Mead holds distinction as the first Australian to sell over a million copies of a record produced in Australia. Arguably the most nonpunk record in our nation's history, the recording featured Clare Moore, future drummer of Sputniks.

Choosing a name that was certain to exclude any serious popularity of their own, Steve Miller and Dave Graney formed the Foreskins in

Mount Gambier in 1977. Realising the band had little chance of prospering in the country town's "proper" music scene, they organised a show at a football social club hall. With only word of mouth and posters for promotion, the band rationalised that the attendance of friends and family would cover costs for the evening. A thousand inquisitive people supposedly arrived to witness the Foreskins.

Graney suggests their workings were not dissimilar to those from other nations where punk was animating restless youth: "Punk was a very interior event for lots of isolated inarticulate kids who plugged into that energy and spun it out into their own weird, provincial lives."[9]

Despite any romanticising of Mount Gambier, six months later Graney and Miller left for Adelaide, where they met bassist Liz Dealey and Sputniks were born. A future punk residing in Elizabeth, Dealey says she had been "playing on my own in my bedroom . . . no one I could find to form a band with out there." Further discouragement came from a music teacher who "told me not to join a punk band because you'll get nowhere, you'll learn bad habits . . . so I stopped taking lessons."

Moore joined Sputniks, formed in 1978, after one show. In his autobiography, Graney revealed a woman vastly more imposing than her Christian rock beginnings suggested: "She wore dark, adult clothes, dark lipstick, and drank black Russians. . . . She had ideas and opinions and could put away as much booze as any decent, hedonistic young Australian should have tried to. Easily."[10]

Dealey speaks glowingly of Moore and how "it was really empowering at that time to be in a band with a really good female drummer." In the "English scene," Dealey asserts, "women were in everything." Conversely, in Adelaide, "All the bands we played with as the Sputniks, mainly they were men. . . . There were women around, but they weren't prominent in many of the bands."

Perhaps a not-so-subtle nod to the band's composition, certain copies of Sputniks' *Second Glance/Our Boys* seven-inch in 1979 were accompanied by badges lovingly reading "You Cunt I Love the Sputniks."

With the group having "played around for a year or so," and feeling opportunities to have been exhausted, Dealey says, "At the end of '79, we decided we were going to move to Melbourne."

Admitting ambitions accompanied the move, Dealey says the idea was "to come here and play gigs and be a really popular band." Instead, "We came here, we lived in a caravan park for three weeks" before improving to "seven of us living" in a "five-bedroom house.... It was a bit depressing and winter came around.... I'd also just bought the Cure's album *Seventeen Seconds*," which did little to enliven the mood. Dealey does, however, qualify the perceived bleakness by insisting, "It was good fun, and I don't regret doing it, but I'm glad I went back to Adelaide."

A homesick Dealey departed as the band began "doing gigs as the Moodists and started to become quite popular."

Exhibiting no envy of the success that Graney has had in subsequent decades, Dealey explains, "He worked really hard, and I think he had it in his mind that he was going to be a notable figure in the Australian music scene." Beginning as an enterprising teen who managed to draw a thousand people to see a novice band in Mount Gambier, Dealey is of the belief that "as he went on, I think his personality and his character was really prominent and people would have seen that this guy has a vision of what he wants and he's going to get it just because of the way he was."

Briefly emerging also in 1979, New Rose unsubtly named themselves after the Damned's debut single. Kelly Hewson, recalling their first gig, which "was at my high school," describes a staunchly unidimensional band: "They only played one song, I think: 'New Rose' by the Damned."

Hewson's own bands, No Tactics and Agent Orange, had their own English punk fixation, the commonality being a shared repertoire of Sex Pistols material. Still, set lists weighted with the supposedly most scandalous band on the planet didn't seem to inhibit their ability to acquire shows: "We did a sponsored tour ... to shopping centres and stuff in the outer suburbs ... just in the car park of the shopping centre on this huge stage they set up. That was pretty weird." Or more accurately, it was "not that great."

If the group was uncomfortable with a gathering of suburbanite consumers, appearing at one of the state's bikie festivals was harrowing in a different way: "We got a bit lost and the drummer got there with his girlfriend; he had yellow hair and bondage pants and everything, and his girlfriend had a checkerboard haircut and stuff, and they shat themselves and left before we got there."

After the remaining members found "two bikies to play drums," the threat didn't appear to abate as "someone was throwing rocks at us on the stage."

Believing themselves to be facing an imponderable fate, the band realised "the bikies weren't throwing rocks at us, it was this blues band that hated us because we were a punk band."

Unrecorded groups such as No Tactics and Agent Orange were indicative of the obscurity and/or briefness of many early Adelaide bands, including: the Wave, Divine Service, the Recoil, the Bad Poets, Urban Guerillas, the monosyllabic Fuck, Void, Kaos, all-female band Razor Cuts (whose vocalist/guitarist/violinist Kathy Bluff later found a place in the Australian Symphony Orchestra), and the almost prophetically named Brain Damage, who, being bashed, broke up shortly thereafter.

The Ulsers, though boasting significantly greater endurance through their five-year lifespan, produced a seven-inch from 1981, *Remember Them*, whose title did little to prevent their consignment to a minor historical relic.

A group of work friends, Ulsers remained outside any music scene, performing at parties and to work colleagues. Their attempts at avant garde were executed with a certain punk quality—including cardboard boxes for both live and recorded drums—as the band crafted the kind of music that confounds those predisposed to more conventional rock formats. Local radio station 5MMM, hosting a segment on worst records ever produced, proclaimed *Remember Them* the winner.

Best known for the track "Life on the Dole," released on a 5MMM compilation in 1980, the Brats were another band skulking on the outskirts of the punk scene.

The Brats made their debut at a Cannabis Law Reform Society party, and the Australian Marijuana Party offered to keep the clock hands at 4:20 by booking the band in mid-1978. In what could have been a classic case of weed-induced paranoia, the show never eventuated: "The gig was cancelled, the AMP said, because all of the punks expected to turn up would cause too much violence."[11]

The band stuck to playing to the familiarity of crowds with dubious character, including at the Austral, a renowned bikie pub, and a show at a juvenile detention centre. Peter Brat, reliving the event, boasted, "There were all these teenage hoodlums in the front row going crazy."[12]

Despite disreputable audiences and shows being shut down by

police, the Brats managed to accrue a respectably sized following. The disintegration of the band, however, saw some members travel north to a most unlikely of live music destinations—Darwin—as members of Exhibit A.

## DARWIN

In 1974, Cyclone Tracy had razed the near entirety of Darwin and forced three-quarters of its inhabitants to be evacuated. A half decade later, the arrival of punk barely elicited a stir.

Exhibit A's Darwin period had been preceded by their Adelaide beginnings, where they were subjected to disturbances of human—rather than atmospheric—origin.

The band performed two shows at the Overway Hotel, and it was reported that the "first show there saw half of the band's following get beaten up. Next gig the other half got thumped, and that was the end of that."[13]

Recommencing in Darwin in 1980, Exhibit A's Stu Spasm joined with former members of the Brats. Expressing dubious belief that the Northern Territory's capital constituted some form of punk music cash cow, Spasm told *DNA*, "We thought when we went to Darwin, we'd make some money."[14]

They lasted only months before returning to Adelaide; Spasm was near incredulous at the band's inability to derive an income. Claiming that the remaining members wished to stay on due to Darwin's proximity to Southeast Asia and the opportunity to smuggle drugs, his replacement, Richard Howard, suggests, "Darwin was that sort of place: full of outlaws and wild-eyed chancers. I loved it for a while, but you do end up drinking beer for breakfast" and "going troppo" (losing one's mind).

Not so much a chancer or smuggler, Howard had arrived in Darwin with his girlfriend on a roundabout way back home to the UK: "We stopped off in the Gulf of Carpentaria for six months, looking for work on the prawn trawlers, and wound up in Darwin.... Richard Ploog [later of the Church] was in the band. I seem to remember a lot of rehearsing and a couple of gigs at the local RSL."

Prior to Howard, the band had opened for Cold Chisel in 1980 to six thousand people, yet the city otherwise lacked reliable venues and opportunities for the group's stand-alone gigs. Finding place at a "musician's ball" in 1981, Exhibit A were wedged between a Greek bouzouki band and a cabaret act. Combining with the Darwin Theatre Group to hold mixed "events," evenings could include any combination of dancers, poetry, acoustic performances, and feminist theatre.[15]

As the band relocated to Melbourne in 1982, Howard finally made the return trip home to the UK. There he found a music landscape evolved from that which he'd left as a teen: "Punk was over. New Romantics had moved in."

# “ARSEHOLE OF THE UNIVERSE”

## WESTERN AUSTRALIA

### PERTH

If Darwin was a remote musical outpost, then Perth, routinely cited as the world’s most isolated city, was somewhere between nowhere and oblivion. But if inhabiting a sliver between expanses of desert and the Indian Ocean was enough to cause geographical malaise, it wasn’t impairing the quality of its more underground art and culture. Ben Juniper relays that “it’s often been said, not just in the musical arts … the isolation of Perth has given it a certain edge.”

Bereft of the grit that marked London and New York, and as beneficiaries of resources investment money, Perth afforded a level of comfortableness to many of its residents. However, when coupled with the homogeneity of the postwar settlement in nations such as the US and Australia, it helped foment a politics of boredom, especially among suburban youth. In a 1972 election speech, Gough Whitlam had highlighted “no greater social problem” in Australia “than the good use of expanding leisure.… It is, above all, the problem of urban societies, and thus, in Australia, the most urbanised nation on earth, a problem more pressing for us than for any other nation on earth.”[1]

Perth bands crudely amplified Whitlam’s sentiment, with the Victims screaming “Perth Is a Culture Shock,” the Exterminators even more explicitly labelling it the “Arsehole of the Universe.”

Local journalist Ray Purvis captured the mood of its participants: “These were middle-class kids from good backgrounds playing punk as they knew it—informed by the trade papers, but otherwise completely insulated from the global movement. In this way the Perth punk scene was completely unique. It had its own flavour … which was ‘I am sick and tired of the mediocrity and sheer boredom of life in this town—so let's make a hell of a racket, and give the establishment the middle finger.'"[2]

Rather than solely directed towards authoritative figures, punk's collective middle finger would be aimed foremost at its existing music scene. It was mired by cover bands, and Ben Juniper recalls that "there was no other place in Australia that was quite like it. Cover bands would be pulling crowds of up to three thousand people in these ridiculously big beer halls."

Neil Fernandes is unswerving in offering Perth punk's view of such groups: "They were the enemy."

Fernandes cites his defining musical moment as the loan of an album by friend and future bandmate Kim Salmon. Like many diligent record collectors and avid readers of music magazines, Salmon had become aware of the Ramones in the lead-up to their first album's release. For modern music listeners accustomed to immediacy, it's hard to conceive the anticipation preceding such a record. Salmon describes the elation when "there was the call from 78s [78 Records] to tell me the Ramones LP was finally in! Bringing it home and putting the needle in the groove ... was one of the perfect moments of my life."[3] Unfortunately for Salmon, Perth failed to feature on the Ramones' Australian tour schedule in 1980.

Cheap Nasties (posthumous self-titled collection LP, 2018) formed in the immediate aftermath of the Ramones debut, but the band played few shows, struggling to gain momentum or interest. Friction over musical direction and irreconcilable differences between Salmon and Fernandes led to the former's departure in late 1977. With Salmon gone, the remaining members became Manikins, with Fernandes continuing as primary songwriter.

As the first of the '77-era Perth bands, Cheap Nasties were shortly followed by a group that superseded them for both popularity and recorded output: the Victims. The drummer in the group, James Baker, recollects, "We did four nights at the Governor Broome Hotel with the Cheap Nasties. That was almost the start of the whole scene."

As a kid growing up in a small country town, Baker knew of solitude more than most rock music fans, having lived in a place that had "nothing to do with rock 'n' roll. You couldn't even buy a record there."

Thankfully, according to Baker, "Rock 'n' roll comes from the heart; it doesn't come from where you live."

Leaving town at fourteen, the outer reaches of Perth at least gave Baker the opportunity to procure records, and provided a pivotal moment: "I met this guy from Detroit in 1972, '73, in a coffee shop, and I had silver boots on, and he goes, 'Wow, man, that's cool, do you like rock 'n' roll?' . . . He turned me on to Iggy and the Stooges and the MC5 and the Velvet Underground and all that stuff I'd never heard of before."

Undertaking an overseas trip in 1976, Baker says it "was surprising when I went to America . . . going out to nightclubs and saying, 'I like the Stooges, the Dolls, and MC5,' and they'd go, 'I've never fucking heard of them.' I come from Kenwick in Western Australia, you bums are sitting here in Hollywood, and you've never heard of the New York Dolls or the Ramones?"

Travelling on to New York and London, Baker took in "the Heartbreakers, the Ramones, the Pistols . . . the Damned . . . the Vibrators . . . the Adverts." He admits to it being an amazing instance of "right time, right place. But also, you had to want to seek it out." Of the shows he saw, Baker surprisingly reveals them to have been "small—two hundred max. Sometimes a hundred, sometimes fifty." Nonetheless, reflecting on being witness to the epicentres of a musical revolution, Baker does confirm some awareness of its importance: "I knew it was something that was happening, like, 'We're the new kids on the block, we're taking over.' I felt that side of it."

Arriving in England in the months preceding the release of the Damned's "New Rose," Baker met Sid Vicious on a bus, who introduced himself as his real name, John Ritchie. Vicious later spared Baker a beating from skinheads at a show by the Clash. Also meeting the Clash's Joe Strummer and Mick Jones at a pub following a Damned gig, Baker became one of the countless replacement drummers the group auditioned.

Aided by such a collection of experiences and anecdotes, Baker became one of Perth's most central figures, Juniper explaining that "James certainly did have a certain cool cachet about himself" and that "coming back from New York and London with an armful of records turned a lot of people over here onto sounds that they hadn't really heard before."

Exhausting his funds overseas, Baker returned to the relative quiet of Perth with ambitions of his own. Seeing an advertisement for the Geeks, Baker tried out as singer before leaving the audition as their new drummer. One of his bandmates, Dave "Flick" Faulkner, would be another pillar of early Perth punk. The duo, as well as Geeks bassist Dave Cardwell, left the band while still in the rehearsal stage, forming the Victims.

The setting for the Victims' first show, "Victim Manor," was a large, squalid sharehouse by the train tracks in East Perth that the embryonic punks had symbolically taken over from its previous hippie inhabitants. Further shows occurred with the only other band sharing a likeness of vision, Cheap Nasties. Baker recalls one particular pub gig: "The Cheap Nasties played early on, and they liked Cheap Nasties. The Victims, they said, 'You're fucked, get out of here,' and they turned the PA off. But they couldn't turn the amps off.... We had a song called 'Disco Junkies.' ... We played it as long as we could.... All these truck drivers, they were walking out giving us the finger.

"I thought, 'Hang on, we can get press out of this,' so I phoned up the *Sunday Independent* and my old buddy... Ray Purvis, and he managed to get a bit in his magazine: 'Punk Rock Band Kicked Out of Kewdale Hotel'—exactly what we wanted. We used to get all this press, which would piss off all the other musicians."

Those musicians, he says, "hated us and we hated them, and that was great.... We won in the end; people don't talk about those bands anymore."

In 1978, talk of the band was even to reach London, their *Television Addict* seven-inch receiving a glowing review in English magazine *Sounds*: "If you and I thought we could never listen to another punk single, then this one is the one for you. An Oz three-piece showing that with the right spirit, sense of humour, production, and care, it's still possible to breathe new life into an area ruined by countless shoddy imitations."[4]

But the band's own breath was by then almost extinguished. The same month they were being heralded internationally, the Victims performed a final show at Leederville Town Hall's "New Wave Festival" alongside the Veneers, Invaders, Sad Sack and the Bags, Hitler Youth, and Blök Musik (who shortly after became the Triffids). A further record—*No Thanks to the Human Turd* seven-inch, 1978—saw its release a few months following their breakup.

Even with the Victims as the city's most vaunted first-wave band, Baker bemoans their failure to last long enough to fully benefit from the growing interest in punk: "Sadly, we sort of broke up before we could capitalise on that." The Victims' combining of a standard punk sound with a nascent penchant for pop was, however, to eventually pervade commercial radio listeners for decades, Baker and Faulkner forming the Hoodoo Gurus in Sydney in 1981.

Sydney being the preferred destination for departing Perth punks, Dave Warner alternately views a shared sociopolitical temperament with Queensland when asserting that Perth "was very conservative in all areas," though he concedes, "It wasn't as repressive as Queensland." Like Bjekle-Petersen, Western Australia premier Charles Court moved to encumber potential troublemakers. His government amended a section of the Police Act in 1976 so that anyone seeking to assemble groups over three people was required to seek permission of the police commissioner, punishable by a month's jail.[5]

Warner contends, however, that such environments are at least beneficial to cultural expression, tending "to generate a very strong climate for people in the arts. Not too much good stuff comes out of places that have got really liberal and leftist-leaning art things. It's usually just dogmatic propaganda."

One of the few performers of original music in pre-1977 Perth, Warner inadvertently questions the sacrosanct narrative of the Saints as Australia's first punk band when discussing his group, Pus, formed in 1973. Warner remembers, "We didn't call ourselves punk, but I think we came from a very similar position.... It was more the attitude; more a conceptual thing about what music's about, and I think that's the similarity.... It's kind of academic in a way."

Warner views Pus's isolation as cause for the lack of familiarity: "Most people don't know about it, I think. Punk history has tended to be written by people in the eastern states.... Especially back in the '70s, it was a different world over there [Perth], there was no press ... no record companies ... no way of getting your stuff out."

Despite the barriers, Warner succeeded in creating more than just casual curiosity for his next band, Dave Warner's From the Suburbs. Their first album, *Mug's Game*, went gold in 1978.

Making a move into writing following their third album, Warner penned the screenplay for the 2000 feature film *Cut*, starring Kylie Minogue and Molly Ringwald, as well as winning multiple literary awards as a crime fiction author.

Believing his band to also have been the first punk group in Perth, the Geeks' Ross Buncle has undertaken a personal online crusade of ensuring their recognition and place in the city's punk genealogy.

James Baker remembers seeing the advertisement for a vocalist, and he relives his own—brief—time with the Geeks: "It wasn't a bad band, but they were not worried about the image at all, which pissed me off.... I wanted everyone to look like the Heartbreakers or something.... I left and took some of the songs that we wrote that ended up being recorded by the Victims."

The Geeks, transposing into Hitler Youth, debuted at the Leederville Town Hall "New Wave Festival." After that single faltering show led to their abandonment, Buncle regrouped as the Orphans.

The Orphans' search for a singer had included auditioning a woman who, in spite of being vocally capable, was suspected of being an acid casualty, especially after claiming to have seen a deceased Jim Morrison of the Doors alive in Sydney. The choice was instead made of Billy Orphan, recently released from Pentridge Prison in Melbourne.

If the troubles of finding a suitable singer weren't frustrating enough, Buncle wrote of that which came from the "woman who lived near our ... rehearsal quarters; she banged on the door between songs one afternoon and pleaded with us to 'Turn down the trumpets!'"[6]

More detrimentally to Buncle, soon after the Leederville show the Orphans played at punk venue Hernando's Hideaway, taking over from the recently broken-up Victims. Hoping to insert themselves as the new leaders of the scene, they were to be confronted by diminishing audiences. "Whereas the Victims had branded themselves with an unmistakable punk identity, we were probably more extreme musically, and threatening in a way the Victims had not been, but did not look like a punk band."[7]

A double CD—*Exposed*—was released in 2006, collecting studio, rehearsal, and live recordings of the Orphans' various iterations.

Where Buncle had hoped the Orphans would take the mantle as Perth's preeminent punk band, that position came to be occupied by the Manikins. Through a more digestible melodic sound, Neil Fernandes recalls the group's successful move from the exclusivity of punk venues to larger audiences and suburban pubs: "One of my proudest achievements was that we had a residency at a place called the Dianella Hotel, which was in the middle of suburbia, and we played there for three or four weeks running before they kicked us out. But for three or four weeks, people who lived in and around Dianella came to see the band without knowing anything about the inner-city punk scene, and just got up and danced."

The open-mindedness of Perth music fans, however, wasn't always obvious. "I did get to meet Peter Garrett [Midnight Oil vocalist and former federal minister] and said to him that the Oils were the only band that the Manikins never supported, and he said, 'Oh, why's that?' and I said, 'Because your fans would have killed us.' We barely got out alive supporting Cold Chisel and the Angels when they came to Perth, and I said, 'But your fans were so diehard that we would have just got bloody bottled.'"

Fernandes was generally appreciated for his capabilities as a songwriter, but the same could not always be said for his heritage. Moving to Australia from India at age twelve, he was the subject of racial epithets: "At the time in Perth there was a bit of a nasty skinhead scene. It was small, but I can remember some pretty violent times." One particular individual "lived down the road from me.... When I drove past, he would wave to me ... but when he was with his friends, I was the 'Paki punk.' But because we were a kind of punk band and they were all into punk rock, they'd all turn up at the gigs, but didn't quite know how to relate to me. And I can remember a number of occasions where things got nasty at gigs.... I felt I was being targeted. I've never made much of this anywhere else, but it's certainly something I recall. I wouldn't want it to be portrayed in a fashion which overstated it, but it was definitely there.... It didn't stop me from doing anything, but it was there."

Cautioning against viewing his persistence as a deliberately political act, Fernandes says, "I was playing in a band, I was writing these songs, and it was about that. To me it wasn't any great cultural or political battle that I was waging."

Manikins' first single, "Models for Mankind," in 1978, presented punk with underlying pop as Fernandes retained a rough guitar tone. With their second single, "Premonition," the following year, the band had lost near all punk influence in the crafting of a polished and formidable power pop song. The loud guitar returned, however, for the third single, "Love at Second Sight," in 1980.

The strength of Fernandes's songcraft brought the band to attention of the Easybeats' Harry Vanda and George Young, producers of AC/DC's early albums. "By that time," says Fernandes, "I'd probably decided that I didn't want to do it, I didn't want to tour—I hated it.... And I'd resigned myself to the fact that this is something that we'd continue to do from Perth and entirely on our own terms."

Contrary to the supposedly universal teenage fantasy of rock 'n' roll stardom, Fernandes confesses that "I can't say it's something that ever drove me, the idea that we could become really big and successful.... I was always a very self-conscious performer." His preference being the bringing of songs to completion, a self-reflective Fernandes notes, "I don't think I had the resilience or the temperament or the discipline that people who do succeed seem to have."

The band's main songwriter, Fernandes says that he "stopped playing in '81" as the band broke up. Pursuing a career in public service, a contented Fernandes does, however, offer a glimmer of lament: "If there's any regret that I do have, it's that I think I could have developed as a songwriter.... I look at my friends, my contemporaries back then like Kim [Salmon] and Dave [Faulkner], and think they've developed. Dave ... in my mind ... he's among the best songwriters that Australia's ever produced."

After his break from Fernandes and Cheap Nasties, Salmon joined the remnants of the Exterminators to become the Invaders, before the addition of James Baker and a name change to the Scientists in 1978.

The *Frantic Romantic* seven-inch in 1979 exhibited a band well versed in melody, guitarist Ben Juniper remembering, "The early lineup of the Scientists was seen as Beatle-esque." Though viewing the association as doing "a disservice to the originality of the music," Juniper says, "I don't really think the Scientists were punk in the English mould ... but people certainly liked the idea that we were, so that's what we called ourselves.... I always thought of the Sex Pistols as a sort of pantomime; a great way to sell records."

Making the distinction between pantomime and unadulterated performance, Juniper says of Salmon that he "certainly put his heart and soul into being a showman.... The Scientists had a very loud, very high-energy show, and you either loved it or hated it." Salmon's memory, though, seems to gravitate towards the latter: "People had got the Victims. They didn't get us. We were loud, loose as buggery, and yet had pop melodies and wore moptops. And loud shirts."[8]

The moptops and melodies remained for the follow-up self-titled seven-inch in 1980. Juniper says that of the records that were pressed, "A lot of them went overseas.... We charted in New York and London on the alternative charts."

Known to record enthusiasts overseas, the Scientists didn't seem to exhibit interest in making forays into the suburbs of their own city. Almost content with their insularity, even if they were being stifled by it, James Baker insists, "We didn't necessarily give a fuck about playing in the suburbs.... We were happy if they accepted us, but we wouldn't change the way we were." Juniper's memory is less dismissive—that despite "a hardcore little following" it "certainly wasn't enough to sustain us. It was pretty depressing."

At something of an impasse, the band decided to head to the eastern states to test the response. "It did seem pretty ambitious," Juniper says, "but we managed to get out of Perth ... and go up and down the East Coast a couple of times. It was a bit of an achievement because of the tyranny of distance. Perth was a very hard place to break out of."

The near-inconceivable distance of the drive compounded the mental barrier of Perth's isolation, as air travel amenable to a punk's budget was still decades away. Many a band have been ruined by the numbing hours spent confined together on Australian highways, exacerbated by financial pressures as well as the difficulty that is frayed emotions owing to sleep deprivation and the aftereffects of drugs and alcohol.

In part an undertaking to find a new audience, Baker says the tour was "just an adventure as well.... We had a couple of gigs with the Boys Next Door, and a couple of gigs with the Lipstick Killers, and the rest was playing with awful bands like Jimmy and the Boys and Mother Goose. The Scientists even supported Sherbet.... It was their first gig as Sherbs when they decided to go new wave and bring their leather jackets in on coat hangers like stage props [*laughs*]."

The second tour east was more deflating, Baker remembering that "they stuck us on this ridiculous circuit" which brought "a lot of mismatched gigs." A concurring Juniper says, "We'd get sent to RSL clubs out in the boonies.... Your sneakers are sticking to the carpet, and you're doing your songs while people are playing one-armed bandits [poker machines] at the same time." Songs concluded "usually just to dribbles of applause. Occasionally you'd have somebody that knew the music somehow, but they were the exception, not the rule."

The band appeared at Sydney music venue Bondi Lifesaver, about which Juniper recalls, "We were on a double bill with Jo Jo Zep and the Falcons.... That was a disaster. It would probably have held two thousand people.... We did this forty-five-minute set and there was a dribble of applause. Angry Anderson [Rose Tattoo vocalist] was in the audience, and he got so annoyed by this lack of response ... that he grabbed a microphone and plugged it into the mixing desk and started berating the crowd."

After limping their way back to Perth, Baker suggests that "I don't even think people knew we went [*laughs*]." Juniper reveals the reality behind the self-deprecation: "I think we'd just appeared on *Countdown* and came home with barely enough money to get back down to Perth. In fact, the boys dropped into my old man's place ... about fifteen miles outside of Perth, and had to borrow twenty bucks for some gas ... and got fifteen dollars' worth of beer and five dollars' worth of petrol."

If nothing else, the band's appearance on *Countdown* had fulfilled Salmon's prediction to his fellow students that he would one day feature on the program. Back in Perth, though, transmission returned to its normal indifference, Juniper remembering, "We played to our normal fifty people. I don't think anyone knew we went, or even saw us on *Countdown*." He quit the band.

The band continued as a three-piece and recorded their self-titled album. Baker considers their conundrum: "It made it hard here. We broke up in the end because no one would come and watch us."

As Juniper "went back to the tactile arts"—his father being noted painter Robert Juniper—he says, "I don't know why or how, but I always felt that Kim particularly—but James also—they'd do well."

The Scientists, resurrected with Salmon and a continually evolving cast of support musicians, dissociated themselves from their old sound as the next half decade saw them become one of Australia's most revered independent acts.

The Scientists were not alone in re-forming, as, having disbanded for a year, the Victims reconvened for a single evening. They had no support band, so those arriving early had hours of drinking behind them by the time the group reached the stage. They were described as showing no hint of their inactivity, and *Roadrunner* columnist Kim Williams wrote, "In the break between the first set and the second, a fight broke out.... I went to the toilet shortly thereafter but was too scared to piss."[9]

Fights allegedly continued as the second set was reportedly halted by police. Baker's memory, however, differs substantially from Williams's, dismissing his account: "No show we ever played got shut down because of violence."

Even years later, Williams recalled it as "one of the scariest experiences of my life.... It was completely out of control. The skinheads breaking bottles everywhere; there were several hundred of them and somebody ended up getting stabbed and some marines came in; they were in town and they ran away.... The gig closed down when the door of the nightclub got smashed off its hinges, somebody got stabbed, the ambulance came in, and that was it. Perth was a much more violent place then than it is now. There were a lot more skinheads, and they would often travel in packs to gigs, smash things up."[10]

Where punk in Australia was viewed as an alternative to suburban beer-barn violence, Perth's scene would endure repeated violent episodes. Quick and the Dead, the main soundtrack to the trouble, gave voice to something more sinister than just middle-class disgruntlement and restlessness. Through uncompromising sound and demeanour, the group—or more specifically its followers—were to supersede all other early Australian bands for violence both of image and deed.

An already large British-born population in Perth, bolstered by significant waves of migration in the 1960s and early '70s, was reflected in the import of British culture, including skinheads. The "boot boys"—or longer-haired skinheads—then listening to glam bands were usurped as the scene underwent revitalisation with the emergence of punk. One of those to make the transition, Mark Webster of Antibodies, provides a snapshot: "We used to go to Hernando's Hideaway to watch the Victims, the Scientists, and a few other punk bands. There was a fierce rivalry with the rockers and bikies, but punks and skins mingled with each other. It was a great time to be a youth."

Quick and the Dead's bassist and stalwart, Murray Holmes, had his interest piqued by the earlier boot boys: "When I was really young ...

Status Quo and Slade played in Perth.... All the old skinheads, immigrant skinheads, the ones that had the longer hair and flares, they were all there, and I was like, 'Jeez, what are all these blokes on about?' It sort of started from there.... 1977 came and the Sex Pistols came out... so we started this band and played at Hernando's.... That would have been Enemy Sounds."

James Baker was one particular fan: "I was really impressed with them. They were like The Damned in the sense that they drove everyone out of the place with such high energy."[11]

The band underwent a name change to Audio Damage, but the warning signs were already present in the pages of *Roadrunner*: "Perth's only punks ... if only they could lose some of their scummy arsehole following."[12]

As punks and skins formed two increasingly distinct and sometimes antagonistic groupings, Holmes says, "We were only invited to do a couple of shows. There was a concert in Fremantle where there was a whole pile of other bands, and that turned into a fucking big riot disaster and punch-up.... I think there was a couple of other places where we played with these other [punk] bands. But of course, it kicked off again. Everywhere we went, it just all ended up in a massive brawl at the end of the night, with everyone and anyone, or between themselves.... I suppose you could say we were on the hardcore side of things with a pretty aggressive audience.... I think we were banned from everywhere in Perth, so that made about a hundred [venues]."

Accepting that "we were a pretty big influence on all the skinheads," Holmes explains, "They went from the long hair, from the flares ... basically evolved into real skinheads with jeans and Doc Martens and Ben Shermans and Fred Perrys and braces.... Nobody else would be game to see us in Perth because they'd get their heads kicked in or something. So basically, our audience only grew through the amount of skinheads in Perth. There weren't very many alternative music people that would come along."

What outside attention they did draw was near always condemnatory, reflected in Kim Williams's 1981 article: "Their jackbooted audience make genocide seem just that much more acceptable."[13]

The month following its publication, ABC current affairs program *Nationwide* featured a segment on Quick and the Dead: "Violence isn't part of the lifestyle of most people in Perth. It's an ugly, unnecessary, and usually unlawful deviation from the easy-going, good-natured living that most people prefer. But these aren't most people; they are loosely called punks or punk rockers, and to them violence is simply part of their lifestyle."[14]

The band's impact and legacy of infamy superseded their popularity. The city's *Weekend News* also made headlines of the group and its followers: "60 Skinheads in Wild Rampage," "Skinheads in Wild Brawl," and "Skinheads in Wild Country Brawl."

Violence would be propagandised in the title of Quick and the Dead's 1981 seven-inch *Another Violent Night*. Their notoriety fuelled attendances to the point, Holmes says, that "eventually we were actually making good money." Not that the band always played the most conventional of venues. "Once again, we had nowhere to play ... [so] what we had to do was create our own venues and publicity, and I just thought we could probably get a bit of recognition playing in a prison.... It suited us really, really well.... Got a bit of a write-up in the paper about it."

Gaining even greater exposure was one Quick and the Dead show as part of what was dubbed their "Bunbury Holocaust Tour." Holmes says that a local football team "were having some end-of-the-season piss-up" and, in a highly questionable decision, agreed to allow the band as the evening's entertainment. "That got into the paper once again."[15]

Appearing to have let their newspaper subscription lapse, the organiser of a show at Fremantle's Victoria Hall

> rang me up and asks us to play with all these other bands, and I said, "I don't think it's really a good idea," and he goes, "No, no, no, it'll be all right, it'll be fine." On one side of the room was all the skinheads and punks, and on the other side of the hall was all these fucking hippies.... A bunch of these skinheads and punks found a chain somewhere, a big heavy chain, and they smuggled it into the hall, and they got up the back—about three of them on either side—and they ran down the middle and mowed all these fucking hippies and tables and chairs down.... There was arms and legs and glasses flying everywhere. The poor bloke that was running the show came up to me and he says, "Can you please get all your gear and leave?" He was just about crying.

Others were again seemingly oblivious to their reputation—though this time, while their presence was appreciated, the tears were for real:

> We played the Mosman Park Deaf School for Children. . . . There was probably about fifty or sixty of them with all their parents. We started playing and . . . they all started putting their heads in these huge speaker things I had either side of the stage. Obviously, they're picking up the vibrations, and after a while they all got fucking aggressive. . . . We finished pretty early because they had to be home. . . . We're packing up the gear and everything, then I see a big half-circle of all these kids . . . and there's about six or seven of them bawling their eyes out, and I thought, "What's wrong with them?" One of the organisers was walking past, and I said, "What're the kids saying?" and she looks down and she says, "Oh, they've had such a good time they don't want to go home."

From sixty to six hundred, Holmes notes that around the same period, "We were playing quite regularly at the Criterion Hotel in Perth, and we had about six hundred people there." But the band had also accrued a list of enemies. Holmes says, "Somebody rang up and put a bomb threat on the place. The police turned up, but they did fuck-all, they didn't even clear the place out." Next, the group organised a river cruise, but this time the constabulary was not so indifferent as the event "turned into a disaster." That "disaster" was most felt by an unfortunate bottle shop owner, Rhys Evans remembering that "they pulled into the jetty and everyone went into the bottle shop. . . . They just took everything, and all hopped back on the boat." Reaching the end of the cruise, Holmes says, "There was about a dozen police vans backed up, with the doors open, and it looked like they were going to arrest everyone. But they didn't get many, because as soon as the boat stopped all the skinheads just jumped off and ran in four hundred directions."

Water or land was irrelevant for their propensity to find trouble, Holmes admitting, "We sort of got used to it. You knew what was going to happen every time we played. I never used to try and incite violence or anything like that, but a lot of people had hate in their guts and they were against the system. . . . Go back to the deaf school for children: they were fucking violent and they'd never even heard of us. I think it's just that sort of music—it's just full of aggression. That mixed with the crowd and alcohol, that's what sparks it all off."

Paring away the accompanying trouble and viewing them simply as a musical entity, James Baker is adamant that "it actually wasn't a bad band." Yet the music and violence became so entwined that they could not be untangled, Baker lamenting that "it was just the audience they attracted. They just wanted to be a bit more violent than what one should."

Paper Dolls were another band whose ability was on occasion obscured by secondary constituents. Bassist Sheila Monkhouse says, "Apparently when we were sober, we were good."

Through a history of "a hundred or so shows," however, the group were impeded by others as much as themselves. After arriving to a "gig we were supposed to play," Monkhouse offers the memory that "they all got so drunk and out of it that the drum kit was smashed up" before Paper Dolls could even play.

In addition to the perils of a glass or two too many, Monkhouse says of the lesser-known bands, "Drugs did get a hold of a lot of them.... I know it was part of the genre, but it was very sad.... A lot of them didn't last very long due to in-house [issues] or they hocked their guitars for drugs. Or they died, unfortunately."

Still, Monkhouse retains a positivity about her time with the band: "I found my identity through that—I found my place.... It led me to places that I never thought I'd go. We got away with a lot with punk rock because you only needed to know four or five bars."

Conceding the Fakes to be one of those "lesser-known bands," singer George Karpathakis says, "We were just a blip on the radar" who expired after "about eight gigs."

Describing Perth as "a very hot scene," Karpathakis employs the adjectives "intense," "intellectual," and "creative": "A lot of the punks were English or of English migrant background, and they brought some of that with them, and some of it was just cultural osmosis." Differentiating Perth from South London, however, Karpathakis says, "We didn't have the kind of problems of Brixton and all the race stuff, so there was no way a Clash was going to arise in our midst." The Fakes were nonetheless differentiated, at least by race. "When you separate us out from the others, we were a 'wog punk' band because we had a Croat, two Greeks, a Maltese, and an Italian."

The group was described at times as a poor Roxy Music, and Karpathakis concedes, "That's a fair statement.... We'd rip off everybody."

A Roxy Music rip-off performing to an audience of hardened outlaw bikers sounds like the ingredients for a bloodbath. It would also, Karpathakis recalls, be the Fakes' final show:

> We had a bunch of bikies—I think they were the Gypsy Jokers—who used to come into the Coronation, and we'd play. They never minded us, and we never minded them, and it was like a good relationship. Then one day a whole pile of bogans ... started abusing us and we abused back. Anyway, a fight broke out and it turned into the most amazing bar brawl I'd ever seen. People were thrown out cowboy-style ... it was completely mad. We didn't stop playing. After that the guy didn't employ us anymore and that was our last gig.

His brief foray as a musician concluding in cinematic style, Karpathakis "went to Sydney and trained to be a filmmaker.... I became kind of a film academic.... I did a thing called *Street Kid* in Perth for FTI [Film and Television Institute], which is the life of a punk."

The Fakes members' own lives had come from backgrounds far outside punk: "There was a guy called Mick Price who came from Captain Matchbox Whoopee Band.... George Blazevic was a journalist at the *West Australian*, ABC TV, and News Corp" as well as being a playwright. "One of the guys who was in the band ... had been in Pus." Karpathakis himself "was in a kind of Australian folk thing in my earlier years ... get in the shed and use a lagerphone.... It was a diverse mob."

The 1980s were to bring a new surge of more fundamentalist "hardcore" punk that eyed much that had come before with suspicion, viewing it as superficial, insufficiently subversive, or preoccupied with success. Not that their fleeting existence ever saw them eye stardom, but Karpathakis is frank in assessing his band's punk devotion: "The Fakes were exactly what they were called: the Fakes.... You always knew there were bands that were trying it out. Like us."

The Saints, 1976. Photo by Jennifer Fay Gow.

The Leftovers, 1980. Photo by Paul O'Brien.

Razar, 1979. Photo by Paul O'Brien.

Radio Birdman, live in London, 1979. Photo by Adrien Boot.

Thought Criminals, 1980. Photo © 'pling.

X, 1978. Photo by Bruce Tinsdale.

Suicide Squad. Photo by Kay Glass.

Tactics, 1980. Photo © 'pling.

Vacant Lot, 1979. © 'pling.

Boys Next Door, 1979. Photo by Peter Milne/M.33.

News, 1979. Photo by Paul O'Brien.

La Femme, 1979. Photographer unknown.

The U-Bombs, 1978. Photo by Paul O'Brien.

Sputniks, 1979. *Messenger Press* photo.

The Victims, 1978. Photo by Robert Baxter.

The Scientists, 1978. Photo by Robert Baxter.

Quick and the Dead, 1982. Photo by Andy Oliver.

Depression. Photo by Liz River.

Cosmic Psychos. Photo by Tony Mott.

Vicious Circle, live on US tour, 1986. Photo by Joseph B. Henderson.

I Spit on Your Gravy. Photo by Joe Holzer.

Gash. Photographer unknown.

World War XXIV, 1983. Photo by Bruce Griffiths.

CHAOS, 1985. Photo by Bruce Griffiths.

Urban Chaos, 1983. Photo by René Muir.

Hard-Ons. Photo by Tony Mott.

Massappeal. Photo by Todd Ingham.

Mystery of Sixes, 1982. Photo by Peter Fischmann.

Crucified Truth. Photographer unknown.

Insane Hombres. Photo by Bazzil.

Perdition. Photo by Liz River.

Exploding White Mice. Photo by Eric Algra.

Pigs Are Guilty. Photographer unknown.

Where's the Pope?, 1985. *Messenger Press* photo.

Matt and Clare of Insurrection. Photo by Andrea Snashall.

INSANE
1982-1989
OLOGY

# "DEAD BEFORE RETIREMENT"

## VICTORIA

### MELBOURNE

1982 is the year punk died. Or so it is eulogised in a somewhat standard narrative. Indeed, the release of the Clash's "Rock the Casbah"/"Should I Stay or Should I Go" single that year could be viewed as punk's headstone and the full realisation of its complete melding into mainstream music production. No cultural movements can maintain their initial novelty, dynamism, or social impact. As Rob Burke observes, "Nobody expected punk to last. Every kind of music up until that point had had a certain shelf life."

Pronouncing punk's death had allowed for pundits, public, theorists, and tastemakers to withdraw their gaze. But while the music was brief and the ideas expressed pithy, it exhibited unexpected endurance, continuing to be played even in new and continually evolving forms.

Following a *New York Times* eulogy in the mid-'80s, the *Sydney Morning Herald* pondered, "Is punk dead, did it achieve anything, and what was it all about?" With surprising insight, it answered, "But punk itself hasn't quite died. Pure punk rock evolved into something ... infinitely faster, louder, and more extreme."[1]

Emerging as punk's uglier and more brutish progeny, "hardcore" was to slough away any artistic pretension or pop residue. "Hardcore punk bands," continued the *Sydney Morning Herald*, "have no aspirations about changing the course of rock 'n' roll. Theirs is a subculture intent on staying that way, the most rebellious expression of rock 'n' roll and fiercely protective of its independence."[2] In its new, deliberately impenetrable form, hardcore more closely defined the performance of pure rage. The fury emanating from suburban youth was no less incendiary than that of

"Anarchy in the UK," and it often manifested in more violent expression. In the US, it spoke to the detritus of the American dream; in the UK, 1982 was a marker for an entire new wave of harder, faster, untempered, and unrefined bands under the loose stylistic banner of "UK82." Despite its initial cries of "no future," punk would not only have a future, but would flourish, as bands like Dead Kennedys, Black Flag, the Exploited, Discharge, and GBH sold tens of thousands of albums worldwide.

By the mid-'80s, however, the halcyon days of punk in the charts, on major television music programs, or quietly selling huge swathes of records were gone. A more underground scene, reliant upon its own initiative, energy, and resources to survive, spread the continents. Yet the evolving of punk into a multitude of subsets beyond merely stolen and sped-up Stooges riffs would be met with incredulity, or even resoundingly dismissed as of no serious historical relevance. Australian music writer David Nichols dismissingly wrote of it as "a punk revival" that "was all style and no substance, and only worth acknowledging as a bizarre phenomenon."[3] As such, 1980s punk would be mostly forgotten from the near entirety of Australian music history.

Entering the initial years of a new decade, the Birthday Party, the Church, Models, the Moodists, Laughing Clowns, and Dead Can Dance appeared at the Ballroom. As bands whose members had a history in punk's first wave, such groups had made stylistic progressions beyond punk, either becoming more complex and challenging or exhibiting commercial accessibility and achievement. Punk's antipathy, truculence, and belligerence, aside from a few small pockets, had receded. A reaction was imminent.

Paul Lindsay observes, "By '81, '82, you had the emergence of bands like Sick Things, Civil Dissident, Depression, Mad Flowers, and there was a totally different vibe. Things had got a lot more aggressive and heavy."

Dead Kennedys, the most popular of the international hardcore bands, performed at the Ballroom in August 1983. They were the first overseas hardcore punk band to tour the country, and unprecedentedly large crowds were drawn to the shows. If punk was dead, as the posthumous observers supposed, then a thousand attendees at one of their Sydney shows was pure corpse defilement.

Even with the passage of decades, Matt Bissett says of the Dead

Kennedys tour: "I have no idea how to explain those shows. I'd never seen anything like it. . . . I still remember the exact hairs that went up on the back of my neck when they first started playing."

As if to confirm punk's continued ability to not only inspire but provoke and offend, in 1982 a Dead Kennedys record had been reason for charges of obscenity brought against Keith Glass of Melbourne's Missing Link record store. The record was played before a Melbourne magistrate, and a warrant was issued for seizure of further copies. But if Dead Kennedys were felons against the public's sensibilities, their offstage demeanour gave little indication. With his band supporting Dead Kennedys at one of their Sydney shows, Dave Briggs met the group as they were engrossed in *The Twilight Zone*, observing, "They're just really nice guys, and they were super straight." He borrowed his brother's car for the big occasion, but after the show the key went missing. Briggs recalled, "They helped me look for it . . . one of the biggest bands in America at that time." However, they were not quite as successful as lost-object locators as they were punk musicians. Briggs says, "I had to call my brother up at two in the morning."

Before the defining event of the Dead Kennedys tour, punk in Melbourne had endured something of an interregnum. As the bands between the end of the 1970s and hardcore were often unsupported and/or forgotten, Lindsay posits that it was "because they were the progenitors. They were the inspiration, like the spark. Some of those bands too, they only lasted for maybe a year." To Mick Turner of Sick Things, "People who were well-adjusted" simply "drifted away. . . . There was no money or future in any of it. The rest of us wallowed in it, playing as much as possible for nothing and joining as many bands as would have us. It was a reckless, beautiful, creative time, with no rules or cliques to worry about."[4]

Beginning in 1980, bands occupying the Sick Things' orbit and the early '80s Melbourne scene included Criminal Youth, Dogs of War, Public Nuisance, FBI, the Mess, and Odious Comparison.

Lindsay vividly remembers his initial encounter of Sick Things and the impression they were to leave: "I hadn't seen a band with that intensity plus that sort of chaos." They were arguably the premier pioneers of Australian hardcore. Turner also relives the self-destruction, dirty dishes, and ultimately tragedy that was their own circle and the scene more widely:

> We were young and unemployed. At one point, I lived in a sharehouse with seven or eight others. I can't remember what we ate, no one cooked or cleaned, and the kitchen was a no-go zone.... Looking back at that house, there's only three of us still alive today as far as I know, although I've not had contact with the other two for a while. At different times after the house dissolved, three people committed suicide [recorded in 1981, Sick Things' *Committed to Suicide* seven-inch was released in 1985] and one was murdered (I heard). The music scene attracted people who played and loved music, and also was a haven for misfits. In a good way, it gave community and support to people who didn't fit in to regular networks, and it still does. The art and music communities are where these people can thrive. Unfortunately, they also attract drugs, and I guess a lot of these people succumbed to bad habits and fell afoul of its consequences.

Given the questionable hygiene of their home, there is perhaps veracity to the rumour that the whole band once contracted Hepatitis B. Whatever the truth, *DNA* was correct in asserting that they possessed a "musical sense well ahead of most of the Australian punk scene."[5] Turner relays, though, that their followers were not always so enlightened: "We'd only played the Duke of York in Prahran, which was a tiny pub, but nice scene there. Then we got a gig at the much bigger Mt Erica Hotel; they even put our name in big letters on their 'What's On' board out the front—it was kinda great. Then when we played, our so-called fans came and smashed the toilets up.... So, they fairly banned us because of a few dickhead fans."

It was not to be the band's only show marred by troglodyte behaviour, with Turner revealing, "There was an infamous Roar Studios benefit gig that marks the end of the Sick Things era." Tim Hemensley later recounted the frenzied evening: "The gig consisted of seven bands for one dollar, with the entry fee entitling the payer to a hot dog dipped in speed upon arrival. Needless to say, the whole event ended up being a completely raucous, drug- and alcohol-fuelled affair—someone rode in on a motorbike and ripped out several floor tiles, toilets and walls got smashed, fittings were damaged—and to top it all off [artist Pasquale] Giardino ripped the TV off the wall and threw it at a skinhead band that had turned up and were singing racist rhetoric."[6]

The gig was also significant for finally exceeding Turner's tolerance: "That for me was the end of the punk scene in Melbourne. The arseholes had taken over."

If punks were predictably prone to violence, the choice of peace-loving hippies as an audience becomes somewhat more explicable. Sick Things made a brief re-formation in 1986 to play a Friends of the Earth benefit show, but Turner can't have been overwhelmed by the response: "I really don't remember the FOE benefit." He does, however, recall a subsequent reunion in 1988 where "we played in Adelaide," but details are similarly sketchy aside from an encounter with a favourite late-night, drunken takeaway snack: "It was okay, I think. I... remember staying at the New Century Hotel upstairs from the venue and finding an ancient half-eaten kebab in a drawer in the hotel room. I guess that summed it up."

Sick Things went into permanent retirement as Turner and vocalist Dugald McKenzie's attention centred on new band Venom P. Stinger. Turner later attained accolade as a member of the Dirty Three.

In chronicling the history of Sick Things, Hemensley wrote of Melbourne punk and hardcore's sometimes tumultuous links to art via organisations such as Roar Studios. Arguably a living artwork in themselves, I Spit on Your Gravy's exploits routinely outraged venue managers, preoccupied St Kilda police, and titillated readers of the *Truth* newspaper. A publication more driven by scandal and sleaze than any journalistic desire for fact, the *Truth* took fancy in the band's antics. The group exhibited an "any publicity is good publicity" attitude, and bassist Mark Carson says of the *Truth* using the band as fertile copy: "It was fantastic.... We never got one positive press report."

Initially the band jammed UK punk covers in the bedroom of a St Kilda terrace house dubbed "Gravy Mansion." Carson explains that eventual vocalist "[Fred] Negro was next door doing the married thing. That is what he was gonna do." A reluctant Negro relented after one practice and joined the band. The matrimonial couple soon separated.

Taking the group's act on the road, Carson says, "We all went on this big trip up to Sydney.... It was just fifty crazies from Melbourne on buses." Contrary to the image of decadent rock 'n' roll lifestyles, guitarist Jason Banner reveals: "We were all really hungry and we went to some donation place... and they gave us a whole heap of these frozen pies.

They thawed out and we'd heat them up with a hair dryer. . . . There wasn't much money going around."

Summing up the period as "bleak but fun times," the "fun times" often saw the band subject to criticism. Aside from the lewd and crude, one particular source of critique was their accompanying group of female backup singers, the Spitettes.

Carson expounds his theory behind the extravaganza that was their stage act, "that people have only got twenty minutes' concentration span. . . . If you've got shitloads of stuff going on—Fred's fucking a [raw or roasted] chook, a couple of girls in the corner, a bloke doing magic tricks—it was a lot easier to engage for a whole hour." Banner implies even the *Truth* was censorious in reporting the band's shows: "Things that didn't get put in were like when Fred did a shit onstage at the Helter Skelter Club and then we piffed the shit out into the crowd. You should have seen them run."

US singer G.G. Allin would meld punk and depravity in near-equal measure. Though aware of Allin and other more extreme punk performers, Negro was really just a fan of American drag queen and actor Divine. "I remember when Fred got sucked off [onstage] at the Princes Berkeley in Adelaide," offers Banner. Negro was far from alone in the outrageousness, though. At one particular Adelaide University show, after partaking of the more-than-generous free drinks, Carson says someone "had organised a motorbike." As a more-than-willing participant, Banner says, "We moved all the chairs and made a track and were seeing who could do laps fastest on the bike. I rode into the wall." Carson corrects Banner's account: "Straight through the fucking wall."

Not willing to catalogue all the anecdotes, Carson says, "We could tell you stories all day. Some of the shit we used to get up to was madness." Not shockingly, "Alcohol was usually pretty heavily involved."

The band's antics were part of the reason for finding themselves on the outside of the punk scene. Carson explains, "We were a punk band, I suppose, by definition, but we never really fit into any of those sorts of groups at all. . . . We actually got summoned to a meeting . . . by the hardcore-ers saying that we were making a mockery of punk rock. . . . We were all friends as bands, but in a way they were trying to do something serious and they saw us as just taking the piss a bit."

Scrutiny from the punk scene was far from the only attention the Gravys came to receive. Qualifying his story by admitting, "I've never seen this," Carson says, "Apparently there was a dossier done by the council.... They had a secret agent following us around and taking photographs.... A lot of it was to do with cleaning up St Kilda, and that's when all the trouble started coming for Fred. They were after him for his artwork, they were after us. We were seen as bringing all the undesirables into the area."

As one of St Kilda's greatest advocates and musical icons, ironically Negro was apportioned blame for the closing of its most valuable venue, the Ballroom. At a Tuesday night show, during a break in their set caused by a broken string, Negro conducted a "small penis competition" among members of the crowd. Such antics usually provoked little more reaction than guffaws from the audience, except this same evening the licensing board happened to be inspecting the venue. Carson, however, suggests something more conspiratorial: "The fact that those guys were there the night we were playing the Ballroom, who were looking to renew their licence—it's just all a little bit too coincidental."

I Spit on Your Gravy released their first album, *St. Kilda's Alright!*, in 1984. Carson recalls, "They raided Missing Link records, the vice squad did, and they got the last six hundred copies of it." He recounts the resulting court case: "There was a stolen stereo out of the police lockers set up in the courtroom, and we're sitting there and they're playing our record. Then the judge said ... 'That's enough, take it off now. I refuse to ban this record because I've never heard anything so bad in my life, and if I ban it, it might become popular, and no one deserves to hear this.'"

Negro also found himself in court on four charges relating to fliers he had drawn. Found innocent of two charges, he was adjudged guilty of drawing obscene articles.

By the end of 1985, the band were struggling for venues willing to host them. Carson says, "We couldn't play under I Spit on Your Gravy."

Beyond the bawdy lyrics, nudity, profanity, and sex acts involving pieces of fruit and poultry, it's easy to forget I Spit on Your Gravy was a musical act. Carson admits, "I got a bit sick of the novelty. Like it was great fun, but it used to hold us back to a certain degree." Banner says, "I think we wanted to play a bit better."

After the band placed a greater emphasis on musical performance, Carson remembers that "the venues got bigger and bigger, packing out the Prince and the Ballroom." Virgin Records signed the band, despite knowledge of their reputation. The group's popularity was reflected in the crowd size when launching their second album, *Fruit Loop City*, in

1987. Carson fondly remembers that it "was huge. There was thousands there."

But if circumstances seemed primed for the band, Banner explains they never quite lived up to potential—mostly of their own doing: "We signed up, did a bit of a tour, came back in massive debt because we fucked everything up, then that was it. Virgin more or less wiped their hands of us."

Carson, too, was finished with the group: "I left the band not long after" a volatile St Kilda Festival show in which a heated Carson and Banner "had a couple pushes. . . . Next thing you know, the jacks [police] were locking us up. Best headline though: 'I Spit Duo in Legal Spat.'"

Banner confesses a degree of regret: "There was a few things we missed out on doing, like we wanted to get to America," a trip which, he reveals, "was very close."

Anticlimactically, instead of the band ending with a grandiose collapse, or simply its members' incarceration, Carson says, "It never really broke up. It just stopped."

As the Gravys were making their own unique legacy, a new series of Melbourne bands took up the sound of a more global hardcore scene. One of those able to make the passage from local popularity to international reputation were Depression, with Dead Kennedys vocalist Jello Biafra touting them as "probably the most powerful punk band we saw in all of Australia; the one band who could probably tour anywhere in the world."[7]

Depression captured their tight and powerful sound in a series of recordings for Reactor Records through 1984 and '85, with the *Money Chain* seven-inch, a self-titled album, and the *Australia Australia* twelve-inch.

Prior to the release of any these records, *DNA* had begun to document increasing fractures among Melbourne's hardcore bands. For a genre that made routine calls for "unity," it was reported that "apparently the punk scene in Melbourne has been threatening to divide in two for a while now, with the dividing line being one's opinion of Depression."[8] Insinuations over money, violence, lyrical content, overexposure, dominance, and the encroaching of heavy metal into their sound constituted the criticisms. Undeniable, though, was their passion and energy in furthering the scene. A disappointed Smeer says, "We gave everybody our gear, let them use our PAs—we gave and gave and gave, and all we got back was people slagging us off." When Smeer was interviewed in 1986, the enmity had not abated, with him making the claim, "I am probably the most hated man in the Australian punk scene."[9]

While contending with outside critique, Smeer in turn began to question the intent of those who "were just going to gigs to get fucked up. . . . We got sick of all that, and there was a bit of violence, and then all the separation bullshit that everyone was trying to create. Then we went to a couple of metal gigs . . . and I thought, 'Just look at the fucking headbangers, they just live for the music.' . . . They like a drink, but they weren't popping pills and taking smack. . . . I thought, 'That's what we need: we need people that appreciate our fucking music,' not just going there to get fucked so you can't even comprehend or hear anything."

Smeer desired to appeal to more than just a punk clique which was either fatiguingly familiar with Depression, using them as a soundtrack to their own self-destruction, or discouraged by the band's allegedly polarising behaviour. Added to this, Depression's contact with metal had come to permeate their own sound. Liz, then partner of Smeer, remembers that he "came home with a Metallica record. . . . We started getting into all that crossover stuff. . . . It was really well played, it was fast, it had some punk elements, they were saying some important things, so we loved it right from the start."

In 1987, Depression released the *Ultra Hard Core Mega Heavy Punk Metal Thrash* live album, its title a statement of their punk/hardcore/metal hybridity.

Giving indication of the reception metal initially received among punks, Paul Lindsay says, "I remember earlier on I wore a Metallica *Ride the Lightning* T-shirt [onstage]. Someone threw a can of beer at me."

An undeterred Smeer says, "We did the first punk/metal gigs back in 1985. . . . Punks would come in and they'd look and go, 'Ooh, don't know if I wanna go in there, there's a whole lot of headbangers.' Then the headbangers would come and go, 'Ooh, there's a whole lot of punks in there.' End of the night, the headbangers and punks were all arm in arm, headbanging, having a ball."

Smeer would also be caught in embrace—instead with his mother—for a *Good Weekend* magazine article in 1986 titled "Punks Have Parents Too."[10]

By the time of their final album, the 1987 LP *Thrash till Death*, Smeer says that the hardcore scene had reached its zenith and "started dwindling off." Added to which: "I had trouble keeping the band together.... It just kind of slowly faded away."

Depression is remembered as one of Australia's foremost punk/hardcore bands through the decade. Smeer says, "I've always thought Australian bands were as good as bands overseas.... I don't know what it is, but it has a certain fucking vibe and it's got real guts.... I'm proud to be part of it."

As Depression impacted beyond their home city, End Result was only one of countless bands the world over lost to relative obscurity despite the quality of their music, having supported Dead Kennedys. Jello Biafra was praising of the band, "who only after two or three gigs had one of the most powerful sounds in Australia."[11] That sound, Jello perceived, was "a heavy-duty Crass-styled anarchist band."[12]

Beyond just a greater severity in sound, a segment of the secondary wave came to adopt a more militantly political tone and style. With End Result vocalist Paul Conroy citing the influence of bands like Crass, the Subhumans, and Discharge, such groups were animated by the political environment of Margaret Thatcher's militarism and the Falklands War, as well as Ronald Reagan and the apex of the Cold War.

English band Crass, the most iconic entity of the anarcho-punk movement worldwide, delivered staccato, military-style drumming aided by the militancy of all-black uniforms. Where the Sex Pistols' "no future" was a message of resignation, anarcho-punk brought a more refined and focused radicalism. Acutely confrontational, anarcho-punk was didactic in approach, and it coincided with protest movements of the period. Conroy says, "Around that time, we were involved in antinuclear campaigns and animal rights campaigns."

But if punk never constituted a credible threat to social or political order, talk of Crass's actions would still reach the highest levels of the ruling party in England. In Australia, their influence was confined to a small milieu.

Contesting its degrees of radical political content, however, punk proved no less capable of reproducing dominant ideology, conservatism, or outright bigotry, as examples of racism, sexism, and homophobia have abounded.

Few bands to emanate from Australia have ever been such an antithesis to anarcho-punk idealism as Scum, an acronym for "Sexual Carnage and Underage Molestation." Band members Jim Filth, Dick Destruction, Nick Off, Brett Straight, and Fuckhead Ferrett played under a banner containing "SS" and the Totenkopf (the German skull and crossbones).

Guitarist Ferrett recounts, "The band was deliberately provocative, especially Jim. You couldn't take him anywhere without him vomiting or upsetting someone. He had a wonderful voice, like the opera, which he used to twist into a snarl for all the songs."

Spurning musical evolution, Scum began performing almost exclusively Sex Pistols covers, including "Belsen Was a Gas." Causing consternation among some punks, this infraction would pale against the lyrical content of their original songs, which proudly exhibited an unadorned nihilism and misanthropy. Ferret says that their lyrics contained "all the stuff the safe little playtime hardcore punks couldn't deal with. We managed to ruffle feathers everywhere we went."

Smeer recalls a particularly unruly show they shared in Bacchus Marsh, where "a guy ran up on the stage and punched the singer in the head, and everyone started throwing bricks through the fucking windows, and the cops came." Ferrett unhesitatingly castigates Depression: "We hated them after Bacchus Marsh.... The cowboys were gonna kill us, and Smeer got up and explained that he didn't want trouble, he just wanted to play his guitar and be all nice.... Someone got up and smashed Nick in the nose, and there was blood everywhere. We were escorted out of town by some locals with shotguns, followed by the police. And where was Depression? They'd run away and left us to it. No love lost there."

Derisive of the hardcore scene, Ferrett asserts that "if there was any trouble all the hardest core would turn and run for their lives. The antiviolent peaceniks left us to patrol the front line." Further highlighting the cleave, Smeer says members of Scum "were in the army reserves, and they were telling me they used to blow up sheep and shoot them, and I was like, 'Dude, I'm a vegetarian.'" A guarded Ferrett admits, "We blew stuff up. I could tell hundreds of horror stories.... We did some pretty extreme stuff.... We'd have done time if we had been caught doing some of the stuff we did."

Unrepentant, Ferrett says, "I don't think we went overboard with too many things." The destructiveness, however, went to an unprecedented level at a party they played in 1984, which degenerated into brawling. One person allegedly died. Deliberately evasive, Ferrett says, "Someone dying at a show we played ... no comment."

With the resignation of their drummer, Ferrett says, "We couldn't find anyone suitable, so we just disintegrated.... After Scum I went about my own business, cut the scene.... I got robbed, I lost the plot with society, and went bush for six years."

Permanent Damage was a restrained and clean-living yang to Scum's yin. Guitarist Matt Daveson reveals the band "was more into exercise and living a healthy life from good food compared to other bands. I can remember playing in Adelaide and our hosts expected us to go straight to the pub, but we wanted to go for a run on the beach or visit a gym."

Daveson, born in Melbourne, had been living in Detroit before returning at age eighteen. On arriving back to Melbourne, he says, "It took me about six months to find the hardcore scene. The reasons were many, but I can remember asking a guy on the street who happened to be wearing a leather jacket with studs and a spiked mohawk, 'What music are you into?' and he said, 'The Rolling Stones.'

"I finally met [vocalist] Manny and he ... mentioned these two guys who played in a Turkish wedding band.... I can remember going with Manny to his house and listening to Jenk play. He blew me away with amazing drumming skills.... What Jenk and [bassist] Izy had learned playing together in the wedding bands is how to play tight."

Such skills were evident on the band's self-titled seven-inch in 1985 and *End of Innocence* LP in 1987. Additional to the wedding waltzes, though, Daveson acknowledges the release of Slayer's *Reign in Blood* between the two records and its resulting influence on Permanent Damage's sound.

If Slayer's satanic themes caused consternation among religious figures for decades, Permanent Damage's first interstate tour in 1985 brought its own conflict with churchgoers. After they played three consecutive nights with Vicious Circle, publication *Trousers in Action* reviewed the shows: "This tour didn't get off to a good start at all ... no band even set up, and yet there's already aggro.... One lad, bottle in hand, threatening to brain another.... The aggro continued" with another fight that resulted in someone "getting a bottle over his head." After the troublemakers failed to heed a tenant's demand for them to leave, the tenant started "waving a fuckin' submachine gun!!! Supposedly only a replica, but that's all very nice to say with hindsight. . . . Anyway, the sawn-off whatever in possession of another of the tenants was real."[13] The police arrived in numbers, but the guns had disappeared, and only a few people were arrested.

At the final show, Vicious Circle's set was cut short "to avoid disturbing a Greek Easter Midnight Mass procession." However, "various audience wandered downstairs and the resulting antagonism between punks/skins and Greeks led to a can and bottle fight."[14] One of those present, Alan Creed, recalls, "There was riot police, TV crews, there was everything."

Of no shock to readers, *Trousers in Action* reported, "Sadly both bands returned to Melbourne, very pissed-off with the Sydney scene."[15]

The same year, Permanent Damage were given further reason to resent the Harbour City after appearing with the Hard-Ons. Hard-Ons bassist Ray Ahn recalls:

> Me and Keish copped a fair bit of "fucken gook" or "nigger" the whole night, but as usual, we just got on with it. . . . Upon exiting the Gaelic, we were dismayed to see a group of skinheads sitting on Keish's car bonnet, the rest were leaning all over it. . . . Back inside, we were greeted by Manny, the lead singer of Permanent Damage, who thanked us for our set. . . . We got talking, and we somehow mentioned the fascists and Keish's car. "What?!" he bellowed. He charged outside and pointed his finger at the skinheads. "Get off my fucken car. Stay off the fucken car. Fuck off! Right now!" . . . The skinheads trudged off back inside sheepishly. Manny mumbled something under his breath, I swear it was "fucken malaka."[16]

Though the band "had shaved heads" and "attracted some skinheads to the gigs," Daveson stresses, "We were not into their message." The wariness or dislike was evidently mutual, Mark Zerafa describing an incident between Permanent Damage and skinheads as "the worst thing" he saw during his time in the scene: "Permanent Damage were playing, and Manny, the singer, got a brick in his face, and the skinheads started—it was pretty gnarly."

Unconscionable incidents aside, Daveson speaks favourably of "a scene that was reasonably healthy, with good attendances, plenty of bands, and you could be into anything and pretty much be accepted."

Within that diversity of interests, he says, "On reflection, the Melbourne scene had all kinds: those into the music, those into the alternative message, those into revolution/anarchy, those who were or saw themselves as different, and lost souls living a hard and maybe short life."

Vicious Circle's Paul Lindsay also speaks to a scene with broad composition, from which some sought to escape traumas and/or inflict damage upon the self: "I think there were a lot of different people that were dealing with different issues from home life and having really hard lives, and sometimes they saw that as an avenue of escape."

Lindsay's early years were the embodiment of difficult but owed to his adopted lifestyle. Where the majority of the scene's bands germinated from the eastern suburbs, Lindsay grew up in the city's west: "I remember when I was probably about twelve or thirteen years old, I was out front of a friend's place, and a guy just pulled up and called me over to the car. I went over and he had a double-barrelled shotgun inside the car. He pulled it up and put the shotgun to my chest and punched me as hard as he could. I was only a kid. He smashed my nose and told me he was going to kill me.... At that time a lot of people had guns and carried weapons.... It was a totally different mindset."

Being a punk within an often-hostile environment also came with further disadvantages: "I got into fights quite often.... The first thing people would do when they would beat me up or fight me was grab my mohawk and hit me. I just shaved it off"—a wise decision considering "It was just like a beacon" in an area where gangs such as the Black Dragons and Lebanese Tigers roamed.

Never contemplating giving up and going back to a life of suburban normalcy, Lindsay impresses that "I'm just not that sort of person." Besides, the punk scene was itself something of a haven. "When I first got into the scene ... compared to some of the yobs that I grew up around, and where I was, the punk scene was a bit tame."

For Lindsay, "The next step was obviously to get into a band, to find people like-minded." That group would be Vicious Circle. Emerging from previous band Politburo, Lindsay recalls that "a lot of the people at that time, say '83, '84, were still into that UK82 thing.... We were sort of more into stuff that was coming out from America, but also stuff from Europe as well.... I was trading tapes and vinyl seven-inch records with people all over the world."

Vicious Circle's more "cosmopolitan" sound would especially confound Sydney audiences during their first tour: "I think initially people just looked at us and were like, 'What the fuck?'" Not willing to inflame the Melbourne-Sydney rivalry by confirming the superiority of his hometown's bands, Lindsay says, "I don't know if it was superior standard, I just think the evolution was different." Yet some in Sydney hadn't quite made the evolutionary leap. "We played a show with the Hard-Ons and there was a bunch of boneheads there and they just wanted to kill us.... I remember we were playing, and people were sieg-heiling and shit got thrown at us."

Unfazed at being occasional interstate pariahs, Vicious Circle were both driven—releasing four EPs and four albums in around four years—and connected. "We just started networking from about '84."

Through such connections, in 1986 Vicious Circle became the first Australian hardcore band to tour the United States. Playing alongside such luminaries as Agnostic Front, Final Conflict, MDC, Attitude Adjustment, GBH, Crucifix, Christ on Parade, and MIA, Lindsay makes the assessment that "I think we held our own."

Touring to the US in the 1980s involved a prohibitively priced plane ticket; touring to Perth in 1988 was a similarly exorbitant undertaking: "The promoters paid ten grand to fly us over there and to put a crew on and put us up."

The same year marked the bicentenary of Australia's federation. Amid various celebrations, the plight of Indigenous Australians was addressed in fanzines and interviews, with some bands acknowledging historical and ongoing mistreatment. Lindsay was one of those particularly vocal: "They spend eight million dollars on some stupid party while the Indigenous people of this fucking country, this so-called country, have got one of the highest death rates in police custody in the world.... It's a real insult."[17]

As the group's vocalist, Lindsay wrote lyrics that were consistently political, addressing Indigenous issues in the songs "Rule 17" and "1988 (John Pat)." Reflecting on the tracks, he says, "It's just something I feel very strongly about as a human being, to show respect to First Nations people.... I used to wear land-rights shirts sometimes, and an Aboriginal flag shirt, and people would literally want to fight me."

Impressed rather than incensed by the band, Virgin made offer of a record deal. "That was just sticking a lot of money in our face and saying, basically, 'We can stick you in a really big recording studio, we can do two film clips.' . . . I don't know what motivated them, but I'm glad how it turned out and we didn't sign with them. . . . It probably would have screwed us for the next fifteen to twenty years."

After taking a half-decade hiatus through the '90s, the band continues today to release and perform, Lindsay explaining, "I never looked at doing what I do as being a financial outlet. . . . It's been passion based, and I need to do it. It's something I thrive on and enjoy."

Harbouring similar ongoing passion, Peter McGrath's life in punk traces back to Brisbane's first wave. Described as the city's "premier punk," McGrath featured in the *Sunday Sun* in 1978, where he was quoted as saying, "We're plain bad, we smell, we're filthy, and we're rotten through and through."[18] McGrath cautions against condemnation of his small-punk, big-mouth act by suggesting, "You've got to remember how old I was. . . . I was twelve, thirteen when we started getting into punk music."

A "rotten" McGrath was subjected to retribution by Stranglers bassist Jean-Jacques Brunel in 1979. Spat on while onstage, Brunel battered McGrath in the head with his bass "Conan-the-Barbarian-style. Split my head right open. And again, I was a child—it was like beating up your kid." McGrath doesn't hasten to add, "Good band, though, back in the day."

If a gunslingin' bass guitarist was a temporal threat, the greater danger came from those with real guns: "The police became overbearing. It was that bad the hidings that we were copping; guns shoved in our mouths . . . insane charges they were hitting us with. . . . It got too heavy, so Sydney was our next stop." The city's more liberating environment did not prevent him and his companions from being arrested: "We got locked up in Long Bay [jail]."

Trying his luck even further south, McGrath admits that "I was a bit lost when I got to Melbourne. . . . The little group I had . . . we didn't fit in, and then one day we went to see this band Mad Flowers. . . . They were great."

With Mad Flowers, the sound of American hardcore was brought to Melbourne. And just as the US came to dominate popular culture, so too would it become the principal reference for Australian punk as the decade progressed. Yet McGrath admits that in 1983 he hadn't heard Bad Brains or Black Flag, as "their records just didn't come here." Forming

Death Sentence in 1984, "We didn't know what we were doing.... We couldn't buy those records in Melbourne.... We'd read magazines and see all these names of bands.... We just created what was written about these bands."

Trading on their interpretation of US hardcore, McGrath says, "We fitted in with the Civil Dissident crew." This despite the fact "they were straight edge [drug- and alcohol-free], and my drug use," McGrath says candidly, "I never hid." Even within Death Sentence itself, "We had Conn [bassist] and he was militantly straight edge, and I was a heroin user." It was hallucinogens rather than heroin, however, that was to fuel McGrath at their first show. Imposing themselves on a bill, an acid-affected McGrath threw up after the first song.

Death Sentence was far from a timorous band. Guitarist Gary McGillivray revealed that "a lot of people hated us, not because of the music but because of certain personal attributes of some members' personalities ... but a lot of people into the scene really got into us, they'd listen to the music and ignore the other shit that was being said."[19] McGrath provides additional insight that "we were feared more than anything else, too. We wouldn't fuck around."

With McGillivray and drummer Scott being replacement members for only three weeks, the group recorded the *Ryan, Thanx for the Support* seven-inch in 1985. The record contained seven songs in eight minutes, and *Family Slaughterhouse* reviewed Death Sentence as too fast to even slam dance to.[20]

If Death Sentence were thought to be extreme in speed, the appropriately named Seven Minutes of Nausea took hardcore punk and evolved it to a near-unprecedented level of severity. After they formed in 1985 as a more conventional punk/hardcore band, the always adventurous John Peel played the group on his program: eleven songs performed in fifteen seconds. Their 1988 EP *Our Culture Is Boring* contained 342 "songs" in thirteen minutes. A pioneering band for the genre of "noisecore," it brought the literal blurring of hardcore and sheer noise.

Yet as Seven Minutes of Nausea still endure three decades later, Death Sentence back then were spiralling towards their own conclusion. Scott, who was also McGillivray's best friend, died of a heroin overdose.

Death Sentence released the twelve-inch *If Pain Mends My Mind* in 1986, and an unreleased album preceded the band's breakup. Citing the reason for their end, McGrath says, "Hardcore finished. We really had nowhere to go; I wasn't going to play metal." As well as being left adrift by stylistic trends, McGrath admits that "heroin had become a lifestyle.... My time had become, 'Where am I going to get my next fix from?' ... It just became a job." Perhaps a nod to his informal vocation, tracks from the unreleased record were released as a posthumous seven-inch in 1994 under the title *Needle Park*.

McGrath, however, is imbued with triumph. Four decades after appearing before readers as the face of Brisbane punk, and having traversed the dangers and tumult of addiction, he declares, "The fact is, I survived and I'm still into the scene.... I've done a lot better than a lot of the others did."

Mirroring McGrath's view that metal's incursion had facilitated hardcore's demise, Civil Dissident vocalist Matt Bissett says, "That was possibly the stepping-off point for me, when metal started to creep into punk.... Hardcore was over by then.... There was some great music that came out of it, but it's okay for things to be over—light a fire under something else."

Civil Dissident's first release, the *Fourth Rate American Thrash Tape* (1984), spoke not only to their undiluted hardcore influence but also to an underappreciated sense of humour: "It was something that was said about our music. We were pretty tongue-in-cheek, despite being reasonably serious ... and that was just a fertile quote to make the most of.... I never quite understood it, but there was definitely a difference between the way a lot of people thought about us and other bands.... People were pretty narrow-minded in a lot of ways, and that perfectly filtered down to subcultures like punk, where you've got to have the gear and the hair.... That didn't make much sense to us."

Acceptance, however, wasn't only confined to attire—drummer Dave Ross was the subject of ridicule for his employment in a bank, as well as driving a decrepit and sometimes smoke-blowing old Mercedes.

Being from Melbourne's outer urban sprawl almost necessitated a car, but Bissett also feels the distance afforded the band "a little bit of autonomy in a certain way to develop maybe our own opinions a bit differently." The freedom to formulate individual perspective was coupled with the ideas encountered through punk at an explicitly political point of its evolution: "It was a process in those days, where you got a whole lot of information.... You could see what worked for you, but at least you were getting that information. The difference, politically, was a lot of kids my age weren't considering the things that are affecting the world."

During punk's initial wave, graffiti had appeared in the basement of the Pram Factory theatre in Melbourne ridiculing the notion of punk's radicalism: "Today's punk is tomorrow's police cadet." In 1985, Civil Dissident guitarist Wayne Mosdall left the band to join the police force.

That same year, the group released its *First Blood* seven-inch. Rejecting emulation of overseas records, at least lyrically, Bissett had sought to address issues that were more immediate or pertinent: "We didn't live through the miners' strikes in England, we didn't have Thatcherism and all that stuff.... We were bored; there was no real suburban evolution or anything like that. There was plenty to get angry about, but I didn't want to adopt other people's issues."

Two further tracks were included on the popular international hardcore compilation *Cleanse the Bacteria* that was compiled by famed skateboarding and music artist Pushead in 1985. Civil Dissident's appearance was a reminder that away from the trivialities of localised scene drama and being an outspoken band, they showed the ability to produce music comparable to that being made anywhere else in the world. "It was 100 percent about the music," Bissett says. "The music was the fire under everything we did. Getting in a room and making some noise was just the best thing in the world."

But where Civil Dissident would generate awareness overseas, Melbourne hardcore's mid-'80s peak brought a slew of overlooked and often short-lived bands, including Armageddon, Balrog, Children of Sorrow, Combined Effort, Internal Haemorrhage, Mental Health, Nobody's Victim, No Control, PFA, and STP.

With links as school friends to Civil Dissident, Society's Victim were another youthful, evanescent group.

Guitarist Shaun Whitmore, as a teen from the leafy outer suburbs, encountered an inner-city scene that "was pretty full-on" and intimidating: "A lot of the people that were coming to the gigs were on heroin at the time, and they were living in squats. That part was pretty wild."

As the band made a timid foray into performing live, Whitmore says Depression "looked after us very well." Yet it was also through the same connection that Whitmore was to find himself disavowing the punk scene:

> Smeer was very much the king punk of Melbourne at that time. So, he's playing away, and this bloke came up and spat on him, and Smeer just lunged at him ... [and] they're rolling on the ground belting each other.... Smeer had a mate ... I remember he had "skins" tattooed on his face. He was like Frankenstein, this massive bloke ... [and] he ended up grabbing this bloke off Smeer with one hand and then just belted him—really smashed him. The bloke goes, "You're all fucked, I'm coming back with a gun."

Multiple guns would instead accompany the arrival of police. As for Whitmore, he reveals, "That was actually it for me. I thought, 'You can stick this up your arse, I can't be bothered.' ... I wasn't even eighteen years old.... It would have been about three weeks after that they ended up doing the Dead Kennedys support gig at the Venue, so I was pissed off that I missed out on that."

During the 1980s, Oi!/skinhead bands in Melbourne were few and, like Bootboys and Justified Hatred, failed to make lasting recordings.

Jason Cardwell acknowledges his own band, No Remorse, as comparably anachronistic among the dominance of hardcore around 1986–87: "There were no other Oi! bands ... so all gigs were mostly with punk bands, many being into US hardcore."

Even if Cardwell remembers relations between punks and skins as more peaceable than other capitals, the presence of skinheads in Melbourne could still deter. A resentful Paul Lindsay told *DNA* that "there were a few Asians coming along to some shows in Melbourne, but they got frightened off by skinheads."[21] The lyrical content of two songs performed by No Remorse gave possible indication for their apprehension. Cardwell addresses the tracks: "There was one song called 'Invasion,' and we did play a Skrewdriver cover called 'Sick Society.' ... Even though I never agreed with the lyrics, I played bass when we performed these two songs, and there's no excuse. I regret this, and decided about thirty years ago that I could never be involved in anything with such a standpoint again."

Cardwell's post–No Remorse band, Bastard Squad, would be confronted by the presence of a skinhead crowd, including a more politicised variant. One of Bastard Squad's committed followers, Dimma, recounts the first gig of theirs he attended:

> They played with this band White Lightning. . . . We even dragged my cousin along. He's got one of those surfie undercuts, and it's all teased up [*laughs*]. . . . I open the door and it's like wall-to-wall skinheads. . . . It kind of felt like everyone looked at us. Maybe no one did, but I shit myself, and I thought, "I'm not going to turn around and walk away, I'm just going to have to go through with this," so we go in. We were sitting there and I'm drinking beers and I'm not feeling it, I'm still terrified. There was this skinhead next to me, and he looked like the most nonthreatening skinhead I'd seen, because he probably had about a number two [shaved head], and I go, "What sort of band is White Lightning?" and he goes "They're Oi! But fast Oi!" I go, "Okay." I'm thinking, "What the fuck is Oi!?" . . . They started playing, and Goonie, who was a notorious character from Melbourne, started hanging shit on Chumley [White Lightning vocalist], and it just kicked off—massive all-in brawl . . . just about every window got smashed.

A questioning Dimma says, "How we ended up going back again after that, I don't know. There must have been something special and important about punk to continue." His faith was further tested when "Stretch," perhaps the most infamous of Sydney's skinheads, "totally caved my mate's face in at the Prince of Wales; just stomped on his face for probably five minutes and everyone was too scared to jump in, because he was a psycho."

Bastard Squad would be a return to the more simplified formula of early '80s England, where the postcard-featuring fashion sometimes surpassed attention to the detail of the music itself. Through two albums—*Hardcore Revolution* in 1990 and *Show's Over* in 1991—Cardwell says that "what Bastard Squad achieved in '87–'92 was without a doubt a revival of the UK82 punk sound. No one else was interested in playing that type of music when we first started."

Among the "mostly studs and leather at Bastard Squad gigs," Cardwell says that "there was still a great variety of people." Such variety, however, included at least one person with more duplicitous motives: "There was a female punk at the gigs who actually worked for ASIO. Once her cover was blown, she didn't hang around for long. I know the police didn't like our version of their badge on flyers, T-shirts, etc., and a few people did get harassed. My place got raided a couple of times, for drugs apparently. On both occasions they mentioned Bastard Squad, and knew we had a song called 'Die Pig Die' and another called 'Police Corruption.'"

Cardwell would experience even more serious police scrutiny in 1993 when arrested for the murder of his girlfriend. He was convicted and sentenced to fifteen years, and the band was rendered inactive. Upon his release, the group recommenced, and they continued to perform both locally and internationally.

Despite its supposedly innovative impulse, punk has been no less immune to imitation or unashamed plagiarism. Forming a band whose existence was mostly entwined with and borrowed from the first span of Bastard Squad, Chaotic Firing Squad vocalist Ed Browne had initially come under the influence of a punk older brother: "Only by virtue of it being my brother did I think it was kinda cool."

But with his brother taking the clippers to his punk persona and embracing skinhead, Browne lost enthusiasm for his sibling's subcultural choice: "I started hearing ... a lot of really fascist skinhead stuff. I remember feeling sort of intrinsically, as a kid, that this is somehow really wrong."

Browne's early excursions into playing live, however, were to exhibit their own form of crudity: "I played on my own, in a pub, this solo thing where I was trying to play electric guitar ... and I called myself 'Max Gangrene.' I think I was fifteen.... I actually snuck out of home with this little Peavey five-watt amplifier."

Progressing to a full band, Chaotic Firing Squad's first show had them banned from the Tote. Inserting themselves onto the bill, the group lasted three songs, including a rendition of "Belsen Was a Gas."

The Tote would not be the most public of their illicit performances. With a rehearsal room that Browne recounts "used to back on to the ANZ bank," the band took all their gear on a Friday evening and performed on its roof. They drew a healthy crowd more awed by the spectacle and "not so much because we were any good," but then police arrived. "We tripped the wire to their alarm system."

Reviled by law enforcement, the band were strangely welcomed by corrections, talking their way into a show at Pentridge Prison. A thankful Browne, though, says a wary drummer "piked out of the show. We were waiting to go in in the waiting room and Andy didn't show up.... I'm really glad because we were just these little kids. We had songs like 'I'm to Be Executed'... [and] 'Bars in the Window.' What do we know about jail when you're seventeen?... We were private school kids."

Conceding his "upper-middle-class" background, Browne had found much to differentiate himself from his peers; he says, "I spectacularly failed at school... always hanging with kids much older than myself." Browne had been drawn to St Kilda and its colourful street life: "I'd stay with my friend Karl—he's now dead—he was fifteen and being kicked out of home, and was taken in by a transgender sex worker, living and working from the top [of the flats].... In a strange way, I felt absolutely safe." But from the perceived safety of the flat, the introduction of drugs "got way out of hand quickly," Browne admitting to being "always out of my depth."

Occupying "fifteen years of my life," Browne says he and others would almost daily "go doctor shopping." A particular practitioner in Collingwood "just wrote scrips for whatever you wanted.... It was fucked-up times." Nevertheless, he says, "In all that time, I very rarely felt scared or intimidated by the street or anything else that was going on."

As punks slavishly adhered to styles from the US and UK, the Cosmic Psychos exhibited Australian tropes set to the soundtrack of a near-unchanging set of mid-paced punk. Far from his trademark flannelette and blue jeans of the farm, bassist Ross Knight says, "As a thirteen-year-old, I had long, half-peroxided rat's tails and a Connie [sharpie cardigan] and used to play football in platform shoes. But I was just a little bloody skeg.... I had too many pimples to get involved in fights—no one wanted to hit me."

As an admitted "skinny little runt covered in acne," Knight says his appearance "suited the punk rock image so much better.... As soon as my mother found out—there was a little article in the paper about how disgusting this punk rock was—she said, 'Whatever you do, don't get involved.' I go, 'Nah, Mum, I'm too much of a KISS fan for that.' Well, I'd pierced my ear with a safety pin and started wearing a Ramones shirt and band badges within about two weeks of that conversation with her."

Leaving Kyneton for the big city, Knight vainly tried to shoehorn his rural sensibilities into Melbourne's art punk scene's expectations: "I used to walk around with a copy of Dostoyevsky's *Crime and Punishment* in my pocket. I never fucking read a word of it, but I thought, 'Everyone will think I'm really smart.' But no, I used to get dragged along to it, and tried wearing the suit, coat, and tie for a bit, but at the end of the day I'd have a few grogs and just want to be a twit, so the country boy would come out.... Melbourne was more about heroin and art I think in those days, and that scene never excited me."

Less interested in the contents of a library than terrorising those outside it, Knight's first band, Rancid Spam, had made a "live performance outside the library in Kyneton, and that went down like a fucking lead balloon. So, we didn't get too far."

That band was followed by Spring Plains, but the sediment of Melbourne art punk could not be entirely removed: "It was all shite arty-farty stuff. That's all we could play, because we were that bad—we had to call it art."

After fittingly playing their first show with touring UK band the Fall, Spring Plains appeared at the debut gig of Painters and Dockers. "We went on and this bloke came out ... with these overalls on, and he had this shit look on his face, and he's standing, fuming. He went back into the bar, and he came back a couple of minutes later with a machete and started hacking into the sound desk. We were lucky we had Neil doing sound: he had fists like wheelbarrows and was a big, tall lanky bloke. All I remember as I was running from the pub, because it was starting to fill up with Port Melbourne wharfies, was Neil punching the shit out of this bloke going, 'I want this man charged.'"

The band then transitioned to Cosmic Psychos, and Knight says, "Melbourne was just getting deeper and darker by that stage." The Psychos reacted with wit and a more simplified formula, crafting their sound around Knight's interminable bass and laconic vocals. "Personally, I only ever played to my ability, which is not much.... Too many bands had advanced too far. It wasn't conscious; I got to a spot where I wanted to be and, personally, I've stayed there and I'm quite happy about that."

Undoubtedly served well by that position, Knight enthuses, "Shit yeah, it's got me a few beers."

Covers of the Cosmic Psychos' 1985 twelve-inch *Down on the Farm*, self-titled LP in '87, and *Go the Hack* album in '89 combined images of Australian blue collar: blue denim, blue sky, beach, bulldozer, and bush. The photos could hardly be more removed from the highly self-conscious punk fashionista traipsing the bleak streets of London only a decade previously.

With a basic, unrefined ethos to complement the record covers, Knight describes the group's reception among the more hardcore bands as "surprisingly good. I used to think they'd fucking hate us, but we actually got along like champions with those guys.... We could drink with anyone and talk the leg off a chair."

Russell Hopkinson, one-time drummer of Vicious Circle, offers admiration while explaining how the scene "wasn't that narrow that you could have this band who was basically the exact opposite of every vegan anarchist in Melbourne and they'd be accepted because they were doing something different and it was cool."

Against the previous charade of his taste for Russian high literature, Knight says, "I still have not written a serious song in my life.... I'm always having a dig at the ultra-cool or whatever, and that probably helped. Instead of singing about some dark being in some fucking cosmos somewhere, I'd rather sing about a dark hot dog in the bottom of my lunch bag or something like that."

Knight identifies, however, a distinct shift of weather within the city's music scene by the late '80s: "I think Melbourne came out of a dark cloud.... There seemed to be a definite turn. It was just more raw—just rock."

Mirroring an international trend for more unpolished guitar music, the band recorded their *Blokes You Can Trust* album (1991) with Butch Vig, who had recently completed similar duties for Nirvana's *Nevermind.* "Yeah, we had Bitch Vig polish a turd for us," says Knight. Yet the Psychos were innovators in a market filling with emulators, and Vig revealed their significance as being "highly influential on the Seattle so-called grunge scene."[22]

Any visions of platinum records and MTV *Unplugged* appearances were mere ephemera, as a straight-talking Knight opines that "musically, we were just left behind, because I don't think we progressed anywhere, really.... I'm glad we were never good enough or marketable enough for anyone to throw that kind of money at us."

The Psychos were never to overreach their status overseas as any more than an Australian peculiarity, albeit one with a sizable and dedicated following that allowed for multiple international tours. Anything else, Knight says, has been excessive to demands at home:

> I have things to do, I can't be running around talking about myself every day of the week—I've got to fucking work.... It's really odd some of the places you end up, people you end up chatting away to, whether it be rock stars or movie stars or whatever.... And then when I come home and I go to work, I get back on the dozer and I go, "Fuck me, I've just been hanging out with blah blah or blah blah." I know people who'd give their eye teeth for that, but it just seems kind of a natural thing to do; I guess I don't feel threatened by them and they don't feel threatened by me. We've always been the guys in the corner of the room with our pants half-down and with a lampshade on our heads. As I said, we can drink a beer and talk the leg off a chair, so I think that's where we belong.

In 1982, the first issue of Melbourne zine *Regression* contained a "Women in Punk" feature that included well-known figures Poly Styrene, Beki Bondage, Siouxsie Sioux, and Wendy O. Williams. No local women were presented.

The following year, *Maximumrocknroll* explicitly addressed itself to women and their presence within punk. The article's introduction noted concern of "a widespread failure to confront issues of sex equality" and the desire to redress it as "not just a low priority but practically unheard of within the confines of punk." It made recommendation that "if women want to change the way we get treated in punk... we must start by taking up, within our own culture, a strong and independent stance: a political stance."[23]

No band in Melbourne through the 1980s would exemplify that strong stance more than Gash. Guitarist Liz explains, "We were the only band in Melbourne where girls were writing the songs and talking about these issues.... I felt a bit responsible that I needed to try and show women that they can do it too." An especially confronting moniker in itself, Liz said at the time, "I suppose the name Gash would draw more attention to us, but any way you look at it, we would still draw attention due to the fact that we are girls playing hardcore music, which is pretty rare in itself."[24]

Initially drawn to pub rock, Liz could not help but note its even greater dearth of female performers: "I used to look at bands like Rose

Tattoo and Cold Chisel and all the international bands that came out—they were all males—and I'd be in the audience thinking, 'I'd love to do that. Why aren't there more women doing that?' ... But I thought, 'If I can't be in a band, I'll be a groupie,' so that seemed the next best thing.... We'd get really drunk and take drugs and dance and have a really great time. So that was my life; I wanted to be around music and rock bands. And then I heard the Ramones."

Newly introduced to punk, Liz says one night

> we were stumbling down Smith St, Collingwood, and we heard this music.... I thought, "That sounds like the Ramones, let's go up and have a look." So we went up the stairs and it was like a dollar to get in and it was a punk gig.... We went up to the bar and started talking to these guys.... We were amazed, they didn't try to get on to us and no one was sleazy. And these guys seemed articulate and artistic and interesting to talk to, whereas the other gigs we were going to it was all drunken yobbos, people coming up and grabbing your arse and trying to get on to you. It was really refreshing.... We found out where more gigs were, and started going to those and got to know a whole lot of people. I found the scene really friendly, and people were really into the music and the image and trying to change people's perceptions, and that really resonated with me.

Conversely, at home Liz was to find no encouragement from her mother: "She used to look at me with my black lipstick and bleached blonde hair and think I was crazy. She would say things to me like, 'You can't go out like that; people will think you're a witch and want to kill you' [*laughs*]."

After she joined Genocide on bass, the band broke up, leaving Liz "really determined to get a girl band together."

With a lineup, attention turned to the perennial headache of a band name: "People were always yelling at us from passing cars ... and someone might have said, 'Show us your gash!' once and it just became this joke.... We were sitting around the kitchen table trying to think of a name, and Smeer ... said to me, 'Why don't you call yourselves Gash? Turn it around and make it fun rather than an insult?' ... We thought, 'Yeah, it could stand for something, an acronym,' so we came up with 'Girls Against Sexist Hype.'"

The band released the *G.A.S.H.* LP in 1986, whose cover parodied glossy women's magazines, replete with subheadlines like "Shock Report! Will he still love you without your mascara?" and "Wonder Diet for Winter: Starve yourself so you too can conform to society's idea of how a woman should look."

Released posthumously the following year, Psychotic Maniacs' *A Tribe of Melbourne* seven-inch featured Liz on bass. Its title alluded to a certain solidarity between Melbourne's diverse subcultures, Liz explaining that "what's happened is people who don't fit into that overall society form their own groups: goths, punks, rockabillies, etc. It's like a safety net.... We all came together that way."

The same fellowship could not be found from the general public. "Smeer and I were shopping ... and this old guy ... he was just staring at us up and down and ... said, 'If I had a gun, I'd fucking shoot you arseholes,' or something like that.... People in restaurants wouldn't serve us. We'd walk into pubs and the barman would just say, 'We don't want your kind here, get out.' ... We were like aliens." Or even worse: hippies. "We used to call ourselves hippie punks because we liked good food and we were vegetarian, and we cared about that stuff."

Attention to health, however, came with a corresponding judgement of people whose lifestyles tended towards the more unwholesome: "Back then we sort of used to look at people that were really into heroin and think they were scummy, and we didn't want to know about them.... We were very judgemental. Now I can look back and say you don't get that way unless you've got very strong wounds ... and stuff you haven't dealt with.... We just didn't like that self-destructive scene."

The band's second album, *Positive Change*, from 1987, attempted to promote a more affirmative message, yet Liz considers its effect negligible: "I think people kept coming to see us because they liked what we were doing, but I don't think they listened much to the lyrics." Interrogating the culture that she had initially found so enriching, Liz emphasises that it was "not so much the music but the drinking and the drugs. I started questioning that a lot. Then I started wanting to get healthy, so I stopped drinking and taking whatever."

Delving into hippie/New Age culture, Liz says, "I started getting into Wicca and all this different natural healing stuff.... It was a natural progression for me. I got into reading tarot, I joined a Wiccan group, I dragged Smeer ... along to this Wiccan festival [*laughs*]."

Though long removed from punk, Liz expresses a curiosity towards its continuation: "I would love to know that there's still punk bands around and people are still holding those values and expressing them and being creative.... But I feel like it's an era I've left behind. It was great and I really enjoyed it, but I'm very different."

Despite the evolution, Liz says her partner is still able to identify its remnants, telling her that she's "never lost that punk attitude." Conceding, "I like hearing that," Liz says, however, that ultimately "I want people to be healthy."

While through the 1980s Liz constituted one of only a modest number of female performers in Melbourne, two novels using the decade's punk scene as their setting employed women as central characters.

Though the title of her later novel *Eat Well and Stay Out of Jail* could have been of great instructive value to Australian punk, *Nature Strip* by Leonie Stevens saw the book's protagonist, Caitlin, develop a relationship with a punk. Through Caitlin, a snapshot of the early '80s scene is captured, where, parallel to the music, heroin becomes a defining theme.

Stevens, in an interview, revealed the work to have largely mirrored what she had witnessed: "I was never quite as involved in the drug scene, but the whole thing of the shared house, the punk scene; that was my scene in the early-'80s. I was right in there."[25]

Nearly two decades subsequent, Ann Witherall's *Fly* chronicled almost the same time period. Semiautobiographical, the book includes mention of numerous bands and squats among the drink-soaked, drug-infused, violence-prone days.[26]

As a child, Witherall had arrived from England to the southern suburbs of Adelaide: "I grew up in this horrible, low-income area that was just full of yobbos. You couldn't walk out of your house and down the street without getting... 'Fat slut, woo, show us your tits.' It was all that, and every time. As a woman you were degraded constantly."

Like most teens just yearning for acceptance, Witherall says, "I wanted to fit in; I wanted a job in a factory after I left high school in Year 10; I wanted to get married and divorced and have five kids with three different men [*laughs*]. No, I didn't want any of that, but I wanted to fit in as all teenagers did.... Then when I was sixteen, I tried to kill myself, and my mum said, 'Go and live with your dad in Melbourne.'"

In sentiments similar to that of Liz, Witherall says:

> I got into the punk scene in the beginning because it wasn't that kind of macho, meat-market kind of feeling when you went out to gigs.... Yes, it was obviously dominated by men, but it didn't feel that way.... You were more respected, and everyone was watching out for each other, and there was a feeling of community.... I don't remember ever feeling scared. I felt very much accepted and very secure there even though there were bad elements, as the book indicates.... It was amazing to me at the time because I had come from such a terrible place in South Australia.

In likeness to *Nature Strip*, Witherall records the detrimental encroaching of heroin: "We were politically active and did so many things ... and then all of a sudden heroin hit and it all fell apart." Constituting only "a little bit" in 1984, Witherall says, "By the time I left Australia ... in '88 I was twenty, but I'd had a heroin habit for a year and a half." More widely, "It ruined the glue that was keeping people together—and it was a fantastic scene—and within a couple of years it just dissolved into drugs and the scene was second."

Witherall died in 2023.

Witnessing a scene at least in part given over to heroin, bands came to openly address its impact through song: Arm the Insane's (*Virus* seven-inch, 1987; *Remember* LP, 1987; split LP, 1991) "Smack Jack" and Civil Dissident's "First Blood."

Ruminating on the differences between punk of the late '70s compared to the 1980s scene she experienced, Witherall offers the increased presence of those with troubled upbringings as a possible reason for the extent of its drug use: "They ['70s punks] were trying to find a different music sound or break out from their middle-class, boring lifestyles. And I could be completely wrong, but I think the early '80s to mid-'80s scene was more of, 'I hate my life, I fucking hate the world.' ... We were angry about something, and most of us came from families that were broken and experiences that were really fucked."

Coinciding with punk's increased extremity of sound and temperament, some viewed a concomitant rigidity and decline of experimentation that had accompanied the first wave. As a member of Charred Remains and Murder Murder Suicide, Rusty Teluk was one of those who felt its constriction: "You had to play hard and fast. We weren't really about that, we were about saying the same things, but we thought, 'We're saying it in our way.' . . . We didn't really fit in with the hardcore bands, although we'd play with them. . . . I guess we were tolerated."

Remembering recording Charred Remains' tracks for the 1984 Melbourne compilation *Eat Your Head*, Teluk acknowledges them as partially reactive: "I actually played melodica and acoustic guitar. I insisted on putting them down to piss off the hardcore punks. Well, not to piss them off, but it was sort of like it was supposed to be about you could do anything, and all of a sudden it had become fairly regimented."

Inclusion of melodica, Teluk says, "came out of dub. . . . We were into punk, but we were into reggae as well." The first wave of punk in London had been entwined with reggae, and Teluk observed that famed DJ Don Letts "used to play reggae singles" at the Roxy "because there were no punk singles." A then-London-based Bob Marley even wrote the track "Punky Reggae Party" about the symbiosis of the two cultures.

By the latter half of the '80s, however, reggae had mostly been expunged from punk's playlists. Punk's continuance, or at least the purity of its identity, was instead being threatened by heavy metal. The fusing of hardcore with metal—"crossover"—came in the shadow of Metallica's 1980s albums. Suicidal Tendencies' *Join the Army*, Corrosion of Conformity's *Animosity*, Agnostic Front's *Cause for Alarm*, Cro-Mags' *Age of Quarrel*, DRI's *Crossover*, and Stormtroopers of Death's *Speak English or Die* were to be defining albums of the new movement. Depression's ignominiously titled *Ultra Hardcore Mega Heavy Punk Metal Thrash* live album in 1987 and the *Thrash till Death* LP the following year gave indication of thrash metal's permeation of one of Melbourne's most high-profile bands. Others included Condemned? and Hard Corpuscles.

Cold War politics and nuclear annihilation would be taken up by many such bands as lyrical and stylistic themes. The cover of the Extremes' 1987 LP *From Both Sides* was an obvious reference to the still-percolating US-USSR conflict; SIC opened their 1988 *Screaming in Churches* twelve-inch with the track "Radiation"; Utter Stench's 1987 album *Cry for Help*, says drummer Mark Zerafa, "was about Chernobyl, because Chernobyl had just happened."

The same year of the Extremes album, Brian Brannon, singer of US hardcore band JFA, appeared on the cover of skate magazine *Thrasher*. Hitting a peak around 1987–88 in the US, skateboarding came with a soundtrack that had taken a significant detour since Jan and Dean's twee, clean-cut "Sidewalk Surfin'" was performed on *American Bandstand* in 1964.

In an era well preceding Tony Hawk video-game respectability, skateboarding mimicked punk's confronting attitude, attracting the same attention and scorn of parents and authorities. An affront to the idyllic and serene suburban image, skateboarding was instrumental in the pushing of punk into its more hardcore sound, with California as its epicentre. As a pastime and soundtrack to the great suburban teen trifecta of isolation, boredom, and harassment, skaters started to form their own bands. *Thrasher* began to feature punk and hardcore and in turn influence an audience beyond just the confines of North America.

Mark Zerafa had been one of Melbourne's early adopters of skateboarding, beginning in 1978. His entry to skating had ironically been facilitated by the abandonment of music: "I got a drum kit when I was eight, but I didn't really know what I was doing.... I sold it and bought a skateboard with the money."

Forming Utter Stench, Zerafa reminisces, "Three out of the four guys were skateboarders." The one who wasn't, he says, "gave shit to us." Band member Chris Paine was a sponsored skater, and the name Utter Stench derived from the associated smell of used skate gear.

As skating was revived in the late 1980s, Zerafa recalls that in 1988, "Steven Hill [cofounder of skate company Globe] rang me up ... '*60 Minutes* want to do a story, does your band want to do it?'" Featuring practice footage of Zerafa's post–Utter Stench band, Terrorize, the segment traced the recent rise of skateboarding. The band's bassist, Borgy, staunchly told the interviewer when queried about people who don't skate, "I don't get along with them."

Zerafa recalls a charismatic and characteristically brash Borgy who "rang me up once. 'I'm in San Francisco, I was at a party, and the guys from Metallica were there. I walked up to James Hetfield and said, *You've got to play with Utter Stench*.'" At home he was no less cavalier. Riding his motorbike through the open doors of the Tote, Borgy avoided the pool table and pinball machines only to crash through a wall, half the bike left protruding.

The vitality that Borgy was as an individual, however, came to be extinguished, a sorrowful Zerafa revealing heroin "got him in the end."

After years of unrelenting hardcore and the slow eroding of audiences towards the end of the '80s, other bands emerged to break the monotony. Insyte guitarist Greg Stainsby remembers, "There wasn't a lot of punk bands mixing it up.... The tribalism existed big time in the '80s."

It was a decade in which the monolithic pop star also arose, and Stainsby had not been immune to the fanfare: "I was becoming a teenager in the 1980s and listening to Michael Jackson or whatever and my sister said, 'Why don't you listen to something more meaningful?' She was a Monash Uni anarchist and soon had me listening to the Clash.... Somehow, I ended up getting into Crass and anarcho-punk in the mid-'80s."

A politicised Stainsby became acquainted with band members Peter and Alice "through the protest scene." Together, he says, "We were all interested in getting [across] a message of equality and animal rights and antiauthoritarianism.... We were also chucking in theatre to try and get our point across. I dressed up as Ronald McDonald at one stage and burned a McDonald's flag."

The group's acerbic live show was to bring them into trouble almost immediately. "I got arrested. We played an outdoor show... and we did a Conflict cover, an antivivisection song. It's got a lot of 'fuck' in it, and we were arrested for indecent language." Peter was also charged, and his court appearance even made the pages of the *Herald Sun*: "Police Prosecutor Sen-Sgt Bob Head told the court it contained the word 'f..., or variations thereof' at least seven times."[27]

The incident would not be the band's only appearance in print, with Insyte the subject of a letter to the editor from an enraged parent who had supposedly confiscated the group's demo tape from their sixteen-year-old daughter. As to its authenticity, or being a cheap attempt at self-promotion, Stainsby remains unsure: "I don't know, but I wouldn't be surprised if it was fake."

All attempts at promotion could have been welcomed, as, being a part of an anarcho-punk and squatter scene, Stainsby admits, "It was small.... A lot of squatter punks were into anarcho stuff, but there didn't seem to be a lot of anarcho bands."

Insyte released their sole record in 1990, the *Squat!/Groove* seven-inch, and squatting occupied its cover and A-side. Stainsby says that "within the punk scene and the sort of leftie, anarchist scene there was definitely a lot of people squatting." To do so, however, he explains, "You needed a degree of exposure and education to know that you could squat and stay, and that's what the Squatters Union was trying to tell people."

Exhibiting their own educational purpose, the band conveyed opinions through the providing of lyric sheets at shows. The more informational or instructive approach would come against what the band perceived as a disinterested, declining, and depoliticised scene. Guitarist Jim diagnosed that "it's losing all its threat. . . . It should be something with meaning behind it, trying to do something rather than just rebelling against your parents."[28] Sharing Jim's sentiment, Stainsby rued that punk was "moving away from the political side of things. . . . [It] sort of had rebellious ideas behind it, but now, with thrash metal and punk, it's losing all its awareness."[29]

With the passage of three decades, Stainsby tempers his critique with a certain concession: "That said, your average thrash band was pretty anti-corporate, anti-government." Besides, says Stainsby, anarcho-punk was similarly guilty of conservatism in the form of parochialism. "The punk scene could be pretty conservative, and I guess we identified that with the chaos punks, but you could say the same about the anarcho-punks or whoever; they're people who like their particular genre. I think it's fine, but it does get a bit narrow-minded."

Hardcore regularly perpetrated acts to confirm its thuggish and buffoonish characterisation. As a member of Alligator Parade and Slush Puppies, Phil Rose says, "I reacted against that in a musical sense . . . that whole kind of masculinity, chest-beating aspect of punk rock. . . . And we didn't look the part. We were these four nerdy teenagers."

Notwithstanding Rose's lack of styling and intolerance for punk's bouts of red-bloodedness, he says, "We made good connections with people, and I tended to find that the friends I made with bands and people during that time were people who were open-minded, which is what punk should have been about anyway."

Beginning during hardcore's mid-'80s peak, Alligator Parade, says Rose, had "almost kind of got co-opted into the hardcore scene." It would be a fortuitous adoption, as Rose's recollection is that it "was massive ... very underground, but it was big."

Not unsusceptible to fluctuations of styles and popularity, Rose says that with the passage of only a couple of years "that original kind of hardcore scene was there, but it had changed a bit around that '87–'88 time." Alligator Parade themselves had also transformed, Rose remembering they "went a bit more progressive and not punk.... It just fell into some nether region and the band just split up."

Forming the short-lived Slush Puppies (*You're So Perfect* seven-inch, 1989), Rose again found himself in an outlier group. They did perform a style eventually aligned with '90s skateboarding; however, drummer Todd McNeair says, "We didn't quite fit into the skater punk mould. We had a song called 'Hate to Skate,' which probably didn't go down too well [*laughs*]." Still more than half a decade before skate/pop punk became a mainstream music current, McNeair admits of their melodic sound that there were "not a huge amount of people probably into it at that point."

Not someone to be preoccupied by prevailing trends, McNeair continued in Seminal Rats, a group whose sound had been rarely pursued by bands south of the New South Wales border. Alongside earlier groups White Elephants and Slaughterhouse (members of whom traced to late '70s band the Virgins), Seminal Rats unashamedly delved into the foreign Sydney/Detroit style—so much so that an article covering the Rats described them as having "got the Birdman shtik down to a degree that'd have a xerox machine looking up 'verisimilitude' in the dictionary!"[30]

Disparaged for supposed impersonation, McNeair today performs the most unsuspecting vocation that could be imagined of a drummer in a flannelette shirt with a packet of smokes in his top pocket: "I'm a tennis coach.... I've sort of come back to it.... I was pretty good, but I was over it by about eighteen. I started playing in some bands and that was the end of it."

Though attempting to balance on the shoulders of giants like Birdman, the Stooges, and MC5, to McNeair's uncomplicated thinking, Seminal Rats "were just some eighteen-year-old kids that played our instruments. We'd go surfing on the weekend, play sport, but we liked punk rock."

Whatever the band's fashion failures and lack of cool, punks and even international rock stars seemed largely untroubled: "They asked Chris Cornell [of Soundgarden and Audioslave] who were his favourite Australian bands, and one of them was the Seminal Rats."

Existing from 1984 until 1999, the band's recorded output consisted of two albums and three singles, none of those releases coming after 1991. Shows also came with infrequency, McNeair revealing that "there'd be five years where we'd play five gigs." Representative of bands who play on, unmoved by being at variance to current taste, singer Michael Harley admits, "It wasn't always easy, we didn't always get big crowds, but there was always a core of people of who were kind of our following."[31]

Not all bands were to remain in permanent obscurity. In 1983, an eleven-year-old self-described "punk anarchist" featured in the *Age*, touting his band Royal Flush. The average age of band members was only twelve, and Tim Hemensley told the paper, "Our material expresses disgust with the system, with schools, society and Government."[32]

Also composed of young, fledgling musicians, Foot and Mouth made the solitary release *The Prophecy of Fossos* twelve-inch in 1986, a record that confounded, reviled, and delighted listeners in seemingly equal quantity. More notably, Foot and Mouth guitarist Sean Greenway and drummer Matt Whittle were to join Hemensley and Joel Silbersher in forming GOD.

If *B Side* magazine described GOD as "a bunch of . . . juvenile retards who all secretly come from cosy, middle-class homes," a less-insulting Dave Thomas said that "they copped a lot of shit for being young."[33]

Youthfulness aside, Todd McNeair believes that they "were either the best band in the world, or the worst." Thomas speaks with uncanny similarity: "They were unreal, GOD, but also shit. You never knew what you were going to get."

Silbersher, then still a kid performing with a mouthful of braces, crafted a song that should have shamed many older, serious Melbourne musicians into pushing their guitars back under their beds. "My Pal," released as a single in 1987, traversed strict genre definition, enduring as arguably the country's most celebrated underground song.

In its following issue, a possibly more contrite *B Side* was left confounded by the genius of such "juvenile retards": "I have no idea how they managed this."[34]

## GEELONG

A new decade, a new sound, and a differing outlook and style saw splintering in Geelong between the "old" and that which was emerging. A teen then making his entry into punk, Willie was firmly encamped in the new: "At SPAC [Deakin University's Sex Pistols Appreciation Club] you had the old[er] . . . punk rockers with pieces of steak safety-pinned to the shoulders of their jacket, and they were like, 'Oh, punk-rock art.' We were snotty little punk kids stealing their drinks and getting really pissed and stoned and puking all over the place."

Born out of SPAC in 1981, Vision of War were no less chaotic, "starting with three-note songs and playing them at a million miles an hour because that was the only way we could cover our inability to actually play. So, we were a very early thrash band. . . . It worked because it was '1, 2, 3, 4, meet you at the end of the song.'"

Transitioning into the Tribe, the band melded anarcho-punk with their earlier, barely coherent thrash. Engaging in unflinching political spiels onstage, Willie says, "I guess it went down well because that was the vibe at the time. I hear it now and it's [*groan*] 'Blah blah blah.'" Their "Social Uniform" tape was no less dogmatic; its title, he recalls, "was basically about how from birth, through school, to work, to death, it was all laid out for you; that's it, that's the best you can hope for."

The band itself quickly progressed through its own life cycle and "just sort of died away." But even if the band itself reached expiration, a sentimental Willie remembers, "Everyone was young and alive."

Given its status as a major urban centre, Melbourne expectedly had a near-constant supply of bands and audiences through the 1980s. More susceptible to fluctuations, regional cities such as Geelong saw their scenes sharply wax and wane, a scenario John Nolan observed of his time in the state's second-largest city: "Geelong is very cyclic; it'll have three or four great years where a lot of people go to gigs, then it will just dry up. A lot of those bands will fuck off to Melbourne; Geelong will die until the next batch of bands come along." The early 1980s in Geelong had seen the Tribe joined by Manslaughter, Napalm Disasters, and Dogs on Heat, followed later in the decade by Off the Deep End, Wasted Brains, Mental Abuse, NTT, and IDK.

After one such ebb in Geelong, Andy Turner says around 1984, "The amount of people in Geelong ready for this music finally hit a critical mass, so Dave Thomas, in particular, was able to nurture a punk scene that had a real audience, venues to play in, fanzines being written, records being released." A nonchalant Thomas simply offers, "I was never one for waiting around for other people to do stuff."

As a teen in thrall of the uproarious rock of Rose Tattoo and AC/DC, glimpsing flashes of the Sex Pistols and early punk on television had Thomas thinking, "'This sounds like AC/DC, this sounds like Rose Tattoo,' but didn't look like the yobbos that wanted to bash my head in."

Hiring a scout hall for the debut of his band No Escape, Thomas says, "I had learnt how to hold a barre chord a month before this gig, and I realised all I've got to do is slide these barre chords up and down the frets and I can play the whole Sex Pistols album, the first Ramones album—so easy."

A brief if formative band, Thomas says of the groups he formed following No Escape that "there was a heap of shit bands like that." One of those excremental acts was Bodies, yet Thomas's deprecating assessment failed to inhibit a guitarist's lofty ambitions: "He comes into a rehearsal once with a feather in his ear and a rising sun headband, and he goes, 'I want us to sound like U2, everything we're doing's shit.'" Thomas, who was then the band's bassist, had a swift response: "'I'm going to buy a guitar.' . . . I just started listening to more sort of guitar-y stuff and the Stooges and 'Oh, wah-wah pedal' and 'Every song's in E' and 'Anything you don't know just play an E chord and hit the wah-wah—it sounds unreal.'"

Of the more hardcore scene, he says, "I kind of dropped out of that."

Thomas soon founded Bored!, and their sound fused the punk and hardcore of his early years with the guitar histrionics of Detroit.

The band rehearsed at Thomas's home. He recounts that "there was a doctor's next door. . . . One day the doctor came over and said, 'Please, could you guys shut up, because there's people coming in with sore throats and we can't hear them.'" While Bored! was still in their infancy as a three-piece, Thomas remembers being "asked to play at a birthday party at Jan Juc Surf Lifesaving Club. . . . It was fucking wild. . . . These guys threw the PA speaker through the window and they pulled down some old planks from the roof and smashed them. There were people pissing off balconies. . . . Dean jumped offstage and broke his arm."

With a solidified lineup, now including Nolan, the band recorded their self-titled twelve-inch in 1988. Nolan remembers Stephen Walker of radio station Triple R "gave it record of the week . . . and literally wrote, 'Hey, why are you buying all these records from fucking Seattle when you've got a band in your own backyard who are doing it just as good?' And that's when it all just blew up for us. We just got every support: Sonic Youth tour, Dinosaur Jr. first tour, Mudhoney's first tour, played with the Ramones twice, Faith No More—that was hilarious."

Having brought Tim Hemensley into the band, Thomas unemotionally declares, "He was the best person I've ever played with." Answering suggestion that the punk pedigrees of himself and Hemensley aided a band like Bored!, Thomas concurs: "That 'Go fuck yourself' attitude is still good to have underlying. . . . Tim—fucking hell, what a wag."

A Ross Knight anecdote confirms both Hemensley as a jester and his combustibility: "I remember playing with Bored! over in Perth, and we're talking about our bass guitars and Tim's going, 'This bass guitar's been with me for fucking ever, I love this bass guitar, nothing's gonna happen to this.' About three songs into their set, he fucking smashes it against the wall, broke into a million bits, then comes asks me if he can borrow mine. I'm like, 'Fuck off.'"

Touring Europe for three months in 1990 was enough to almost break Bored! itself, fragmenting as Nolan and Hemensley left to form Powder Monkeys. But by then, proclaims Nolan, Melbourne—via Geelong—had already usurped Sydney's Detroit legacy: "In Sydney, things were starting to peter out. . . . When we drove back to Melbourne in the van, it was like we were bringing the rock 'n' roll cup back to Melbourne after it had been in Sydney for all those years."

Entwined with the rise of Geelong's status, the Barwon Club's affiliation with heavy music had been secured early in Bored!'s history. Thomas says, "I remember one of the owners coming up to me and going, 'Your band is so shit, but you get so many people here and they just get fucking wasted—we sell so much beer—when do you want to play here again?' Everybody had a good time, there was never any problems. The bouncers that I knew there, they used to go to me, 'I prefer to work here than work at the Geelong Hotel because I know here the crowd looks rough and it looks wild, but I won't have to punch someone. But if I work at the Geelong Hotel, I'll have to punch about three people and get someone in a headlock.'"

Thomas's memory is perhaps clouded by a certain selectivity. Paul Smith, whose band Frontal Lobotomy played their first pub show at the Barwon Club supporting Bored!, remembers the show "ending in a riot with the pub being closed down.... Everybody was kicked out of the pub.... Bottles began flying, police cars were (apparently) tipped over, and in the end eleven people were arrested, including our singer, Stitchy, for offensive language. I had to do a runner through the Toyota car yard to escape being locked up myself. Thankfully I got away, because I was still only seventeen at the time and that wouldn't have been good for the publicans."

A far more benign hazard of the Barwon Club was the voiced approval or disavowal of some of its crowd. Thomas reflects, "It's an interesting art form, music: you put yourself open to abuse and criticism.... I know people growing up ... that could play guitar, they were awesome, but never played in bands. And I'd go, 'Do you want to come and join Bored!?' ... 'Nah, I don't want to play in a band, I'm happy just playing.' Because they wouldn't be able to do it; they couldn't handle that kind of thing.... When you meet people in the building industry, they have a bit of, 'Oh, you played in a punk rock band, did you have a mohawk?' and all that and have a laugh. But then they'll come up to you later and go, 'I was in a band when I was eighteen, I played a bit of bass—best time I ever had.' Or they go, 'We were so shit I had to stop playing.' ... They all tell you some story."

Thomas's own story was to conclude in 2020, the consequence of cancer.

Nolan passed away a year later.

## MARYBOROUGH

One of the most unrevealed biographies of any Australian punk bands remains Robert Trimbole's Hat (ex–Brain Spazms). The man who resided under the hat had departed the country seven years before the group's sole recording—the 1987 *Suntan* seven-inch. A decade prior to the release of the record, anti-drugs campaigner Donald Mackay vanished from a hotel car park, killed by a contracted hitman. One of those named as the architects of his murder was Robert Trimbole, an alleged member of a Calabrian crime gang. Mirroring the opaqueness of Mackay's murder, little information is available on the band, their dark '80s sound surpassed by even more darkly shrouded origins.

# "COG CITY"

## TASMANIA

### HOBART

Though the dangers posed to punks by outsiders were rarely fatal, to be dressed in any form that brought attention to oneself was likely to cause some kind of confrontation. This was especially true of 1980s Hobart, as Anthony D'Ettorre says: "We had the shit kicked out of us every time we went into town." Reliving a war of attrition, he says that "there was twenty-four of us [punks] in the school, which was nice because we kind of needed a gang.... By the time we were seventeen" that clique had been reduced to four. "The others just went, 'No, it's too much, there's too much violence.'"

An "all-boys public school," D'Ettorre says Newtown High "was a fucking insane school. There was rapes going on, constant beatings." Future perpetrator of the 1996 Port Arthur Massacre (thirty-five fatalities) "Martin Bryant was the same year as us.... We were all raised on op-shop clothing and single-parent pensions.... We never had any money." Post-school, D'Ettorre recollects, "Your choices were either the zinc works, Stanley machine works, the Blundstone factory, Cadbury's factory. University was unheard of."

Composing part of a larger group of outsiders, D'Ettorre says, "We were art school punks, the weird university crew, the bohemians, the hairdressers, gays, artists, just anyone who wasn't middle of the road." Included was "people like Lou Razor.... Everyone who hung around with her was hardcore.... They were breaking into chemist shops every night.... There was another crew we used to call the 'Apteds,' this is because there was five brothers.... Four of them were punks—full-on Catholic family." Together, he says, "We just didn't fit in—none of us had ever fit in—and all of a sudden there was something which was ours.... We were really proud of it."

Accompanying the pride was also the artificially induced feelings: "We were drinking and doing heaps of Valium, smoking pot, sniffing lots of glue, sniffing petrol, sniffing Skefron, dropping pills—just whatever we could get our hands on."

Aside from their suspect and illicit activities, D'Ettorre recalls, "The *Mercury* did a bad story on street kids, which had focused on the problem of all the street kids hanging out in the mall, which was most of us with nothing to do."[1] Slighted by the article's perceived slander, D'Ettorre remembers, "We went down and kicked in the front display windows of the building."

Ousted from his band Masochist "for them to become more serious" as post-punk band Zoo Infantry, D'Ettorre says, "We then got Verbal Warfare together."

Surveying the extent of the scene at the time, D'Ettorre tallies "Carnage, who never played a show," and "Verbal Warfare, who only ever played one show—and we were the two 'real' punk bands."

Cessation of Verbal Warfare precipitated the even less subtly named Holocaust. But with the duration of Holocaust also brief, D'Ettorre joined Tin Soldiers. Juxtaposing the delinquency of punk mall dwellers, D'Ettorre describes members Keith and Ian (later of the Philisteins) as "good private school boys.... We rehearsed five days a week. On Fridays we rehearsed up to seven hours.... Hobart's one of those places; there's nothing to do, so you just sit in your bedroom and do what you do, whether it be musical or artistic, literary."

Offering memory that "it was really rare for bands to come down to Hobart," for D'Ettorre and friends, fun often needed to be sourced elsewhere. "We would go to nightclubs" and "wave singles in front of the DJ and every now and then they'd play 'Never Again' by Discharge or 'Hitler's in Charge' by the Exploited." With the floor cleared, "it would be our turn, we'd go onto the dance floor and soon as it finished Soft Cell would come on, we'd exit the dance floor, and everyone would go back on." The tolerance of the clubs and their patrons would be returned by "stealing their drinks all night."

Outside of club nights, D'Ettorre remembers, "The gig at the time was at the Orient Club.... I was really pissed and ... a bunch of bogans were in the main back bar and I started hurling abuse at them. I'd written this song called 'Cog City,' which is what we used to call yobbos in Hobart [cogs] . . . and the cunts just went for it and there was this riot. . . . Everyone knew me as 'Matt Bastard,' and I fucking lived up to it."

No longer able to perform as Tin Soldiers, the band's future had already been determined: "I was already booked to move to Melbourne, because that's what you do, you don't stay in Hobart." He had previously visited the city for the Dead Kennedys tour in 1983, about which he says, "My ticket was like ticket five hundred and thirty or something, and it's just this mass of mohawks and studded leather jackets. . . . You go back to Hobart and it's like, 'This is shit.'"

# "Y BOTHER"

## NEW SOUTH WALES AND AUSTRALIAN CAPITAL TERRITORY

### SYDNEY

A new decade, and still the legacy of Radio Birdman's "New Race" didn't look to be abating in Sydney, *B Side* magazine positing that "maybe Birdman's coattails were long enough and strong enough to drag an entire scene along."[1] Spanning the better part of the decade, bands such as Minuteman, Mushroom Planet, Eastern Dark, Reptiles at Dawn, Trans 262, Asylum, Howling Commandos, Naked Lunch, Space Juniors, Bits of Kids, and Vanilla Chainsaws expanded on the blueprint laid by Radio Birdman and the Detroit bands.

In addition, the Celibate Rifles, the Hitmen, and New Christs were drawing large audiences, the city being well into its time as the epicentre for Australian pub music. It was a halcyon era now fondly idealised, and Tony Bambach whimsically recalls the Lime Spiders' own place within a golden age: "You sort of realise that it was a pretty special time. Bands were playing six or seven nights a week continually.... Tonnes of venues, tonnes of people going out.... I feel very lucky to have grown up then."

During the Dead Kennedys tour, Jello Biafra could not help but note Sydney's "several Radio Birdman clones and offshoots.... It's the most fruitful garage rock scene I've ever run across. They put an emphasis on making it sound hard and severe."[2]

Of those bands, Jello was particularly impressed with Bambach's Lime Spiders, describing them as "the most extreme band of its type I've ever heard, as far as taking sixties punk and making it more abrasive and annoying as any way possible."[3]

Revealing that "the '60s punk influence mainly came from Mick [Blood, vocalist]," bassist Bambach says, "I was more into the '70s punk.... Everyone at school and in the neighbourhood seemed to have a copy of *Never Mind the Bollocks* when it came out." Even Flowers, the precursor band to '80s mainstream icons Icehouse, had not been unsusceptible to its hype: "They played nearly every song off *Never Mind the Bollocks*."

The Spiders had also been birthed in the late '70s at a one-off show. The guitarist for that gig, Eric Grothe, left the band, becoming a National Rugby League legend for the Parramatta Eels.

After some further false starts, the group won a battle of the bands in 1981. Receiving recording time as part of the prize, the band recorded and released the *25th Hour* double seven-inch. The Spiders, however, broke up again before its release.

Re-forming with a changed lineup, the Spiders asked Bambach to join the hyped outfit. Less than a year later, their track "Slave Girl" topped the independent charts, Bambach admitting he was fortuitously able to "jump on the bandwagon" as the band spread its fan base among the insatiable pub dwellers of Sydney.

Whatever excitement had germinated came to a sudden conclusion as the band broke up again following release of their next single, "Out of Control." Yet in what was now becoming a formality, the band re-formed after being asked to contribute a song for the 1988 Yahoo Serious film *Young Einstein*. "Weirdo Libido" reached number twenty-five on the mainstream charts, the song's film clip being the first video ever played on *Rage*.

Virgin offered the Spiders a three-album deal, and the band looked to be on the precipice of a new level of popularity. To Bambach's thinking, this would "be a good opportunity to not have to worry about getting a job for a few years, to travel, and to behave like a delinquent." His parents were somewhat more sober in their enthusiasm: "For my parents, no rock musicians were 'real' musicians.... I think they wanted me to work in an office as a lawyer or accountant, so probably quite a disappointment from that point of view."

Disappointment could also be a word used by Bambach to describe their first full-length offering for Virgin, their *The Cave Comes Alive!* LP: "Virgin were pretty keen for us to be successful.... I think we underachieved in relation to their expectations.... One thing I always remember is the 'Volatile' single [photoshoot]. . . . They said, 'We want you guys to look really tough and volatile.' The end result was this really awkward-looking photo with the drummer holding a pair of nunchucks."

Bambach's dissatisfaction with the album was compounded by a slow desertion of their shows: "By the time 'Volatile' came out, and we were doing our regular sort of gigs, that's when I noticed the crowds were dropping off. . . . All bands have waves of popularity, and, for whatever reason, we weren't able to sustain ours. . . . That's about when I decided to pull the plug. I'd decided I was here for a good time, not a long time."

Attracted by the strength of a music scene that Bambach describes, bands from other capitals made Sydney a destination.

Beginning as Gun Control in Adelaide in 1981, the band relocated to Sydney on a manager's suggestion. The group's guitarist, Kelly Hewson, offers candid rationale: "We were going to hit the big time, of course, what do you reckon [*laughs*]?"

Making a final appearance at the Tivoli before departing Adelaide, Hewson, through a certain haze, has a memory of a particularly unmemorable individual performance: "There was hardly any people there, and we were on last. . . . I would never normally smoke a joint, but I was like, 'There's hardly anyone here, I'll be right.' . . . Then I looked outside and it was totally packed. . . . I was freaking out, and we went on and I was totally out of it. I started playing and I was like, 'Oh yeah, I'm into it, I'm into it,' and everyone changed into a new bit and I was like, 'What the fuck happens now?' It was just the worst gig I've ever played. Ever."

After an initial period of productivity, some smaller-city naivety saw the group, now in Sydney as Funhouse, discover the dangers of the big smoke. While the band was on route to a show, opportunistic thieves took off with the entirety of their equipment. "That sort of killed us. . . . We tried to keep going, but it was pretty hard. . . . No one had any money."

Hardly revelatory, given their name, Funhouse's 1984 *Conspicuous Consumption* seven-inch located them within the post-Birdman categorisation. But as a man with more than enough of a history in punk bands to know one if he saw one, Hewson says that despite existing in Sydney for over a year, "We didn't really come across any punk bands. . . . There were, but we never knew them somehow."

Hewson's observation highlights the existence of two scenes that were often unaware or inattentive of the other's activities. As a member of one of the earliest bands of the second wave of punk in Sydney, Positive Hatred vocalist Mark Creus says of the Detroit-influenced scene, "We didn't come across them very much." On the occasion that he did, Creus describes an appearance of "winklepickers with tight blue jeans and black T-shirts, cigarettes up their sleeves, and long hair."

In late 1979, *Roadrunner* had speculated whether the Birdman legacy could be unseated from the city: "The ghost of Radio Birdman stalks the streets of Sydney, waiting for someone powerful enough to put it to rest."[4] Though punk's strength was initially as emaciated as many of its participants' physiques, the second-wave bands in Sydney attempted to capture hold of the city's underground music scene.

Arriving from England to Sydney, Creus says that alongside brother and bandmate Julian, "we heard that there was thirteen punk bands at Rags. We went there and stood out like sore thumbs because we looked like, at that time, English punks—pasty, pale." But what they lacked in beachside complexion was more than compensated for by their citizenship, Julian revealing, "Having that accent, it gave you a definite in. People were interested in talking to you."

Guitarist Paul Berwick met and befriended Mark and Julian, and they became regulars at integral Sydney punk venue the Civic Hotel. Berwick suggests, "I had the money. They didn't have any money. I was prepared to buy some drinks for the guys, and here we are [*laughs*]."

He helped construct the Civic's stage, but Berwick self-deprecatingly offers that "I could play guitar, but I was not very good at carpentry."

While Berwick was incapable of deriving an income as a handyman, Positive Hatred were also making few dollars as musicians. He explains, "We were never generating money out of our shows, not making enough to go and record. . . . There was a guy we knew who worked at a studio, and he got us some time to do a free demo. He worked for Polydor Records or something, and he said, 'I'm going to get you in front of the A&R guy.' He took it and came back and we said, 'What did he say?' and he said, 'It was crap.'"

A realistic Julian recalls, "We didn't have any visions of grandeur that we were going to make it big. We were just really living in the moment." A posthumous self-titled album released in 1985 was to stand as the band's sole stand-alone output.

With the influx of a second wave, the presence of punks and skinheads on the city's streets and in its pubs couldn't evade notice of even a cultural monolith such as the *Sydney Morning Herald*: "Sydney punks and skins live in a delicate embrace" and "usually get barred from the same pubs together."[5] Or engage in rioting together. In December 1981, a two-hour drunken frenzy through the city was reported by the major newspapers and became the subject of the Anti-Hierarchy song "George St Riot." Bassist Chip Wardale relives the events that followed their removal from the Sussex Hotel: "They were literally walking down the street . . . smashing shop windows and smashing windscreens and fighting people. So, there was cops coming up on horses, just a proper scene—big articles in the papers. . . . There was probably thirty arrests, I reckon, because I was one of them."

For whatever its flaws, or at least periodic outbursts, Jello Biafra had written that the city did have "a good street-level punk scene, plus a wilder and slightly more violent outer-suburban scene."[6] With ties to the city's outer northern suburbs, Progression Cult, as well as supporting Dead Kennedys, were the first band from Sydney's second wave to release a record (*New Blood* seven-inch, 1982).

Progression Cult's songs differentiated themselves from the often standard two-to-three-minute rock/pop formula of punk's initial wave. Vocalist Anthony Lange says they "were super hard and fast. One of them lasted only twenty seconds. We figured our audience didn't have a long attention span, so we made all the songs really short."

Of similar brevity was Lange's patience with the dole office: "I told them I hadn't received a cheque to pay rent. The bored desk guy said, 'You know what? I've heard this story twenty times today.' I reached across the counter and grabbed him by the scruff of the neck and rammed my head into his. I quickly got my counter cheque."

For Sydney punks of the early '80s, an additional source of income to the dole was the Paddington Markets. A ritualised part of the lifestyle, punks charged visitors for photos, as Lange says those congregated would "basically drink and cadge money off passersby."

As a member of first-wave band Rejex (*Niagara Baby* seven-inch,

1979), Johnny "Rejex" bemoaned that by 1982 the punk scene "had become diluted from its original impetus back in 1977. Now it was a lot of angry drunk people, it had lost its intellectual edge, it had become an excuse to get angry and get out of it."[7]

Lange responds to the criticism: "Understandably, intellectuals like Rejex would have been disillusioned by the stack of new Discharge/Crass/GBH street-anarchist types, plus the Oi! skinhead bands that really were just into it for the violence. . . . Changing the world by taking personal responsibility was a totally foreign concept to drunks and drug addicts that all wanted something for free. . . . Nearly all would best be described as destructive hedonists that liked rock 'n' roll."

Drugs and alcohol were being openly celebrated among Sydney bands: Decontrol released the *Pull Cones Not Triggers* tape in 1985, and the same year, CHAOS, whose name was an acronym for "Cannabis, Hash, and Overproof Spirits," released their *Urgent* seven-inch.

Bruce Griffiths, who released many of the Sydney bands of the period, reflected on those being drawn to the scene: "The punk thing in the early '80s to me was a whole bunch of people who did not fit in, which is probably why a lot of them are dead now,"[8] and, "It was a group of people seeing how far they could go musically, or chemically or whatever."[9] Lange's own experience did little to dispel Griffiths's summation: "I was drinking and taking loads of drugs, so I left Sydney for six months to dry out, came back six months later, and started the Bedspreads. . . . Within that six-month period, everyone started taking heroin." The fulfillment of punk's often fatalistic mindset, Lange says, "By 1985, I counted up twenty-three dead friends. . . . Deaths were mostly heroin and suicides, yet some jail too."

One of the most publicised deaths of Sydney punks was to occur in 1983. Taken into custody for intoxication, David "Macca" McIntosh died two hours after being detained. His official cause of death was recorded as a mixture of drugs and alcohol, the findings met with heavy scepticism. Where Darlinghurst's gay community had collectively resisted harassment since arrests at the first Mardi Gras in 1978, punks were also being subjected to mistreatment by local police. University of New South Wales student newspaper *Tharunka* highlighted the situation preceding Macca's death: "In the past six to eight weeks there has been a concerted drive against the punks in Darlinghurst, who constitute approximately 80% of Sydney's punk population."[10]

Recorded the following year, Vigil-Anti's track "Darlinghurst Police" vocalised the contempt felt towards the area's officers, who were subsequently highlighted for misconduct in a Royal Commission report.[11]

Returning to his own life-endangering behaviour, Lange says, "I changed my life slowly and difficultly. That era had left most people from the hardcore scene shell-shocked and badly damaged from drugs, death, violence, and hate. Most were like survivors from a lost war zone—it was depressing.... Luckily for me, yoga then martial arts turned my life around from an early death."

Lange today runs a respected Brazilian jujitsu gym.

Preceding Progression Cult, members of the band had played in northern beaches group Government Downfall. As a punk-enthusiastic teen, Alan Creed soon found himself residing in their ill-famed Manly sharehouse and then becoming a member of the band: "I left school at fifteen, I left home shortly after. I didn't have a great home life at the time, and I moved into this house. They called it 'Cockroach Castle.' ... There was thirteen of us living in there." Residents included a "drug dealer living upstairs" and "a weird guy living in another section.... He wound up in jail for all these sex crimes.... One night we were tripping on acid and the upstairs bathroom literally fell down, it was that rotten. It just gave way about ten minutes after someone had been taking a shit."

Given the sordid nature of the home, and its secondary use as a rehearsal space, it seems a formality for Creed to explain that "we'd always have the cops coming down.... Whenever anything happened in Manly, they'd turn up there first."

Scrutiny also arrived from the media, Creed recalling an "article from the local paper where we did a gig.... A bunch of cars got trashed and broken into. 'Drugs Peddled at Local Dance,' I think was the headline."

Having brought minor local infamy to themselves, Creed says that contact with the inner-city punk scene was unnerving: "The inner-city guys had all the studs and leather and bondage gear and perfect hair.... It was inspiring but intimidating.... It was aggressive and violent, and all the drugs and crime. There was no safe space; you went there, you kind of knew. You hung around with your mates and looked out for each other.... In some ways that added to the air of danger and excitement."

Creed's post–Government Downfall band, Aberration, were themselves an intimidating entity: "We probably looked like a punk Rose

Tattoo, all sleeve tattoos, boots," who "attracted more of a skinhead following. A lot of the problem was getting shows, and in the end it was very difficult for us to get gigs because a lot of violence would happen.... The original lineup fell apart. The bass player, Greg, was pretty heavily into heroin.... Liverpool the drummer... wound up in jail on an armed robbery charge."

This was not the only appropriating of cash in which the band was involved—on another occasion, they were to be its victims. With anarchist bookshop Black Rose acting as guarantor for a loan, live recordings were to be made with a view to their release as a compilation album. "We did the recordings. Then one night we were out at the Mosman Hotel, we'd been selling some hash and had all these deals, and were sitting smoking joints in this yellow Mini in the carpark. Cops came and found us." The police detained two of the car's occupants, and Creed says that "we went home.... Later on, I'm at home and get a phone call saying, 'This is Redfern Police, we know what you've got there, we're coming down, we want it all out on the table. We'll have the dog squad down there; we'll tear your fucking house apart.' I actually had bags and bags of dope, sheets of acid, ounces of hash."

Gambling that the police didn't know the extent of his stash, Creed "dug a hole under the neighbour's fence and buried most of it ... and put like half an ounce of hash and some deals out on the kitchen table." One of the guys detained at the pub "took the rap for it.... But when it came to the court case ... they [police] took most of it. He basically just got a fine rather than a heavy sentence or anything. He used the money that was going to fund the recordings to pay the fine, then disappeared, and that was the end of that record."

A tireless performer with a multitude of other bands, Creed confesses, "I don't know why I'm still doing it after thirty-five years [*laughs*]. Not really had what could be deemed any kind of success, but I still love it."

The early biography of World War XXIV's Rob Burke in part mirrors Creed's: northern beaches, the discovery of punk at an early age, and discontent with family life. While forming the band, guitarist Burke says they too felt an inhospitable attitude from the inner-city punks: "They thought we perhaps didn't belong there, and that punk shouldn't come from what they perceived to be a very rich area.... At the time,

Warringah Shire [covering the northern beaches] had the second-highest youth unemployment rate.... Many of us felt we were lost souls."

Embraced among the surf-heavy northern beaches, Burke says that "everywhere you went, *Radios Appear* was on everyone's stereos all the time.... Our first single, 'Azaria'/'Y Bother' [1983], ... it was definitely a homage to Radio Birdman, the Stooges, and the whole Detroit sound."

More than just a homage, the single showed a band inhabiting two time periods, its A-side carrying the remnants of Birdman, the B-side exposing an embrace of hardcore.

Perceiving a disconnect between the relatability of the first and second waves of punk, Burke says, "Our roots were definitely in the '70s, but the message was becoming very lost to us." US hardcore bands such as Circle Jerks and Angry Samoans, Burke says, were "more appropriate to where we came from—they were skaters, they were surfers. It was a natural step for us, and punk had to move on. You couldn't keep playing 'Born to Lose' [the Heartbreakers]."

Their first show, though, saw the band consigned to relics before the gig even began: "Stupidly we did a sound check and played 'Submission.' ... You could almost hear the groan from the bar next door thinking, 'Oh fuck, they're going to play the Pistols.'"

However, after beginning their set, "in a second the whole room was full and bouncing around and having a ball.... I think we sort of won them over that night.... It turned out to be a really good gig"—if not without incident. "It was a benefit for the Marijuana Party. There was all these bowls of pot around the place.... These skins arrived and just started stealing it all, stuffing it in their pockets. And then a massive brawl started.... Everybody in the place was fighting. Bizarrely, at the time we were playing 'Y Bother.' At the end of the night, after they stole all the pot, bashed everyone up, robbed the guy who was taking the money on the door at knifepoint, some guy apparently got thrown off the walkway across Parramatta Road."

Throughout the entirety of punk's history, bands have never experienced a lack of surreal, unsuited, and disastrous shows. Escaping to the New South Wales ski fields, where they performed as part of a pub's punk-themed dress-up night, the band had "actually stopped and played at a pub" on the way: "There was three people in the crowd. [They were] yelling, 'Play some Stones, play some Stones.'"

Locally, the band enjoyed much more favourable reception, as their self-titled album in 1986 "went to number one [on the independent chart] and hung there for six weeks." But despite the popularity, when questioned on their inability to secure shows for the band, the group's manager retorted, "You're fuckin' banned from everywhere."[12]

A 1984 Sydney scene report in *DNA* observed, "There might be loads of bands around, but there are very, very few places for them to play at."[13] In the early to mid-'80s, a series of unique buildings—mostly squats—therefore acted as provisional venues, including Side F/X, an old Marist Brothers high school, and former naval facility the Gunnery.

More dire than the depletion of supportive spaces was the omnipresence of heroin. Burke describes what would "become a real heavy anchor, and it in fact killed our bass player.... It was one of the worst things to ever happen to me.... 'Don't' is [a song] about heroin use. Heroin had started to have an impact on me.... I think in a way it was me starting to talk myself out of it."

A member of World War XXIV since 1981, Burke left the group in 1987 as well as departing Climate of Fear:

> I was high and had a horrible three years after that, and I had a massive overdose in 1990. I crushed my sciatic nerve and was unconscious for five days—paralysed my leg.... My kidneys shut down, I had renal failure.... I was in hospital for a couple of months and it wasn't like I had any great epiphany.... Either I was going to end up in jail for a hell of a long time—in and out of jail—or I was going to die. I guess I still had enough—I don't know if I'd call it common sense—but I wanted more from my life, and that was enough.... A year later I went to university.

If World War XXIV's beachside residence drew them to the sounds of Californian hardcore, Anti-Hierarchy's outer-western-suburban English-migrant upbringing brought a greater affinity to its UK counterpart. Describing the area as "brilliant," bassist Chip Wardale nonetheless concedes it was "nowhere for music, though."

As a result of their isolation, Wardale says, "We had our own little world going on out in the suburbs. It actually took us ages before we bothered to hang around the bigger scene in the city." There, says Rob Burke, the name Anti-Hierarchy "came as a response to the cliquey older punks." Asserting that "they had a superiority about them," Wardale also notes their aversion to the newer hardcore groups like Anti-Hierarchy: "They saw that whole sound as really bad."

The formation of Anti-Hierarchy had not been indubitable, as tragedy befell the group while under their initial name, Espionage. On Christmas Day 1981, "Before we got to play, Brett [original singer] got killed.... There was this ongoing aggro at the time with these Lebanese guys.... There was a bit of an altercation on the street.... He [Brett] and one of the Lebanese guys were wrestling, and they both went under a car and they both got killed."

After relocating to the inner west, the band's irrepressible ways would not go without notice there also, Wardale estimating he got arrested "every third week."

A particularly notable evening saw Wardale detained alongside one of Sydney's New Zealand punk contingent following a Harbour cruise gig: "Something had gone wrong, and the ferry driver just turned around and pulled in to where the police vessels were, and there was a lot of cops there.... I got grabbed.

"In the back of the paddy wagon ... the whole way he's abusing the cops ... and I'm going, 'Shut the fuck up.' They opened the back and dragged him out, and they didn't even wait to get into the cop shop, they just started laying into him straight away.... I saw him the next day and he could hardly walk. Everybody was hobbling around, blood on their jackets from being bashed by cops—brilliant fun."

Such fun, though, when repeated with regularity, becomes drained of its effect. Eventually, says Wardale, "I was ready for something a little bit more progressive. I wanted more interesting music. I wanted to be more artistic."

Remembering that "it must have been around '83 or something," Wardale says that Red Eye and Black Eye were two Sydney record labels who gathered the more artistic, avant-garde, or just plain confounding bands. On the response to it, Wardale says, "A lot of punks couldn't handle it, but I actually loved it.... The music was kind of crazy and interesting.... They pushed it even more extreme than the punks. Lubricated Goat's antics, there was no punk band doing some of the stuff they did. Bands like that were playing punky kind of music, but they just weren't part of that scene."

Bruce Griffiths adds, "What they pretty much all have in common is roots in punk . . . but they kept moving, didn't stay still, and kept innovating. With no disrespect to any of the punk bands playing in Sydney at that time, I was seeing a lot more imitation than innovation."

Under his Aberrant Records label, Griffiths released bands entwined with the new vein of progressive, underground music. Inclusive of bands Grong Grong, King Snake Roost, and Bloodloss, each is acknowledged for their influence on the emergence of grunge in the US.

Like many of those involved in the more experimental scene, Griffiths's background was in punk and hardcore, releasing three compilations: *Flowers from the Dustbin* (1983), *Not So Humdrum* (1984), and *Why March When You Can Riot?* (1985). The latter's cover provided the following rationale: "This is to give them the chance to be heard."[14]

One of Jello Biafra's observations of Sydney had been that "many of the bands make so little money, they don't make an effort to save and record their own record. They figure that no one would help them distribute it anyway. . . . Most of the recent punk records are poorly produced, and are very hard to get a hold of."[15]

Anti-Hierarchy was one band to never appear on record. Some of those otherwise unreleased bands that appeared on Griffiths's compilations include Queen Anne's Revenge, Vellocette, What?!!, Itchy Rat, Vigil-Anti, and Beggars Court.

A stand-up comedian and comedy writer, Griffiths reveals, "At the time that I was doing Aberrant, I was writing for Doug Mulray on [radio station] Triple M, which effectively subsidised the label." In 1982, Mulray, as the Rude Band, released a seven-inch including the satirical track "I'm a Punk." Lyrics for the song presented a mocking of the mindless interpretation of punk:

> I don't stand up for cripples on a peak hour bus
> I'm a punk (He's a punk)
> I never help me mum do the washing up
> I'm a punk (He's a punk)
> I take drugs and get drunk

For Griffiths, however, the parody would become all too prescient:

> What it [punk] became not only left me questioning my own involvement, it left me questioning wanting to have any part in "promoting" it, or, more specifically, promoting what it

> had become. The final straw for me came in 1985. I was walking through Central railway tunnel on the way to a gig at the Vulcan.... Ahead of me were three Punks (uppercase *P* pertinent) and ahead of them, a busker. They veered over to the busker for a moment, then continued on their way. When I reached the busker, he was in tears. These "Punks" had taken every dollar he'd made. The scene had become *that*.

Moving to release the noisier, more experimental acts, Aberrant featured one band, Feedtime, whose sound, while not distinctly punk, possessed an equally intense and disconcerting atmosphere. They also performed at some of the same punk venues. Bill Quarry recalls one pub in particular: "Feedtime used to play these shows down at the Central Markets Hotel.... I never went because—it seems ludicrous now—these skinheads used to go to these Feedtime shows. They wouldn't necessarily go and see them at other gigs. You were wary about some shows you would or wouldn't go to. You'd get beat up if you went there."

Liz of Gash says, "We were shocked at the violence everywhere in Sydney." A Depression show at Bondi in 1984 saw Smeer struck in the head with a glass, while another unfortunate punter was stabbed with a drumstick. Ray Ahn recalled that "one of the bouncers was hiding away all the blood."[16] Smeer reveals, "It was a skinhead fight ... and I jumped in the middle and tried to break it up.... Then I went in the dunnies to have a piss, and then guys came in and tried to bash me up."

Trouble with skinheads became so problematic that groups were banned from the city's premier alternative venue, the Trade Union Club. Police requested that the club cease booking punk bands, and boots were also prohibited, with patrons abandoning them at the door to spend a night drinking in their socks.

Skinheads, however, were not one homogenised, violent mass, but a collection of differing tendencies and tensions that became more diffuse as the decade progressed. Chip Wardale describes the nuances: "There was a group of skinhead guys who were more old school, and they used to hang around at the Sussex Hotel with the mods.... These guys ... were into ska and stuff. The nasty ones were into Oi!"

Skinhead's origins had been in late '60s England and a taste for Jamaican ska. A revival, dubbed "2 Tone," saw ska blended with elements of punk, as the Specials, Madness, the Selecter, and the Beat reached the top of the English music charts in the early '80s. In Australia, only a handful of bands took cues, including the Allniters in Sydney and Melbourne's Strange Tenants and No Nonsense. Gary, a Sydney skinhead, recounts that, mirroring England, "ska fizzled after a couple of years. . . . It was a natural progression to get into oi and that."[17]

Freed of any art-school pretension, Oi! incorporated football terrace culture and a purer working-class rebelliousness. The results weren't always palatable, though, to those who had championed the first wave's supposed radicalism. Yet Oi! enjoyed considerable popularity in England, as, pushed by *Sounds* writer Gary Bushell, bands such as Cockney Rejects and Angelic Upstarts appeared on *Top of the Pops*.

Some skins would not make the transition to Oi!, as an irreparable split occurred. At a time when the most emotive division in the country was likely Ford versus Holden, Karl Kelsall explains, "The hardcore Oi! sort of thing didn't really mix with the ska ones. I'm sure there were cases, but in general there was a split." The divide was even reflected in differing attire, as the Oi! skins' bleached-blue jeans and singlets accompanied even shorter hair. Of those choosing the Oi! path, Kelsall says their number "wasn't massive. In my estimation, in Sydney, there was a couple of hundred—a hundred and fifty."

Local bands popular with or composed of skinheads included the Crims, the Cutters, CI5, Crash Course, Growling Frenzy, and Kelsall's band Joyful Killing.

An arrival from Auckland as a teen, Kelsall had sought to establish his own band in Sydney. Cultivating a sound reminiscent of the first-wave English punk of Stiff Little Fingers, Kelsall acknowledges that "the music wasn't that sophisticated. The people coming weren't expecting Beethoven or anything."

Sometimes the people coming weren't even interested in the music so much as the band itself: "The police, I don't think they were big fans of Joyful Killing, because we did some gigs for the Prisoners Action Group to raise money for the families of prisoners. . . . I remember at one gig . . . the police came and raided the place. . . . After that, the police must have been reading the gig guide or something—they kept turning up to gigs. Sometimes they were there before we arrived."

Together the transplanted New Zealand punks and skins developed a "bit of a reputation." Admitting that "it definitely got quite lively at times," Kelsall cites "punch-ups and fights and cops and paddy wagons. . . . Back in those days, I used to be quite an aggro person myself, so it didn't really bother me that much." Offering almost a hint of gratitude, though, Kelsall says, "There was some dodgy situations I got myself into, but I came through it all right."

For all the emphasis on what occurred around the band, Kelsall boasts that musically they were more than adept: "We won the [Vulcan Hotel] band competition, people recognised us, we did have some ability." However, for all the promise, "We sort of ended up running out of places to play, and I think we might have even changed our name twice. . . . It's a pity we didn't put more down and record properly. . . . In a way it was just a big fucking party. . . . They were good times, there was some good gigs, it was a good era."

The skinheads' revelry made great content for the city's papers: a front page of the *Daily Telegraph* in 1983 contained a photo of over a dozen skins on the ground being questioned by police under the headline "Flat Out on Broadway." Other articles highlighted more nefarious elements: "Oi skinheads . . . hate foreigners, homosexuals, anarchist punks, hard drugs, and yobbos." Giving the *Sydney Morning Herald* a glimpse into their lifestyle, Michell Vandermerr told its reporter, "We go out a lot, drink, listen to music, just talk, and the boys get into a lot of fights, which they enjoy talking about. We have been kicked out of nearly every place in town."[18]

Skinheads would again feature in the *Sydney Morning Herald*, this time presented on a front page in 1986. An investigation into the "Tribes of Sydney" featured Brinley, a nineteen-year-old skinhead with a dislike for "faggots" and "foreigners." Admitting to accompanying other skinheads "poofter-bashing," and with an analogous distaste for punks, Brinley spoke candidly, saying, "Sometimes I'd walk down the street and see someone and think, 'I'd like to punch him out.' It brings on a satisfaction."[19]

As someone initially drawn to their company, Alan Creed says, "I did hang around with a bunch of those guys in the early days, but I just drifted away from them. I wasn't into that—the racism, the hatred of gays, hate of anything different—it was just fascism, it wasn't punk to me." Active within the scene from the early appearance of Oi!, Rob Burke remembers:

> They pushed themselves to the really radical extremes. It was just machoism gone mad.... Probably the most violent thing I saw... [was] this skin with sixteen-hole Docs—he was about six foot four inches, really big guy—knocked him [a punk] down and started jumping up and down on his head, bringing his knees right up to his chest and slamming down on his head. I remember looking across at the guys and thinking, "What the fuck do we do? Do we stop?" They looked back at me with the same sort of bewilderment, and we just kept playing.... To this day I don't know if that guy lived.

Burke speculates that "some people who misread punk, the message of punk, may have even been attracted to it so they could behave like that, so they could get into fights because they thought it was acceptable. It wasn't.... But I think it also relates to the '80s as well; there was a lot of violence everywhere."

While the violence may have been similar, extreme politics differentiated a section within the skinhead scene. Karl Kelsall explains that "Oi! skins and bootboys were fairly similar, then you had the Nazi skins, who were a bit political and had their racist thing going on, which never interested me.... A younger lot came through probably about mid-'80s ... who had that white power going on."

In the mid-1980s, as skinheads were marauding the inner city and its drinking establishments, Sydney's media were playing up race wars in the western suburbs between Lebanese and Vietnamese gangs. For the more politically minded and active skinheads, Sydney was the centre for the country's foremost white nationalist organisation at the time, National Action. The most prominent of its members, Ross "the Skull" May, often appeared in media attired in full Nazi uniform.

Though the politics would inevitably find their way into a handful of bands, others simply attracted a skinhead following through their own branding. Singer of the Stukas, Guy, says, "We weren't skinheads" but "I think we were the closest thing, because we were called the Stukas and they're Nazi planes and they associated us with the Germans.... They loved us.... We played all over Sydney and they would come anywhere.... They'd salute us, they'd wear swastikas.... We had a ... residency and that ended straight away. They said we attracted a bad crowd."

Offstage, Guy was not without his own personal troubles: "We played around for a while, then I got pinched and locked up and so the band was on hiatus. . . . Every time we'd get anywhere, I'd get pinched and go back to jail. . . . Crime wasn't my forte. I never got away with much [*laughs*]." The remainder of the band weren't always merciful either: "The drummer was kind of a bikie, and he once sent a guy to come up to me in jail and threaten me and say, 'I'm here for life, if you come back, I'm gonna rape you, I'm gonna bash you.' . . . It was pretty hectic in the Stukas."

Guy offers the thought that

> it's definitely a mystery how I'm still alive. . . . A lot of the things I don't remember with the Stukas. I was smashed, I was a junkie, I'd just turn up and play. Sometimes I didn't know what venue I was at and what bands we were playing with. . . . I remember one time I was hanging out for heroin, and I got really drunk. Halfway through the set I pulled the blanket out of the drummer's kit, laid down on the stage, and just went to sleep. They just played on as an instrumental. . . . Lobby Loyde was there to do our mix and said, "You guys are the most punk band in Sydney."

Mutant Death was a band that also experienced prison, but with the luxury of returning to their own beds at day's end. Member Andy Nehl says, "We played a gig for the prisoners inside Bathurst Jail."

Having even "learnt a few prison songs," the band were scheduled for the "lunchtime gala day," which was the one day a year that partners were permitted to mingle with the prisoners. Obligingly, says Nehl, "Their wives and girlfriends had smuggled in alcohol and marijuana. They were going off into these tent marquees and having sex. Half of them were virtually having sex standing in the line for the barbeque" as the band toiled futilely at the other end of the recreation yard. "I think they essentially hated us."

With members of Mutant Death involved in prisoners' rights activism, their *Trapped* seven-inch in 1984 included the song "Police Verbals." Acutely aware of police attaining "verbals"—fabricated verbal confessions—Nehl reveals the extent to which the practice was known: "Heaps of the lawyers around town knew it, all the people who were politically active in the prisoner's rights area knew it, all the legal centres knew it. The New South Wales police, at that stage, a whole bunch of them were really corrupt. The armed hold-up squad ... would give what was known as the 'green light' for some robberies to go ahead. The cops used to deal drugs, [former detective sergeant Roger] Rogerson used to kill people. That was all known, but I guess legally proving it was another matter."

As members of the New South Wales police force were (allegedly) evolving their job descriptions, bands such as Impatient Virgins, Brain Thieves, No Class, and the Rejected (*First Offence EP* seven-inch, 1985; *Final Offence* LP, 1987; *No Offence* LP, 1988) were still anchored in earlier English sounds.

Ragadoll was another to embrace the punk pastiche, with member Jimmy Willing quite literally adorning punk to escape his conservative and regimented surrounds: "I had been in boarding school for eight years and I wanted out. We're talking old-school soldier discipline here: church four days a week, and no girls. The school had a policy of weeding out punks and removing them, so punk rock became my ticket to freedom. . . . I and several other students attached bondage straps, zippers, swastikas, safety pins, etc., to the Kings School uniform."

With his newly acquired liberty, Willing says, "My second concert ... was the Bedhogs at Side/FX, and it was hardcore. . . . Side/FX was an alternative venue that ran from a Darlinghurst squat. It was wild, anarchic, expressive, and very violent."

Willing's observation was that "the bands were more than just bands, they were gangs. . . . The wildest, most colourful gang was led by Eager Penis (if you can call it leading). . . . Eager was the living embodiment of punk anarchy—he had run away from home at twelve or thirteen to join the gangs. He wore his hair in a series of glue-hardened spikes, somewhat resembling a World War Two shipping mine. . . . I must say that I was not in these gangs, just a schoolboy who looked on wide-eyed."

Willing's wariness was justified, as he says, "The violence with boots and glass ... revolted me, and was the major factor that caused me to drift away from the gangs. It was pointless and destructive." His band had also not been graciously received by the more austere gang members: "The hardcore punks did not embrace us. Our eclectic influences also made us ... difficult to define."

Despite Ragadoll being rejected by its more extreme segments, "punk," says Willing, "was now the flavour of the month and saleable. . . .

I think we could have been very successful if we had listened to our manager.... Shelley wanted us to remain punk, but it meant to me to not grow up.... I have never forgotten Shelley berating us backstage.... 'I've handled your long hair,' she said, 'and the lashings of psychedelia and truckloads of LSD, but you cannot go onstage before the Dead Kennedys and play a song by the Byrds.'"

Not content to be a mere copyist, Willing conversely views himself as having been an early innovator: "Our dyed, feathered, furred, and patched dress code became a revolution in cult fashion, and we undoubtedly created a prototype for what later became known as 'feral' [an amalgam of hippie, punk, and environmental activist].... I moved to the North Coast [of New South Wales] in 1988.... Not long after this, the next generation of punks, who were now morphing into 'ferals,' arrived on the scene. They were attracted to my lifestyle, marionette show, and rock 'n' roll band."

Despite any shared ethos with the region's countercultural remnants, Willing says, "There were some among the older 'hippie' generation who attempted to shut us down and take away our voice.... I remember very clearly one self-appointed Aquarian elder writing off my whole generation as being 'Sid Vicious murdering Nancy Spungen and then overdosing on heroin.' I was shocked and speechless. Punk for me had been empowering and inspiring."

Previous to his Sex Pistols infamy, Sid Vicious had been a member of the Flowers of Romance, alongside female members Palmolive and Viv Albertine. That group was more a footnote to English punk history, but both women were to continue in the Slits, a band of particular inspiration to a subsequent wave of female punk and post-punk performers. Miriam Williamson could not help but be another to cite their influence.

Joining with Williamson to form Wrong Kind of Stone Age, guitarist Gavin Williams wanted a greater breadth to his songwriting following the conventionality of his previous band, Identity X.

Supporting Dead Kennedys, their exploration proved effective, as an absorbed Jello Biafra remembered Wrong Kind of Stone Age as "one of the best morbid-ambient post-punk bands I've ever seen or heard."[20] Despite the morbidity described in their sound, Williamson says, "We weren't really part of the local goth and death-rock scene." The group still found a place on bills with punk bands, but at a Rehearsal Room show not all who attended did so for the enjoyment of the entertainment: "It was very close to Redfern, and relentless police harassment of Aboriginal people could be seen on the street every day. The local station was later featured in [ABC TV's] *4 Corners*. They were following someone they claimed had run into the venue, or were going off a tip-off. I'm not really sure, but it was chaos. It was dimly lit, and there was a fog machine pumping out fog so thick it was hard to see. Next thing all these heavily armoured cops arrived. It was like something out of *Judge Dredd*."

In 1984, the band released the *Flying Low to Batavia* seven-inch. But as "punk had burnt out in Britain, and people involved were re-forming, or their bands were morphing into a different sound," Williamson says the group's brooding style took on an increasing dub influence: "We became more influenced by Adrian Sherwood's On-U Sound stable of bands and production styles with dub production.... We were probably the only band in Sydney playing this style live.... Affordable new technologies were being embraced, like Roland's earlier synths bringing more electronic sounds into the scene, and a wider influence including reggae, ska, and dub.... It was a refreshing change following on from the frenzy of punk."

Just as perplexingly named, Box of Fish inhabited similar terrain to Wrong Kind of Stone Age, both aurally, and, as bassist Bill Quarry relays, through caution or a reluctance to strictly adopt punk as a signifier: "In a lot of ways, bands like them and probably us, because punk had become so codified, it was like you didn't want to be *that*.... A lot of that punk 'rock' was just how it sounded to me: like rock. I wanted to listen to the stuff that wasn't rock.... I could never immerse myself entirely into one specific genre.... If people ask me now, I go, 'I'm a punk, but I'm not your version of it, probably.'"

Quarry's distance from punk had stemmed in part from its more irritating representation:

> The mainstream media presents what punk is, so a bunch of kids come and do exactly that: spitting, breaking bottles, being a complete jerk—they follow the cliché. That used to frustrate me.... I was being a bit cheeky to the punk rockers about their anarchy symbols, and ended up in hospital. I don't remember a hell of a lot about it... got my face stomped on, basically....

> I used to get frustrated with it because it was so full of shit. That whole thing about open-mindedness and individuality and everything was just words.... A lot of people ... they weren't into it as some kind of rejection of society or anything like that, it was just rock 'n' roll. There was no undercurrent for them.

Of forming Box of Fish, Quarry says, "I don't think there was any conscious decision to make it anything separate from that [punk], but it became evident." Releases followed, with 1983's *Erosion* seven-inch and 1985's *Slap Em Round the Gills* LP. Tentative interest came from Virgin and Festival Records.

Despite their distinctiveness from the static UK82 style, Box of Fish's musical connection to punk ensured its own limitations. Quarry speaks of the predicament: "Outside a few small inner-city venues, all the other ones were agency-run.... When you're playing that style, you're just stuck there, because they're not going to put you on anywhere else because you don't fit the bill." Singer Andrew Johnson, giving assessment in 1985, said, "Our music's never going to be accepted by the mass, we'll always be kept at that level, we'll never be able to break out."[21]

The band broke up the same year.

Two bands both concurrent and connected to Box of Fish blended darker and post-punk sounds with anarcho-punk. The singer of Dusk Furrow, Andy Jarvis, later joined Quarry in Toys Went Berserk, while Quarry also spent time performing with the also puzzlingly titled Be Kind to Beavers.

Newly arrived from England, the Beavers' bassist, Kol Dimond, had attended a legendary Midnight Oil gig at the Stagedoor Tavern in April 1980. The venue's last show, it was advertised as "Midnight Oil Destroy the Stagedoor." Grossly overpacked, and with hundreds left outside, Dimond describes what eventuated: "There was a major riot.... I thought it was the best thing to happen. The cops were chasing us all around Railway Square and down George Street."

Despite the excitement, Dimond explains, "I came out a punk rocker, and wondered what the fuck was going on or why I'd done it, because it seemed like a dead end.... I wasn't expecting it to be that much behind the times, but it was quite backward when I came out."

In spite of finally locating a community in Sydney, Dimond professes, "I was just chomping at the bit to get home again, thinking it was still going to be like it was when I left," but "it was fucking all over pretty much in England."

Reenergised by anarcho-punk, Dimond says, "My whole thing was the Crass scene.... I went to live with Crass.... At that time, you either went with the leather, studs, and mohawks, or there was a massive scene to keep punk individual and alternative, and to not become a format and a costume." While describing the UK82 groups as "all really good early English bands," Dimond observes:

> They were fully into the studs and leather jackets and shock value and glue bags and cider. That was about the only thing for a while, and then the whole CND [Campaign for Nuclear Disarmament] campaigns were where we all started hanging out.... That all led up to 1984 ... and the miners' strike in England, and that was the peak of anarcho-punk in the UK.... That started politicising the left wing again, and out of that the anarcho-punk scene went one step further and started pushing nonhierarchical and consensual community-based living and mutual aid—the policies of anarchism—and the bookshops opened up, and the squats. So, people went the other way; it wasn't so much about how you looked, it was about what you were doing.

Back in Sydney, punks organised a "Stop the City" protest on Hiroshima Day in 1985, influenced by similar demonstrations in London. Audio samples of the event opened the Beavers' *Wide-Eyed with Alarm* tape.

To Dimond, anarcho-punk represented the division between bands promoting a message and those animated primarily by the music: "There was a whole different crew in Sydney then. There was the anarcho-punk scene, which was quite obviously politicised, and then there was the Hard-Ons/Massappeal guitar heads who weren't really politicised, but they were part of the punk scene. It sort of veered off a bit, and we got more into the punk stuff and the politics. Everything we did was benefits and trying to raise money, squatting places, and all that sort of stuff."

With a principal love of professional wrestling and high-energy music, Psychotic Turnbuckles seemed to encompass Dimond's categorisation of apolitical guitar heads. To them, however, their struggle was no less real in seeking to redress what they viewed as the lifeless state of Sydney's music scene. Directly addressing the title of their first album, 1986's *Destroy Dull City*, Steve Lorkin describes the band's perception of "no exciting, explosive rock 'n' roll going.... I just wanted to kick people up the arse and just go crazy, turn your guitar up to ten and just play some garage punk."

Replete with customary yellow and green wigs and wrestling spandex, the band's theatrics trumped even the most stridently clichéd punk performers. Conducting interviews while impeccably remaining in character, the Turnbuckles cultivated a mythology of their origins in the fictitious Pismo Beach, California, and having been forced to emigrate after their banning from the Pismo Beach Wrestling Alliance.

Not all were enamoured by their ostentation. Lorkin remembers that "rock music writers in the papers back then were very serious and articulate, and for someone to come along with purple hair, screaming about ... it was not very credible.... You'd rarely see interviews anywhere or anything written about them."

Consigned to being a jocular aberration by journalists, Lorkin counters with the band's ability to enrapture crowds: "The fans loved the Psychotic Turnbuckles. They did very well live.... It was just nuts onstage.... People in the crowd would start wrestling with each other. You'd see full-on wrestling matches in the crowd."

Among the band, says Lorkin, "Everyone was just wrestling-nuts.... We were on tour once and *Wrestlemania* was on TV.... We wouldn't leave the hotel room to go down and play until the wrestling had finished."

A wistful Lorkin reflects on a time when "there were tons of gigs, pubs everywhere. You didn't really think it was a special time, you thought, 'This is how it should be.' You can go out on a Wednesday night and do a gig and there's four hundred people there.... There was no distractions; you'd just go and see a band for something to do."

A band that translated beyond just the inner city, Lorkin says the "Turnbuckles did hundreds and hundreds of gigs all through the suburbs." One of the city's most popular independent acts, the group could "get anything from a couple of hundred to about eight hundred, nine hundred, a thousand people.... Getting that sort of crowd now," observes Lorkin, "we'd be getting a record contract with some major label."

• • •

A Yugoslavian, a South Korean, and a Sri Lankan walking into a bar sounds like the premise for a dubious 1980s punchline. Instead, it would be the routine for one of Australia's most successful independent bands of the decade, the Hard-Ons. A crudely named trio from the multicultural confines of Western Sydney, in their initial incarnation they toured twenty-three countries, boasted seventeen consecutive number ones on the local independent/alternative charts, and sold a quarter of a million records worldwide.[22]

Arriving to Australia at age nine, bassist Ray Ahn had been directed towards musical tuition: "My parents . . . put me in the Bankstown Police Boys Club Band. I played the trumpet . . . played in a marching band, did ANZAC parades, did solo recitals which I won medals for."[23] But if brass was to be his initiation, Ahn soon succumbed to the corruptibility of rock, even if the volume was initially too overwhelming for him as a kid: his first concert being a free AC/DC show in a Punchbowl park, Ahn admits, "We only stayed for like two songs. It was so ridiculously loud. I remember all the kids had their fingers in their ears. . . . It was too much for a ten-year-old."[24]

Friends since primary school, Blackie (guitar) and Keish (drums and vocals) had begun jamming as teens, with Ahn admitting, "I was kind of envious." He successfully hassled his parents for a bass, but the band had already filled the position with a "popular guy with flowing blond hair" who was a "super-talented sportsperson and a pretty smooth bass player."[25] Their first show, playing under the name the Dead Rats, took place in a suburban scout hall and was broken up by police.

As the "smooth" bass player departed—along with his sandals and leather bandanna—Ray was provided his opportunity. Together for two weeks, the trio played their first gig at Keish's uncle's birthday party; Ahn described the scene as "forty Sri Lankan people there—they loved it."[26]

Over the next two years, the band perfected their blending of a Ramones template with varying levels of pop and metal, appearing at "high school dances, birthday parties, church halls, scout halls, people's backyards."[27]

With Blackie the last to reach legal drinking age, the Hard-Ons played their first pub gig in 1984. Peter Zounis was there from the outset: "I bumped into Ray, and he was putting flyers around town, 'Return of the Legendary Hard-Ons from the USA,' and the place was fucking packed. We thought it was a great laugh."

The group was already well-honed, and Ahn admits that "we had absolutely no qualms about getting up there and thinking we were going to be better than anyone else."[28] The response reflected their self-belief. But then, says Ahn, came the reaction: "It was good for the first couple of months, then people started hearing about us and talking about us, then the fascists started to turn up, and it was pretty unpleasant at times." The unpleasantness was to encompass "beercans, bottles—full and empty—spitting, death threats, racist jives, jumping on our cars, etc., etc.," as well as crowd calls of "Channel 0 [multicultural TV station]" and "United Nations."[29]

The Hard-Ons' slogan, "Young, Loud and Multicultural," was bold in a decade of immigration debate, a time when future prime minister John Howard criticised multiculturalism and questioned levels of Asian migration. Ahn later told the ABC of their means to counter the hostility: "We came up with plans to combat booing and racism and stuff. One was to play as hard as we can ... so there would be no chance we could ever get blown off the stage by another band or give anyone the chance to yell at us. Play as loud as possible, play as fast as possible, and, if possible, not have gaps between the songs."[30]

As gallant as their efforts may have been, it failed to immune them, Ahn remembering, "We were getting death threats and stuff, so we made handbills that said 'No Racists' and 'No Fascists.' It got to the stage where it wasn't fun anymore.... In a way it was almost like [racists] were an accepted part of the punk scene.... People who would wear mohawks and the studded belts, they tended to be the more fascist and racist. I would feel more comfortable going to a hard rock gig in the suburbs than a punk gig."[31]

One of the band's most confronting shows was the sieging of their venue in Ravensburg, Germany, by neo-Nazis. Likely agitated by their tour poster—a cartoon drawing of the band in Ku Klux Klan uniforms accompanied with "White People Suck"—something akin to a riot ensued, with the band barricaded inside the building.

Early in 1985, the group recorded their *Surfin' on My Face* seven-inch, at the time one of the biggest-selling independent records ever in Australia. Their *Smell My Finger* twelve-inch, the best-selling alternative EP of 1987, solidified their place as Australia's foremost punk band. Its cover featured Ahn's drawing of an elderly woman removing her finger from a snot-filled nostril, as popularity failed to prevent criticism of the

Hard-Ons as puerile. A defensive Ahn told the *Sydney Morning Herald* in 1992, "I mean, we're called the Hard-Ons. We're three moronic dudes from the suburbs. What do you expect our lyrics to be?"[32]

The cover for their *Hot for Your Love, Baby* LP in 1987 contained a photo of the three band members lying on the sand as a former *Playboy* Playmate of the Year glided by. Russell Hopkinson remembers the parley the band was then producing: "There was so much discussion on the Melbourne scene of 'Can you really like the Hard-Ons? They tick all the racial boxes, but are sexist.' My thing was: you go to a Hard-Ons gig and it was the first time I'd seen girls dance at a punk show.... It's not as macho and hardcore."

Alongside the perceived sexism, the band also continued to have to defend their name, as if much coherent could be made of the mind of fifteen-year-olds, aside from awkward lust.

Forced to play as the Hard O's when having trouble with venues, at a show in northern Queensland they were simply billed as "Band." Ahn offers some context: "I mean, calling the band 'The Hard Ons' ... we're not a macho band.... We're puny migrant kids into punk. We're just making fun of it, rather than being it."[33]

A reflective Ahn recognises that "there were a million things we did or said that we would not partake in now, but nobody is perfect. Once we found out how easily people got upset, we kind of just ran amok." Interviewed in 1986, he had said, "We never saw music as a medium to put across any messages. We saw it as an end in itself."[34]

Regardless of any feigning of simplemindedness, Jay Whalley believes that "they were sort of political by default, just by being a multicultural, long-haired punk band touring the world." Despite not being a band with a deliberate message, Ahn did later acknowledge that the group achieved more than just filling people's record collections with their sizeable discography: "I think we opened a lot of eyes and broke down a lot of stereotypes."[35]

Contrary to the gripes of detractors, the band continued to release popular records and draw huge audiences, and they became one of the most important independent acts in the country. But devotion to the Hard-Ons was not simply confined to the island continent. In addition to their swathes of international followers, which justified five European tours, a character on a national German soap opera wore a Hard-Ons T-shirt on the program.

Supporting Soundgarden in the US and Red Hot Chili Peppers in Australia, the Hard-Ons came to inhabit a space between underground and mainstream. On being given a glance into the sordid tent that was the major music industry, Ahn's recollection is, "We understood it for the horseshit that it was, but we never said no to high-paying, high-profile gigs just because they were mainstream. It is incredible fun rubbing shoulders with industry cokeheads for a while."

Wary of repetition in their recorded output, the band diverged with its *Too Far Gone* album in 1993. Both fans and their label were not as enthused or appreciative of its experimentation. The response was compounded by pressures associated with being reliant on the industry for an income, and Ahn says, "We found playing in a band more like a job, so we stopped doing it.... The music industry is run by arseholes, not fans of music, and we didn't have any more energy,"[36] and, "It just wasn't as fun as when I was a young kid."[37]

The Hard-Ons attracted hundreds, and sold by the thousands, through a distinct and Australian take on punk which also dispensed with attentiveness to fashion. As the 1980s progressed, punk's flamboyancy of leather, studs, and charged hair would be jettisoned in place of US hardcore's suburban humility of jeans, sneakers, and flannelette. *Rise Above* zine reported that "flannelette fibrosis seems to be the latest Sydney punk fashion disease ... more economic than a leather jacket at least ... also seems most punks these days don't bother about haircuts."[38]

Massappeal, the band that most exemplified the US influence in Sydney, had also developed a relationship with the Hard-Ons. Vocalist Randy Reimann says that the affinity came through musical devotion and a deprioritising of the trivialities of cool, cliques, and cachet: "I can relate to the Hard-Ons a lot, and it was at a Hard-Ons gig that Massappeal formed.... They were kids from the 'burbs too that got into it because they loved those records.... So, when you had the opportunity to make it yourself, it wasn't that you were doing it for some fucking lifestyle."

Reimann's memory is that "I was really into skateboarding and living out in the western suburbs.... I had no idea what was redundant or what was fresh, I was just this kid." Unpersuaded by earlier UK punk, Reimann says that US hardcore "just made total sense to me ... this really high-energy music."

While Reimann tentatively broached the inner-city venues, punk elitism was again to rear itself, with him as its sometimes target: "It could have been my first gig at the Trade Union Club and . . . this guy was coming down the stairs and I recognised him from Fairfield and I was just excited to see somebody else from Fairfield, and I said, 'Hey, you're from Fairfield.' He just spat on me and threw me down the stairs."

An extra-vigilant Reimann says, "I felt I always had to watch out. My firsthand experience was there were violent skinheads and punks and none of them really liked us. . . . Whatever gig I was at, I was one of their targets."

Attending one of Permanent Damage's Sydney shows, luck, or at least a rare show of strength, spared Reimann: "On the dance floor the skinheads just went for me, and grabbed me and were just going to pull me into the pit and beat the shit out of me. So, two skinheads had my hands, and my brother and Kevin [McClear, bassist] had my feet, and they were doing a tug-of-war . . . and my brother and Kevin won, they got me, and we escaped."

Deliberately distancing themselves from the UK-inspired scene, Massappeal "was a deliberate backlash against what was going on," guitarist Brett Curotta says, "the destruction and the violence and the drugs. The whole stupid English influence that was there at the time."[39] Conversely, they sought to promote "just positive attitudes. Being sensible. Because there was so much stupidity here it was ridiculous. It was so negative and staid."[40]

For all they endured in harassment, on releasing the *Nobody Likes a Thinker* album in 1986, it immediately became a minor phenomenon. While unobservant of how many records were being sold, the accompanying T-shirt was harder for Reimann to ignore: "I was working in the city at the time . . . 'Oh look, it's another one of our T-shirts, isn't that weird?' . . . It was funny seeing people like the guy from Metallica [James Hetfield] wearing them."

With three years between this and their follow-up album, *Jazz*, the band lost some of its momentum. Members of the group had also moved on stylistically, Reimann remembering, "I'd discovered industrial music, and so had Brett." This new influence was partially reflected in their sound, and Reimann admits, "It wasn't as popular [*laughs*]. . . . We had to stay loyal to people's expectations of what hardcore was, and I found it hilarious."

The band lasted until 1994. Reimann says that from the height of playing overflowing venues, "The last tour we did of Melbourne was so horrendous.... Sixty people or something, and they're yelling out, 'Play fucking Nirvana!' ... All of a sudden this grunge thing happens and all these surf kids who wouldn't have heard of Black Flag or Negazione or *Raw Power* or anything like that think they're cool as shit because they know Nirvana.... I remember going into the carpark, it was still daylight, and sitting by the van and weeping.... It ended with gigs like that.... That was my favourite period, musically, but it was the least popular."

Massappeal's prior popularity was to be exceeded by that of Reimann's own stepson, Jake. Massappeal was asked to re-form in support of Henry Rollins in 2003, and thirteen-year-old Jake accompanied Reimann to the show. He established his own metal/hardcore band, In Hearts Wake, and their *Skydancer* album peaked at number two on Australia's mainstream chart in 2015.

The year following Massappeal's re-formation, and in recognition that the "passion to make music is relentless," Reimann helped form Tralala Blip, a group composed of differently abled members. Reimann says, "I was doing support work for people with intellectual disabilities, something I started back in Massappeal.... There was these people doing music programs ... and it was so bad it was insulting.... Sitting around singing other people's songs, everybody was bored. But a light bulb went off in my head of what was possible. I was way into electronic stuff by then ... so I came home and started devising a way that would allow people who didn't have any background in music and the ability to do conventional type of music a way of making original music."

Decades earlier, Reimann had given assistance to Sydney label Waterfront when asked to compile a hardcore compilation album. Released in 1989, the *Thankyou Charles* LP featured Lethal Overdose, Under the Influence, and SSDC, who had all yet to make appearance on vinyl, as well as Fester Fanatics (*What Choice Do We Have?* LP, 1988).

Other Sydney hardcore bands in the second half of the 1980s were not as fortunate to be captured on record. Consigned to tape releases or remaining undocumented, such groups include Stigmata Party, Nuclear Disgrace, Skate Demons of Hell, Drokk, Death Mission, and Terrible Virtue.

A band who was to share history—and frustrations—with Massappeal was My Heart Bleeds for You (*Stressout* twelve-inch, 1988). The band's guitarist, Jamie Fonti, offers similar sentiment to Reimann, that "it seemed like there was this new code we all had to adhere to.... People who didn't even write music or play in bands tried to dictate what you should play. I was already moving in new directions.... The last My Heart Bleeds for You songs," he says, "had raps going on in them."

After breaking up the band, Jamie took on the role of Massappeal's live mixer as his brother Sean joined on bass. Citing a particularly fond memory of his time with the group, Jamie unmasks Henry Rollins's mystique with the image of "him dancing around to Prince's 'Kiss' backstage."

Given people's broadened tastes of hip-hop and the Artist Formerly Known as Prince, it was foreseeable that the Fontis had already been collaborating on a project far removed from punk and hardcore. Culminating in "techno-grunge" act Caligula, Jamie recalls, "Pretty much everybody in Caligula were ex–hardcore band members. There were loads of other bands that all moved on, and we were among old friends.... Friends of the hardcore bands like the Hummingbirds and Ratcat were getting signed to majors, and while we didn't have our eye on that target... it just sort of happened."

Ratcat was a band that was to triumph at the top of the mainstream chart, with Bruce Griffiths revealing that they "very much came out of the Sydney punk scene." Singer/guitarist Simon Day had been part of a contingent of North Shore punks, founding member Victor Levi came from Decontrol, and second drummer Andrew had previously played in Bedspreads.

With the eventual cessation of Caligula, Sean Fonti joined Def FX, another popular Sydney electro-alternative act. The group's singer, Fiona Horne, also had a history rooted in punk as vocalist and guitarist for the Mothers.

A vexatious youth and home life had been reason for Horne being so receptive to punk's often troubled underpinnings: "Authority figures were cruel, friends were cruel, life was cruel—that's just what life felt like.... I left home very young—at fifteen—and hung out with people who also felt rejected and angry at the world.... We were all looking for an identity. The Dead Kennedys ... was the first tangible experience I had of punk with a political message.... I remember pissing Jello Biafra off because I kept grabbing his microphone cord and swinging it around while he was trying to sing. I was a little dork getting carried away, but I was starting to learn."

That education, though, was at variance to the environment she was surrounded by: "I was hanging around with a bunch of skinheads.... They would go down to Central Station with nunchucks and beat random people up—seriously. They snorted and hit up a lot of speed and hated heroin. They also raped girls. I dated one of the guys briefly, and one day he told me to go downstairs and get rid of the girl they had all just gang-raped. I was so insanely naive, and I'm so lucky I wasn't gang-raped too. Blitz's 'Someone's Gonna Die Tonight' was always on the turntable."

Escaping the grim scene, she says, "I could barely play guitar, but I wrote what I could and played until my fingers bled—literally." A compendious Horne reflects, "I was an insecure teenage girl, so I don't remember much except trying to be cool, screaming my head off, and trying to play a good lead break."

Any associated pain was vindicated as the Mothers released their *Drives Me Wild* seven-inch on Waterfront in 1987. Horne remembers the process as "so fun.... There was an immediacy of passion, everything was just, 'Yes, let's go!' ... It was a fuckin' awesome time." Such fervour was reflected in its reception, as the record reached number four on the independent charts. A tour with visiting UK hardcore band the Stupids took place the same year, while a twelve-inch, titled *12 Incher*, followed in 1988.

Not content with just some minor local recognition, Horne says, "Now I've been on the planet more than half a century I can say I want to live life to the fullest." Included in wringing all that's possible from her life has been everything from becoming a commercial pilot to having an affair with Tom Jones to being part of a world-record skydive formation. Foremost, however, Horne developed her national public profile as "the face of modern Witchcraft," publishing a dozen books on the subject.[41]

An older, meditative Horne returns to what punk was to offer a disturbed teen lusting for answers and acceptance, as well as its continued influence: "Back then I just wanted to get away from my suburban hell upbringing, and I wanted to be something different to what I thought I was, which was a piece of shit. That's what I'd been brought up to believe. Punk and the street culture of the time gave me a path of escape, a path to explore and try to work out what the hell I was. I was so impressionable and trusting, but I was drawn to rebellion, not conformity. This attitude still resonates in me."

Commenting on the bands and scene associated with Waterfront, Horne says, "I don't think we realised just how blessed we were to be a part of that scene.... It was definitely an incredible wave to be a part of." Spunk Bubbles were another of the label's artists with whom the Mothers shared stages; guitarist Peter Zounis says, "Waterfront itself was a big thing in the scene at the time."

Yet even if its significance was undeniable, some were not as enthused by the label's band signings. Zounis says:

> You used to bump into guys like Rob Younger in Waterfront Records.... He was always in there bitching to the guys that they were putting our records out.... It was kind of disappointing, because here was this guy who I thought was a hero and anti-establishment, and he's bitching because we're swearing and putting rude things on our record covers.... That's what makes the Australian stuff good—for want of a better word, that Aussie "larrikin" comes out in them: irreverent. Because punk quickly became another cliché; it really did become a uniform and a set of guidelines. I think for a lot of us ... that wasn't what we were into it for. We got into it because it was supposed to be about tearing down walls and doing what you want.

That irreverence, coupled with their non-Anglo backgrounds, saw Spunk Bubbles release their sole album, *Speak Lebanese or Die*, in 1987. Zounis, explaining its title to have been "an in-joke," admits, "I often look at it and laugh and think, 'Jesus Christ, imagine releasing that now.'"

As well as being an exercise in unfettered free speech, Zounis points out that "there was a bit of a problem too at the time with racism.... I don't look that Greek, but Graham looked like a Leb. He had long, curly black hair, black face hair, he'd always play without his shirt, he looks like an Arab [*laughs*]. And I remember one gig we did ... the first song ... he came out of the toilets dressed as Jesus carrying a big crucifix. The skinheads went nuts, spitting all over him. That night I thought we were going to get killed."

Not that the enmity was confined to skinheads: "We had to fight our way out of the Royal Hotel ... one night because we wouldn't play

Joe Cocker. It was literally like a *Blues Brothers* scene. Me and Dean had the mic stands and guitars and were whacking people off while the other guys were bringing the car around."

Another who was anxious to beat a hasty exit was the engineer of their 1986 seven-inch, *Metal Wench*, Zounis believing, "I don't think he could wait to get out of there. He said, 'I've never seen a band like it, I don't know how they're functioning.' … Even the tours, when we came down to Melbourne and Adelaide, they were like a lawless wagon ride to the Wild West." After inquiry into how many exasperated managers the band went through, Zounis says, "I think four in two years."

Owing to their anarchic tendencies, Zounis says, "I think we basically ended up with two venues in Sydney that we weren't banned from." But then, what did one expect when dealing with a group whose members included pseudonyms such as Ug the Caveman, Arty Bumfart, Bosom, and V.D. Brothel Brain?

Most contentious for the band, however, had been their track "Suck Me Off and Gargle It," in spite of Zounis's admission that "I really didn't expect that reaction from it."

Contextualising, Zounis says, "We were being kids. … I was sixteen when the first single came out. … We just didn't take much of it very seriously. … You just didn't see it at the time that you had an audience. … It was wild days, but I've got to say we didn't do anything to hurt anybody. But we were pretty crazy. … We burnt and went out with a bang very quickly."

Other people, believes Zounis, didn't know when to make an honourable exit:

> Recently I bumped into a bunch of the old crowd at a gig I went to and I thought, "They're like the walking dead; like zombies, their brains are gone. I'm glad I got out of that." … I think for whatever reason, a lot of them didn't make that next step in life, they just got stuck there. … I always thought you've got to progress. … I don't just want to go play to a pub of ten or twenty people who are old punk rockers asking them to "Suck me off and gargle it." I enjoyed it, I had a great time, but I'm not into nostalgia too.

Despite his suspicion of sentimentality, Zounis gives the opinion that "I don't think there's been a scene like that since. … Selinas fits, I think, two thousand; we played that a couple of times with the Hard-Ons and Massappeal and filled that up.... We just didn't realise back then in the '80s what we had."

Ben Brown, however, of the band Hellmenn, fellow signees of Waterfront, cautions against revisionism: "I think people look back now and glorify it a bit." Yet Brown makes it hard to resist doing so when recalling that "we got seven hundred people" at the launch for their first album, a figure that in the new millennium is usually reserved for international touring acts.

Brown was one among a cadre of punk surfers on Sydney's North Shore, which also included Barton Lynch, a world champion and elite figure of the sport. Brown explains, "I was good friends with Barton, we went to school together. He was a real punk for a while, probably before us guys." Fellow former pro surfer Matt Branson says of Lynch, "I went to his house one time, and he showed me his record collection, and it was Crass and all this brilliant punk rock stuff, and I was blown away—never took him as a punk rocker." Alan Creed offers another well-known name to their contingent: "We used to hang out with [women's world-champion surfer] Pam Burridge in those days.... She was hanging out with us, partying with us."

More noted for his band Hellmenn than as a surfer, Brown says, "You'd always get a core of surfers that showed up that just liked high-energy sort of music.... They were pretty mad, a lot of drunks, and probably too much fighting."

Hellmenn formed out of earlier band Fourth Degree, and Brown says, "We never had a real idea about the sort of music we wanted to play. It all evolved." Release of their *Herbal Lunacy* LP in 1987 saw Hellmenn following the Birdman/Detroit sound and heavy rock popular among surfers, executed with hardcore's power.

Brown's observation, though, is that "there were a lot of bands like that." One of the most emblematic and impressive exponents were fellow Waterfront group the Splatterheads, whose *Filthy Mile* twelve-inch and *Ink of a Mad Man's Pen* LP shortly followed Hellmenn's releases.

Feeling the "Waterfront sound" to have "run its course a bit," Hellmenn made a divergence through their following releases, which included a brief dalliance with a major label. Asked about the main change that accompanied such a signing, Brown forgoes any accounts of high-priced drugs and celebrity: "We flew rather than driving.... We always at the time felt lucky.... You realised you were on a good wicket."

However, Brown gained greater renown as a visual artist. Beginning with iconic artwork for local bands, he says that without punk, "I reckon I would have done art, but I wouldn't have had the springboard to get enough of a name." In the proceeding decades, his profile has allowed for the producing of posters for Nirvana, Silverchair, Pearl Jam, Blink-182, Hoodoo Gurus, Sonic Youth, Mudhoney, and Frenzal Rhomb, in addition to his work for Mambo, Hurley, Volcom, and Rip Curl.

Avoiding any desire to mourn the passing of his loud music and party days, a contented Brown now says, "I had my dash, it was good fun. I just like hanging at home and drawing."

Vultees guitarist Craig Sinclair is another to sentimentalise the mid to late '80s era. Describing the years 1986–87 as when "the Sydney scene was at its peak," he contrasts it to only a few years previous, "when the scene was at its worst—heaps of violence. I was very young then and just got really disillusioned. It was like they'd sing about one thing and listen to records saying one thing and do the complete opposite.... That's why I left those circles."[42]

Previous to Vultees, bandmate Scott Deegan had also begun in the darker period of which Sinclair speaks before becoming similarly dissatisfied. The source of Deegan's disaffection had been the witnessing of punk's realpolitik of violence:

> This skinhead ripped a fire extinguisher off the wall and was going around threatening to bash people's heads in with it.... I was fifteen or sixteen and totally middle-class and innocent.... That scared the bejesus out of me.... I played in a punk band [named AIDS] and wrote for a zine and dressed mainly in black, but I was too young and well-behaved to be involved with those who would call themselves the Sydney punks.... I wasn't particularly into pissing people off—the nihilism side of punk.... I was drawn to the leftist politics of the Clash, and then Crass. It was all such a revelation to a kid, though I had an incredibly naive view of the world. That interest in politics has never faded.

Deegan, who became an English teacher in his mid-thirties, reveals the endurance of punk's politics not only within himself but as a pedagogical tool: "I do include Discharge's *Realities of War* in a presentation I give about antiwar literature. That makes the buggers wake up.... There's a Clash poster on my classroom's back wall, a gift from a student. There are kids who think what I did musically is very cool, and others who don't give a shit. A lot of them find 'Heaven' [Vultees' *Heaven/Breaks My Heart* seven-inch, 1986] on YouTube and play it to try and distract me when I'm teaching."

Beyond just inquisitive or disruptive teens, inadvertent recognition for Vultees came in the early 2000s, as cult Norwegian rock band Turbonegro covered "Kick It Out" and included it as a bonus track on the reissue of their *Never Is Forever* album as well as on their *Small Feces* compilation.

The band's greatest indirect fame, however, arrived some three decades following their breakup, with the appearance of drummer Nasser Sultan on reality TV series *Married at First Sight*. A *Daily Mail* headline proclaimed, "'I've Slept with over 1,000 Women!' MAFS Star, Nasser Sultan Reveals His Enormous Number of Sexual Partners."[43] The station's publicity, touting him as "50 going on 30," also featured photos of Sultan from his playing days, including with Vultees. But "after life of being on the road in the music industry," it continued, "Nasser is hoping to finally settle down."

## CANBERRA

While punk reinvigorated protest in music, its looseness of definition allowed for customisation into often disparate factions or scenes. In engaging politics, punk's remonstration could therefore come down on either side of the ideological divide, from Crass's experiment in the living commune and anarchist collective to Skrewdriver's boots-on-the-street neo-Nazism.

Intriguingly, for the most socially progressive state or territory in the country, Canberra punk in the 1980s came to be populated by a sizeable segment who tended towards expressing political reaction, and even racial intolerance. George Howson, present for Canberra's first wave, explains the tensions that stirred early: "There was a lot of hostility initially between the skinheads and punks.... I got out of Canberra at the end of '80 ... came back for a few months at the end of '81. I guess there was a certain sense that the scene had changed; it had got a bit meaner and nastier."

With his late '70s band Capital Punishment re-forming as the Slammers in the 1980s, Trog also witnessed the shift in interpretation: "The music which was labelled as punk had changed into something horrible. In Australia we were trying to copy the English Oi! bands and sing about blood in the streets, and we seemed to take pride in talking dumb."

Whatever the opinion of Trog's criticism, indisputable was the music's ability to consolidate substantial numbers. David Mahl of Urban Chaos gives a rough quantitative measurement that "there must have been a couple of hundred—at least a couple of hundred. That was more the punks, and if you added the skins and all the followers of theirs, there was another couple of hundred, I suppose."

From the same northwestern suburb as Mahl, Dave "Spasm" notes the area as having been a fountainhead for the city's punks and skinheads: "I went to Belconnen High, which was pretty much the punk high school of Canberra. . . . At lunchtime . . . there was a band, Third Detail, that would play in the hall. . . . I would say there would have been twenty punks and about fifty skinheads . . . ranging Year 7 to Year 10."

Much of the hostility that Howson identified had seemingly dissipated, as Mahl, himself a punk, reminisces that "the punks and the Oi!'s, we all got along really well." But while those within Canberra itself were fraternal, the arrival of outsiders did not always bring an exhibition of universal love. Describing the event as "fairly legendary," Chip Wardale recalls the excursion "where the whole [Sydney] punk scene moved to Canberra for a weekend" to attend "Canberra Must Burn" in 1982: "It ended badly. Lots of fights." Another of those present, Mahl, says, "I'll never forget the day: I was sitting at the Hotel Civic having a beer . . . and all these buses were pulling up and we were going, 'Okay, better get on the phone.' They were mad, those boys; they were up to no good a lot of the time." In addition to the fights, the event's name took on extra appropriateness, as "there was fires lit up at a place called Ainsley Village. So, it got a little bit nasty."

With no one appearing to have learnt from the experience, relations between the cities soured again a few years later. Following a poorly attended show at Canberra University featuring some Sydney bands, an explicit threat was made via review of the gig in *Rise Above*: "For your own safety, never come up to Sydney, as you may well find that the only beds you'll crash out in will be in St Vinnie's hospital."[44]

• • •

It's a long, long way from the chest-beating, hurly-burly world of skinheads and Oi! to singing "I'm a Little Teapot" on a national children's television program, yet Rhys "Stinky" Muldoon, Car Killers vocalist in the early '80s, joined the *Play School* cast in 1999. Describing him as "a friend of mine," Mahl says, "He was hilarious in the early days." Revealing that Muldoon was tattooed with a graphic of classic UK Oi! band Blitz, Mahl says, "He got Blitz's *Voice of a Generation*, but they spelt 'Voice' wrong."

From the innocence of children's programming to the R rating of serious violence, Mahl says, "Back then you used to have to fight to survive, because a lot of people didn't like you.... We had a big mob around Canberra called the 'War Wogs,' and they used to try to single you out." At one particular show at the Stakeout with Club of Rome, "the War Wogs," says Mahl, "came with nunchucks and weapons.... I've been stabbed in the forehead; I've been bashed with star pickets."

But if incidents at their own shows were infrequent, as Mahl insists, some within Canberra had no aversion to disrupting a succession of touring bands.

As part of their 1983 tour, Dead Kennedys made an unwise detour to the capital. A segment of the crowd was particularly hostile, Dave Spasm remembers: "One of them [skinheads] flicked a cigarette butt and it hit him [Jello Biafra] square in the eye.... Then he [Jello] introduced them all to stage diving, and as soon as he stage dived, that was it, the boots went in. They were all standing around booting him.... Because it was Canberra, that's what they did."

Such behaviour highlighted the more objectionable side of the double entendre that was a local band named Skin Disorder, who had formed the same year.

Familiar with the public's health and safety, as well as punk, in 2014 the *Sydney Morning Herald* reported on centre-right Liberal Party member of Parliament Sussan Ley under the headline "From Punk Rocker to Health Minister." The article read, in part: "A high school student in Canberra in the 1970s, Ley walked around with no shoes, black lipstick, spiky purple hair, a dog collar, and a nose piercing connected to the razor blade in her ear. Over thirty years later, she still describes herself as a 'recovering punk rocker from a time when it really mattered.'"[45]

• • •

Another punk with a strong political connection, David Pope of 4 Minute Warning and 4 Thousand Million, attained position of political/editorial cartoonist for the *Canberra Times* in 2008. Yet where some of the scene stomped through Oi!, Pope's bands increased the pace as well as political content. All vegetarians, 4 Thousand Million told *Object-Dismembered* fanzine in 1985 of their anarchist-inspired beliefs: "We are anti-authoritarian; we believe in the capacity for people to run their own lives."[46]

When they performed at a community hall show with Deranged and Hell Yes in 1984, that capacity for self-management came into serious question. Dave Spasm relives the evening: "I've got a live tape of it.... You can hear people getting whacked with broomsticks and mops.... They [skinheads] were just cutting a swathe through people ... and they stole all the money off the door."

Spasm asserts that "I just never got involved.... What can you do? There's fifteen to twenty of them and they're all nutters.... You just had to put up with it. Most of them were friends—we went to school with each other—you'd sort of put your politics aside, it was just such a small place.... It wasn't like they were out to cause trouble at every gig, it was just some gigs something would snap in their head. Somebody would look at them the wrong way or somebody would be wearing an Aboriginal flag and they'd just nut off.... They wrecked a few good shows, that's for sure."

With two years having passed since the Dead Kennedys show, Anti-Nowhere League fared little better. Mahl remembers, "That was where they started doing the 'Out in the Wasteland' type stuff.... They came out dressed up in stupid top hats and tuxedo tops, and they got a bit of a pummelling that night. They still played, though, to their credit. I guess they'd seen worse."

In 1981, the drummer of local band Tidal Wave had covered his kit in swastikas, more as a (by now) predictable act of punk "transgression" than any expression of political identification. Yet for some of the new generation in Canberra there was no obfuscation of their political intent. In an interview with *Shit on Brisbane* in 1986, Massappeal chastised the city's scene that "allows bands like A.S.L. [Anti-Slopehead League] to survive."[47] That same year, Massappeal appeared on a bill with the Hard-Ons and SSDC under the heading "Thrash Against Racism." Undoubtedly encouraged by the sentiment, skinheads turned out in number, with the touring bands almost disbelieving of how many were assembled.

Dave Spasm estimates that of the Canberra skinheads, "90 percent of them" were drawn to political racism. Members of both Spasm and Mahl's own bands, Under Siege and Urban Chaos, were to eventually join White Lightning, the most known of Canberra's white nationalist bands.

The history of white power punk groups had been rather meagre, with the National Front in England having only two affiliated bands as part of their "Punk Front." It took a re-formed Skrewdriver and the release of their *White Power* seven-inch in 1983 to act as catalyst for a wave of followers. A movement coalesced as "Rock Against Communism" (RAC), acting as counterbalance to the left wing's (recently defunct) "Rock Against Racism."

White Lightning formed the year after the release of Skrewdriver's overtly political *Hail the New Dawn* album in 1984. Former member Simon gushed when reliving his memories of Canberra for Dutch neo-Nazi zine *Out of Order* in 2000: "All my mates were into oi! and white pride as well. I did not know any skinheads that were into oi! and were not white and proud of it. Lefty skinheads would never dare to show their face on the street for fear of getting severely beaten."[48]

Spasm is near disbelieving of his former bandmate Nigel Brown's eventual path: "It was really weird; his parents and his family were just really, really nice people, and then I don't know how you can change from being down the line to crossing the fence to be like that—hating gay people and hating Blacks and Asians."

A member of White Lightning, and previously Order of the Boot, Brown relocated to England in 1991, where he performed with some of the continent's most well-known white power bands. Arrested for inciting racial hatred while recording in Holland, he was deported in 1996.

Assembling Apparent Death in 1987, Spasm was still unable to be free of the skinheads' presence. When the band performed at the Boot and Flogger, he says, "All the boneheads came there and wanted to get in because none of them had any money." Devising a punitive entry fee, Spasm says, "It was upstairs, so we made them carry all our gear up."

Apparent Death made up one of a small grouping of late '80s hardcore bands, including Village Idiots, the eclectic Csabai Testicles, and

SSDC. The latter band's vocalist especially suffered from the skinheads' targeting, Spasm revealing that they "hated Simon because he used to be a skinhead, then he turned into this anarchist guy and started wearing Aboriginal flags and stuff, so they wanted to kill him." In interviews and the song "Honour and Obey," Simon also inadvertently attacked certain inherent precepts of the skinheads' culture, principally hypermasculinity.

Having already disrupted Japanese touring band the Star Club's Canberra show in 1986, skinhead antagonism reached a crescendo in late 1987, Simon being one of their main targets. With SSDC billed to support Massappeal and Texan thrash band DRI, flyers for the show contained a blunt message: "No Nazis." Like a red commie rag to a short-haired bull, some took up the challenge.

When opening the show, Spasm says Simon was making some political statements. "Then all the boneheads showed up and cans started flying.... And then Massappeal played and the cans started flying more, and then they sort of had a bit of a dig at them."

Massappeal's Randy Reimann later wrote, "By the time DRI hit the stage, the skins had moved down into the pit and were picking off dancers one by one."[49] Refocusing their attention to the stage, Spasm says, "One of them got up and pulled the Star of David earring out of the bass player's ear. Then he got hit over the head by the high-hat stand, and then it just erupted." Within the ensuing melee, Reimann recalled "someone swinging one of Tubby's cymbal stands around like a baseball bat and collecting more than one bald head."[50]

Mahl was not only one of those present, but, he says, "I was with the skins on that occasion." Describing the conflict as more than just a political objection, he asserts, "It was also a lot to do with drugs as well." Whatever the motive, he remembers, "That was a very hard fight.... You were throwing punches in every direction; you didn't know where to go. There was only about a half a dozen [of us], maybe a dozen at the most, but there wasn't many. It did turn really ugly.... We thought they were all peaceful people like Crass, but no, that wasn't the case."

By contrast, Spasm had unintentionally found himself caught up in the fracas: "I was standing at the front of the stage, and one of their [DRI's] road crew ... starts punching me in the head.... He goes, 'You fucking skinheads!' and I'm like, 'Dude, dude, I've got a studded leather jacket on,' and he goes 'Oh shit, sorry man.' Then the crowd turned on the boneheads, because there was only about ten of them. And then the cops came and dragged them all out and the show continued.... It was great."

Reimann offers some gruesome detail of what happened when the trouble abated: "Later I watched Tubby wipe/peel skin and blood from his drum stands."[51]

The episode would be the near finality of years of skinhead harassment, Spasm saying that "they all kind of disappeared after that. I think their dominance had been shot."

In agreement that there was a subsequent dwindling, Mahl identifies external reasons for the decline: "Everybody was starting to look at themselves, and sick of being broke, and everybody was getting jobs or careers or going to uni. Everybody was starting to have a bit of a change, so it did drop off a bit."

Reliving all the incidents, Mahl says:

> There's danger and there's *danger*. Like there were a few people who got shot in a few of the local areas, and we had a few problems with the bikers, but we earned a lot of respect because they knew that we were not going to back down. We were going to beat you.... I'm lucky to be alive. There's a few moments there I didn't think I was going to make it. I'm sure that goes along with most of the people there.... It certainly formed good character.... A lot of us grew up together, from fourteen years old to twenty-five to thirty years old, and you still see them these days. Hairstyles have changed a little bit, but the attitude and the morals are still there.... What a blast, those years.

A fear of skinheads, however, didn't recede with their waning—a residual anxiety remained for those able to remember. Arriving to the city, Doug Smith recalls the reaction his appearance was to cause:

> I moved to Canberra just after all those guys had started to kind of disappear.... I was a young, skinny kid, walking around in boots with a shaved head and stuff, and people would be getting out of my way as I walked down the street, and I'd be thinking, "God, this is weird, what's people's problem down here?" And then you start hearing the stories about this group of guys that

> absolutely dominated Canberra. They wouldn't queue for a drink, they would just go to the front of the bar and everyone would shit their pants and they would get served.... I would end up seeing a few of them around, and I saw them fight, and they were fearsome guys. And the stories weren't just from Canberra; when they would travel to other cities, they got a fearsome reputation as well. Guys went over to England and became Skrewdriver Security and stuff, which was the legendary badge of being the baddest dude over there.

Along with the reputation and legacy, some of the older skinheads, Smith diagnoses, "ended up basically with PTSD." Of a friend, says Smith, "the stuff he did during that period, he can't live with himself. He's got psychological problems because he was violent and committed acts of violence on innocent people in the name of what he thought he believed in at the time."

## WOLLONGONG

Attempting to identify a reason for the proliferation of Canberra's Oi! and skinhead scene, George Howson suggests "that atmosphere of being on the dole, of high youth unemployment. Particularly that late Fraser era where unemployment was, I think, nationally about 10 percent." Indeed, Oi!'s germination in England often centred on youth unemployment, but while Australia did not suffer jobless figures as drastic as the UK, Nick Southall asserts a correlative relationship of joblessness and punk in the setting of early 1980s Wollongong: "As youth unemployment grew, so did punk culture."[52]

As the barely concealed class war of Thatcher and Reagan played out overseas, 1980s Australia was a period of the entrepreneur and corporate largesse, of Christopher Skase and Alan Bond. At the opposite end of the income scale, and with the unemployment rate reaching into double figures, it was "normal" Australians now standing in queue with punks at the dole office. With the economy labouring, the Australian electorate turned to drinking in the form of Prime Minister Bob Hawke, a recognised world champion of yard-glass beer-sculling.

Yet unemployment and a harsher socioeconomic environment did not presuppose the manifestation of shaved heads and right-wing ideology. Southall says, "In Wollongong, punk's focus on cultural rebellion and individual autonomy mixed with the more overt political struggles that erupted during the early-'80s."[53] Central to that political engagement were the organisations YAPO (Young and Pissed Off) and its successor, WOW (Wollongong Out of Workers Union). Pushing back against the pillorying of the unemployed and their consignment to a mere reserve army of labour, Southall highlights the group's largely punk composition: "For many, WOW was seen as a group of punks. And while not everyone involved in the union was into punk, many of the more active members were."[54]

Conspicuously establishing premises in a squat opposite the Department of Social Security, WOW's space acted as both office and home to about twenty members.

After leading Wollongong's 1983 May Day march, WOW headed to Canberra to join a hunger strike in protest of the Hawke Labor government's first budget. Unappeased by the announcement of an increase in unemployment benefits by a paltry five dollars, "WOW members took their protest to the National Press Club, disrupting Treasurer Paul Keating's speech, in front of a national TV audience."[55]

Like WOW's ejection from the Press Club, Wollongong band Raw Power were accustomed to being removed from music venues. Securing work as a teen at BHP in nearby Port Kembla, Raw Power's Steve Abrahall was particularly attuned to the region's fortunes being dictated, in part, by the health of its steelworks.

Abrahall was born in England but migrated in his youth, and his cousin was Colin Abrahall, vocalist of UK punk legends GBH. But where GBH became central figures of the early '80s hardcore sound, Steve's Australian upbringing and proximity to Sydney saw his band come under sovereignty of Radio Birdman and Detroit.

By the time of Raw Power's breakup near the middle of the decade, UK punk's influence in the city was, like Sydney, much diminished. Though groups like Oi! band the Firm still existed, the second half of the decade, to varying degrees, saw punk used more in combination with garage, '60s punk, and proto-punk. Bands like the Stayns, Abrahall's the Mutated Noddys, and the Unheard took up residence at the Ironworkers Club as the studded leather jackets were outnumbered by paisley.

• • •

Regardless of the composing material of one's attire, Dave Curley's memory is that "as soon as you met anyone who was in a band that wasn't playing top forty, there was a sense of affiliation there, because we had a common enemy."

Like WOW, a further common target of Curley's was youth deprivation: "The first real job I ever had was working at a youth refuge—working with homeless kids, basically. So, therefore, I was tuned into WOW.... I met all those old punk guys. They knew me as a youth worker before a guy in a band."

One of six brothers who eventually became the near-dynastic family of Wollongong guitar music, Curley cites eldest brother Pat as deserving of "a lot of credit for the whole thing." Tutoring his younger siblings to play, Pat "one night in 1980 or 1981... brought home this record and said, 'Dave, listen to this, I think you will like it.' It was *Radios Appear*. It changed my life, without sounding like a wacko."

The three Curley brothers of Dave, Lenny, and Jay made up the majority of Proton Energy Pills' lineup. Bringing inspiration from another working-class city whose lifeblood was also revenue based around steel, Curley says, "We were much more Detroit." Through a curtain of long hair and guitar noise, the band infused the Stooges/MC5 sound with '70s punk, hard rock, traditional metal, and a hint of pop.

In contrast to Wollongong, where "we had to work really hard to get a gig anywhere," Curley says, "All of a sudden we were getting gigs quite easily [in Sydney].... We did seem to get accepted pretty well straight away."

Touring with the visiting Mudhoney in 1988, Curley notes the hype that was building around the early stirrings of grunge: "It was the next big, cool thing.... I didn't like it, to be honest; I didn't go for all that Seattle stuff.... The rock 'n' roll that I loved, that had an edge enough to be referred to as punk in some circles, kind of got lost in all that grunge stuff that was happening."

For the recording of their second single—"(Less than I) Spend," in 1990—Waterfront enlisted "godfather of grunge" J. Mascis of Dinosaur Jr. as producer. [56] Guitarist Stewart Cunningham reveals a personal lost opportunity from this visit: "J. Mascis went on to say how he dug my guitar playing, and that he knew a band back in America looking for a guitarist and that I'd be a perfect fit for them... [and that] he would call them up for me and arrange it if I was interested.... But I was twenty years old and . . . was having the time of my life and there was no way I could get my head round leaving my own band and mates that I loved to go and live in the USA. I hadn't even been on a plane before!"[57]

That band was Nirvana.

Cunningham would be left to rue the "what if?" as, following the release of a further twelve-inch, his own band broke up during the recording of their debut album. The remainder of the group became the initial members of alternative band Tumbleweed, forming in 1990.

The group played on marijuana imagery, and Dave says, "There's a very famous little sign on the highway heading towards [the Curleys' hometown] Tarrawanna, and Jay famously just put little lines on each side of the cross of the *T*: 'Marrawanna.'"

Though only "in Tumbleweed for basically six months," Curley says that contrary to any waft of weed, "I was straight-y one-eighty because of my job. And having worked with homeless kids, I didn't see the party side of drugs, I saw the death side of drugs. . . . I can totally understand how they would be over their big brother telling them not to drink."

Harbouring anxiety after his ousting from Tumbleweed, Curley says, "I don't talk about this much, but when I got kicked out of Tumbleweed, one of my biggest fears was, 'Well, who's going to look after Jay now?' Basically no one did."

With heavy music proving more than amenable to Australia's hard-drinking culture, Curley identifies the music industry as no less complicit: "From the age of sixteen, seventeen, you go to work and get given as much drugs and alcohol as you can handle. Then all of a sudden, when your band is not the flavour of the month anymore, we just dump you then leave you as an alcoholic. Basically, he [Jay] never recovered. It's disgraceful; in any other industry you'd have a duty of care."

Jay passed away in 2014.

## NEWCASTLE

Obvious are the comparisons that can be made between Wollongong and Newcastle at the beginning of the '80s: blue collar, beach locales, and dependencies on BHP steelmaking in providing jobs in cities with otherwise higher unemployment. But though Newcastle did not develop an overt and organised political project in likeness to WOW, it was able to foster a tolerant scene that could inoculate itself from the sometimes-quarrelsome divisions observable in Sydney. His brother having relocated to Newcastle for further study, Jamie Fonti says, "He discovered a scene up there that had mods, punks, rockabilly, skinheads, goths, and the gay scene all in one big melting pot, as it was a small place."

Highlighting the city's magnanimity, and a seeming imperviousness to trends, Newcastle's most notable band of the decade, the Porkers, hybridised punk with a genre that one could have been excused for believing was all but defunct: ska.

The band's vocalist, Pete Cooper, had futilely sought to form a band for two years, his abilities as a performer confined to his workplace, where he "became in charge of in-store promotions at Big W."[58] Adding insult, a very early incarnation of the Porkers practiced in an apartment downstairs from Cooper, who admits to becoming irate at their intrusion into the sanctity of his Sunday mornings.

They finally made their debut in 1987 as the Pork Hunts at a skinhead house-demolishing party, where sections of the dwelling were utilised as fuel for a bonfire. They were only intended to be a one-time party band, but favourable reception convinced them to continue. Drummer Donny Annecchini, though, was not as allured by their then-more-traditional ska sound, leaving the band after only the third show. A mainstay of Newcastle punk, Annecchini played through the decade in the Mansons, Ramones cover band the Marones, Cash from Chaos, and Raw War, alongside other local punk bands Dissection Committee and Fractured Black.

The band was sagely convinced by the booker of the only receptive venue in Newcastle to change their name; the Porkers was a pseudonym some members had used for inquisitive family members. Releasing their *Tired of Being Pork Hunts* seven-inch in 1990, the band not only exhibited a crass humour but would also reach number six on the Australian independent charts.

For every band accolade, there is indubitably an anecdote of struggle, misfortune, or malevolence. Appearing at their first Sydney show, Cooper ominously observes, "Basically it was skinheads.... So, Pete had a smart mouth, Pete dedicated 'Black Superman' about Muhammad Ali... to the white power guys up the back, which they didn't like." The band was only able to reach the song's chorus before the targeted skinheads invaded the stage. "I managed to roll off the side of the stage and ended up under the DJ table." In the ensuing melee, Cooper describes "girls fighting girls and then the bouncers were into it. It was just one of those movie scenes."[59]

Subsequently, Cooper says, "I was labelled a 'race traitor' by the white power movement, and it was really hard to play in Sydney for a few years."[60]

If Sydney was verboten, another continent was unspoilt territory; the band toured the US in 1992. There, a nascent ska scene saw bands like the Mighty Mighty Bosstones, Operation Ivy, No Doubt, Voodoo Glow Skulls, and Skankin' Pickle adding a more pronounced punk influence. An inspired Cooper was taken by "that mixture of punk and ska, and I kind of went, 'That's what we need to be doing.'"[61]

A rejuvenated sound culminated in the album *Grunt* in 1994, as well as further international tours to Japan and Europe. A "third wave" of ska that had begun in the late '80s impacted the mainstream charts from the mid through late '90s. Yet despite a stream of further records through the '90s and 2000s, the Porkers were unable to emulate that level of popularity. Though ska punk waned from its '90s peak, Cooper and the band have continued to play, unmoved by the fickleness of music audiences, remaining a cult Australian act.

# “NON REGULATION FUN”

## QUEENSLAND

### BRISBANE

Returning to the saga of Joh Bjekle-Petersen and the state’s political, juridical, and law enforcement climate, one of its effects had been to drain the punk scene not only of vitality, but also people, as many retreated to the southern states. Viewing the repressive environment firsthand, a somewhat worldly Jello Biafra wrote, “I felt safer walking around on the streets of East Berlin than I did in Brisbane.” It “was the closest thing to a heavy, heavy, junta-style police state I’ve ever been in.”[1]

The regime’s disdain for any form of alternative expression would be symbolised by two events in 1982: the demolition of music venue Cloudland under dubious circumstances and the conducting of the Commonwealth Games. With the games impending, Bjekle-Petersen declared a “state of emergency,” ensuring increased police powers and rendering protests illegal. (Fast-forward a few years, and exhibiting the sometimes redundancy of satire, Joh received an honorary doctorate of laws from the University of Queensland.)

In defiance of the government, large protests were held, highlighting the discriminatory impact on Indigenous people of the crackdown. The same year, the Clash enlisted Australian Indigenous reggae band No Fixed Address and activist Gary Foley as support during segments of their Australian tour. Active in the establishment of Canberra’s Aboriginal Tent Embassy in 1972, Foley made an appeal to the Clash’s audience to march in solidarity for Indigenous land rights.

Attuned to the state’s entrenched racial antagonism and discrimination, Biafra told a Brisbane audience, “We’re in Queensland, the Sunshine State. It’s just like Florida except there are more race riots.”[2]

Dead Kennedys' drummer and guitarist were arrested together outside their Brisbane show. Making the pages of the *Courier Mail*, guitarist East Bay Ray asserted that drummer D.H. Peligro had been detained owing to harassment for being Black. In an accompanying photo, Ray wore a shirt depicting the outline of Queensland with the words "The Police State" daubed across it.

Though not explicitly a punk band, the Parameters offered, with their 1983 track "Pig City," one of the strongest musical censures of Bjekle-Petersen's regime, and the song was taken up as an underground local anthem. The band's vocalist, "Fats," gave his summation of its lyrics: "The things I've talked about in the song are familiar enough to anyone who's lived here long enough and had anything to do with the political scene or the music scene, or looks or acts in any way 'different'—or even innocent bystanders.... Practically all my friends have been harassed more than once by the police on the streets, in their homes, coming out of dances.... It's part of the way of life here—there's a whole atmosphere of paranoia."[3]

Within the air of suspicion, Jello was unable to observe even a precarious local punk movement: "There is no real scene in Brisbane at the moment."[4] But, as if to offer stirring symbolism of punk's defiance, a decade following the Saints' Club 76, a punk sharehouse still stood on Petrie Terrace. A small cabal of bands also remained to brave the conditions. Active since the first wave of punk in Brisbane, Rod McLeod noticed the few shoots of a new germination: "Everything was getting so lame—rockabilly, for god's sake.... But then we started to notice some of the jokers that used to come and see us play ... were starting bands that had the same sort of energy and intensity we had: Mystery of Sixes, Public Execution. Again, just young suburban fans of punk music who thought they had something worthwhile to say."

Himself a restless suburbanite, Public Execution drummer Fred Noonan remembers a city then more than a million people that would be desolate after 10 p.m.: "The popular thing of a Saturday for the yobbos from the suburbs" was to "do laps in the city—drive around the block, looking at girls, and honking their horns and doing burnouts."

Harbouring hoon tendencies himself, Noonan confides, "Before I got my drum kit, my ambition was to be a mechanic and race cars ... then I got the drums and was 'screw cars' [*laughs*]."

Passing through an obligatory first band, Malicious Joy, Noonan says that when he moved on to Public Execution, they had "that more militant message.... The aggression of the American punk and that sort of harder edge is what we were looking at," an expression of undiluted anger rather than overwrought critique. Noonan quips, "Most of the punks didn't even go to school, couldn't spell 'punk,' where the Go-Betweens kind of crowd would talk about Nietzsche and fucking Warhol and Picasso."

While performing live, says Noonan, vocalist Terry was "not scared to challenge people with his lyrics or stage persona." Jello Biafra was less understated, declaring "Public Execution ... were probably the most maniacal of the Australian bands I saw. The singer was a genuine nut onstage, with a really demented look in his eye."[5] Insinuating that such performance was reflective of living circumstances, Noonan observes, "Things were volatile back then; just finances, trying to stay alive and stuff like that.... I was a pretty sedate and suburban boy during the week, just because I lived so far away from everything, but these guys were all living in squats and stuff like that—money, drugs."

Substance use was to be part subject of their *Methadone Slave/SS Brigade* seven-inch in 1982.

Unlike others who were to succumb to the lifestyle, Noonan says, "I always had the music and the long train ride home." Beyond the myriad of harmful temptations, Noonan suggests that punk instead offered him an invaluable sense of self-worth: "It was the first time I had something that I could say I could do. I was crap at everything else until then. I was never going to let go of that, and I've kept playing and gone through all this stuff because of it."

Alf Lunghi speaks to an unexpected longevity, both of himself and punk as a musical movement: "Here we were thinking, 'Why bother going to uni and getting a career when we're going to have mutually assured destruction?' We should have known better [*laughs*].... So, for us it was live fast, die young, and no one expected to live past twenty-five.... I never thought it [punk] would last; I thought it would just be a phase, but it has developed into a wild sort of phenomenon and it's lasted."

Like Noonan, Lunghi had felt a particular disconnect to his surrounds and pull towards the inner city: "I hated the suburbs.... I found more acceptance in the city with the punks—they didn't judge you."

Lunghi and his housemates, though, were not so averse to judging the neighbours: "In '80–81 ... there was only two sets of terrace houses in the whole of Brisbane, and one was on the way to the governor's house, and we turned it into a squat.... We put a couch up on the roof; we'd throw things at the governor's car and generally harass people."

Endowed with boundless leisure time, Lunghi's first band, Sabotage, was formed out of the terrace houses, with the addition of Lindsay Dalgleish: "Every morning he'd come around with a six-pack of beer and his guitar and we'd jam all day.... He's dead now, but he ended up playing in Mystery of Sixes and Public Execution."

Not himself an original member, Lunghi says, "The Mystery guys, I jammed with them for quite a few years.... They were very polarising.... They weren't innocent little boys who were being picked on, they were provocative, and they didn't mind a fight." More threatening than the band itself were its fans, Lunghi remembers: "They had a following ... and they used to bash people and cause trouble and steal things. So, the band gets a bad name, of course." Highlighting the risk, Lunghi recalls of the singer of La Fetts that "he got stabbed in the crowd at the Nash at one of the Mystery shows."

Another evening saw a reversal, with band members being armed: "The manager of the pub handed us all bits of wood and iron bars—it was like a movie. All the band guys were inside, and there was just wave after wave [of skinheads] charging the door, and we were just hitting bald heads and hands. And then the cops turned up and they all just disappeared. That was crazy—the doors were bowing in."

As well as the volatility of their audience, Lunghi says that musically, "They were different, and that seemed to be the thing; you'd have straight-looking people ... playing the bentest music that wouldn't be played anywhere else.... They did have a rough element, but people came to see the Mystery of Sixes simply because they were really good. They were a cut above all the other bands."

For all the effort and danger faced, however, Lunghi says, "I played with the Mysterys for two years, and then when we went to record and do a show, they got another guy [*laughs*]."

The band's recorded output consisted of two self-released seven-inch records, in 1982 (*Sample*) and '83 (self-titled).

Their first recorded track, "Azaria," was to cause angst, allegedly banned for six years by the Australian Broadcasting Tribunal. The song related to the case of a missing two-month-old baby—Azaria Chamberlain—whose story had captivated the country as the child's mother was convicted (and later exonerated) of murder, her defence being that a dingo had taken the newborn.

Like the plausibility of a dingo in Azaria's disappearance, stories of the band began as rumour and became legend regardless of any factuality. Addressing speculation that the band was shot at during a rehearsal, Lunghi does little to aid or dispel the tale: "I did hear that someone laid some shots while they were rehearsing."

Following his ousting from Mystery of Sixes, Lunghi joined Rabid Souls, yet he says, "We were being told that all the [band] money was being put into an account and it wasn't.... The guy took off.... That stuffed that up." Lunghi's fortunes seemed to have reversed when asked to drum for the already established and revered Insane Hombres: "We rehearsed and we rehearsed."

The band broke up after one show.

Lunghi only partially laments that "I've always been part of it, but I always just seem to miss out," reassuring himself that "I've had a lot of fun and met a lot of good people all through it; and I've seen it all and I can remember it."

Becoming musically active simultaneous to Lunghi, Sebastian Nemo and his band Subversive Rash were one of the first of the harder-styled groups in Brisbane. Explaining that "punk was always evolving," he says that the process involved "trying to find ways to be more extreme than the wave before. Because the original '70s punk became quite acceptable ... you needed ... to go even further." Concomitantly, of the newer bands, he says, "They've gone underground because they're not interested in being in your pop charts, so they've become more extreme." What proliferated was an attitude of, "Well, we're going to do it ourselves because we've got no one to do it for us.... Right from the start, Australian punk grabbed the ethos and did it outside the mainstream, made their own rules, made their own everything.... All across the world we were networking.... People all around the world were fascinated with what was happening in Australia.... I used to write to Olho Seco, a band in São Paulo in Brazil—trading stuff with them."

Subversive Rash, however, never had a significant opportunity to influence beyond their local scene, their bassist committing suicide in 1982, after which members formed Pictish Blood.

Though taken by the new current of punk, Nemo speaks of an aversion to hardcore as a masculinist expression: "I hate hardcore, because it was basically an American term, and they created things like the mosh pit and slam dancing.... If you're small or you're female you don't want to be slammed around by a bunch of guys.... You're creating exclusivity that never existed in punk before.... The original punks, they'd pogo; everyone would come to the front of stage and dance, peacefully."

Such progressive thinking, however, was discordant in a state Nemo acknowledges for its then intolerance. Offering illustration, Nemo recounts the attempt of Pork and Corpse of Christ to play Toowoomba in 1982: "We walked into this bar.... This guy came over and said, 'You get your toughest guy, we'll get our toughest guy, and meet you outside.'" If only they had viewed the full experience of both bands, that challenge may have been rescinded: "Back at that period, Pork or Corpse of Christ were dissecting pigs' heads onstage and hitting pigs' heads with hammers."

Nemo passed away in 2019 after a battle with brain cancer.

As Nemo was skirting the fringes of extreme music, bands such as Screaming Tribesmen (*I Don't Wanna Know* seven-inch, 1982), Vampire Lovers (*Buzzsaw Popstar* seven-inch, 1983), Post No Bills, and Tapeloops (*Fire in Heaven* seven-inch, 1984) infused more tempered influences, including post-punk and garage. Proving that Brisbane was also not entirely devoid of the Detroit/Birdman influence, the Girlies were performing a cover of Birdman's "Burn My Eye" a decade following its original release.

Like a man adrift waiting on the Gospel, the Girlies' drummer, Heyden Wilson, says, "There was a lot of shit music coming out, like commercial stuff, and I thought, 'There's no guitar music around anymore.' Then I went over to my mate's place and his older brother had the New Race album.... I went straight down to the record store and bought it."

Wilson surrounded himself with fellow Detroit enthusiasts, and the Girlies' first show was at a notorious Brisbane establishment: "The venue was called the Love Inn. It was owned by a gangster, Hector Hapeta." It was one of the Valley's (supposedly nonexistent) unlicensed casinos and brothels. Wilson says, "I don't know who could possibly believe they didn't exist.... It was so blatantly obvious.... We did ... photoshoots and film clips in the brothels—Hector's brothels."

Receiving no retribution, the band were also fortunate not to have incurred the wrath of animal protection after reportedly leaving kittens in cages outside Brisbane radio stations to coincide with release of their first single, "Pussycat," in 1987. Wilson, however, is scant with detail: "I'm pretty sure we did do that . . . just to get their attention. . . . We did it more just to stick it up them, to say, 'We exist.'"

Lacking attention from mainstream radio, the band risked oversaturation in live venues. Wilson reveals, "In 1987, we did over a hundred shows." One of the group's more awkward appearances came on Channel 7's Saturday morning program, where prerecorded audience squeals reverberated through a smoke haze to only heighten the unease. "It was seven o'clock in the morning or something, we had to mime live. . . . We went along with beer and were smoking a joint, and then we went in and there was all these little kids—'Holy shit.'"

Some stage anxiety is undoubtedly uncomfortable, but the band being placed at the centre of a murder investigation following a boat cruise show was enough to sober any high: "The boat took off from a suburb called Murarrie, and a girl had been murdered there around about that time. And the last thing she said to her mum—and it's really sad—before she was going out was, 'I'm going to do an audition with the Girlies.' We never knew anything about this. So, the police rang up George, our manager, and said, 'Can we see you about something?' and he said, 'I've just got to go over to Murarrie,' and they said, 'What? Murarrie?' So, they dragged him in. . . . We were all suspects in this murder thing for a while."

After relocating to Sydney, the band managed few live performances. Wilson remembers them to have "kind of petered out." Likely lured by the city's legacy rather than any present reality, Wilson concedes, "We were a bit late."

As the trickle of punks out of Brisbane continued through the decade, Andy Nehl was a rare instance of migration in the other direction: "I moved to Brisbane in the middle of 1980. . . . I applied for a job at 4ZZZ, and they gave me a job as a radio announcer/producer."

Far from ignorant of the state's regimen and treatment of its politically and culturally defiant, Nehl says that "I'd already been arrested two years before."

In spite of such spectre, Nehl's memory of 4ZZZ had been that "it was full-on playing all these bands. . . . There was really serious journalism.... It was 4ZZZ and a couple of people at the ABC basically fighting the good fight, exposing the corruption and malpractice of the Bjekle-Petersen government and the police, whereas most of the local media in Brisbane was fairly compliant to the government at the time."

For Nehl, his primary impression was a "pressure cooker of oppression on top of you... and that pressure was coming down on Aboriginal people, it was coming down on gay and lesbian people, it was coming down on punks, it was coming down on alternative politics, it was coming down on art. Anything that didn't fit the super-straight, boring, innocuous version of what the Bjekle-Petersen government thought Queensland should be, they came down on you."

Sebastian Nemo doesn't hesitate to offer blunter analysis: "It literally was a police state. So, it's not a police state the same as it was in South America where police just go and shoot people, but they could do whatever they wanted to anybody."

Glenn Brady catalogues just some of their unchecked abuses:

> They would pull you over on the street, strip-search, maybe a punch or two to the head or a telephone book around the face, back at the station.... The police watchhouse in the bowels of the city was a filthy, evil cunt of a place, and always full on Friday and Saturday nights with drunken yobs, punks, skins, and Aboriginals; blood up the walls from beatings, and people screaming abuse at the cops who were your typical fat-gutted, racist bastards.... House raids were just part of the day-to-day life of punks and skins.... They would simply kick in the door, threaten you with mass violence, then smash the house apart and leave.... Everyone had a story to tell about the cops then, and all were bad in varying degrees.

Nemo relives one particularly deceitful, if unsuccessful, action: "Six police cars turned up because there was three punks in the park on a Sunday morning." While the three were still in custody at the park, having attained their home address, police "planted drugs while we were there. Luckily a friend of ours was turning up at the same time and was watching them from next door. He saw them planting grass underneath the house, so he took it and went home and smoked it. So, then the police came back and there was nothing there."

Beyond just personal harassment, punks, in the midst of Brisbane's barely concealed and illicit nightlife, were witnesses to the entrenched corruption of the city's police: "We used to play gigs at the Outpost and there was a [illegal] casino upstairs. That's why we didn't get raided by the police.... We saw people handing money to the police."

At the expiry of his contract, Nehl returned to Sydney as his band, Black Assassins—composed of 4ZZZ workers—fell into inactivity.

As one of few outlets willing to confront the Bjelke-Petersen government, 4ZZZ predictably came under the scrutiny of authorities. In 1985, a recording by La Fetts—"SEQEB Scabs"—was seized from the station by police, a minor act in the escalation of conflict between Joh and the trade unions. Anti-union laws meant penalties were applied to those deemed to be harassing "scab" replacement workers during a strike. With the song receiving considerable play on 4ZZZ, police raided, confiscating the tape. The band had difficulty in gaining further shows.

The master tape for the song is today housed at the State Library of Queensland.

Not all bands had the desire or temerity to deliver explicitly political content, yet Fred Noonan gives the assessment that simply existing as a band under the rule of Bjelke-Petersen ensured that "you're a political band whether you want to be or not."

Noonan joined New Improved Testament, and he suggests that a praxis of US hardcore ferocity guided them more than any theory of politics: "When it came to New Improved Testament, speed... was one of the things we looked to as a guiding light.... The thing that fascinated me was watching the guitarist's hand—it was just a blur."

Demonstrating the often-denied links between punk and the earlier countercultural movement that it supposedly repudiated, Noonan says the band effectively "dropped out.... We moved to what we called the 'New Improved Testament Research Farm,' which was a little house out in the sticks.... We could make as much noise as we wanted. So, we were really like hippies living out there, we were smoking our pot and practicing. We would spend six hours a day just playing, jamming, eating mushrooms, and tripping out."

Irrespective of one's evaluation of societal withdraw, such experiments in remote communal living at least brought respite from the glare and insults of a public who tended to reflect the government's arch-traditionalism. Noonan offers a secondhand account that reinforced any desire to distance oneself from fellow Queenslanders: "Ron Peno [Died Pretty vocalist] . . . was walking with Nick, the singer of New Improved Testament. I think he'd just come back from tour in Europe [in 1986], and he's walking down the street, and someone yelled out, 'Fuck off, you ugly little faggot!' And he just turned to Nick and said, 'In France, I'm a king. Here I'm an ugly little faggot.'"

The Sick Boys, a collection of Brisbane's toughest and unruliest punks, would not be subjected to public derision without consequence. Glenn Brady describes their background: "They were just suburban and wild and mostly came from fucked childhood homes. They embraced a lot of the English punk, with its drunken, pilled-up glory and hatred of a society that never wanted any part of them."

Reportedly beating up someone at a party and scrawling "punk and proud" with the victim's blood, Bad Ronald and Blowhard member Rollo's memory was that "they'd fight anyone." Placing their number at "probably a good twenty or thirty of them, maybe, when they were really going off," he says, "They all ended up dead or in jail."

Adding further menace to Brisbane's punk landscape, a group of Nazi punks had also materialised. In his own memoir of the city's scene, Marquis H.K. tells of being handed a party invite around the middle of the decade that contained the instructions "BYO booze, NO blacks or fighting."[6]

Alf Lunghi identifies the Nazi punks' central figure as a woman: "Big Liz. . . . She was about six foot one, six foot two, and big, broad shoulders. . . . She used to bash a lot of people. . . . I've seen her push bouncers through plate-glass windows."

Glenn Brady's initiation into punk had come through the befriending of another striking and audacious female figure: "She had inch-high spiked green hair, tights, and studded wristbands, and basically at that stage of suburban Australia's collective mind it would have been more normal to see someone walking around on fire. People stopped dead in their tracks to stare, cars slowed down as they walked past, and I stared as well, thinking that, surely, they will be beaten before they got home."

Describing himself as "a slightly troubled teen" with "average grades," Brady makes the claim that "my future was already sealed. . . .

I had left school and had just started to get into pot and drinking with several other yobs my age from Geebung who had also been bitten in the brain by punk. We had no careers, no aspirations, or even girlfriends, so we kind of banded together through the love of this new music."

The youthful resignation, though, was quickly usurped, as

> hearing the Dead Kennedys for the first time changed a lot of things for myself and I imagine many others.... Most of all it contained "information," stuff that had not been taught to us in our Christian and state schools. None of us knew about what was behind corporations, banks, the CIA, the church, death squads in South America. Looking back now, it's incredible what we were taught... there was another way to go in life.... With all this newfound info, four of us decided we wanted to make some noise and scream stuff.

Where Jello Biafra had prognosticated a dead scene, by the mid-'80s and onwards the ease of forming a band produced a wealth of groups, including Brady's DPO, as well as Bodycount, Rabid Souls, DFH, 5th Column, Psycho Circus, Death of a Nun (posthumous self-titled seven-inch, 2017), NTT, Strange Stains, Prince of Weasels, Criminally Insane, the Tony Mitchell Gang, and Rampant Scabies (split LP, 1990) in Brisbane; the Grogans in Ipswich; and Complete Chaos, Social Cancer, Ultra Deviates, Subterranean Destruction, M-16, Squadron Leader (*For So Long/1-2-3-4* seven-inch, 1984), and Thrust (*Getting Closer* seven-inch, 1988; *Go Insane* twelve-inch, 1988; *Mindless* LP, 1989) on the Gold Coast.

The proliferation of bands was also reflected in the breadth of Brady's new social group:

> So, in a short time I had a lot of friends in the scene and was sharing houses and moving around a lot—lots of piss-ups and parties. Gigs were a bit rarer, as at times there might only be one or two venues, and sometimes none at all.... Our first gig was also the first time that I had ever been to a live venue and seen a band. We were scared young punks, sculling cider outside the venue... while we watched dozens of punks and skins roll up. The one thing I really recall was the amount of skinheads; there must have been fifty easily, and about seventy punks. In between bands, the skins, all pissed-up, started sieg-heiling.

In 1985, Brady and Marquis H.K. were themselves captured sieg-heiling mid-pose, the photo featuring on the front page of the *Daily Sun*. The target of their taunting had been police gathered at a peace rally. In an attempt to further antagonise the city's constabulary, Brady's next band, though musically more measured, took on the name Barbeque City Cops, but ultimately their desire for a decent payday came at the expense of Brady: "The other blokes in it wanted to make it big, and I didn't have the voice that they needed for stardom and glory."

As his musical endeavours ended, Brady returned to an earlier passion of visual art: "I gave it away when punk took over my interest, and it wasn't until around 1991 when I came back to Brisbane that I thought I would give it a go again.... I had been refused entry into art school twice, and revenge became a motivator for me. It was, 'Fuck art college, fuck the art scene, ya pompous cunts.' I was angry, and still am. It kept me going through the '90s when I was in psych wards a dozen times, shock treatment, hundreds of pills, and surrounded in the wards by mad cunts ... but I hung on, as I knew I had something valid to say and share with this stupid but beautiful world."

Whereas Brady was being denied entry to school, Martin Lee had himself expelled from it. But then Lee's extracurricular activities were not those generally favoured by more diligent students: "I went to school with Ian Haug from Powderfinger.... There was a place called White Chairs, and a lot of the English punks would drink there, and we'd go there. We were thirteen or fourteen—it was crazy." Later joined by "a guy called Julian," Lee says, "We were both fifteen, sixteen.... We were in these full-on punk rock venues getting raided by the police."

Lee, however, already had a familiarity with Brisbane's felonious entities: "My family had a Chinese restaurant in Fortitude Valley.... I'd see all the criminals were there, all the police, all the lawyers.... Every fucking criminal would be sitting at my father's restaurant ... but my father was left alone.... By the time I started doing the punk rock thing, all those venues in the Valley that we played, they were all fronts for drug operations, casinos."

In the vicinity of criminals, Lee instead came under the influence of more "senior" punks: "Everyone was older.... Because I could play the drums, they were like, 'Come on, man.' ... So then I got in with that crew, and did Bengt Snarl and another couple of punk rock bands."

As for the thoughts of his parents, perhaps punk was simply viewed as less risky than other forms of Brisbane nightlife: "My mum was quite supportive.... She actually took me out of school so I could go on tour.... They were like, 'Just keep him away from drugs.' At the time I was very straight edge ... so drugs and alcohol didn't interest me. It was all good—came back alive."

Though Lee was unscathed, the band's troubled guitarist, he says, "literally disappeared—never heard from him again." With him also went the band. "Then I hit sixteen and got kicked out of school, and I said to an older dude, 'Man, let's go to the US.'"

In Los Angeles, Lee experienced the downside of its legendary punk scene: "I loved the Bad Brains. They were finally playing when H.R. was in the band, at a place called Fenders in Long Beach. These skinheads turned up, and they only played like two and a half songs because of the violence—they called it off. So, I never got to fully see the Bad Brains."

Just as Bad Brains added metal to the collection of influences that composed their *I Against I* album in 1986, Lee followed a similar orientation, if not without greater accolade: "I started getting exposed to the metal part; Corrosion of Conformity, DRI started getting more metal, so I started investigating that, which took me into the early Chili Peppers stuff.... My heart was always in the hardcore, do-it-yourself thing, but my musical horizons opened a bit more.... So, by the time Regurgitator came around, Ben [Ely, bassist] and I loved that music, but we just wanted to explore.... That's when he said, 'I know this Vietnamese dude,' and that was Quan Yeomans, and next thing you know we had three songs and we got a record deal."

That record deal for Regurgitator culminated in two platinum albums and one gold album in Australia by the time Lee departed the band in late 1999.

Paul Hanlon reveals Regurgitator's homage to his own band, Crucified Truth. Choosing to exhibit their punk roots, "Regurgitator used to cover one of our songs, 'Cops Are Cunts,' when they first started. They played it all over the world."

The apparent incongruity of Regurgitator and Crucified Truth is even more pronounced as Hanlon cites his own group's influences being bands that very much personified their names: "Disorder and Chaos UK, we were mad for them. It was so loose and drunken, and that was a big thing for us early on. But then ... we got into Black Flag's *Damaged* ... Circle Jerks' *Group Sex*.... It sort of opened up a big thing for us.... We started the whole ... 'support your scene' thing.... We basically grabbed that from America. It was all about solidarity, support your scene, and being a part of something.... It was trying to put a positive message."

Such positivity also acted as possible counterweight to the "negativity" experienced from police. "You look back now and think, 'I can't believe that happened.' ... It's been understated. I can't stress that enough."

The greatest peril Hanlon cites, however, was the public, rather than police: "Probably the worst thing was just the random violence—not at shows. I couldn't tell you how many times I was just walking down the street in the suburbs and all of a sudden a car stops and three or four guys get out, sometimes with a piece of wood, and like, 'Right, we're going to kill ya.' ... You've got to expect—and I don't mind—people having a reaction or even having a laugh if they're not used to seeing something ... as long as they're not malicious. But there's a line you don't cross."

Given the anecdotes, Hanlon can rightly say, "We did have some unique tales, and went through some unique situations that I think definitely gives you a bond."

As the strength of band members' personal relationships were being reinforced, they were also making valuable connections overseas: "We were really into networking. I'd probably get a couple letters a day from all around the world.... I've actually got the first Offspring single sent to me by Dexter [Holland, vocalist of the Offspring]. He read the review [of Crucified Truth] in *Maximumrocknroll* ... and he basically sent this thing with a handwritten letter, saying, 'Hey, can you send me a copy of your cassette, this is my band, we're called the Offspring.' ... So, a lot of people weren't organised, and they never got anything done, whereas we were very conscious."

That conscientiousness is documented in Crucified Truth self-releasing their *Communication* seven-inch in 1986.

Regardless of the level of a band's organisation, nothing can prepare for unforeseen events. Act's Cal Crilly relives their tragic beginnings: "We had a rough start, because the young drummer we had died of a brain haemorrhage when he was seventeen."

Though not life-threatening, the band's first evening of socialising in 1984 had been far from incident-free: "We all got too drunk on Brandavino when we met up. Shane, who sang in Act, he ended up getting in a fight and going to the hospital. I just ended up getting put in the watchhouse because I collapsed on the pavement."

The band only managed to reach their second show before further incident. "The anarchists had put on bands, and Shane just got too drunk and he dropped his pants and called everybody fascists. It was guaranteed to have feminists there, and they said, 'We'll cut his balls off.' It was an appalling sort of gig. We straight away got notoriety for being a bunch of drunken scumbag punks."

Contrary to perception of Act as simply befuddled drunks, Crilly says, "I've always been more into the political side.... We landed in Ireland the day before Bloody Sunday.... 1972 was probably the most violent year of the Troubles, so you can imagine a seven-year-old kid going to school with all these soldiers.... Every Friday the town [Derry] would be hit by five or six bombs—it was pretty crazy times. So, I was already political in certain ways, or had that awareness, so when punk came along ... I saw punk as actually saying something."

Act gave one of their most forthright performances in solidarity with inmates protesting conditions and mistreatment at Brisbane's maximum security Boggo Road Gaol in 1988. Setting up opposite the prison to perform for the protestors, Crilly says, "We were able to play loud enough that night.... You could hear them all cheering and were having a good time.... We probably played about twenty-five minutes that night and then thought, 'All right, we've done enough.'" Quickly packing the gear into a borrowed minivan, Crilly remembers that "literally minutes later the cops came past with a floodlight, checking the street looking for this band.... We did the same thing the next day." Vision of the band performing made television news.

Eschewing pure victimhood, Johnny "Hombre" asserts punk's acts of resistance: "We weren't victims. Far from it. We were making our own choices, and choices have consequences.... Oppression begets pushback."

Forming Insane Hombres in 1986, Johnny identifies his band as one that transcended strict demarcation—if not only in what they played, then to whom: "I'd like to think we had something to do with breaking down the unnecessary divisions that existed between the tribes that were so exclusive back in our day. When we played, we imposed, in part, a rebel truce, and ultimately crossed the subcultures over."

In 1988, the group released their Brisbane scene classic, the *To the Core* twelve-inch. Demoting importance of the physical artefact, however, Hombre again centres their supporters, offering, "The best memories are of the people; it was always about the people." Acknowledging that "we didn't appeal to everyone," Hombre says, "those we attracted were zealots.... It was like they had 'found' us. So yeah, we were never going to be a household name, but man, so many of those who came to our gigs were passionate."

Through four years together, Insane Hombres exhibited a lifespan that few other bands within the tough environment that was 1980s Brisbane could manage. Against the impediments, though, Hombre says that "when the Hombres threw it in [in 1990], the scene ... was no longer proving itself.... Punk rock never died in this town. It can't. Brisbane is where it was born—it's our heritage."

But if punk can never die, its behaviours are certainly able to exasperate and exhaust its participants: "It seemed that the more I sang about 'aggression is not violence,' the more they did not get it.... We were attracting more and more skinheads, and too many of them Nazis.... And of course, the little skins started carrying knives, didn't they." Or as Sebastian Nemo recounts, even more novel weapons: "A thing that skinheads used to do in the '80s was take darts out with them so they could throw darts at people."

Even "Rock Against Racism" benefit gigs were not a haven, Hombre revealing, "I had to put a bodyguard detachment on my mum (who had come to see us for the first time), and rightly so, because before the day had ended there was a massive skinhead brawl down the front which shut down the benefit.... Don't get me wrong, we had a lot of support from the skin community, but clearly some had views we could not and would never support. And while we stood up for those values, we were not being heard, ironically, at our own gigs."

Knowing the value of not further inciting violence, others just sat back and watched the barbarism play out before them. Supporting metal band Mortal Sin in 1987, Bad Ronald (*Working Your Life Away* seven-inch, 1988; *River Pirates* seven-inch, 1989) vocalist Rollo recounts the evening: "We ended up wearing tights—packed our tights out—and wore wigs, and took the piss out of them a bit. We were told they were a cock-rock band—they weren't." Mortal Sin's singer "got up onstage and went, 'Skinheads and metalheads in the room, total mix, I wanna see some violence.' ... This big skinhead bloke ... got up and just hit him. Me and my mate Grant were sitting at the bar, and it was like one of them Western movies where you see the big brawls.... There were chairs flying everywhere. We just sat behind the bar and didn't move a muscle."

Bad Ronald's drummer, James, had previously been a member of Oral Injury, described by Malcolm May as the first Oi! band in Brisbane. Possessing a bass drum painted with the Southern Cross and "oi," the group left little confusion as to their genre of preference. Their politics, explains Rollo, weren't quite so obvious: "They were a skinhead band. I don't know if they sang much right-wing stuff.... I remember one song about girls' bottoms [*laughs*].... James wasn't like that, he was like a yuppie, I suppose. A yuppie with no hair."

Oral Injury's bassist, Mick, however, was a far more confronting figure: "He was a huge bloke. I think a bit dangerous at the time, but he just said to me, 'Rollo, as long as you don't talk politics, we'll be great mates.' I just looked up at this giant, mountainous man and went, 'Fair enough.'"

As Oral Injury's drummer moved on to a band with an identifiable left-wing critique, their bassist took an opposite bearing, joining with Malcolm May. May recalls, "There wasn't really any skinhead bands [in Brisbane]." But if bands were meagre to begin with, their number began to germinate. "It was really small to start with, then mid-'80s onward it just went crazy." A witness to the growth, Paul Hanlon remembers that "Brisbane had a huge skinhead population. Probably one of the biggest in Australia."

Originally from Melbourne, May, who was enlisted in the army, was despatched to Brisbane in 1981. Not alone among his army colleagues in having the interest in punk, May says, "There was a couple of us—not too many.... I had to be careful, because doing what I was doing on the weekends was, in the army's eyes, not that of a soldier. I got arrested a few times, spent nights in the watchhouse, and a couple of times they found out. They weren't really impressed.... They couldn't tell me I couldn't do it, but they were aware of it."

May further explains that "I was in the army from '81 to '87, and

I was hanging around everyone," but "it wasn't until I got out of the army that we started the bands." May's first band, Bride Wore Boots, did not have similar endurance to his military career, lasting "maybe six months.... And then we formed the next band, which was Australia's Pride."

With connection to skinhead bands in other states, May remembers that "someone organised for us to go down and play" in Sydney. Following a "big fight" and "a chair through the front window of the pub," May describes an after-show incident that, if not for a different city, could easily have been a deleted scene from *Romper Stomper*:

> We left the gig and were in a hire van.... We pulled up at this set of lights, and there was a Mercedes with these Asians in it. They started abusing us, and we started abusing them.... Next thing one of them hurled a beer and it hit the side window of the van and smashed it. We drove up the road further and it had come to a bit of a stop, so we blocked them, and the angle they stopped blocked the road. We got out of the van, and as we were ... the boot of the Mercedes popped up and a couple of these Asian dudes jumped out.... They grabbed a tyre jack and "boom!" straight through the windshield. And then we had this big, massive, full-on fight with them.... There was big casualties on both sides.... And we could hear the police way down the street ... they were getting closer and closer.... So, we picked up our wounded and threw them in the van, and they did the same, and we drove off. We jumped the median strip ... and drove between the corner of this building and the traffic lights, and drove on the footpath and sideswiped the van on the corner of this building, raced down this side street, and pulled into this block of flats. We heard the coppers go past up the street a bit.... The minivan, by the time we returned it in Brisbane, it was trashed.

After the dangers of Sydney, in Brisbane the Treasury Hotel became something of the skinheads' own fiefdom: "This old Italian guy used to own it—Silvio—he used to let us get away with blue murder. He really liked us."

As well as the congregating punks and skins, the venue also drew the attention of a thrill-seeking public: "There was a dare going around Brisbane in the late '80s ... on a Friday night: walk in the front door and through, out the back door, without getting harassed. It was full of skinheads and punks."

Eventually the punks were "moved on" to the Lands Office Hotel, a fight in the pub fracturing an already uneasy peace.

Any fissures within the various subcultures were further exacerbated as a segment of skinheads took on a more overt political tone: "They sort of changed the scene, because a lot of the punks were real leftie, peace-and-veggie-style punks, and me and my crew headed in that hardcore Oi! lane.... Not everyone was into it, but the majority of Brisbane skinheads were.... A lot just happily drifted over to the hardcore side, because, man, they were fucking hardcore times."

Adding to the fraught times was the emergence of a new group who became a natural foe to the skinheads: "We used to get in a lot of fights in the city with—at the time we used to call them—'bombers.' They were like rappers ... that was at the start of hip-hop/rap.... In the height of the day, walking through the city ... you were constantly looking over your shoulder, because skinheads didn't have a really good name. Everyone had a skinhead story. There was a lot of people that wanted to have a crack at you."

Unsurprisingly, May's observation is that "you sort of had to be pretty hard to do it."

After years of unimpeded habitation of the Treasury, the exceeding of tolerance for the skinheads' behaviour meant a new venue had to be sought.

Their newly established "Eureka Club" bar became the epicentre for the city's "hardcore" skinhead scene, and a witty Rollo quips, "Unfortunately, we were always busy when we were asked to play that joint." He would not be alone in his aversion, May revealing that "we stayed there for a couple of years ... then the pub got sold.... This gay dude bought it and turned it into a gay parlour."

As one of the older and more seasoned figures within the Brisbane scene, May speaks of a generational change that also signified the beginning of its decline: "Everyone just started drifting, and the scene was sort of on a downhill run. By this stage it was early '90s.... It kept going along, but it was a lot smaller.... It just wasn't what it was in the heyday, in its prime. And it will never go back to that, either."

Comprehending the extremity of his past, May says, "I look back and think, 'Fuck, I did a lot of things I shouldn't have done and weren't really right,' but at the time, it was what it was.... We were all in our twenties, full of testosterone, full of piss and bad manners, thinking we were six foot and bulletproof. We had a pretty full-on reputation around town, and we liked it. We got that reputation for a reason.... I remember there was one or two incidents where it was like, 'Fuck, man, we're lucky we didn't die,' looking back on it."

While suggesting a tempering of his outlook, May also identifies a certain spirit in him that remains undiminished:

> It just suited my personality, the type of person I was.... I'm still a forward person, but I'm a lot more tolerant these days.... It's still in my blood to this day; I still wear Doc Martens and I still wear Fred Perrys and I've still got short hair. I don't dress as a skinhead as such, but it's still there.... I've got a bar here in Thailand; mate, they'd never heard half of the music I play in the bar.... They were wild days.... You couldn't do it again now like we did it then—no way, not a hope in hell.... No place had CCTV back then.

Scrutiny instead came to be placed on Joh Bjekle-Petersen himself, but not before his regime had caused a detrimental decline of the city's punk population. Rollo recounts the juxtaposition that was Brisbane and the destinations of those flowing outwards from it: "You'd go to Melbourne or Sydney for a weekend and there'd be four hundred people at a gig, and they'd be having fun.... Cars didn't stop and jump out and chase you.... So, I think generally, everyone just filtered south."

Cal Crilly gives a more quantitative account of the exodus: "I was doing the treasurer's job at Triple Z in the early part of 1988. I think I did it for about three, four months, and I didn't get a single subscription in that time." Crilly attributes the lull to a coordinated campaign of harassment and venue closures in the lead-up to Expo 88, a six-month international cultural fair that attracted more than fifteen million visitors. "When Expo happened, Joh really went to town on anyone who looked alternative. It got really heavy; they brought in the Drugs Misuse Act in 1986 and used that to harass everyone off the streets."

Yet by the time the gates to Expo opened in April 1988, the nineteen-year reign of Joh had already unravelled; he was forced to resign in late 1987.

Investigation into Queensland's police had begun as far back as 1976, with unfavourable findings. The Fitzgerald Inquiry, tabled in 1989, went much further, documenting corruption and gross abuses of power within Queensland's political leadership and police force. For all of Bjekle-Petersen's posturing of moral purity, the report exposed the same criminal behaviour punks had witnessed firsthand for a decade: illegal sex clubs masquerading as massage parlours, money taken from venues by police, drugs, illegal gambling.

By year's end, the Country/National Party's thirty-two years of continuous government was over. Like many, Cameron Borg vividly recalls the day: "I remember being at Livid Festival.... Everyone just cheered their heads off and got so drunk because we'd finally got rid of the Nationals."

Johnny Hombre, who played through the pre- and post-Joh years, recalls the accompanying easing of persecution and bringing of renewed hope: "Joh's demise saw conditions improve for punks. We emerged above the parapets. Putting Queensland politics and justice back together meant we were no longer an opportunistic diversion for the coppers. They instead started weeding out their own. The task force was disbanded."

Yet as if to give a reminder that Queensland was not going to quickly extract itself from its dark past, Rocking Horse Records was raided in February 1989. Records seized included Dead Kennedys and Hard-Ons.

## TOWNSVILLE

With the tumultuous events of the state capital unfolding, Queensland's regional bands continued unperturbed. But as Tim Steward suggests, such composure was often accompanied by a normalisation of harassment: "Pretty much the moment you stepped out of your house, the yelling would start. Yet it became normal after a while—you didn't care."

Of suitable age when the hardcore bands emerged in England, Steward says, "My mum let me go to gigs, and that was around when the second wave of punk was happening, so I got to go and see Discharge and Subhumans.... My thing was that real straight-ahead, early '80s UK sound."

Transported from the fury of UK82 to Townsville 1983, Steward reveals only a retrospective culture shock: "When you're a kid, pretty much everything's normal, so you just accept it and roll with it, whatever happens. But by the time I got to Townsville I was really . . . living this punk thing, but all in my own little bubble in this suburb of Townsville."

In an era lacking easy global connectivity, Steward highlights both the isolationist nature of marginal cultural forms and also their sometimes-unexpected and welcome artistic outcomes: "You were so isolated, and you didn't hear much music, so when you read something in the papers about this thing called punk that was happening in England and America, you more or less had to guess at what it sounded like yourself. . . . You were just pretty much making it up. Which was kind of cool, because all these bands came up with bizarre, crazy music which had nothing to do with what had come before, but it was just their take on it."

Enlisting "a bunch of suburban kids who were really young" and barely versed in punk, Steward's band, initially christened Psycho Skate Smurfs on Smack, slightly moderated their name to "Lethal Injections, before we changed to Madmen."

In Brisbane, Cameron Borg remembers Madmen appearing alongside a band who was to become one of the country's highest-ever-selling acts, Powderfinger. It was "one of Powderfinger's first shows. . . . We went there expecting to see some full-on punk stuff. . . . The Powderfinger set consisted of all Neil Young covers, and it was freaking atrocious."

Though not making a shift in sound to anything as easily digestible as Powderfinger, Steward says, "Our life as a punk band sort of naturally came to an end, because I was already tired of writing those kinds of songs. . . . I guess in a way, having lived in Townsville . . . I was still rooted back in the early '80s thing, and the world had moved on, but I hadn't caught up with that yet. . . . Starting to hear stuff that was current and suddenly going, 'Oh my god . . . music's expanded, music's gotten amazing, there's all these different angles you can take,' it was just a big eye-opener. Especially hearing something like Hüsker Dü, because they had that punk element at the bottom but built so much amazing stuff on top of it."

Relocating to Brisbane at the end of the decade, Madmen soon evolved into indie band Screamfeeder.

## ROCKHAMPTON

As Steward built a following and sizeable discography in his new city, others never reached beyond a handful of shows, and instead remain the subject of local legend. Rockhampton teenage hardcore band Noise embodied one such entity. Amassing a storied three-gig history, Noise also released a tape whose title located them on the city's cultural map: *Like a Stain in Your Toilet.*

Response to their first practice was the arrival of police and threats to destroy their equipment. Second practice: again the police were alerted. Moving to an alternate location, their third attempt attracted not only the police but also the local newspaper.

Making their live debut again brought the attendance of police, including detectives. Days later, one member of the band, escorted to the police watchhouse, was charged. Boldly seeking a second show, some of those gathered at the hippie party attempted to confiscate the group's guitars after a performance of "Sex and Violence" by the Exploited—though, at the least, police had finally been thrown off the scent. A third and final show was organised at a hall, attracting an audience of four punks and skins. Singer Ruth, collapsing during the set, was taken to hospital.

Whatever expressions of punk that occurred in Rockhampton in the 1980s can likely be attributed to the singlemindedness—or perhaps foolishness posing as tirelessness—of Cameron Borg. But where many would see too great a challenge, Borg saw liberation: "Being based regionally, it gives you more freedom, in a sense. You get less opportunity to play gigs and meet people, but you have a little bit more freedom, because you're not dictated to by this kind of scene, or something." Not that any deranged positivity was shielding him from the frustrations. Within a larger city, says Borg, it "seems like: just get the band together, get some decent songs, and you're going to have some level of success. Regionally, it's more like: slug your guts out and you're going to keep hitting a brick wall. But that's cool, because it hasn't been a motivator for me." Rather, Borg's modest initiative was to "make some good changes in my life and my mates' lives."

At the least, his efforts made him the subject of the 2010 short film *A Piss in the Ocean: Cameron Borg; Ripples in the Mainstream.* Describing it as surprising, Borg says, "People in the day seriously just didn't want to know, they were appalled. . . . To this day, my parents still aren't into it. All my bosses I ever had when I was working and in bands hated it, and would lecture me about bringing their workplace into disrepute. . . . So, if I was faking it, I would have chucked the towel in a long time ago."

Borg's initial foray into band-naming seemed to preempt the

revulsion his bands would elicit. Forming Cyst in 1982, he says, "Older punks were dismissive, insisting, 'It's all finished now,' like only their period counted.... But we were kind of buoyed, because it was really kicking off, the second wave in England at the time, and even in America.... We're thinking it's not finished at all, it's just the older guys who think it's all wound up."

Perhaps they had a point, though, since Cyst, says Borg, "was just shambolic" and "only ever played at a party. It fell to bits, because the guy we had singing was actually AWOL from the air force, and the service people were tracking him down, and it was getting too hot for him. So, he took off, and then the band folded."

A frustrating period elapsed before another band could be cobbled together: "Until I met Dick [Richard 'Dick' Dale] I couldn't find anyone like-minded to get anything started.... I just kept holding out."

Explaining that "Rockhampton was a really small town, with only fifty thousand people or something back then," to therefore "meet a guy like that who was also into it, and the same mentality... it was great.... We knew of each other's existence, but it took about two years before we finally bumped into each other somewhere—'You're that dude.' All my mates had met him, and all his mates had met me... I was starting to think this guy was mythical."

Choosing the equally displeasing name of Smegma, Borg says the band "was basically an excuse, from my memory, to get really pissed." Amassing only six shows in two years would afford them ample spare time to indulge. The reason for the paucity of gigs, though, would be quite obvious to any small-town punks: "We were freakin' pariahs. The whole town hated us. The cops hated us; they were really gunning to bash Richard every chance they got—seriously. The musos hated us; I'm a pacifist by nature, but I'll stick up for myself, and I actually got in running fistfights with the wankers from the musos club."

Reminiscing about the deceit used to acquire their second show, Borg says, "They had an ad in the paper looking for a country and western band to play at a twenty-first [birthday] at the North Rocky pool. So, we said, 'Yeah, we can play that,' and we turned up and set up this huge, massive PA, and we actually had the plug pulled halfway through the second set. They just hated us. But we got paid."

Curiously, Borg says, "The people we had that came to our shows, once we started getting known a bit, it was mainly—and this is really weird... all these railway workers and meat-working yobbos.... Maybe we just struck a nerve with them or something." Adding to the smattering of punks in Northern Queensland, Borg says that for their third gig "we ran this thing called the 'Punks Skins Festival.'... We had a lot of people who had got on to the band all through regional Queensland, all the mining towns.... All the punks up in Townsville had known about us. So, we had all these people congregate in this guy's private big warehouse... and it was fantastic."

The band's concluding two appearances came at a wine bar, the last being a particularly fitting finale: "Twelve cop cars to break up a punk band.... Richard and Adam got arrested out of the band, and three punters who had big mohawks got arrested. When the cops came in, all they had was the flyer for the gig, and it was hand-drawn by Richard, and it was just stick figures with mohawks, and the cops were going in using this little hand flyer as who they were going to arrest."

The band refused to limp off without a final statement, releasing their *A Stain on Your Society* cassette in 1987. "That was actually a bit of a dig at Rocky, really, and at Townsville and the whole Queensland society.... When I was based in Rocky, I was always being really positive." Championing the town, Borg says, "I wouldn't let people bag it.... But once I got out, mate, I don't know that I want to go back there [*laughs*]."

# "CAN YOU DANCE TO FEEDBACK?"

## SOUTH AUSTRALIA AND NORTHERN TERRITORY

### ADELAIDE

While most bands barely manage to crawl out of the practice room, Fear and Loathing (*Wait till the Cat Licks It Up* twelve-inch, 1989; *The Odyssey of the Trojan Meatball* LP, 1989) are recognised as the longest continually running punk band in Adelaide. Birthed in 1981, theirs is a history replete with chaos, dysfunction, innumerable lineup changes, and a disjointed sound, suggesting revolving personnel and influences. For a band whose initial intention was supposedly to sound like Discharge, their eventual output gave indication that they'd been listening to those records on the wrong speed, covered in dirt, filth, and beer.

The biggest punk stirring of 1981 had not been the arrival of Fear and Loathing but the slated event "Dead Azaria and the Dingo Dance." A playful take on the Azaria Chamberlain case, the gig garnered the attention of all the major media in Adelaide. Adding to the already provocative name of the event, half-price entry had been offered to those who arrived with a toy doll. Following the adverse publicity, the venue's owner refused to allow the gig to proceed.

Skunks singer Mark Hayes, a member of one of the bands set to appear, says the group almost stalled: "We laid low for some time after that."

Though the topic of child and dingo would be too contentious, the band's tracks "Dance with the Fuhrer" and "Violent Night" had no problem finding place on their 1982 *Scratch 'n' Sniff* seven-inch.

For any talk of unruly behaviour, though, Hayes reveals, "I was a choir boy during my primary and secondary schooling." The Skunks, says Hayes, "walked a similar path as the Sex Pistols and other bands of the late 1970s.... It was the shock element that provided the impetus.... All of those punk bands flirted with the violent factor. Whether intentional or not, there was a fine line between that."

Addressing the tension in *DNA*, Harry Butler wrote that the track "Dance with the Fuhrer," especially, "symbolized the problems inherent in the band's attempts to manipulate their image. A substantial proportion of the audience thought it was fun to sieg-heil and goose-step around the place when this was played." Despite the questionable seriousness, it inevitably brought a Newtonian response of equal and opposite reaction: "Another faction though was rabidly anti-Nazi (not a bad thing in itself), however they took the antics of the aforementioned people very seriously, and promptly proceeded to clobber anyone displaying supposed pro-Nazi sympathies."[1]

Clobbering certainly wasn't confined to punk shows, as it constituted a passionate local pastime, Kelly Hewson recalling that "Adelaide was a really violent place.... If we went out, all your average people were massively violent."

Confusingly, for a band that maintained an uneasy embrace with violence, in their early period Skunks had covered the Cure and Siouxsie and the Banshees. Yet, according to Hayes, any taste for the morose—or a whole lot of makeup—did little to quell the dangers that stalked the band: "The older skins would beat up on the punks and younger skins (Oi! skins) inside the venues. Then, after the shows, the rockers would wait outside to beat you up as police stand by and watch.... We also had run-ins with a certain bikie group. You either stood and fought or ran as quick as you could."

Rather than solidifying bonds between maligned subcultures, Skunks were not shy in expressing disdain for them, be it mods—"Do the Mod Stomp"—or hippies—"Kill a Hippie."

If the trouble inside venues, or rockers lurking outside, was not already sufficient, Hayes recounts the cat-and-mouse strategies that often played out in and beyond Adelaide's central business district: "The Rundle Mall was a battleground ... same can be said for Hindley Street.... Both were looked upon as the rockers' turf. But we flirted with that and still played shows there. As well, rockers would drive in their cars to the northern and southern suburbs to beat up punks and skins."

Rockers, however, were not the only group disrupting the fluid functioning of Adelaide's retail precinct. Opening in 1983, a skinhead shop—Unionjack Clothing—was pressured into closure after only two months following complaints of customers' unsociable behaviour.

Tainted by their own followers, Hayes explains that Skunks also ceased operation: "Lack of venues, but mostly the violence, helped split the band up." Even a Skunks re-formation show in 1987 suffered from the same turbulence, Hayes remembering that it "was the same problem that saw us disband in 1982. The violence of some spoiled it for most, and we stopped playing."

Dismissive of the danger they faced within Adelaide's subcultural struggles, Hayes speaks to punk's collective empowerment: "Never thought of giving up; we took strength through each other. We were a close bunch of friends, and a lot of us still are."

Appearing with Skunks at the Commercial Hotel, members of Head On likely felt the cost was not worth the effort, as skinheads brandished knives at them following the show. One of the band's members was also beaten, before Mark Hayes intervened.

The group's desperation for shows saw them debut at a golf club, alongside a reggae band, to a surfie crowd. Further Head On gigs included a Mile End hippie commune, a birthday party, and a scout hall show where, despite amassing an eight-dollar profit from the door, the group trashed their own gear and microphones.

At least still in possession of admirable self-deprecation, the group released the five-song tape *Can You Dance to Feedback?* (1981).

Joining Malicious Sods, former Skunks drummer Chris Hayne again occupied a band impeded by audience behaviour. A succession of members also ensured the group never gained real momentum, only performing three shows. The most propulsion, it seemed, was to come from Hayne himself, future bandmate David Hassell remembering Chris "falling off the back of the stage and knocking himself out at one of them. He was drumming and must have been vibrating backwards."

One of their remaining two gigs, the "Aurora Punk Show," saw Malicious Sods, Stinkpots, Scum, Alternative Living, and the Anti converge at one of the only venues still tolerant of punk. As the last band on the bill, aggro reached a crescendo during Malicious Sods' set as the show ran "out of control, fists and boots flying, blood spilled."[2] *DNA* lamented that a "whole bunch of kids had decided to come out and have a look at what was being offered, but I'll bet many never go to another gig after this night."[3]

The main casualty had not in fact been wide-eyed and traumatised teens, but one of the bands themselves. Peter McIver of Alternative Living remembers what "did turn out to be our only gig, and our drummer may well have left because of the trouble at the gig."

Young and still largely sheltered from any extremes in Adelaide's scene, skinheads existed to McIver more as rumour than anything real:

> It was all just hearsay to me. I was a giddy kid; I could hardly believe I was about to play my bass in front of a crowd of people. I wasn't thinking about much else other than, "Don't mess this up." . . . I'm not sure who was playing when the skinheads burst in the back of the room, causing immediate havoc, but someone from the stage shouted out, "We are not here to fight!" "Well, we are!" was the response from the skins. . . . It was hard to work out who was who and what was going on in the melee, but it was brought home to me soon enough as I saw the guy in front of me get glassed by a skinhead. There was panic, but weirdly I just stood there in shock, almost unable to move. For reasons I'll never know, they left me alone. It was all over as quickly as it had begun.

McIver may have avoided danger through luck rather than resolve, but the more severe repercussions came when arriving at home: "The guys were making a real racket loading gear into my folks' house, and Da came to see what was going on. . . . 'What the hell is going on!? There is a guy on the front lawn, and he looks like he is dead!' One of the rabble had passed out rather than passed away, but it was all the same to Da. . . . I was 'encouraged' by my parents to have no further part in the scene, as the word spread about the violence at the gig. We never found another drummer, and Alternative Living must have faded away."

Alternative Living were not the only group to disband after a violent episode. In 1983, the vocalist of Total Absence also lost enthusiasm after being punched at a show.

Similar to Alternative Living, Scum suffered repercussions following the Aurora Punk Show, as their bass player was caught for underage drinking and their drummer fired for incompetence. The group disbanded.

After the barely active Malicious Sods broke up, the lengthy friendship between Chris Hayne and Scum's David Hassell easily facilitated a new band. As the Droogs, the group drew upon a set consisting of UK Oi! and punk covers, Hassell observing, "We were about the only one, really, that was playing that type of music."

Attempting to recollect how many shows actually composed the Droogs' live history, Hassell poses the question, "What constitutes a show? How many songs? [*laughs*]." He describes sets as consisting of "sometimes three, four songs, lucky—the cops were there. You'd see a table go flying here or there, behind the main crowd, and that was it.... That's eventually pretty much why we stopped as the Droogs.... Word gets around ... no one wants to play with you.... It was wasting your time at the end."

Hassell is sure to offer, though, that "we had some good ones as well, don't get me wrong."

As Hassell retreated to the relative sanctity of the local pub, he says, "Chris was still floating around doing things." The pair reconvened for the formation of Northern Drinking Cult (*Drink Up the Cider George EP* seven-inch, 1991), but the setting of the pub seems to have erased more detailed memories of their origins: "I honestly can't remember how we started again.... You've gotta remember we were all pretty pissed back then [*laughs*]."

Still inclined to the occasional re-formation, Hassell speaks of the entwined friendship between himself and Hayne that has surmounted the decades of beers, brawls, and broken bands: "Over all them years, in one way or another, me and Chris have been in bands together.... There's not many people you can say you're still good mates with that you went to primary school with."

As Hassell rues the trouble that accrued outside the band, *DNA* reported that Debortion experienced a greater issue: conflict among themselves. Filling their set with US hardcore cover songs, it was not to be slam dancing that precipitated violence at their shows, but rather the band members' own partners: "Apparently most of their girlfriends hate each other.... At a recent gig they had an all-new floorshow to go with the music—the various lady friends started discussing their differences via their fists."[4]

Poeticism, rather than violence, is one of punk's more unacknowledged associations. Yet Discharge's war-themed haikus or Dead Kennedys' sociopolitical rhapsody were presumably not quite what Aristotle had in mind when forming his *Poetics*. Unconcerned by poetry's lack of cool, Dave Scunge, vocalist of Septic Saw Blades, gave readings of his lyrics in the Rundle Mall while the band was in periods of inactivity. Performing under the name of the Subversive Poet, he incurred a ban, shoppers having to be shielded from his censure "of this false, greedy, ignorant, and racist society."[5]

Foreseeably, Septic Saw Blades were ascribed as "Adelaide's most non-trendy, non-fashion, non-cliche punk band."[6]

Beyond that which was fashionable and/or formulaic, Jello Biafra had correspondingly written that "Adelaide is considered the most eccentric of the cities, meaning even most of the punks both tolerate and support some very, very unusual bands."[7]

A more sceptical Butler remembers that most punk fans failed to display "any interest" towards the "unusual" bands, "even if such outfits were obviously displaying a punk attitude through their free-form and no-rules approach to music.... Those bands took the exploration of music to amazing new heights and depths" and "were 'punk' in that they took on the 'no rules/anything goes' ethic to try and do something new.... By contrast, the punk bands chose to limit themselves musically and rejected anyone who didn't conform accordingly, both musically and in personal appearance."

The punk bands did, however, sometimes seem capable of inventiveness, or at the least just being plain quirky. The initial conception of SUBDeK had been to perform a two-hour operatic musical piece based on the theme of nuclear holocaust. A combined lack of equipment and drug intake at rehearsal meant the vision never came to fruition. Eventually incorporating other members to become a more "conventional" band, SUBDeK instead attempted to infuse as much speed as possible into their music.

Contemporaries—and fellow fiends for velocity—Ribcage Wrestlers' fast hardcore was not to be played in a standardised form, but a fluctuating, terrifying swirl of hardcore and noise, including the use of vibrato effect. Lyrical content was, at times, even more unconventional—a song on their 1989 *Are Playing* seven-inch featured the lead singer of the Exploited's mother as its subject.

In perhaps the most unsettling example, however, Stinkpots made use of an improvised instrument that was either unfamiliar or fear-inducing to most punk sharehouses: a vacuum cleaner.

The group that personified Adelaide's "unusual bands," Grong Grong, mesmerised and haunted Jello Biafra, who recounted, "I lay awake for about two nights after seeing Grong Grong, still wondering if I actually saw what I really saw."[8] Harry Butler, seeking to locate the very source or influence of their inventiveness and brilliance, was instead told by guitarist Charlie Tolnay, "We weren't even confident that we'd even be able to write songs."[9]

Beginning in 1982, the band's name alone gave indication of the damaged entity Grong Grong was to become, as they were "named after an incident in which [singer Michael] Farkas consumed acid during a road trip from Adelaide to Sydney.... After losing his grip on reality somewhat during the trip, he arrived in the rural New South Wales town of Grong Grong, the name of which Farkas found hilarious. Later, when in Sydney trying to get into a local club for free, Farkas pretended to be in a band named Grong Grong to gain access. The ruse worked, and Farkas decided that the name was lucky."[10]

Supporting Dead Kennedys in Adelaide, their unbridled cacophony so transfixed Jello that he offered them a record deal, later releasing their self-titled album in 1986. But others were not nearly as enamoured. Supporting the Saints in 1984, Grong Grong were removed after only four songs, Tolnay telling *DNA*, "They cut the sound short and said we were driving away customers, that we were too loud, that we were the worst band they'd ever seen. By far."[11]

Still the high-profile supports continued, but along with them a dose of misfortune. On Christmas Day in 1984, having just supported PiL, Farkas overdosed. Reports suggested he flatlined more than once in the ambulance. He was comatose for over six months, and half-brother Tolnay was even asked to consider the removal of life support, though this was fortunately premature. During his initial stages of recovery, Farkas—who had dressed in a bondage hood that had bewildered and terrified audiences—was unable to speak. While he eventually recovered, but with lasting physical reminders, the band broke up.

Tolnay later collaborated with Jello Biafra on his Tumor Circus project, which released a self-titled album in 1991.

Grong Grong re-formed in 2009, with a CD/DVD suitably titled *To Hell and Back* released to coincide with the reanimation. Unable to foresee further tragedy, Tolnay died in 2017.

Recording their single the same year as Grong Grong's founding, the Assassins were composed of three members of the Dagoes, including Greasy Pop Records founder Doug Thomas. But where the Dagoes lacked any discernible lyrical theme, Assassins provided a darker, political hue. Their A-side track, "Assassination," originally titled "Kill the Prime Minister," included the line "Australia needs this man dead," referring to then-leader Malcolm Fraser. If not for its obscurity, the song would likely have piqued the interest more of domestic intelligence rather than any music-buying public.

A one-off endeavour, the record's back cover stated the songs to have been "recorded during the depression" in 1982. While this was slightly hyperbolic in prognosis, 1982–83 was, however, Australia's largest recession since the Second World War. Counsel for such pronouncement was perhaps best sought from a man who was to become acutely familiar with the nation's economic fortunes, as well as the Greasy Pop catalogue: Guy Debelle, deputy governor of the Reserve Bank. The *Adelaide Advertiser* wrote that in the '80s, Debelle was to be found "pogoing across 'the beer-stained red/purple carpet' of the old Tivoli Hotel in the city to the tuneful chaos of bands such as The Spikes, the Exploding White Mice, Lizard Train, and The Mad Turks from Istanbul."[12]

Before his transplant from the fetid carpets of the Tivoli to the sober surrounds of the Reserve Bank, Debelle's wild days coincided with the peak of Greasy Pop's release schedule in the second half of the 1980s. Jeff Stephens, whose band Exploding White Mice were a favourite of the label's acts, speaks of Adelaide's "really vibrant scene. I remember when we were playing . . . there'd be too many bands to go and see."

Such a plethora of options possibly meant Stephens's show schedule was already too full to take in the very band he came to join: "I didn't see their first show; I think they'd been going for two months when I joined." The Mice started in 1983 with the intention of being a one-time covers and party band, but favourable response prompted them to continue.

Jettisoning the covers through four albums and seven singles, the group's Ramones/Detroit/Sydney sound was distinct for Adelaide. As to thought of relocating, Stephens says, "I think maybe someone brought it up once at practice, and everyone just went 'No.'" Confessing it "might have been mentioned by me," the lack of recollection is reflected in Stephens's overview of his time with the band: "It's just a bit of a blur, really, that whole 1985 to 1995. We toured three to four times a year," each trip being "pretty long and pretty arduous." As well as the stupefying long-distance drives between Australian cities, the band also made the long-haul flight to Europe, touring there in 1990 and '96.

Stephens posits an additional intensity when seeking to account for the foreign attraction to Australian bands: "I've read so many people from overseas saying when they go to see an Australian band . . . [that] there's a bit of an edge to it that maybe the local bands don't have. . . . They were pretty good, some of them, but they lacked that—I don't know—that sort of going-for-the-throat thing that the Australian bands had at the time."

Continuing, Stephens says, "There's a theory that someone who is influenced by something usually takes it to a bit more of an extreme level. . . . In Australia we latched onto the MC5 and the Stooges, and Radio Birdman and the Saints took that to another level. . . . You take your influence and you intensify it, or you make it more of your own . . . and sometimes in doing that you accidentally invent your own style, which is what the Saints and the Ramones did."

Named after a scene in the Ramones-starring film *Rock 'n' Roll High School*, Exploding White Mice also found their place on the big screen. In 1987, their song "Dangerous" appeared in the feature film *The Allnighter*, which ingloriously holds a 0 percent approval rating on the review-aggregate website Rotten Tomatoes.[13] In likeness to the film that gave them their name, the 1994 Australian feature *The Roly Poly Man* saw the Mice cast as a bar band. With a budget nearing a million dollars, the film reportedly grossed the most meagre of takings at the box office: $4,067.

The Exploding White Mice were producing a more reasonable

return for their time and effort, even making a small impression on the Australian charts with their debut album, *Brute Force and Ignorance*, in 1988. The album, and the years until its follow-up in 1990, were, Stephens says, the high point of the band: "I think we still did some pretty good music in the '90s, but really by the end of the '80s the interest in us had plateaued. . . . I guess we were never going to become wildly successful, and that was never our aim. . . . First and foremost, most people who play in bands like us are fans—started out being fans and still are fans. We're doing it because we want to play and hear that sort of music—we love it. We're not doing it to make money."

Today, Stephens is a record store operator in Adelaide, a vocation that in the age of digital procurement is as much a labour of love as a source of income.

Not boasting near the same cachet as a record store worker, the Insurgents drummer Jay Goodger was at the time a qualified accountant. As most bands squandered what savings they had on a largesse of pub drinks, Goodger set up an account with which they were able to pay for equipment, practices, and the recording of a demo. Yet perhaps they could have been even better served by the employment of an imposingly sized manager, after finding out why they were so welcomed at a particular Adelaide venue: "When we went into the back room one night, we found him [the owner] counting out wads of hundred-dollar notes—he was making lots of money."[14]

Band member Stuart Silcox notes the manipulation more as a matter of microeconomics: "The arrangement between bands and venues was exploitative, but nobody was shocked by this. It was a simple matter of supply and demand. If we didn't like what was on offer, there were plenty of bands willing to replace us on the bill. The alternative was hall shows, which could be great," but they also had potential to end "in carnage, so it was just easier to play pubs and clubs."

As unintended principal of an earlier carnage, Skunks' Mark Hayes had not been swayed from continuing to perform. But where Hayes recalls that Perdition began "pretty well from where the Skunks left off," Jello Biafra failed to note a seamless transition: "Perdition is more thoughtful than the Skunks were, who had a reputation for starting fights at their shows. I found that hard to believe after seeing them live."[15]

Further differentiating Skunks from Perdition, the latter band's source of troubles had shifted from skinheads to their employers, Hayes revealing to *DNA* that "in the last six months I've been called into the office three or four times and told that I've got to put work before the band."[16] Bassist Tony Loader expressed comparable frustration: "The same thing happened to me.... I got dragged into the office and told off about my appearance, and it just went downhill from there."[17]

The year following their 1984 seven-inch *The Intoxicated EP*, US label Flipside released a Perdition/Vicious Circle split album to coincide with an intended tour. But once again, says Hayes, Loader's boss would do as bosses do: "Unfortunately Tony couldn't get the time off work, and Vicious Circle did that tour without us."

One of Adelaide's leading punk/hardcore acts, Perdition then proceeded to confound fans with the release of their *How to Teach Your Budgie to Talk* LP in 1985. Presented in a yellow cover with a graphic of four budgies, Hayes admits the inapposite presentation had been calculated, if it was also to their detriment: "It certainly didn't conform to the punk norm, but that was an intentional decision of the band to do that. As a consequence, the *Budgie* LP did get a mixed response, and we may have suffered saleswise because of that."

Explaining that "we still played punk gigs," Hayes adds that "by 1987, Perdition were attracting a metal crowd as well as punks, and we were covering Black Sabbath's 'Paranoid.' But worldwide, punks and metallers were mixing at gigs as the crossover of both gained momentum.... As well, I was a bit older than most, so had a hard rock and metal background before punk came along.... I grew my hair long again."

Further regression to Hayes's formative years came in 1988, as, a decade after first performing in bands together, Hayes, Kelly Hewson, and Michael Feeney again shared a stage as Dead Ringer. For Hayes, though, any symbolic return to his youth would be challenged by adult responsibilities, including navigating the time and needs of a wife, children, and five concurrent bands: "It definitely strained my relationship with my wife, Janet, to say the least. She was and always has been a great supporter of what I have done, and still do, and possibly I could not have done as much without that support. We are truly best friends; we've had a great journey together, and to this day our relationship is stronger than ever."

Returning from metal's blazing guitar solos and bursting leather pants to the relative simplification of garage punk and the Detroit sound, Twenty Second Sect, the Plague, the Things, the Shanks, the Insurgents, and the Iron Sheiks kept faith in Adelaide through the decade. The latter, adding an element of theatrics in a pre–politically correct era, adorned Middle Eastern headdress for the cover of their 1988 twelve-inch. Titled *Do You Sell Beer Here?*, it would pair nicely with the Filthy Scumbags' *Lager Drinkers from Hell* tape the same year.

Stuart Silcox is blunt in elucidating Filthy Scumbags' unsurprising ambition and methodology: "Getting wasted was the prime objective in this band.... I kind of insisted playing guitar for them because of the nihilist mindset behind the band, which translated into frenzied performances." Performances, he says, that "did attract the attention of the plod on numerous occasions, with raids on our gigs and rehearsals.... We were banned from a number of venues, and we seemed to thrive on this reputation."

Just one contributor to their notoriety was a Hindley Street nightclub show: "We were first on the bill, and with a crowd building outside, the management decided they didn't like the look of our audience, locked them out, and cancelled the gig. People outside took matters into their own hands and busted the door open; crowd poured in, and we ran for the stage, getting through about three numbers before the cops arrived in force with a dog squad, several paddy wagons.... Somehow we eluded them."

Returning from a trip to Melbourne, the band was not quite so elusive, and they were arrested in Horsham. In addition to a series of charges relating to illegal driving and drug possession, Kelly Hewson says police "beat the shit out of them with phone books. They stripped them naked, then sprayed them with the cold hose, and they kept them there for like a week and had to go to court."

Even accounting for all the bannings and arrests, Silcox says, "I had the most fun of almost any band I played in."

Relocating to Sydney in the 1990s, Silcox says, "[I] accidentally fell into photography, snapping oddities on my Redfern mail route with a crude phone camera.... I have always had some interest in art.... This has since grown to include exhibitions and a book."

Silcox was not the band's only creative of note, as Giles Bettison has forged a career as an internationally renowned glass artist. "He's like a multimillionaire," declares Kelly Hewson. Attending Bettison's first Australian exhibition, Hewson remembers, "I'm looking at it . . . $50,000, $250,000 for this big one, before enquiring, 'Is there anything cheap?'"

Composed of Bettison, Hewson, and two members of Filthy Scumbags, the Hot Tomatoes in 1989 put out the LP *With a Pinch of Salt*, which has occupied dusty record stores rather than any haughty art galleries. Featuring colourful clown artwork, the album's sleeve together with the innocuous band name concealed the US-inspired skate punk within.

Reviewed in skate and surf magazines, punk and hardcore took hold among the surf communities of Adelaide's mid-South Coast. Hewson remembers, "We'd play huge shows down south. . . . They were surfies, but they were pretty hard—they were full-on."

From a similar region, Doomsday Hour and the Shitheads were followed by a succession of bands into the '90s, that, unlike Hot Tomatoes, left little trace of their existence. Another to offer lasting remnant, the Bearded Clams (self-titled CD, 1993) ran concurrently to Hot Tomatoes, playing a self-described form of "surf thrash rock."

The same year as the Clams' formation, the *News* featured twin articles on the "new" phenomenon of slam dancing.[18] A half decade late in their discovery, the article described its risks, accompanied by a warning from the president of the South Australian branch of the Australian Medical Association and a condemnation by a spokesperson for the Legal Services Commission. Where's the Pope? was mentioned in the article's accompanying list of bands; bassist Robert Stafford does admit, "I still have a scar from slamming and sliding across the brick paving."

As Where's the Pope? became highly influential among Adelaide's surf scene, Stafford's own introduction to punk had come from loitering at one of the city's most popular beaches: "I was hanging around Henley Beach and met a few friends who were into new music." Little would he know that his own band was to one day torment its local residents. "We did a show in Henley Square, where we got Frank Portolese [maker of Woogie amplifiers] to supply this huge PA. . . . It was so loud, a friend of mine said he had fallen asleep at home and it woke him up, and he was half a suburb away!"

As disrupters of local sanctity, the band's track "There Goes the Neighbourhood" was arguably more applicable as their record title. The song featured on Where's the Pope?'s *Straight Edge Holocaust* twelve-inch in 1988, and Harry Butler's review emphasised the record's appeal to those "put off by the seriousness and elitism of many of the other local punk/thrash bands. It's probably a good set of themes and even a veritable soundtrack for the lives of a hell of a lot of basically ordinary suburbanites."[19]

The choice of name for their full-length album would further invoke 1980s Australian suburbia: *Sunday Afternoon BBQ's*. It was released in 1989, and its cover depicted the band with an obligatory carton of beer, cooler, and skateboard, walking into a gathering of well-dressed adults. Including tracks "We Want Your Beer" and a cover of Gang Green's "Alcohol," it gave the appearance of a "party at all costs" ethos. Stafford, however, insists it to be somewhat less facile: "People remember the fun beer songs, but most of our set was driven by Frank's intense chorus lines and one-liners like, 'Above all, think.'"

Today, says Stafford, Frank Pappagalo is an educator of the nation's youth: "As a schoolteacher, he is hoping to have a positive influence on kids becoming good people and lifelong learners who show empathy and compassion for all ... which is the natural evolution of singing in a band where you had a message that tried to inspire fresh ideas and thought, as well as having a great fun time with friends."

Kelly Hewson, whose band Order of Decay occupied the same period to Where's the Pope?, remembers a scene that, while still offering quality shows, was appearing fatigued. By the late '80s, he observes, "there was quite a lot of bands ... but they were just running on their own energy. They were still awesome, but it's almost like the lost years of punk and hardcore is '87 to '91—all around the world, I reckon."

Within the black hole of Hewson's punk history, Order of Decay released their *Bite or Be Bitten* seven-inch (1989) and self-titled LP (1990), as well as finding an audience to justify repeated tours: "We toured Melbourne like twenty times."

One trip east, though, shattered a certain illusion the band had been harbouring: "We did this interview.... We said something like, 'We're the most full-on, fastest hardcore band in Australia.' Then our first gig is in Geelong.... There's this band of these surfers.... It's probably the only gig they ever played. . . . They're faster than us. . . . The first gig we play and the band that supported us was faster."

Unfortunately, Order of Decay's tempo could also not keep pace with the fast living of their vocalist, Phil Partridge, who died after falling from the roof of the Century Hotel, the venue of the band's first show. Hewson speaks of an almost fatalistic sense that had propelled Partridge: "It was like he knew all the time, and he wanted to do everything quickly. He's like, 'C'mon, we should record more, we should do the other songs, we've gotta do it now.' It was like he was running out of time—it was weird. . . . He was the most hard-living, full-on dude I've ever met in my life."

Though the loss of Partridge was a reminder of punk's often reckless engagement with life, it was far from the only subcultural form willing to teeter on the edge. For Matt Jonsson, punk had offered salvation rather than him becoming another of its youthful sacrifices. Growing up "in the rolling, working-class foothills of Adelaide," Jonsson remembers

> totally crazy days. . . . Mass fights . . . riots and demolition parties that became the rage, smash-and-grabs, ram raids, countless stolen cars and buildings set ablaze, patrolling helicopters. . . . There was drugs, jail, and death. But the real point with all of this is that punk gave me a choice of being a rebel with a cause, and plucked me out of the mayhem. . . . Punk educated me, the bands showed me the big picture, got me thinking, researching, forever pushing me to grow, reevaluate, to read between the lines, to look for truth in all things. I became a pacifist. . . . I started going to protests and became a vegetarian.

Jonsson, through Mutants and Festered Vestoons, had given his own musical expression to that enlightenment. But with the years came an exhaustion—of form rather than content: "Our musical style was broadening; we felt this freedom from years of hardcore, which had exponentially tightened into a narrow formula compared to the free experimental days of early punk. . . . We still loved hardcore, but as musicians had a need to explore."

In Adelaide, bands such as Hoot McKloot attempted to balance the inspiration of punk with reggae, country, thrash, and rock. Jonsson says that, at least visually, "I had been pushing the Vestoons . . . to make masks and engage in more theatrics. . . . My grandfather . . . was a circus performer in a knife-throwing act with my grandmother. . . . He was also in a clown act."

Amid a waft of smoke, stage chaos, and clown face paint, Clowns of Decadence were constructed.

Shunning the evil clown archetype, the band presented little danger, even if Victor Harbour police thought otherwise. Under the headline of "Police Fear Punk Band Violence" and claims of confiscated weapons, the *Victor Harbour Times* reported that "police are concerned about an influx of troublemakers into the town whenever a certain punk rock group appears."[20]

In fact, the only implements the band possessed that could be construed as weapons were swallowing swords. Matty Blade, a part of the Clowns' touring show in the 1990s, later "set a new Guinness World Record by swallowing fourteen 60cm swords simultaneously. . . . He also held the record for most swords swallowed in a year—3782 in 2003—and appeared in the 2007 *Guinness World Records* book after swallowing a sword that weighed 20.1kg."[21]

Blade, however, was only one act of what Jonsson—stage name Snatcha Razoo—describes as a multivariate stage show that included "jugglers, unicycle antics, dancing girls, fat-a-gram stripper, chainsaws, smoke machines made from vacuum cleaners turned on reverse with coffee tins full of a smouldering ounce of weed," pie fights, acrobats, comedians, rubbery puppets, "pyrotechnics, glitter, and confetti bombs. . . . Fire-breathing became a permanent fixture by three members" even if "all got singed at one time or another" in a "supremely dangerous mix with alcohol."

The spectacle would count for little when they appeared on television talent quest show *A Touch of Elegance*, the band placing last. Conservative radio talkback host Bob Francis scored them a zero, stating, "Rubbish like that would get a grant from the government."[22] Rather than a grant, singer Marc Fenech won Most Outstanding Male Vocalist at the inaugural South Australia Music Industry Awards.

Purchasing a Coaster bus, the band became an interstate roadshow. Jonsson depicts both the spectacle and logistical nightmare that ensued: "We would get free food from late-night eateries, just because they got carried away with the bizarre encounter they were having. Or, on many occasions, service stations would go into lockdown as we approached in the middle of the night.... Trying to regroup the next morning ... was chaos. Trying to piece together the events of the previous evening to locate lost members—or found ones—still in party mode, and trying to get them on the bus, could be a daunting task."

This was a task that for Jonsson began to lose its novelty: "I started to loathe all the drinking. I felt a microcosm of man's decadence right in the very bus I was riding in.... To me, the band had become the mirror of itself, and no longer cared—even for all the good intentions, that was being smothered."

Whatever the drift from their original purpose, Jonsson reflects on the memorable and likely otherwise-unfulfilled journey that punk was to provide: "Soaked in sweat, kerosene, and grease paint, and stuck in a rambling twenty-two-seat Coaster criss-crossing Australia, playing everywhere and anywhere, with everyone and anyone, has been a strange, bewildering dream."

## WHYALLA

An even bigger bus—a forty-five-seater—had ferried four bands to Whyalla to perform for Easter in 1987. A declining industrial town, which had until the late '70s been the location of Australia's largest shipyards, Whyalla had experienced only fleeting exhibitions of punk since the music style's inception. The Tongues in 1977–78 worked a set consisting largely of Sex Pistols and Clash covers. The next band of note, Punk and Disorderly, were similarly occupied by Sex Pistols covers, managing only a couple of shows in 1983.

In 1985, a "Whyalla Scene Report" appeared in *DNA*, alerting readers that the scene had doubled to two bands, Domestic Vermin and Flag of Peace, with shared members. By the following year, the city of twenty thousand and only twenty punks had again been reduced to a solitary band, Random Chaos, with Vicious Rumours to follow in 1987.

## MOUNT GAMBIER

Sitting halfway between Adelaide and Melbourne, Mount Gambier was even further removed from musical evolution and subcultural manoeuvrings. With members of Sputniks having left more than a decade previously, punk remained practically dormant until Psycho Zombies and the 1990 release of their *Cry Baby Cry* seven-inch on Greasy Pop Records.

## DARWIN

Contrary to the overwhelmingly white/Anglo demographics of rural and regional Australia, Ant Banister reminisces of the more diverse city of Darwin, "It was probably the most multicultural city back in the '80s, when I was growing up there. Because it was so close to Asia and it had a really high turnover of people, everyone was transient.... The other thing was that the average age of Darwin was twenty-five. It was pretty wild; we could ride our bikes off into the bush and see buffalos and kangaroos and all that.... Hitting my late teens and there were so many bands, and clubs would stay open until dawn.... Parties would go as long as the beer would last, sometimes two or three days."

Spurning the stereotype of a big-drinking Territorian, Banister was a teetotaller. Adding to his distinctiveness, he says, "There was a period where I was the only goth in town." This in a city with an average maximum temperature of 32 degrees Celsius (90 degrees Fahrenheit).

Putting together the band Spring Rolls, Banister says, "We had an old, broken kit of drums, out-of-tune guitar, the synthesiser, and a drum machine.... We were just banging away at first.... We'd give the audience food, eggs, and stuff to throw at us while we played." Counterintuitively, Spring Rolls became a punk band when "we all became better at our instruments." They were not alone in their pursuit, as Banister recounts there were "probably five fairly active punk bands" in the small city.

With local journalists among the broader music coterie, Spring Rolls were aided in gaining exposure: "We'd get in the newspaper pretty regularly. We had an article on how we won the 'worst band.'" They also featured in the first edition of the *Territory Times*, which posed the question, "The Spring Rolls—a scum band or Darwin's worthy dilettantes?"

In 1986, the *Northern Territory News* publicised the band's most infamous performance: "Darwin's contribution to the International Year of Peace, a peace concert, ended up not as peaceful as planned.... Many spectators became extremely violent towards local fringe band Spring Rolls, and threatened band members and people in the audience.... A woman was dragged screaming from the stage and about seven people were forcibly removed from the backstage area after threatening the band with violence." Drummer "Mr Action ... said they were reacting to the lyrical content of the songs, which he described as offensive and in bad taste."[23]

Spring Rolls released a recording of the event, and the tape was suitably titled *Kill Some Hippies and Break the Peace*. Included were the between-song taunts, jeering, and insults. Banister offers his memory of the vitriol: "We were a comedy punk act. . . . It was satire and people weren't subtle enough to get that. . . . It was just all pure shock value; songs about incest and poo. . . . [Singer] Chris was very much into Divine, and to be the most disgusting you could possibly be. It was normal at a party, if someone fell asleep, to shave their eyebrows off and shit on their chest."

As Darwin eventually became too small for those with larger horizons and ambitions, according to Banister at least one band member would seek to forget their time as the city's most infamous musical entity: "Chris, the singer, moved to Sydney, because he's a lawyer. . . . He very shortly after leaving Darwin made himself scarce whenever we tried to contact him. He didn't want to know, because we knew about his history. He was a pretty wild guy. He did some pretty crazy stuff—illegal stuff, seedy stuff."

## EAST-NORTHEAST OF DARWIN

Even further to the north, Papua New Guinea had gained its independence from Australia only in 1975. A decade later, correspondence sent from Port Moresby to *DNA* announced the existence of the Papua New Guinea punk "scene," consisting of a single band, the Screaming Dead. The group had formed after some English rock music fans met a punk from Melbourne in a local pub, and they were joined shortly after by an Indigenous Australian on drums. Their first show likewise took place at a village pub. The *DNA* letter gave account of the gig: "Everything was going good until Bondage got pissed and started to give the blacks shit (the stage then became flooded with rocks and beer bottles, so the band made a quick exit)."[24]

With a few more shows supporting the country's only heavy metal band, *DNA* reported that the Screaming Dead "were getting quite well-known as the new white band with a radical sound." As for being the vanguard in creation of a new movement, "There are a few punks on the streets of Port Moresby but not many." In the aftermath of their final show, a group of locals formed their own band, named Ibos. "The Screaming Dead tried to start something, but thought they'd leave it to the blacks to see if they can bring out the protest of the people on the street through music rather than violence."[25]

# “CONSERVATIVE TRASH”

## WESTERN AUSTRALIA

### PERTH

If violence formed a strong undercurrent to 1980s punk and hardcore, then isolation or the reputed ill effects of WA’s Emu Export Lager could not alone account for the antisocial aspect of Perth’s scene. Its disquiet instead continued to centre on Quick and the Dead.

The band was the subject of a further current affairs television segment, during which the presenter posed the question, “Do their Nazi decorations suggest some political stance?” Addressing the concern of the program, singer Andrew “Bored” disavowed use of swastikas by themselves or fans as anything but “creating an image.”[1] However, flirt with something for any period and you risk it annexing your consciousness. Tony Pola of late ’70s/early ’80s bands the Transplants, Rex Humbard and the Retirement Fund, Avoid Upholstery, Utensils, and Modern Wimps—and later Kim Salmon and the Surrealists and Beasts of Bourbon—had also found brief place in Quick and the Dead. Much to his disillusionment, Pola says, “I played one show with Quick and the Dead and recorded a demo with them. Then I worked out they didn’t like coloured folk.”

Bassist and band stalwart Murray Holmes reveals that on his return from a trip to England in 1982, “That’s when we sort of turned political. . . . We evolved into a band with a right-wing purpose. . . . A couple left because of the persuasion of going right-wing. . . . It was hard to find members.”

After ceasing as Quick and the Dead in 1983, Holmes again travelled to London, and before leaving was requested to bring his bass. Summoned to join Skrewdriver, he began recording with the band the day after his arrival. The album *Hail the New Dawn* was released in 1984, with the revived Skrewdriver having dispensed with an earlier political ambiguity, instead embracing an unflinching neo-Nazism.

Recalling that "I went to a few National Front meetings," Holmes, with Skrewdriver, played a South London show for the organisation. "There was about three hundred skinheads. The National Front had knocked off a container of beer from Holland, and they were selling these cans of beer for, I think, 50p.... I think we all got paid ten quid each. They [National Front] would have made a fucking fortune."

Returning to Perth, Holmes describes the city as also having been fertile for the far-right message: "I think there were a lot of sympathisers. What we had in Perth years ago was the ANM, the Australian Nationalist Movement.... They used to come along to the gigs [after Quick and the Dead], and they were recruiting a lot. They had meetings around at skinheads' places, and a barbeque. A lot of the skinheads were doing poster runs ... back then it was anti-Asian." Members of the ANM were convicted of firebombing five Chinese restaurants in Perth between September 1988 and May 1989.

Burdened by notoriety as Quick and the Dead, the band had been forced to employ some subterfuge to continue finding shows: "We went through a few name changes to throw people off the track a bit.... That was sort of like the later part of it. We went to Final Solution, and then finally White Noise."

White Noise released two albums for white-power/far-right-wing label Rock-O-Rama Records in 1989 and 1990, without Holmes.

As reported in *DNA*, the last drummer of Quick and the Dead had persuaded the group to perform the track "It's the Greatest Working Class Rip-Off." Eventually made aware of the song's origins, anarcho-punk band Crass, they removed it from their set and sought a new drummer.[2]

Contrasting the short hair, short temper, and right-wing disposition of many of its skinheads, anarcho-punk and left-leaning politics had significant influence on the remainder of Perth's scene. Rhys Evans recalls the divide: "It sort of split. It went on to all the anarchist sort of stuff, and then Quick and the Dead were on the other spectrum.... They [Quick and the Dead] used to have a big punk following, but it changed."

Accentuating the division, Russell Hopkinson is uncategorical that "the worst thing that happened to Perth punk was Quick and the Dead.... Early on it ... was not as politically motivated," instead embodying

> the ethics of chaos and Sid Vicious style. But it became much more like a little far-right gang.... I actually got to know the guitarist, Mark. He was a nice guy, and surprisingly he was actually Jewish, and was going to quit the band because it started as a bit of a joke, but people started to take the whole Nazi thing seriously.... Murray [Holmes] basically ran with that Nazi skinhead thing.

But then, as Hopkinson was to discover, not everything is always as simple as black-and-white binaries: "The scariest Nazi skinhead in Perth was a Jewish guy. We found that out, because he used to come over to our house to buy pot off someone and I saw his dole card one day and I went, 'Rosental? Your last name's Rosental?'"

Hesitant to always exhibit his own affiliations, Hopkinson says Holmes "was a refrigeration repairman, and he had a wig in his glove box that he'd wear if he had to go to any little old lady's house or something like that."

However, forgoing a skinhead appearance didn't always indicate a more tolerant disposition: "There were these things called the 'punk's picnics,' and that was generally your entree to the punk scene.... I was wearing a Dead Kennedys T-shirt, and this older punk ... said, 'You can't be into the Dead Kennedys. Three reasons: one, they're American, two, they've got a Black drummer, three, they've got a song 'Nazi Punks Fuck Off.' ... The Dead Kennedys dodged a bullet by avoiding coming here on the advice of the promoters, because it would have been the most violent gig you could imagine."

According to Jello, it wasn't just the advice of promoters which had dissuaded them: "We were supposed to go play Perth.... There were a lot of threats coming towards us, and whether anything would have happened to us, we'll never know ... The police then hand-delivered notes to our promoters, saying something to the effect that, 'If you think we had fun at Rose Tattoo, wait till you see what we're going to do to you.'"[3]

Both Perth shows were cancelled.

Hopkinson's early musical endeavours (Circle A, Genocide, Zoo Rejects, Dismembered, Cult of the One Armed Bandit, Mob Vengeance) were significantly less scrutinised, as he says near all of these bands faltered before playing a single gig: "A lot of your early bands usually contain people who like the idea of being in a band but don't really understand what it entails."

Of those bands that did actually make it to a live performance, attempts were made to create an alternative space, but ended with a far too familiar outcome: "There was not a lot going on apart from house parties, which you would try and hopefully make sure no skinheads knew about." Unsuccessful in their subterfuge, Hopkinson says, "Every time we played a party, we'd have to know certain Cockney Rejects songs ... to avoid someone putting their boot through my kick drum.... It was difficult, so it really just became a small social scene, and when it got too difficult, we all fucked off, basically."

Hopkinson notes that "you couldn't afford a [plane] ticket so you had to get the bus." Yet after the tribulations of Perth, and a torturously long bus ride out of it, Melbourne must have seemed a fulfillment of fantasies, as Hopkinson soon found himself in one of the city's most popular hardcore bands, Vicious Circle. Further travel came then, not as escape, but touring. "There was a couple of worthwhile punk scenes. The Sydney one ... it was way more chaotic; it was more how I imagined one of those Black Flag shows at the Olympic Auditorium [Los Angeles] in the early '80s—pretty close to anarchy.... There was one gig that made the cover of the *Telegraph*.... A famous, violent Sydney punk called 'Eager Penis'—he's probably a story in himself—ended up smashing somebody over the head with a wine bottle after an argument over the wine bottle." Together they "left the gig arm in arm, blood pouring down their faces, and it made the cover of the *Telegraph*."

Such shows, says Hopkinson, "proved your resilience.... It wasn't a friendly environment.... The first time Vicious Circle played Sydney ... this skinhead guy just grabbed me from behind and this other guy went, 'No, no, he's in the band,' and he said, 'Oh mate, I thought he was a faggot.' They were bashing gay people on Oxford Street before going to a punk gig. So, you had that element, where Melbourne was just really cool ... [and] didn't seem as wild to me, but maybe that's because I wasn't as wild as other people."

In Melbourne, the greatest bother for Hopkinson was having to respond to the bemused inquiries of Finnish tourists: "I was obsessed by Finnish hardcore, and I was walking around Melbourne one day, and these two Finnish backpacker girls came up to me and said, 'Why do you have all these Finnish words written on your arm?'"

More tiresome than having to explain Finnish band names, Hopkinson says eventually that Melbourne became "really weird, and lots of people were getting into heavy drugs, so I thought it was time to get out."[4]

He left Vicious Circle and returned to Perth, as his reasons for initially departing his home city had finally receded: "I think there was a small cabal of people who sort of went underground and then eventually the Quick and the Dead dissipated.... When I came back in '86, it had pretty much blown over."

With the menace gone, Hopkinson instead identified an evolution that he found hard to reconcile with his initial motivations: "The organic nature ... is what I really liked about the punk scene. And then by the mid-'80s it was starting to become corporatized, like the crossover metal stuff, and suddenly you had a band like Stormtroopers of Death.... [Their album] probably sold more in Australia than any hardcore record outside of the Suicidal Tendencies album.... I thought, 'This is the death of hardcore,' basically."

Making the progression to professional musician, and with a celebrated career in You Am I, Hopkinson nevertheless reminisces of his punk years that "it was cool. I mostly have positive memories of it, of that whole scene, and still very good friends. But as someone who wanted to become a musician, you have to try and make that step up eventually. It seemed like the right time.... I think you have an eye on what you want to do; for some people it was getting out of it, for some people it was the politics, for other people it was the music, and for some it was all three, equally.... They all serve their purpose."

Rhys Evans, former bandmate of Hopkinson, made a similar transition away from the rough hardcore of their youth. Trading a stage for a DJ booth, Evans explains that he "ended up doing raves.... I got right into it. Even had my own club for a couple of years.... A lot of people I'd hung out with, they became punters.... It was a natural progression, in my eyes.... I never made any money playing in bands at all—I used to make a living out of it [DJing]."

The lack of pay among punk bands was hardly revelatory, especially given Evans's admission that with his band Disabled Youth, "I'd never played an instrument before. I just said, 'Yeah, I can do it.' It was fucking awful.... I got better, I practiced."

Evans joined Division Four, which, like other Perth bands Eep of the Gra and King Pig, was situated within the crossway of punk and post-punk. They released a 1983 demo that was put to vinyl three decades later. Evans also continued to maintain an affiliation to rough, pummelling hardcore through the band Threshold of Pain. Taking on unintended pertinence in their name, Evans says that musically, "People didn't like us—too confrontational for them.... We were together for quite a while, but no venues would take us."

As well as Disabled Youth and Threshold of Pain, other acts to accept the new and seemingly too distressful UK hardcore sound included Rival Tribes and Black Sheep. Evans reveals the latter's guitarist, Jeremy, to have been something of a peaceable enigma: "He'd been over to the UK and met up with all the guys from Crass. He stayed with them for a while. He was a contradiction; he was a full-on Christian vegetarian."

No less direct than the English anarcho-punks, the political preoccupation of Insurrection was self-evident. Drummer Clare McAndrew explains:

> You didn't dress up, you lived it. We were vegetarian and protested for animal rights, pacifist, and very antiwar. This was a lifestyle choice for sure; it was showing your dissatisfaction with the mainstream and what was happening in the world.... I lived it as much as I could, while still being a schoolgirl. I got expelled from the private Catholic school I attended for my hair and fights with nuns. We were very antireligion, and this didn't really gel well at school. I punched a nun (she hit me first), but my parents were (weirdly) very supportive. It was a very difficult time for me, as I was constantly in trouble at home and school. Playing the drums was probably a great outlet for the aggression.

While most teenage musical interactions were confined to distant fixations on Queen, the Village People, and a still untainted Michael Jackson, McAndrew was a whole different kind of cool: "I was getting tuned in to what was going on in the musical scene at a very young age. I also started sneaking out of my window at night to parties. There was mods, skins, punks, rockabillies, indie/Cure heads."

Yet even within Perth's more daring subcultures, McAndrew came to view her own influences as insufficiently adventurous; her band Identity Crisis "seemed tame and lacked edge. I started to hear bands like the Exploited, GBH, and Conflict, and loved the energy, angst, and noise.... While all of my school friends were making themselves look pretty, I was revelling in this much more edgy, hardcore style. The hair, clothes, styling, it was all very important at that young age."

But much like her disavowal of beauty norms, McAndrew came to question some of her musical discoveries, though more through guilt by association: "I always felt some of the more hardcore punks seemed to merge too much with the skinhead movement for my liking, and they certainly did in a small scene like Perth.... I had absolutely no tolerance for the racism or violence that this whole scene embodied."

She correspondingly shifted her listening to anarcho bands "Conflict, Subhumans, Crass, Discharge," and then some uninvited guests to a party held by McAndrew helped precipitate forming a new band: "As luck would have it, Mob Vengeance gate-crashed.... We had a party at our house.... It was a good party, but my parents were both Irish doctors and we lived in a pretty conservative suburb.... The night was a disaster—police, angry parents, grounded for a hundred years—but I knew then that I wanted to play in a band and be an integral part of what this movement was."

The formation of Insurrection was not without its own minor difficulties for a still teenage McAndrew: "It was tricky for me, as I was still at school, but with a bit of ducking and diving I made it to rehearsals and gigs. Being so young made it all that much more exciting, breaking out from my little cocoon of suburbia.... Absolutely no one cared about money or where the band was going, just that we were performing and getting a message across."

As the vocalist of Insurrection, Lydia, through her lyrics, confronted sexism as well as offering elementary feminist themes. With anarcho-punk affording a greater space to women, McAndrew says, "There were some great feminist writers and artists in the anarcho-punk scene also. For me, Crass's *Penis Envy* is a classic feminist punk record, and I wore this record out, and still listen to it regularly and play it to my children."

Even accounting for the scene's myriad misdeeds, McAndrew says, "I did feel like I was part of something very special. We all loved music, and believed in the messages we were putting out, and were so driven to perform."

Similarly driven in her post-music career, the vehemence of anarcho-punk's anticapitalist critique appears to have lessened. Becoming an internationally recognised art economist and academic, McAndrew has authored the books *The Art Economy: An Investor's Guide to the Art Market* and *Fine Art and High Finance: Expert Advice on the Economics of Ownership*.

With Insurrection broken up, McAndrew continued to play in the aptly named Resurrection, who, amassing only half a dozen shows, performed mostly alongside Greenhouse Effect (*Squirt!!!* seven-inch, 1987).

In the mid-1980s, people promoting any such message of climate change were generally consigned as crackpots or dreadfully dull alarmists. Whether having just a topical band name or actually being conscious environmentalists, Greenhouse Effect were arguably more preoccupied by the known effects of ale. Bassist Guy Maddison remembers their beginnings: "Ringo [guitar] . . . came round my flat with some beer to visit my roommate. We drank the beer, talked about music we liked, and decided to start a band."

A punk since high school, Maddison reveals, "I snuck in to see the Quick and the Dead when we were sixteen at the East Perth Tavern." Seemingly unmoved by the theme of "another violent night," Maddison says of Greenhouse Effect, "Initially we were more into Black Flag and Black Sabbath. . . . Ringo was a big Scientists and Cramps fan, and we definitely tried to ape all these sounds. We had no idea what we were doing, and could barely play."

Developing a degree of competency, and following the lead of Insurrection, the band travelled eastward: "We went to Melbourne because we had heard there was a big punk scene there, and we thought we could get gigs. . . . It was all very exciting in the eastern states. We perceived Perth as a boondock backwater, the far distant edge of the empire."

After returning from the east, Maddison refused to become static: "Punk was changing by 1986, as was I. My tastes were becoming more industrial and experimental." Moving to Sydney, Maddison joined Stu Spasm in Lubricated Goat. "I loved Lubricated Goat. It was a great scuzzy, arty punk rock band, even though Stu would contest the punk part. . . . We got signed to Amphetamine Reptile in the US, which was essentially the same sort of punk/art/experimental crossover stuff.... Punks with mohawks would attend Lubricated Goat shows, as would goths, art weirdos, and long-haired paisley shirt people."

Leaving Lubricated Goat and relocating to Seattle at the beginning of the 1990s, Maddison played in Australian transplant Bloodloss, which included Mark Arm of Mudhoney as a member. Maddison is today Mudhoney's bassist.

Against the exploratory and challenging threads at the recesses of Australian music, a barely teenage Bevynn Wilkerson had been loyal to the unaffected, rudimentary rock of AC/DC and Rose Tattoo before punk's intrusion. Identifying "a small, dedicated punk scene in Perth," Wilkerson says, "most of us had watched the *UK/DK* video and been influenced by the bands on there." Featuring the unruly sounds of English bands Chaos UK, Disorder, and Varukers, Wilkerson says that accordingly, "Our music was very raw and abrupt, and I guess we were quite angry-looking, with black beanies, black singlets, boots, and shaved heads. We were drunk at most gigs, and Glenn was a very intense drunk/front man." Their choice of band name only served to aggravate the marginality: "Newspapers refused to print the name of our band, Pigs Are Guilty, as it was deemed offensive, so it was very hard to advertise gigs."

Appearing unable to deal in any subtlety, the group performed songs such as "Brick a Butcher." But while the veneer was of staunch political incendiaries, Wilkerson reveals that they "weren't taken that seriously, as we were basically punk pissheads." Nevertheless, Pigs Are Guilty continued to publicise support for environmental and animal rights direct action. Wilkerson, however, cautions against being considered an extremist, even if others made such presumption: "I did protest against animal cruelty a few times, and against wood chipping of old growth forests, and vividly remember all these men in dark suits snapping away with their cameras at the protesters.... They must have taken a good photo of me, as our house was raided by the police soon after. Pigs Are Guilty's lyric sheets were thought to be propaganda, and we were beaten up, arrested, and taken to the East Perth lockup."

Responsible for the band's astringent lyrics, Wilkerson says that Glenn, singer in both Pigs Are Guilty and Memento Mori, while "quite intimidating to look at, ended up lecturing politics at Canberra

University. His dress sense probably didn't appeal to the general public, but he was a smart fella."

Memento Mori's drummer, Russell Hopkinson, says that with Glenn no longer vocalist, the band "morphed into this joke metal band," Cremator. Dispensing with the far-left political tracts as lyrics, Wilkerson says Cremator "was more dark, black humour.... We were too drunk to be evil." Observing that "there was no thrash metal or anything like that" in Perth, Hopkinson says that "you take it east and you realise there wasn't room to be humorous about it, because these people were really into metal."

With Cremator touring Australia with Vicious Circle, Wilkerson says it "was a huge event." He gives some memories of the undertaking, conducted over five weeks, and the fertile scenes he found on the eastern seaboard:

> We were all on unemployment benefits. We arranged for friends to put our forms in for us so we could eat, and then piled into a Toyota van, gear and all, and drove more than five thousand kilometres to the other side of Australia.... The shows in Melbourne and Sydney were an eye-opener, and it seemed they were closer to what the rest of the world was doing. The scenes were very healthy, and the bands we played with were fucking awesome.... I would return in a few years to live and play in Sydney.

Some of the fondest memories are not always those of big audiences and major accolades: "Playing the Shenton Park Hotel with Cremator in Perth around '87 to a hardcore, angry crowd, people are stage diving off speaker stacks, and I turn around while onstage to see my grandma with her smiling face pressed up against the back window. It made it very hard to keep up my angry, hardcore face."

Despite the depiction of a lively—and with the addition of his grandma, slightly diverse—crowd, Wilkerson says that "Perth was limited at that time." Having already spoken favourably of his experience in the eastern states, he and the band chose to relocate. It would not be without vicissitude: "We got on a Greyhound bus, and drove for three and a half days to our new home in Sydney. An unfortunate incident came from the move which is still ever-present in my mind today. Our bass player, John Cook, decided to hitchhike across to the east coast and was hit and killed by a truck at night. He was a true free spirit, and I know he died living that way."

As alluded to by Wilkerson, Kim Benjamin says, "By the time I started hanging out in the scene, circa 1986–87, I think all of the earlier Perth bands had split up or were pretty much defunct."

Benjamin's awareness of punk had come almost a decade earlier: "It was 1978, I was fishing with my dad at night. We used to take a transistor radio with us to listen to music. I remember the announcer saying something along the lines of, 'There is a new youth cult in the UK called punk rock, and one of the main bands behind it is called the Sex Pistols, and we are going to play their single next, titled "Anarchy in the UK."'"

The song implanted in Benjamin, and a few years later he acted on the memory, even if by then punk had inexorably evolved: "Pestilence was originally influenced by the UK82 bands," but "as we got hold of more extreme hardcore, we also took that on board. . . . All of the mid-'80s UK hardcore (Britcore) bands started reaching us: Ripcord, Heresy, Electro Hippies, Deviated Instinct, Concrete Sox, Extreme Noise Terror, etc." Added to this was the further influence of "cheap wine, cider, pot."[5]

Benjamin suggests the band had barely fifteen minutes of coherent music, but they were afforded a chance at fifteen minutes of (minor) fame when asked to appear on ABC's Saturday morning music-based television program in a "segment regarding Perth hardcore and skating. At first, we thought someone was having a joke with us, until we realised it was legit."

Where many musicians sought some form of recognition or acceptance, others continued to pursue more polarising sounds. Punk music, already condemned as an aural abomination in the late '70s, would undergo gradual evolution into areas of increasing extremity, speed, and heaviness. The blurring of genres in the back end of the 1980s saw bands fuse punk, hardcore, and metal to varying degrees, outcomes, and successes.

Having passed through a number of progenitors, Napalm Death's 1987 *Scum* LP was a landmark in the creation of an unprecedentedly severe subgenre: grindcore. The music featured a near-incomprehensible tempo, and Benjamin remembers, "A huge amount of hype and mystique surrounded Napalm Death before the *Scum* LP came out—the fastest band in the world!"

Pestilence and Benjamin's next band, Resolute, were exemplars of the new development in extreme music. Despite the city's isolation, punks in Perth were greatly attuned to progressions overseas, and led in their uptake. Emanating primarily from England, as well as record labels Earache (home to Napalm Death) and Peaceville, Benjamin says "the early Peaceville/Earache influences ... those bands were very popular in Perth at the time.... That particular raw sound and style didn't really exist in Australia; it was being played in other countries."

Identifying a certain uniformity that was to develop, Neal Bodel's band Controlled by Fear had come under the influence of the same groups: "We all had similar taste, and we were captivated by the brutality and rawness of early grindcore.... We wanted to re-create that sound."

The new sound gave impetus to a scene that was recovering from some lean years. Bodel also provides account of the affinity that the revived scene helped develop: "The punk scene was quite big when I first found it.... There were many other bands forming, and it was an amazing time. We all knew each other, lived together, and partied together. We all seemed to share common values initially, and the message we tried to convey, as simplistic as it was, we all felt the same way.... The counterculture was quite hidden, but it was there." There, standing in opposition to a general culture that Bodel describes as unfamiliar with—and intolerant of—punk. "People didn't really understand why we dressed like we did or acted like we did. We were met with either fear or aggression. People would either cross the road to avoid us or cross the road to try and bash us."

Even within a progressive family like Bodel's—"we used to go to protests and marches as a family"—resistance came against his new pursuit: "I guess my dad in particular had his own unconscious bias around punk, assuming that it was about drugs and violence.... I think he thought I'd grow out of it, but I didn't. My mum was always the peacemaker. She was happy I wasn't a Nazi, and just wanted me to be safe." Her fears for his safety were confirmed, though, when Bodel was attacked during ongoing conflict with racist skinheads. Beaten unconscious by a group of skins while he was alone, Bodel also sustained a fractured jaw, four broken ribs, two broken fingers, and swelling on the brain.

His activism having preceded punk, Bodel says, "I was attending large amounts of protests and would participate in direct action. Some of the things I did back then with my comrades would have put me in jail for a long time if I was caught." That commitment, let alone a continuity of political vision, was not mirrored in the people he was encountering within the music scene. "I realised pretty quickly that not everyone in the punk scene shared the views or enthusiasm for politics that I had. I realised after a year or so that only a small amount of people in the scene were motivated to create change."

Also came recognition of the untreated trauma and grief of many attracted to punk and, despite its attempts at collective self-care, that self-medication, self-harm, and outward violence routinely accompanied its people. As Bodel remembers:

> By the time I was twenty-six, I had been to thirty funerals of friends who'd died of overdoses. Punk attracted damaged people. I wasn't without my own baggage; I'd been sexually abused multiple times by the father of a friend of mine when I was eight. Throughout my years at school following the abuse, I found it really hard to connect with people, and lacked a sense of belonging to anything. I found belonging in punk, as did many people who were finding a place to be accepted. With this complex array of damaged people came a complex reaction to the damage. There is a saying: "hurt people hurt people." I knew people who were excessively violent or self-destructive; their histories read like a horror story, so boundaries and self-control were lost on a lot of people I knew. . . . For me, punk was a monumental catalyst for positive change. For some, not so much.

Meanwhile, Controlled by Fear (posthumous LP *The Only Good Cop Is a Dead One*) had barely lasted a year. Bodel, who then joined the band Cuchulainn Powerhead, says, "The scene at that time was starting to split." His own priorities diverged also, and he declares, "My ideals were far more important than the scene, especially when it started to turn into something that clashed with my ideals."

Undertaking work with at-risk youth in 1993, Bodel says that his experiences of punk meant

> there was something distinctly familiar about it. . . . The violence I witnessed during those punk years enabled me to deal with violence between clients in a calm manner, even if they were

> armed. I gained a reputation for being able to form a rapport with clients with whom no one else could. When I was asked about it, I would always say, "The punk scene and a paedophile prepared me for this." My life, my ideals, and my choice to be a punk has led me to this point I'm at now. I've worked with close to four thousand young people since 1993. I'm so proud of what I have achieved. Now I deliver training about suicide prevention, mental health, domestic violence, and crisis intervention.... My life, my career, and my friends are all intertwined into the intersectional web that is governed by my values.... I'm still an anarchist, and I still listen to punk.

Overseeing the recording of Controlled by Fear's studio tracks, Paul Sherriffs, along with his band SDI, had come under the sway of a similar vein of punk and politics, the latter he asserts even superseding in importance: "For the SDI guys, the politics was more important than the music, and that showed with our songwriting—but we were at least having fun.... SDI was primarily interested in anarchism and anarcho-syndicalism.... We started a northern suburbs anarchist group that went nowhere, but mostly we went to gigs and drank alcohol. We were listening to Crass, Flux of Pink Indians, Conflict, and general Crass/Mortarhate Records kind of bands that were devolving into dirty street punk meets country dropouts."

As someone who came to be drawn to libertarian politics, Sherriffs got his introduction to punk through a dropout, albeit an ex-policeman uncle: "He was English, and would have seen the first of the punk scene in the UK, so that was my first impression of punk—mostly negative 'broken Britain' type stuff. The other thing about my Uncle Paul was he was very left-wing—odd for his career path—and he started giving me lessons in politics at around fourteen. He'd emigrated to Perth, as my mum had done ... and generally dropped out of society."

With travel scheduled to the UK, Sherriffs encountered his own epiphany, but one that instead saw him drop out of punk: "Rave culture was starting, Bristol was starting to happen, Maggie [Thatcher] was leaving, and England was a lot more intense than Perth (we dismissively called it 'Dream Land'). England had a massive effect on me, and I basically decided ... I wasn't a crusty or punk anymore."

Exhibiting his own act of inspiration—or exasperation—the drummer of Sherriffs's post-SDI band, Storm of Perversion, had made the decision to relocate to Sydney, where he would transmute from crust/metal/punk to the top forty with indie band the Clouds.

Prior to the departures, Storm of Perversion recorded its *Non-stop Wombling Picnic* LP (1990), and the album was pressed in Sherriffs's absence: "Apparently the record-pressing plant was a subsidiary of EMI—a big no-no in the punk world. . . . It wasn't like we were signed by EMI, but because we were so right-on politically—or maybe just me—it was an issue. I don't blame [bandmate] Ian in any way . . . but when your friends are chanting 'EMI, EMI' at your record launch, that does hurt."

Some bruising ridicule thankfully failed to translate into a punk consumer boycott, Sherriffs remembering that "when I got back from the UK, I was told that the record was number one on the local charts. And it was nice to have people actually singing along at the launch—that blew me away. . . . But after the launch I pretty much turned my back on the local punk scene. . . . It was only three years for me, but it taught me a lot, and it has resonated for the rest of my life."

Not affected by prevailing currents or trends, Costas Xoufarides expresses love for "it all, from Pistols to GBH to Crass to Napalm Death." Conveying a particular preference for the UK82 sound, Xoufarides says, "At the time, the crust scene seemed to have plenty of bands, but no UK82-style bands." Seeking to alleviate its absence, and fuelled by the intoxicating effect of fermented grape, Xoufarides formulated "Perth's first self-proclaimed Gooncore band."[6] He remembers, "A bunch of us went down for a boozy punk rock road trip, and one night, whilst drinking a goon bag [cask wine], talking about starting a band . . . somebody said . . . Elf and the Goon Gut Babies. We all fell about laughing, but the seed was sown. Back in Perth a week or so later . . . we wrote some songs that day, and played our first gig that night."

As Perth's political and corporate elite cosily sipped champagne together before their unravelling in the "WA Inc." scandal, the Goon Gut Babies blended boxed wine, ample spare time, and penchant for a laugh: "Most of us were unemployed, and shared houses, usually with about six people in them, so quite often the goon bag was reached for quite early."

Coming to find the name for their 1990 cassette would bring a foreseeable result: its *Where's the Goon?* title was accompanied by a "Party 'til You Puke" slogan on its cover and a crucified Jesus enquiring "Where's the Goon?" Punk, cheap humour, and cheaper wine had clearly substituted as the band's Holy Trinity.

The Goon Gut Babies' showpiece, however, was unveiled at an all-day gig at the Old Melbourne, Xoufarides explaining, "For us it was a massive gig, so something special had to be done." As singer, Xoufarides appeared in a piece of stage attire to rival that of Elvis's jumpsuit, the Beatles' Sgt. Pepper's marching outfits, Angus Young's school uniform, Michael Jackson's "Thriller" jacket, and Madonna's cone bra corset: the "goon suit." "The goon suit consisted of a pair of trackie pants with goon bags safety-pinned all over them and a singlet with a goon bag attached to the front and back."

Though lacking any costume, gimmick, or even a stated liking for goon, Lachlan Gurr suggests his band Thrombus were propelled by a similar sense of fun, despite it sometimes violating personal boundaries: "Onstage we ran amok. We abused each other, we wrestled, threw drinks at each other, one band member would encourage the audience to spit on another band member. The drummer would regularly get naked onstage, we got thrown off occasionally, we offended each other and everybody we could, just for our own amusement."

Confessing that he initially "was more into psych rock and indie," Gurr suggests punk offered a cheat to those unwilling to sacrifice half a lifetime in the bedroom perfecting guitar heroics: "It was easy, it was fun, it felt like a way onto the stage without following the stupid rules of the local pub rock establishment. I was hooked; I cut my hair and spiked it up with soap and glue."

But with the hardened hair came a more hardened response from police:

> When I wrote "Policeman" . . . I had only been locked up once and that was for a bit of trespassing. . . . But as it turned out, Thrombus was occasionally targeted by the police for a few reasons: our crowd, the venues we played at, the activism of a particular band member. They had a police truck, just like in Jello's song [Dead Kennedys' "Police Truck"]. They parked it outside our gigs and liked throwing our mates in it. Once, one

> of the band members challenged them over it, causing a detainee to escape while they were distracted in the debate. They then targeted that band member, raiding their house regularly for a few weeks. I got locked up a couple more times. In those days the police had the state in their grip.

Yet still the band continued to exude a playfulness often lacking within the surrounding brutality of the scene, exemplified by releases titled *Blind Spasm*, *Shopping with Mum*, and *Turd in My Stocking*.

With the years passing, the jokes dried up, Gurr remembering that "our creative process had stalled" and "my personal life had taken a turn for the worst." Further, making the sacrilegious revelation that "I had been consumed by the rise of '90s death metal," Gurr "didn't want to play funny punk anymore. My last official gig was at the first Perth Big Day Out [national touring festival], and it was huge. I was happy to leave the band that day."

It's a long way from Perth's Hollywood High School—the scene of Thrombus's first show—to tales of Hollywood, California, and the big hair, rock excess, sleaze, and scandal of Mötley Crüe. Paul Miles, however, is the most knowledgeable Mötley Crüe historian in the world. But just how a good private school boy got to be the authoritative figure on one of the world's most outrageous rock acts would first take a detour through punk as vocalist of Barbary Corsairs: "I grew up in a traditional, loving family. I played a heap of football and went to Wesley College for all twelve years of my schooling. This Christian all-boys institution certainly gave me a very good education, but I think it also made me question things more. In hindsight, I believe my English literature classes—that taught me to look under the face value of text to understand deeper meanings—started to extend into life."

Miles's literary deconstruction combined with mutually assured destruction as he began to discover a more fitting soundtrack: "So, as I was trying to figure out the world, with the Cold War threat of nuclear obliteration hanging over us too, the music I was listening to started to change as well. . . . On the one hand I was waking up to these dark things that were occurring in the world, but also just partying and having a fun time with the air of youthful invincibility, because the world was probably going to get nuked soon anyway."

Within the confines of a well-groomed youth and education, punk most suited Miles's questioning of—and reaction to—shibboleths and expectations: "One appeal of punk was that it ran against the grain, and I had never been able to really do that in my life to that point. It had always been about uniforms and striving for what was considered to be the best, not what happens if you think and act differently."

Also making unwitting—if underage and underfunded—attempts at Mötley Crüe's party lifestyle, Miles says, "During my late high school days, we would go to house parties a lot.... A lot of these were awesome parties, like one-hundred-plus kids in a two-storey mansion in the richest suburbs.... Houses like that always seemed to have a great bar to raid and an amazing stereo system.... It was how you met other misfits from that schooling system, and those that dug the same music or turned you on to new things."

Some of those people included the band Stool Pigeons, who, acting as support to Barbary Corsairs at their first show, Miles says, "probably had more of a Stooges vibe going on.... They were fronted by Hamish Fitzsimmons.... He's now an award-winning journalist with the ABC."

The pilfered fancy booze perhaps clouds Miles's memory of Barbary Corsairs' meeting and formation in 1987: "I don't recall a specific moment of when I met the other guys in the band.... I think one of the main reasons the Barbary Corsairs came together was an absolute mutual love of GBH, English Dogs, and Discharge." But like those bands that came under the increasing sway of metal, Miles says that "back in '87, the whole crossover and thrash movement was happening.... Things just seemed to be turning more metal, which we hadn't really listened to before, probably because it was much more of a bogan thing than for private school kids in Perth."

Mötley Crüe, as one of the most epitomising and dominant bogan bands, eventually came to pursue a more blues direction, parting with singer Vince Neil. Analogously, the interests of Barbary Corsairs members also began to divide:

> I think we were all just changing so much in those days, and exploring different things in life, that we really just went our separate ways.... My head was about to explode from all the thrash and metal, so I slowed it down a bit and listened to more hard rock.... Mötley just became my favourite band.... They

> were just the real deal—they lived it and never pretended. They went to number one, but also went to jail and died from overdose and came back to life. Such stories pulled me in further, and when I first got on the internet in 1995 I decided to create a website that documented all their sex, drugs, and rock 'n' roll tales of debauchery and excess. . . . It brought about all sorts of cool experiences, like touring all-access with them around Australia and Japan.

Repeating Mötley Crüe drummer Tommy Lee's assertion that "Paul knows more about us than we know," Miles says that as part of the process of author Neil Strauss compiling the band's book *The Dirt*, "[he] got me to proofread it, and provide an analysis of sorts, so it could be the best book possible."[7] Miles also contributed the liner notes for Mötley Crüe's double live album, and, he says, "I also proofed the movie's [*The Dirt*, 2019] manuscript."

Miles's own authorship saw the publication of his book *Sex Tips from Rock Stars*, which he says "gave me the opportunity to spend many, many hours yakking with platinum-selling and Grammy Award–winning rock stars and asking them all sorts of wonderfully strange questions."[8] Though the book was devoid of any Mötley Crüe anecdotes, the band's studio albums up to *Dr. Feelgood* had themselves been platinum and multiplatinum sellers, as well as receiving multiple Grammy nominations.

The concluding track to 1989's *Dr. Feelgood*—"Time for Change"—would contain unforeseen prescience for the coming decade, as the fluctuations of mainstream music trends saw hair metal wane from its '80s zenith. Punk, incapable of topping the charts since the Sex Pistols, found renewed interest and exposure. In an unexpected turn—and including the accumulation of its own platinum records and Grammys—the 1990s would see punk's ascendancy towards unprecedented popularity.

# AFTERWORD

As punk music burgeoned into a diversified spectrum of sounds and styles in the decades following its pronounced arrival, it made mockery of prognostications of its death. Propelled—literally—to the top of the charts in Australia, punk, through some of its multitudinous variants, became firmly enmeshed in mainstream cultural production.

Though punk is now a readily purchasable musical form, largely unacknowledged has been its impact and influence on broader Australian culture and society. Surpassing what its numerical marginality would suggest, prominent individuals with backgrounds in punk have spanned from government members to actors to journalists to world champion sportspeople.

But for all those who prospered into adulthood, there are innumerable others who never made it, or in surviving exhibit the mental and physical wounds of a culture not noted for its temperance and restraint. With so many lives tragically wrecked by the false indestructibility of youth, the meaninglessness inherent in the belief in "no future," or an inability to surmount their own grief and trauma, this book is dedicated to them.

RIP.

# NOTES

## INTRODUCTION

1 "The Punk Rock Craze Is Heading Our Way," *Sydney Morning Herald*, July 17, 1977, 91.
2 Simon Thomsen, "40 Years Ago Today, Punk Music Was Born in Australia," *Business Insider Australia*, June 12, 2016, https://www.businessinsider.com.au/40-years-ago-today-punk-was-born-in-australia-2016-6.
3 Clinton Walker, "The New British Underground," *Roadrunner*, vol. 2, no. 4, May 1979, 17.

## "I ONLY PANIC WHEN THERE'S NOTHING TO DO"—QUEENSLAND

1 David Malouf, *Johnno* (St Lucia, QLD, Australia: University of Queensland Press, 1998), 118.
2 *Australian*, February 4, 1998, 13.
3 Clinton Walker, *Stranded: The Secret History of Australian Independent Music, 1977–1991* (Sydney: Pan Macmillan, 1996), 13.
4 John Robb, *Punk Rock: An Oral History* (London: Ebury, 2006; Oakland: PM Press, 2012), 250.
5 David Nichols, *The Go-Betweens* (Portland, OR: Verse Chorus Press, 2003), 23.
6 *Sounds*, October 16, 1976, 37.
7 *Juke*, September 25, 1976.
8 Robb, *Punk Rock*, 251.
9 Nicholas Rombes, *A Cultural Dictionary of Punk* (New York: Continuum, 2009), 238.
10 A. McMillan, "Dirty Deeds 'n' Haloes Don't Mix, Do They?," *RAM*, no. 53, March 11, 1977, 21.
11 S. Matheson, "'What's for Dinner?' Leftovers," *Roadrunner*, vol. 2, no. 7, August 1979, 10.
12 "The Brisbane Devotee," *The Cane Toad Times*, June 1979.
13 Matheson, "'What's for Dinner?,'" 10.
14 "The Brisbane Devotee," *The Cane Toad Times*, June 1979.
15 "Hansard," Queensland Legislative Assembly, November 30, 1976, 1918.
16 David Nichols, *The Go-Betweens* (Portland, OR: Verse Chorus Press, 2003), 18.
17 Allan Gardiner, "Punks and Police: Baroona Hall, Caxton Street, Paddington," in *Radical Brisbane*, ed. Raymond Evans, Carole Ferrier, and Jeff Rickertt (Carlton North, VIC, Australia: Vulgar Press, 2004), 300.

18 Gardiner, "Punks and Police," 300.
19 *Fad Zine*, no. 2, 11.
20 Tony Moore, "Street Struggle: What It's Like to Be Homeless in Brisbane," *Brisbane Times*, January 4, 2011, https://www.brisbanetimes.com.au/national/queensland/street-struggle-what-its-like-to-be-homeless-in-brisbane-20101229-19a0r.html.
21 *Prehistoric Sounds*, vol. 1, no. 3, 1995, 43.
22 Cal Crilly, "The Brisbane Punk Movement 1976," YouTube, April 14, 2017, video, 9:13, https://www.youtube.com/watch?v=uxWfQ8SPp_4.
23 David Nichols, *The Go-Betweens* (Portland, OR: Verse Chorus Press, 2003), 65.
24 Everett True, "Prehistoric: The Punk and Politics of Brisbane's Darkest Days Rebooted," *Guardian*, September 24, 2014, https://www.theguardian.com/stage/2014/sep/24/preshistoric-brisbane-punk-and-politics-1970s.
25 D. Call, "Police Act on Noise," *Queensland Times*, September 24, 1979, 1.
26 "Jim Dickson Interview," I-94 Bar, April 22, 2017, http://i94bar-dev.info/ints/Jim_Dickson1.htm.
27 Henry Griggs, *Cuttin' It in Townsville* (Golden Square, VIC, Australia: Moonlight Publishing, 1995), 33.

## "DESCENT INTO THE MAELSTROM"—NEW SOUTH WALES AND AUSTRALIAN CAPITAL TERRITORY

1 Vivien Johnson, *Radio Birdman* (St Kilda, VIC, Australia: Sheldon Booth, 1990), 31.
2 "Punk in Australia," Double J, *The J Files*, radio program, June 16, 2016, https://www.abc.net.au/doublej/programs/the-j-files/punk-in-australia/10274672.
3 Keith Cameron, "Come the Revolution," *Guardian*, July 20, 2007, https://www.theguardian.com/music/2007/jul/20/popandrock2.
4 F. Villante, *B Side*, no. 12.
5 Johnson, *Radio Birdman*, 112.
6 "Deniz Tek and Angie Pepper Interview on 19th of January 1991," Divine Rites, accessed January 23, 2024, http://www.divinerites.com/in_tek6.htm.
7 *Spurt*, no. 1, 1977, 18.
8 Clinton Walker, *Stranded: The Secret History of Australian Independent Music, 1977–1991* (Sydney: Pan Macmillan, 1996), 25.
9 *Australian Women's Weekly*, January 4, 1978, 67.
10 "David Virgin of Sekret Sekret Reflects on the Birth of Sydney Punk," I-94 Bar, August 18, 2008, http://i94bar-dev.info/ints/davidvirgin.
11 "When Lipstick Killers Stalked the Earth," I-94 Bar, May 29, 2001, http://i94bar-dev.info/ints/lipstickkillers.html.
12 T. Cresswell, "Lipstick Killers," *Roadrunner*, vol. 2, nos. 11 & 12, December 1979–January 1980, 30.
13 *Spurt*, no. 2, n.d., 14.
14 "When Lipstick Killers Stalked the Earth," I-94 Bar, May 29, 2001, http://i94bar-dev.info/ints/lipstickkillers.html.
15 *Spurt*, no. 3, 1978, 44.
16 A. Ryan, "Sitting in the Front Seat: XL Capris," *Roadrunner*, vol. 4, no. 4, May 1981, 8.
17 Various artists, *Why March When You Can Riot?*, Aberrant Records NUMBA3, 1985, LP.
18 Kirstie Clements, *The Vogue Factor* (Carlton, VIC, Australia: Melbourne University Press, 2013), 110.
19 Clements, *Vogue Factor*, 111.

20 Clements, *Vogue Factor*, 113.
21 Jack Boulware, "Murder at the Pink Tarantula," *SF Weekly*, June 18, 1997, http://archives.sfweekly.com/sanfrancisco/murder-at-the-pink-tarantula/Content?oid=2134317&showFullText=true.
22 "No More Lies," *Spurt*, no. 1, 1977, 9.
23 Janine Barrand, *Rock Chicks: Women in Australian Music* (Melbourne: Victorian Arts Centre Trust, 2010), 28.
24 Shane Homan and Tony Mitchell, eds., *Sounds of Then, Sounds of Now: Popular Music in Australia* (Hobart, TAS, Australia: ACYS Publishing, 2008), 200.
25 Troy Ferguson, "When Ak Punk Ruled Ok?," *NZ Herald*, November 14, 2008, http://m.nzherald.co.nz/entertainment/news/article.cfm?c_id=1501119&objectid=10543043.
26 Ferguson, "When Ak Punk Ruled Ok?"
27 "The Barman Talks to Roger Grierson of the Thought Criminals," I-94 Bar, January 12, 2006, http://i94bar-dev.info/ints/thoughtcriminals.html.
28 *DNA*, no. 49, April 1986, 23.
29 F. Villante, *B Side*, no. 10, 1985.
30 F. Villante, *B Side*, no. 10, 1985.
31 *B Side*, no. 4, 1984, 15.
32 Evan Kanarakis, "The Gascan Interview: Ashley Thomson of the Kelpies," *Gascan Magazine*, August 2, 2014, https://gascanmag.com/2014/08/the-gascan-interview-ashley-thomson-of-the-kelpies.
33 Chris Shakallis, Robina Gugler, Cody Anderson, and Steve Nebauer, *Head Full of Flames: Punk in the Nation's Capital, 1977 to 1992* (Hughes, ACT, Australia: Robina Jane Gugler, 2013), 212.
34 Shakallis et al., *Head Full of Flames*, 5.
35 Young Docteurs official website, last modified 2016, http://youngdocteurs.com.
36 J. Meldrum, "Cool Clash Concert Rocks Punk's Image," *Canberra Times*, January 26, 1978, 9.

### "AFTER A FASHION"—VICTORIA

1 J. Apelgren, "Spitting on the Public Schoolboys," *Age*, April 21, 1978, 33.
2 *DNA*, no. 45, September 1985, 8.
3 Stuart Coupe, *Gudinski: The Godfather of Australian Rock 'n' Roll* (Strawberry Hills, NSW, Australia: Read How You Want, 2015) 94.
4 *Pulp*, 1978.
5 R. Stapleton, "The Rise and Rise of Michael Gudinski," *Roadrunner*, vol. 2, no. 4, May 1979, 8–12.
6 J. Burt, "Suicide Survivors," *Roadrunner*, vol. 2, no. 2, March 1979, 9.
7 Vivienne Shark LeWitt, "So This Is Real Life?: The Continuing Dissensions of New Wave Music," *Tasmanian Review*, no. 1 (June 1979): 1.
8 Burt, "Suicide Survivors," 9.
9 Clinton Walker, "Planting Seeds," in *Cultural Seeds: Essays on the Work of Nick Cave*, ed. Karen Welberry and Tanya Dalziell (Farnham, UK: Ashgate Publishing, 2009), 39.
10 J. Rule, "Old News Goodbye," *Roadrunner*, vol. 2, no. 1, February 1979, 9.
11 Shane Maloney, "Here Come the News, Punks," *Age*, February 17, 1978, 4.
12 Maloney, "Here Come the News," 4.
13 Michael Coomber, "Dirty Lies/Chop Chop Chop," Biography of the Original Punk Band News website, last modified 2000, http://www.oocities.org/babeez_news/13lies.html.

14 Tim Finn, "45's," *Roadrunner*, vol. 2, no. 3, April 1979, 22.
15 Harry Butler, "John Murphy," *B Side*, no. 24, 1988, 20.
16 *Spurt*, no. 3, 1978, 16.
17 Ian Cunningham, "Chosen Few," Break My Face, accessed May 11, 2017, http://www.breakmyface.com/bands/chosenfew.html.
18 Cunningham, "Chosen Few."
19 *Spurt*, no. 2, n.d., 44.
20 James Freud, *I Am the Voice Left from Rehab* (Milsons Point, NSW, Australia: Random House Australia, 2007), 19.
21 Freud, *I Am the Voice*, 24.
22 Freud, *I Am the Voice*, 27.
23 "Punk Arrives," St Kilda Music Walking Tour, accessed September 23, 2018, http://www.skmwt.com.au/history_3.shtml.
24 Freud, *I Am the Voice*, 4.
25 *DNA*, no. 6, February 1980, 8.
26 Jeremy Story Carter, "An Old Punk Talks to a Young Punk," ABC News, September 2, 2016, http://www.abc.net.au/news/2016-09-02/a-tale-of-two-punks/7806000.
27 Harry Butler, "John Murphy," *B Side*, no. 24, 22.
28 Lorraine Ali, "Cross Over," *Alternative Press*, November 1993, 7.
29 H. Thomas, "Benefit Concert—For Posterity," *Age*, September 4, 1981, 44.
30 Sylvie Leber, "Why Is the Australian Music Scene Such a Boys Club?," Right Now, November 3, 2015, http://rightnow.org.au/opinion-3/why-is-the-australian-popular-music-scene-such-a-boys-club.

### "SHITPILE"—TASMANIA

1 "The Launceston Riots," *Mercury*, February 9, 1974, 2.
2 Stuart Coupe, "White Riot," *Roadrunner*, vol. 3, no. 1, February 8, 1980, 8.

### "LIFE ON THE DOLE"—SOUTH AUSTRALIA AND NORTHERN TERRITORY

1 Rocka, "This Day Tonight—'Adelaide Punk Rock' (1977)," YouTube, July 28, 2011, video, 7:23, https://www.youtube.com/watch?v=aYvTl1act-w&t=69s.
2 Stephen Hunter, "Adelaide Bands Together," *Roadrunner*, vol. 3, no. 9, October 1980, 6.
3 A. Bunney, "St Vitus Dance Package," YouTube, January 4, 2016, video, 8:03, https://www.youtube.com/watch?v=cg7TU5NAoaQ.
4 *DNA*, no. 1, October 1979, 5.
5 S. Rogerson, "Irving and the U Bombs," *Roadrunner*, vol. 1, no. 4, July 1978, 9.
6 Ian King, "This Perfect Band: An Oral History of Dagoes," Popmatters, June 25, 2015, http://www.popmatters.com/feature/193196-this-perfect-band-an-oral-history-of-dagoes.
7 *DNA*, no. 6, February 1980, 1.
8 D. Robertson, *Roadrunner*, vol. 2, nos. 11 & 12, December 1979–January 1980, 46.
9 Dave Graney, "How the Pistols Brought Punk to Mount Gambier," *Age*, June 3, 2002, https://www.theage.com.au/entertainment/music/how-the-pistols-brought-punk-to-mount-gambier-20020603-gdu9kk.html.
10 Dave Graney, *1001 Australian Nights: A Memoir* (Mulgrave, VIC, Australia: Affirm Press, 2011), 38.
11 *DNA*, no. 6, February 1980, 4.
12 *DNA*, no. 6, February 1980, 6.
13 *DNA*, no. 38, October 1984, 9.
14 *DNA*, no. 38, October 1984, 10.

15 David Nichols, *Dig: Australian Rock and Pop Music, 1960–85* (Portland, OR: Verse Chorus Press, 2016), 525.

### "ARSEHOLE OF THE UNIVERSE"—WESTERN AUSTRALIA

1 "Australian Federal Election Speeches," Museum of Australian Democracy at Old Parliament House, accessed June 16, 2017, http://electionspeeches.moadoph.gov.au/speeches/1972-gough-whitlam.
2 Julian Tompkin, "Frequencies from Planet Perth: Punk Rock and Western Australia's Sesquicentenary Celebrations," master's thesis, Curtin University, 2012, 39.
3 "The Scientists: Pissed on Another Planet," Bad Music for Bad People, accessed November 28, 2017, https://badmusicforbadpeople.com/the-scientists-%E2%80%93-%E2%80%9Cpissed-on-another-planet%E2%80%9D.
4 *Sounds*, May 6, 1978.
5 Paul Murray, "Charles Court," *West Australian*, November 9, 2006, 4.
6 Ross Buncle, "The Orphans Story," Perth Punk, accessed May 30, 2018, http://www.perthpunk.com/the-orphans.
7 Buncle, "Orphans Story."
8 "Scientists: Pissed on Another Planet."
9 Kim Williams, "Live: The Victims, Adrian's Nightclub, Perth," *Roadrunner*, vol. 3, no. 9, October 1980, 14.
10 *Uzurlikzurli*, no. 3, February 1998.
11 Kim Williams, "Hubble, Bubble, Toil and Trouble," *Roadrunner*, vol. 2, no. 8, September 1979, 6.
12 C. Mitchell, "Perth," *Roadrunner*, vol. 3, nos. 11 & 12, December 1980–January 1981, 27.
13 Kim Williams, "Plastic Perth Melts Down," *Roadrunner*, vol. 4, no. 4, May 1981, 3.
14 Blatantly NatSoc, "Quick and the Dead!," YouTube, October 17, 2007, video, 8:33, https://www.youtube.com/watch?v=sYoC_UDiXzg&t=116s.
15 Blatantly NatSoc, "Quick and the Dead!"

### "DEAD BEFORE RETIREMENT"—VICTORIA

1 *Sydney Morning Herald*, June 29, 1986.
2 *Sydney Morning Herald*, June 29, 1986.
3 David Nichols, *Dig: Australian Rock and Pop Music, 1960–85* (Portland, OR: Verse Chorus Press, 2016), 249.
4 Tyler Curtis, "Venom P. Stinger," *Bomb*, October 24, 2013, bombmagazine.org/article/7404/venom-p-stinger.
5 *DNA*, no. 52, August 1986, 21.
6 Tim Hemensley, "Solid Gold Shit," liner notes for Sick Things, *My Life's a Mess*, Stolen Records, 1999, CD.
7 "Looking Back on the Dead Kennedys' 1983 Australian Tour," *Rest Assured*, May 8, 2013, http://restassuredzine.com/looking-back/1807-looking-back-on-dead-kennedys-1983-australian-tour.
8 *DNA*, no. 33, October 1983, 19.
9 *DNA*, no. 48, January 1986.
10 "Punks Have Parents Too," *Good Weekend*, July 12, 1986.
11 "Dead Kennedys' 1983 Australian Tour."
12 "Dead Kennedys' 1983 Australian Tour."
13 *Trousers in Action*, no. 12, May–June 1985, 14.

14 *Trousers in Action*, no. 12, 14.
15 *Trousers in Action*, no. 12, 14.
16 Ray Ahn, "Gaelic Theatre, 1985," *Ray Ahn: What I Did During My School Holidays* (blog), April 24, 2016, https://rahn666.wordpress.com/2016/04/24/gaelic-theatre-1985.
17 *DNA*, no. 65, August 1988, 34.
18 F. Robson, "Naughty Boys of Punk Pinning Hope on Rock of Rage," *Sunday Sun*, October 18, 1978, 35.
19 *DNA*, no. 61, November 1987, 39.
20 *Family Slaughterhouse*, no. 3, 1985.
21 *DNA*, no. 65, August 1988, 34.
22 *Cosmic Psychos: Blokes You Can Trust*, directed by Matt Weston (Kew, VIC, Australia: Australia Umbrella Entertainment, 2013), DVD.
23 Ruth S., Erikka, Lynn, and Anna, "Annihilate Sex Roles: Survey for Women—Poll Results," *Maximumrocknroll*, no. 7, July–August 1983.
24 *Rise Above*, no. 5, 1987.
25 "Take Two," *Age*, February 23, 2003, http://www.theage.com.au/articles/2003/02/22/1045638538654.html.
26 Ann Witherall, *Fly* (self-pub., CreateSpace, 2012).
27 T. Giannoukos, "Protest Song 'Indecent,'" *Herald Sun*, 1988, 3.
28 Giannoukos, "Protest Song 'Indecent,'" 12.
29 Giannoukos, "Protest Song 'Indecent,'" 12.
30 A. Turner, "And More Rats," *B Side*, nos. 17 & 18, October–November 1986.
31 T.J. Honeysuckle, "TJ Honeysuckle Talks to Mick Harley of the Seminal Rats About Their Retrospective Compilation on Bang! Records," I-94 Bar, August 5, 2007, http://i94bar-dev.info/ints/seminalrats.html.
32 "Children in the City," *Age*, February 4, 1983, 8.
33 *B Side*, no. 21, 1987, 5.
34 *B Side*, no. 21, 39.

### "COG CITY"—TASMANIA

1 S. Marshall, "The Generation on the Outside," *Mercury*, June 6, 1984.

### "Y BOTHER"—NEW SOUTH WALES AND AUSTRALIAN CAPITAL TERRITORY

1 A. Turner, "And More Rats," *B Side*, nos. 17 & 18, October–November 1986.
2 "Looking Back on the Dead Kennedys' 1983 Australian Tour," *Rest Assured*, May 8, 2013, http://restassuredzine.com/looking-back/1807-looking-back-on-dead-kennedys-1983-australian-tour.
3 "Dead Kennedys' 1983 Australian Tour."
4 T. Cresswell, "Radio Birdman," *Roadrunner*, vol. 2, nos. 11 & 12, December 1979–January 1980.
5 "Wild Animals, White Trash, and the Milky Bar Kids," *Sydney Morning Herald*, July 7, 1984, 36.
6 "Dead Kennedys' 1983 Australian Tour."
7 Chris Shakallis, Robina Gugler, Cody Anderson, and Steve Nebauer, *Head Full of Flames: Punk in the Nation's Capital, 1977 to 1992* (Hughes, ACT, Australia: Robina Jane Gugler, 2013), 308.
8 Shakallis et al., *Head Full of Flames*, 308.
9 Shakallis et al., *Head Full of Flames*, 196.
10 "Punk Dies in Darlinghurst Cell," *Tharunka*, May 23, 1983, 9.
11 Royal Commission into the New South Wales Police Service, Sydney, 1997.

12 *Trousers in Action*, no. 13.
13 *DNA*, no. 37, July 1984.
14 Bruce Griffiths, liner notes for *Why March When You Can Riot?*, Aberrant Records NUMBA3, 1985, LP.
15 "Dead Kennedys' 1983 Australian Tour."
16 *B Side*, no. 22, 1987, 11.
17 *Barcode the World*, no. 22.
18 R. Fishman, "Life Among the Urban Tribes," *Sydney Morning Herald*, January 23, 1983, 102.
19 L. Schwartz, "The Oi Way: Fists, Boots an' All," *Sydney Morning Herald*, January 16, 1986, 1.
20 "Dead Kennedys' 1983 Australian Tour."
21 *Trousers in Action*, no. 12, May–June 1985.
22 Liner notes for *Tales from the Australian Underground: Singles 1976–1989*, Feel Presents FEEL 01, 2003, CD.
23 Richard Kingsmill, *Wide Open Road*, radio series, November 1, 2008, produced by Cath Dwyer and Tom Morton, ABC Radio National, Australia, https://www.abc.net.au/listen/radionational/archived/intothemusic/wide-open-road-road/3187742.
24 Ray Ahn, *Depth Perception Podcast*, October 11, 2015, podcast, 1:45:42, https://www.dppod.com/dppod-s04e07-ray-ahn.
25 Ahn, *Depth Perception.*
26 Ahn, *Depth Perception.*
27 Ahn, *Depth Perception.*
28 Ahn, *Depth Perception.*
29 *Spare Parts*, no. 1, 1986.
30 Kingsmill, *Wide Open Road.*
31 Kingsmill, *Wide Open Road.*
32 J. Marx, "Upright Citizens," *Sydney Morning Herald*, August 20, 1992, 29.
33 *B Side*, no. 22, 1987, 10.
34 Murray Englehart, "Stiff Luck!," *Juke*, August 16, 1986, 11.
35 Englehart, "Stiff Luck!," 11.
36 Sacha Molitorisz, "Hardware," *Sydney Morning Herald*, December 1, 2000, 61.
37 Ahn, *Depth Perception.*
38 J. Macdougall, "Sydney: A Short Visit," *Rise Above*, no. 5, 1987.
39 *B Side*, issue 23, 16.
40 *B Side*, issue 23, 16.
41 "Fiona Horne: Rockstar, Author, Pilot, Witch," official website of Fiona Horne, accessed October 17, 2018, https://www.fionahorne.com.
42 *Rise Above*, no. 4, July–August 1986.
43 Ilaria Brophy and Monique Friedlander, "I've Slept with over 1,000 Women!' MAFS Star, Nasser Sultan Reveals His Enormous Number of Sexual Partners," *Daily Mail*, February 19, 2018, https://www.dailymail.co.uk/tvshowbiz/article-5406613/Nasser-Sultan-reveals-enormous-number-sexual-partners.html.
44 *Rise Above*, no. 3.
45 Gareth Hutchens, "Sussan Ley: From Punk Rocker to Health Minister," *Sydney Morning Herald*, December 22, 2014, https://www.smh.com.au/politics/federal/sussan-ley-from-punk-rocker-to-health-minister-20141222-12c643.html.
46 *Object-Dismembered*, no. 1, 1985, 4.
47 *Shit on Brisbane*, no. 5, 1986.
48 @ndy, "Angry Anderson: No Violence?," Slackbastard, March 2, 2010, http://slackbastard.anarchobase.com/?p=7958.

49 Randy Reimann, liner notes for Massappeal, *Nobody Likes a Thinker*, Desperate Records DEFCON 12, 2015, twelve-inch.
50 Reimann, *Nobody Likes a Thinker*.
51 Reimann, *Nobody Likes a Thinker*.
52 Nick Southall, "The WOW Factor: Wollongong's Unemployed and the Dispossession of Class and History," *Illawarra Unity: Journal of the Illawarra Branch of the Australian Society for the Study of Labour History* 8, no. 1 (2008): 73.
53 Southall, "WOW Factor," 73.
54 Southall, "WOW Factor," 76–77.
55 Nick Southall, "The WOW Factor: Wollongong's Unemployed and the Dispossession of Class and History," Revolts Now, August 23, 2010, https://revoltsnow.wordpress.com/2010/08/23/the-wow-factor-wollongong%E2%80%99s-unemployed-and-the-dispossession-of-class-and-history-2.
56 Paul Lester, "J Mascis: 'I Never Took It That Seriously'," *Guardian*, August 3, 2012, https://www.theguardian.com/music/2012/aug/03/j-mascis-dinosaur-jr-interview.
57 "Revisiting Proton Energy Pill's 'Less Than I Spend' 7 Inch," *Rest Assured*, June 6, 2018, http://restassuredzine.com/looking-back/5904-revisiting-proton-energy-pill-s-less-than-i-spend-7-inch.
58 Pete Cooper, *Depth Perception Podcast*, July 24, 2016, podcast, 1:19:43, https://www.dppod.com/dppod-s06e05-pete-cooper.
59 Cooper, *Depth Perception*.
60 Cooper, *Depth Perception*.
61 Cooper, *Depth Perception*.

### "NON REGULATION FUN"—QUEENSLAND

1 "Looking Back on the Dead Kennedys' 1983 Australian Tour," *Rest Assured*, May 8, 2013, http://restassuredzine.com/looking-back/1807-looking-back-on-dead-kennedys-1983-australian-tour.
2 Marquis H.K., *Thirty Years of Anger* (Salisbury, QLD, Australia: Boolarong Press, 2016), 29.
3 *DNA*, no. 45, September 1985, 18.
4 "Dead Kennedys' 1983 Australian Tour."
5 "Dead Kennedys' 1983 Australian Tour."
6 H.K., *Thirty Years of Anger*, 51.

### "CAN YOU DANCE TO FEEDBACK?"—SOUTH AUSTRALIA AND NORTHERN TERRITORY

1 *DNA*, no. 31, March 1983, 4.
2 *DNA*, no. 31, March 1983, 27.
3 *DNA*, no. 31, March 1983, 26.
4 *DNA*, no. 31, March 1983, 26.
5 Liner notes for Septic Saw Blades, *Septic System*, El Crapo Productions EC-008, 1986, cassette.
6 *DNA*, no. 59, September 1987, 7.
7 "Looking Back on the Dead Kennedys' 1983 Australian Tour," *Rest Assured*, May 8, 2013, http://restassuredzine.com/looking-back/1807-looking-back-on-dead-kennedys-1983-australian-tour.
8 "Dead Kennedys' 1983 Australian Tour."
9 *DNA*, no. 52, August 1986, 5.
10 Patrick Donovan, "Grunge Legends End Hiatus," *Age*, October 9, 2009.

11 *DNA*, no. 52, August 1986, 7.
12 Michael McGuire, "Meet Guy Debelle: The Punk Who Keeps Our Economy in the Pink," *Adelaide Advertiser*, May 30, 2014, http://www.adelaidenow.com.au/lifestyle/sa-lifestyle/meet-guy-debelle-the-punk-who-keeps-our-economy-in-the-pink/story-fnizi7vf-1226935826659.
13 "The Allnighter," Rotten Tomatoes, accessed May 22, 2017, https://www.rottentomatoes.com/m/allnighter.
14 *DNA*, nos. 57 & 58, April 1987, 13.
15 "Dead Kennedys' 1983 Australian Tour."
16 *DNA*, no. 34, January 1984, 4.
17 *DNA*, no. 34, January 1984, 4.
18 *DNA*, nos. 57 & 58, April 1987, 55–56.
19 *DNA*, no. 77, February 1990, 2.
20 Steve Davis, "The Adelaide Podcast Festival Part 2," *The Adelaide Show*, March 8, 2017, podcast, 48:23, https://theadelaideshow.com.au/podcast-episodes/185-adelaide-podcast-festival-part-2.
21 Liam Croy, "Sword Swallower Matty Blade Dies," *West Australian*, March 27, 2014, https://thewest.com.au/news/wa/sword-swallower-matty-blade-dies-ng-ya-368256.
22 Doc Boom, "Clowns of Decadence—A Touch of Decadence (Official)," YouTube, January 30, 2014, video, 4:55, https://www.youtube.com/watch?v=7y6TWYRqLtc.
23 G. Stein, "Rowdy Scenes at Peace Concert," *Northern Territory News*, August 5, 1986.
24 *DNA*, nos. 39 & 40, January 1985, 27.
25 *DNA*, nos. 39 & 40, January 1985, 27.

### "CONSERVATIVE TRASH"—WESTERN AUSTRALIA

1 LoudProudandDrunk, "Quick and the Dead," YouTube, September 27, 2012, video, 10:43, https://www.youtube.com/watch?v=szortgXRLgA.
2 *DNA*, nos. 39 & 40, January 1985, 19.
3 "Looking Back on the Dead Kennedys' 1983 Australian Tour," *Rest Assured*, May 8, 2013, http://restassuredzine.com/looking-back/1807-looking-back-on-dead-kennedys-1983-australian-tour.
4 *DNA*, no. 65, August 1988, 23.
5 "Nailed Down Interview," *Problems They Persist* (blog), June 9, 2012, http://problemstheypersist.blogspot.com/2012/06/nailed-down-interview.html.
6 *DNA*, no. 81, October 1990.
7 Sarah Guppy, "Rock DJ Paul Miles," *Tone Deaf*, February 19, 2013, https://tonedeaf.thebrag.com/dj-paul-miles.
8 Paul Miles, "Paul Miles: Rock n Roll Photographer, Author, DJ," official website of Paul Miles, last modified 2020, http://www.paul-miles.com/Paul-Miles-Story%20So%20Far.htm.w.

# INDEX

Page numbers in *italic* refer to illustrations. "Passim" (literally "scattered") indicates intermittent discussion of a topic over a cluster of pages.

# ABOUT THE AUTHOR

**Tristan Clark** is a Melbourne-based educator, musician, and writer. His involvement in punk has spanned over three decades and encompassed a gamut of roles: band member, roadie, merch person, show organizer, Food Not Bombs volunteer, and community radio DJ, as well as having written sporadically for local zines and other publications. He now routinely encounters the young students he spends his week working with at local DIY shows and is heartened by punk's continued ability to self-reproduce.

## ABOUT PM PRESS

PM Press is an independent, radical publisher of critically necessary books for our tumultuous times. Our aim is to deliver bold political ideas and vital stories to all walks of life and arm the dreamers to demand the impossible. Founded in 2007 by a small group of people with decades of publishing, media, and organizing experience, we have sold millions of copies of our books, most often one at a time, face to face. We're old enough to know what we're doing and young enough to know what's at stake. Join us to create a better world.

**PM Press**
**PO Box 23912**
**Oakland, CA 94623**
**www.pmpress.org**

**PM Press in Europe**
**europe@pmpress.org**
**www.pmpress.org.uk**

## *Punk Rock: An Oral History*

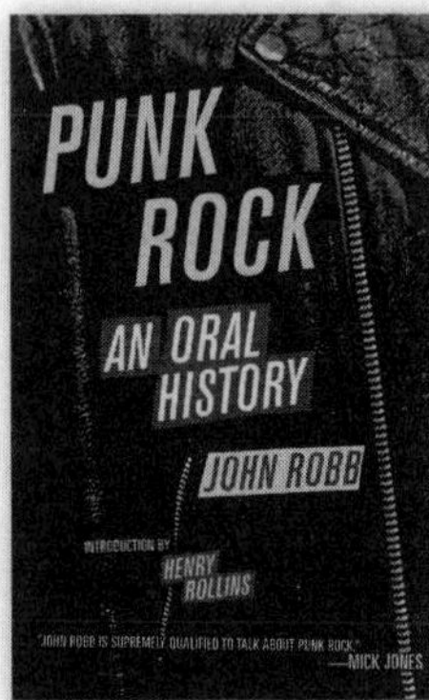


John Robb
with a Foreword by Henry Rollins

**ISBN: 978-1-60486-005-4**
**$19.95 584 pages**

With its own fashion, culture, and chaotic energy, punk rock boasted a do-it-yourself ethos that allowed anyone to take part. Vibrant and volatile, the punk scene left an extraordinary legacy of music and cultural change. John Robb talks to many of those who cultivated the movement, such as John Lydon, Lemmy, Siouxsie Sioux, Mick Jones, Chrissie Hynde, Malcolm McLaren, Henry Rollins, and Glen Matlock, weaving together their accounts to create a raw and unprecedented oral history of UK punk. All the main players are here: from The Clash to Crass, from The Sex Pistols to the Stranglers, from the UK Subs to Buzzcocks—over 150 interviews capture the excitement of the most thrilling wave of rock 'n' roll pop culture ever. Ranging from its widely debated roots in the late 1960s to its enduring influence on the bands, fashion, and culture of today, this history brings to life the energy and the anarchy as no other book has done.

*"Its unique brand of energy helps make it a riot all its own."*
—*Harp* magazine

*"John Robb is a great writer . . . and he is supremely qualified in my opinion to talk about punk rock."*
—Mick Jones, The Clash

*"John Robb is as punk rock as The Clash."*
—Alan McGee

## *NoMeansNo: From Obscurity to Oblivion: An Oral History*

Jason Lamb with Paul Prescott with a Foreword by Fred Armisen and Afterword by W. Buzz Ryan

**ISBN: 979-8-88744-014-9**
**$29.95 336 pages**

They were unlike any other band in the punk scene they called home. NoMeansNo started in the basement of the family home of brothers Rob and John Wright in 1979. For the next three decades, they would add and then replace a guitar player, sign a record deal with Alternative Tentacles and tour the world. All along the way, they kept their integrity, saying "NO" to many mainstream opportunities. It was for this reason the band (intentionally) never became a household name, but earned the respect and love of thousands of fans around the world, including some who became big rock stars themselves. They were expertly skilled musicians playing a new kind of punk: intelligent, soulful, hilarious, and complex. They were also really nice Canadian dudes.

*NoMeansNo: From Obscurity to Oblivion* is the fully authorized oral and visual history of this highly influential and enigmatic band which has never been told before now. Author Jason Lamb obtained exclusive access to all four former members and interviewed hundreds of people in their orbit, from managers and roadies to fellow musicians, friends, and family members. The result is their complete story, from the band's inception in 1979 to their retirement in 2016, along with hundreds of photos, posters, and memorabilia, much of which has never been seen publicly before.

For established fans, this book serves as a "love letter" to their favorite group and provides many details previously unknown. For those curious about the story and influence of NoMeansNo, it reveals an eye-opening tale of how a punk band could be world-class musicians while truly "doing it themselves." Their impact and importance cannot be overstated, and *NoMeansNo: From Obscurity to Oblivion* is the essential archive.

"*With* From Obscurity to Oblivion, *Jason has documented every part big and small associated with the story of NoMeansNo, isolating them into a book filled with an explosion of posters, clippings, and interviews. Yes, what he has created is worthy of a run-on sentence! This is it! The definitive tome!* From Obscurity to Oblivion *has so many subplots and stories I don't know how Jason edited it! A fascinating read and look (did I mention all the tidbits and pictures?) into the legendary Victoria, BC, band.*"
—Nardwuar the Human Serviette

## *Queercore: How to Punk a Revolution: An Oral History*

Edited by Liam Warfield, Walter Crasshole, and Yony Leyser with an Introduction by Anna Joy Springer and Lynn Breedlove

**ISBN: 978-1-62963-796-9**
**$18.00 208 pages**

*Queercore: How to Punk a Revolution: An Oral History* is the very first comprehensive overview of a movement that defied both the music underground and the LGBT mainstream community.

Through exclusive interviews with protagonists like Bruce LaBruce, G.B. Jones, Jayne County, Kathleen Hanna of Bikini Kill and Le Tigre, film director and author John Waters, Lynn Breedlove of Tribe 8, Jon Ginoli of Pansy Division, and many more, alongside a treasure trove of never-before-seen photographs and reprinted zines from the time, *Queercore* traces the history of a scene originally "fabricated" in the bedrooms and coffee shops of Toronto and San Francisco by a few young, queer punks to its emergence as a relevant and real revolution. *Queercore* is a down-to-details firsthand account of the movement explored by the people that lived it—from punk's early queer elements, to the moment that Toronto kids decided they needed to create a scene that didn't exist, to Pansy Division's infiltration of the mainstream, and the emergence of riot grrrl—as well as the clothes, zines, art, film, and music that made this movement an exciting middle finger to complacent gay and straight society. *Queercore* will stand as both a testament to radically gay politics and culture and an important reference for those who wish to better understand this explosive movement.

*"Finally, a book that centers on the wild, innovative, and fearless contributions queers made to punk rock, creating a punker-than-punk subculture beneath the subculture, queercore. Gossipy and inspiring, a historical document and a call to arms during a time when the entire planet could use a dose of queer, creative rage."*
—Michelle Tea, author of *Valencia*

*"I knew at an early age I didn't want to be part of a church, I wanted to be part of a circus. It's documents such as this book that give hope for our future. Anarchists, the queer community, the roots of punk, the Situationists, and all the other influential artistic guts eventually had to intersect.* Queercore *is completely logical, relevant, and badass."*
—Justin Pearson, The Locust, Three One G